Simply Sara

HILLARY MANTON LODGE

HARVEST HOUSE PUBLISHERS

EUGENE, OREGON

Cover by Left Coast Design, Portland, Oregon

Cover photos © Sonja Pacho / Flame / Corbis; Craig Tuttle / Design Pics / Corbis; Radius Images / Alamy

Author photo by Danny Lodge

Hillary Manton Lodge is represented by MacGregor Literary.

This is a work of fiction. Names, characters, places, and incidents are products of the author's imagination or are used fictitiously. Any resemblance to actual persons, living or dead, or to events or to locales, is entirely coincidental.

SIMPLY SARA
Copyright © 2010 by Hillary Manton Lodge
Published by Harvest House Publishers
Eugene, Oregon 97402
www.harvesthousepublishers.com

Library of Congress Cataloging-in-Publication Data
  Lodge, Hillary Manton.
  Simply Sara / Hillary Manton Lodge.
      p. cm.
  ISBN 978-0-7369-2699-7 (pbk.)
  1. Young women—Fiction. 2. Amish—Oregon—Fiction. 3. Oregon—Fiction. I. Title.
  PS3612.O335S56 2010
  813'.6—dc22

                                                                2010019038

Printed in the United States of America

       10 11 12 13 14 15 16 17 18 / DP-SK / 10 9 8 7 6 5 4 3 2 1

For Danny.
We did it. I love you!

First thanks go to my husband, Danny, who worked through every step of this process with me while working overtime hours *and* completing his master's program. He kept me on track, helped me set goals, and waded through my meltdowns. He also made me laugh.

Deep appreciation goes to my parents, Scott and Ruyle; my sister, Susannah; my brother, Geoff, and his lovely wife, Amy; my parents-in-law, Ray and Denise; as well as my brother-in-law, Isaac, and my Aunt Jill.

Many thanks to Aimee Madsen for the multicolored three-by-five cards, highlighters, and Post-it notes that helped me plot the second half of the book. To Carrie Sue Halupa, who read drafts and talked through plot developments with me when I was in a squeeze. To Anna Kintigh, who opened her home for an extended plotting session.

To Kara Christensen, whose words of encouragement have always brightened my heart, even when she is far away. To Rachel Lulich, who kept a close eye on Sara's voice and made sure the characters stayed consistent throughout. To my draft readers—Aimee, Bobbie, Carrie Sue, Danny, Kara, Karen, Rachel, and my mom, Ruyle.

To Rhonda Bergsten, whose winning recipe fit so perfectly into the storyline. To Jared Swezey, who suggested the word *foliage* (as seen on page 54).

To Sandra Bishop, for being my agent and for telling me to do a synopsis. It helped. To my editors Carolyn McCready and Kim Moore, who helped me shape Sara and who supported me in prayer. To Gene Skinner, who tidied up the manuscript into the lovely thing it became. And to everyone who fed us while I worked on the book.

Lastly, many thanks to my readers. I've loved hearing from you. I hope you enjoy *Simply Sara*!

read the letter over again in the privacy of my bedroom.

Pass.

I'd done it. The months of work had paid off—I had earned my Graduate Equivalency Degree.

Me. Sara. An Amish runaway who came to the big city with an eighth-grade education. I allowed myself to feel a little pride.

A little would not hurt.

My life hadn't merely changed in the last six months—it had turned a somersault. I left my life as an obedient farmer's daughter in the center of the Willamette Valley to be something else. I wasn't the first person in my family to do so though. Levi, my oldest brother, left first. He got his GED, attended many years of college, and now worked in a large glass building in Portland.

Maybe Levi inspired me. Or maybe I would have left on my own anyway. But the arrival of Jayne Tate on our family's doorstep changed things. She was fancy and brave, everything I wanted to be. When Jayne left, so did I.

I don't know why people say *run away*, because I don't think a lot of running is usually involved. I suppose a lot of people take the bus. I hid in the trunk of Jayne's car. She's still not very happy about that. Says it wasn't safe.

It probably wasn't. Maybe that's why I've been extra safe ever since.

I'm not the person I thought I would be after I left. I look in the mirror in Jayne's bathroom (so funny that it's called a bathroom, because Jayne's apartment doesn't even have a tub), and I feel as though the person in the mirror is the same person who hid her fashion magazines underneath the floorboards in her old bedroom.

I know in my head I'm not the same person. I don't even much know what I looked like before because I didn't grow up with many mirrors. But the image in my head and the image in the mirror seem the same.

The same, even though I have earned my GED and live in the city with my brother's fiancée.

I must stop. I must change.

I want to apply for college. I want to find clothes that I like, not just more modern versions of the things I wore all my life. I want to learn to drive. I want to find a job so Levi can stop leaving money in my purse when he thinks I'm not looking.

College. The idea makes me sit up straighter. I, an unbaptized Amish girl, could go to college.

❈

"Of course you passed," Jayne's friend Gemma said when I called a few moments later. "Listen, do you guys have plans for dinner? Come on down to the restaurant tonight. We're trying a new special."

Gemma's parents tried new specials a lot at their restaurant. I think Gemma saw them as excuses to get everyone together and make sure we all ate properly. When she mentioned a new special, we felt a bit less like her culinary charity cases.

I told her I'd ask Jayne, promised I'd call shortly, and said goodbye.

"Gemma wants to feed us again," I said, entering the living room.

Jayne and Levi stood in the kitchen surrounded by mixing bowls, measuring cups, miscellaneous other utensils, and a generous dusting of flour. "What are you doing?" I asked.

They exchanged glances.

"We're making you a pie," Jayne said, pushing her short dark hair behind one ear and leaving a streak of flour in the process.

"Oh." I brightened, and then lifted the phone in my hand. "Gemma wants to feed us?"

Levi dusted off his hands. "Another special?"

"Is that yes?"

"Only if you can eat Italian food *and* pie."

I shrugged. "I'll find a way."

❈

Two of Jayne's other friends met us at the restaurant—Kim, who also worked at the Oregonian with Jayne and Gemma, and Joely, a police officer. Joely tugged at my hair. "How's life, Ethel?"

Ethel was her pet name for me. She thinks I'm an old soul.

I gave her a hug, mainly because Joely isn't a huggy person. "I passed my GED."

"I heard. Planning for college now?"

"College." I exhaled, mentally steadying myself. "Yes. But I would also like to find a job."

"Really?" Kim asked as she slid into the restaurant booth. "I may be able to help you with that."

Before I could answer, Gemma's father arrived at the table with a steaming platter of appetizers. The conversation broke off as everyone dove in.

"You guys are really quiet eaters," Gemma said, a slice of crostini in her hand.

"We're chewing," Levi answered. "With our mouths closed. Doesn't lend itself to easy conversation."

"Italians don't let a little chewing slow them down," Gemma retorted. "You need to speed it up a bit. Talk, chew, swallow, and repeat."

"And repeat." Jayne took a sip of her water. "Repeat, repeat, repeat."

"I never said my family wasn't dinner and a show." Gemma lifted her water glass. "A toast for Sara, to her courage and success."

Everyone else raised their glasses and clinked them around.

It was kind of Gemma to say so, but I didn't feel that courageous. Or successful. Finishing my GED was like crossing a creek when I had an ocean ahead. Just thinking about it made me dizzy.

College wasn't the only factor I had to consider. I needed some sort of employment, a driver's license, and, to be honest, friends of my own.

Not that I didn't love Jayne's friends. They were more than kind, letting me tag along all of the time, taking an interest in me. I felt like Jayne's kid sister though, trying to join in on a world I didn't understand.

"What are your plans?" Kim asked.

"I need to start on my school applications," I began. "I want to see more of Portland than Powell's and Elephants Deli."

"Not a bad combo though." She pointed at me with her fork. "My mom's cousin owns a bookstore. It's pretty close to the Art Institute campus. He's always looking for good help—I'd be happy to introduce you."

I sat up straighter. "A bookstore? Really?"

"She's been reading like crazy ever since I found her in the trunk of my car," Jayne said.

Levi elbowed her.

"Well, it's true!" Jayne protested. "I found her in the trunk of my car, and she started reading everything I own."

"That's a lot of books," Kim said as she took a sip of water. "Anyway, I'd be happy to introduce you. We can go over tomorrow if you're available. We'll just leave out the part about you and the trunk when we talk to Rich."

※

A little bell jangled over the door as we entered. The moment I stepped inside, all I could see was books.

Sure, I expected to see a lot of books in a bookstore. If not, I'd be worried. But there were so many books in this space that I felt like all of Powell's Books were crammed into a hall closet. The shelves went from floor to ceiling. A ladder on a rail invited customers to climb to higher shelves and maybe swing to the other end, like Belle in *Beauty and the Beast*.

The more I thought about it, the more I thought Belle would like this shop. Granted, I didn't know Belle very well—I'd only watched the film with Jayne and Levi a few weeks ago.

So many stories...so much information. My fingers tingled to reach for one of the volumes. But I didn't because two men stepped forward to greet us.

One was older, with gray at his temples and a wide smile. He wore a striped collared shirt, a burgundy wool sweater, corduroy pants, and tassel-topped loafers. He wiped his hands on his sweater before offering one to me. "Richard Cameron. Welcome to R.G. Cameron Books."

I accepted his hand as Levi taught me and tried to shake it the way he'd shown me.

"Sara Burkholder." I winced inwardly as I said my name. It sounded so Amish.

"Nice grip, there," Richard said.

I released my hand immediately. Did I shake too hard? Was I making a bad impression? I stood and worried, barely paying attention as Kim hugged Richard and made small talk.

The other man, much younger, wasn't paying attention to them either. Instead, he looked at me as if I had facial hair.

I probably didn't look English enough. I wore Jayne's blouse and cardigan, but I wore them with a skirt about the same length as the dresses I wore back home. My hair hung down my back in a long yellow braid.

Dressing like an English person turned out to be harder than I used to think it would be. After a few weeks in Portland, I apologized to Jayne for criticizing her wardrobe. How could I tell her how to dress when I got nervous wearing a skirt that showed my knees? No one had ever seen my knees before, and I wasn't yet ready to reveal them to the world.

And now this English man looked at me as if I had come from the "Worst Dressed" pages of last month's *InStyle*. He wasn't so well put-together himself. His wavy hair flopped around his ears, and he hadn't shaved for several days. The shirt he wore hadn't been pressed, and his jeans were faded.

What was he doing wearing jeans at work anyway? This was a bookstore, not a woodshop.

As he scowled at me, I fought the urge to scowl back. Instead, I forced myself to stand up straighter and meet his gaze.

"This is my store manager, William," Richard said.

William's expression didn't change as he shook her hand and then mine. Richard smiled at me. I smiled back.

"Kim tells me you're looking for a job." Richard motioned us farther into the bookstore. "Do you have any retail experience?"

"I've made and sold my own quilts," I said, knowing as I said it that it wasn't enough.

"Quilting. That's, ah, that's neat." Richard rubbed his hands together. "You like books? You know books?"

I think William rolled his eyes.

"I love reading. In the last six months, I've read Jane Austen's complete works, some Anne Lamott, *The Princess Bride*, *The Chronicles of Narnia*, the Brontës, John Steinbeck, Ernest Hemingway's *The Sun Also Rises*, Ruth Reichl..."

"In six months?"

"I like books."

Richard crossed his arms. "If someone asked you for a recommendation for a romance, you'd suggest—"

"Jane Eyre."

"Interesting."

"What about political satire?" William asked. "What would you suggest?"

I read the books, but I couldn't remember what *satire* meant. "*The Princess Bride*," I said. It was a book with romance, horror, sport, and comedy, so it was possible there was some political satire also.

Richard laughed. "Very interesting pick. Goldman's handling of the royal family and the references to Vietnam." He looked to Kim. "She's a sharp one." Back at me. "We've got a nice little store here. We cater to the literate crowd that prefers not to need a map to find things. There is a part-time position available. It's yours if you want it."

"Really?"

"Really."

I hesitated for the tiniest moment. William the Crank wouldn't be pleasant to work with. But maybe I wouldn't see him much. And the job would pay, so I could start supporting myself.

Supporting myself and being surrounded by books couldn't be that bad. "I want it," I said with a grin.

No one but me noticed William's frown deepen.

⊰※⊱

Richard didn't waste time. While I was there, he photocopied my Social Security card and the student ID from Portland Community College that I'd acquired during my GED studies. Kim helped me figure out the W-2 form.

William glowered the whole time before leaving for a lunch break.

"I'll start you off doing inventory," Richard explained as I filled out the paperwork. "William and Zach will deal with customers and the register. You'll meet Zach when you start work. I deal in both new and rare antique books. William assists me with the acquisitions of the collector's volumes."

"How many antique volumes do you keep stocked at a time?" Kim asked.

"Anywhere between fifty and a hundred. At the moment I have a first-edition *Anna Karenina*."

"Seriously?" Kim's eyes went wide. "Can I see it?"

"Sure. It's in the workroom." Richard gestured toward me. "We'll be right back. Are you doing okay? IRS forms are a pain."

I smiled. "I'm fine."

The moment they stepped out, William stepped in. I had no idea he was still lurking around. I tried to ignore him, but then I remembered why I was here—I had to stop hiding.

"Anything I can help you with?" I would not let him frighten me.

"For starters, don't even think about touching the antique volumes. The oil on your fingers can damage them."

"Okay. I won't, not unless Richard asks me to."

"He won't. Richard's rarely at the store. It's just me and Zach."

"And me."

"For now."

I struggled to keep my temper in check. I might not have attended high school, but I wasn't stupid, and I didn't like to be bullied. I squared my shoulders. "You need a haircut."

"Excuse me?"

"And it wouldn't hurt you to shave."

"Don't talk to any of the customers."

I looked back at him innocently. "Don't wear orange. It's not your color."

Richard and Kim's voices floated down the hallway and filled the room as they returned.

William crossed his arms. I wondered if, as a child, he'd made that face and it froze on him, just as his mother said it would.

"Finished?" Richard asked.

I signed my name one last time on the tax form. "Yes."

"Excellent. Oh, and if you'd like your paycheck deposited into your account, I'll need a blank check or a deposit slip." Richard collected and glanced over my papers. "When would you like to start?"

"As soon as possible is fine with me."

"Monday, then? We're closed Sundays."

Monday gave me only two days to ready myself. "Monday," I agreed.

Richard shook my hand again and we said our goodbyes. William avoided my gaze. I gave him a sunny smile. "See you Monday morning!"

Chapter 2

Monday?" Jayne stopped sweeping the kitchen floor. "That's fast. Kim says he's got an amazing selection of rare volumes. I've never been, but now I'll have to. Are you excited?"

"I am." I swung my legs, enjoying my post atop the kitchen counter. "I do think though…" I tried to figure out exactly what to say, but the words left in a rush anyway. "I think I need new clothes."

"Yeah? And?"

"What do you mean?"

"You left your home for a lot of reasons, one of them being that you wanted to design clothes and enjoy fashion. Not that you're frivolous, but you're interested in the interaction between people and fabric the way painters think about canvas and paint. That said, the fact that it's taken you this long to update your look…well, let's just say it's surprised all of us."

"Who's all of us?"

"Me, Levi. Gemma. Kim. Joely. My mom. Beth. The mailman…"

I crossed my arms. "You've all been talking about me and my clothes?"

"Well, we can only talk about the economy for so long."

"Thanks."

"You're welcome. So you think you're ready?"

"I have to be ready."

"How are you feeling about your knees?"

I rested my hands on my knees, feeling the bony protrusions through my skirt. "They help my legs bend."

"Very true. I meant, how do you feel about skirts maybe a bit shorter?"

"I don't know…"

"Or pants? You told me once you were dying to get into a good pair of jeans."

"They rub my legs funny."

"But…" Jayne knelt to sweep her dust collection into the dustpan. "They also keep you warm in the fall and winter. Especially with the Gorge winds around here. You might just give them a try."

"I'll try."

"Want me to call Gemma? I don't think you want to go out with just me."

"You look very nice these days."

"Thank you. Still, for something this big, we need to call in the pros."

Levi bequeathed me with his credit card for the day. I promised to pay him back when I started earning a paycheck.

"We need a plan," Gemma said Saturday afternoon. "What we don't finish today we can finish tomorrow. We're shopping with goals—you need at least one pair of well-fitting jeans, black slacks, a white blouse…"

"Why don't you let us know what we're looking for as we shop?" Jayne suggested.

"Because you need to know what we're looking for."

Jayne rolled her eyes, but I appreciated Gemma's sense of purpose. I loved clothes, but I had no idea how to go about shopping for them.

We started off at Gap because Gemma felt certain I needed jeans.

I chafed inside the indigo-dyed pants. I tugged them up—no help. Tugged them down.

"Stop fussing," Gemma said. "Turn around."

"They're too tight."

"Jeans with any sort of stretching agent should feel a half-size too small when you buy them. They'll stretch."

"These are two sizes too small."

"If they were two sizes too small, you wouldn't have been able to zip them up. Come here."

I made the mistake of obeying. Gemma stuck her finger down the waistband. "These feel about perfect."

Reason finally won out. I knew that if I wanted to be English, I had to have blue jeans. I bought one trouser-cut pair and one with slightly flared-out legs that Jayne and Gemma said made my bottom look cute. I don't think anyone had called my bottom cute since infancy.

Gemma chased us to TJ Maxx, where we hunted down a crisp white button-down shirt, a black skirt, gray trousers, assorted print tees, and a couple colored cardigans.

At Nordstrom's, we found a couple silk shells marked down significantly, a beautiful black wool pea coat, and a red corduroy blazer. I almost bought a black dress, but both Gemma and Jayne stopped me. "It doesn't fit," Gemma said, tugging at the extra fabric beneath my armpit.

I studied it in the mirror, taking in the seaming. "I could alter it."

Jayne and Gemma exchanged glances. "If you're going to alter it, it had better be a steal." Gemma fingered the price tag. "At sixty dollars, it's not a steal. Not yet, anyway."

In the end, I gave in, returned to my dressing room, and shrugged out of the dress.

"Now, are you interested in makeup?" Jayne asked before we left the department store. "Sephora's isn't far. We can at least get you matched with a foundation."

Before I quite knew what was happening, I found myself packed back into the car, this time surrounded by shopping bags, and driven to another part of the mall. Jayne pushed opened the doors, and I worked to take in my surroundings.

Everywhere I looked was some sort of makeup. As I walked slowly past the displays, I took in tubes and tubes of lipstick, bottles of flesh-toned foundation, shimmery blushes, and eye shadows in colors I didn't know people would want to put on their eyes. The displays seemed to be divided by brand, some of them with strange names. Urban Decay. Cargo. Smashbox. Nars.

Women milled through the aisles, trying on lipsticks and eye shadows and making faces in mirrors. I even saw a few men in the store, though they seemed to be working there.

The English were so strange.

While I wandered around, Gemma and Jayne set to work. Gemma collected bottles of makeup to try on me. Soon enough, I was sitting in a tall white leather chair under a lamp, facing a mirror as a girl about my age showed me how to match a foundation to my skin ("So smooth!"), use a blush to highlight my cheekbones ("Very pretty bone structure!"), line the upper ridge of my eyelashes ("So thick!"), and apply a dab of gloss to the center of my lower lip ("Nice, full lips!") after lipstick.

I scrutinized my image in the mirror when she finished. I looked like myself but…brighter? I noticed the shape of my eyes and the structure of my face in a way I hadn't before. For the first time, I felt I looked a bit like the person I was on the inside.

I bought the basic cosmetic items as well as a couple lipsticks. Gemma promised to look through her lipstick collection for tubes she didn't use that I might like.

Jayne fingered the long strands of my blond hair. "Have you decided if you're going to change your hair?"

I took a second look at myself. The new clothes, the different face…no, I couldn't change my hair. Not yet.

I told Jayne as much. She nodded. "You don't really need to do anything to it. You have lovely hair. Leaving it makes you look artsy."

Once we completed the shopping, we headed back to Jayne's apartment, where Gemma and Jayne helped me put things together.

Gemma called it an exercise in playing with clothes, and I had to admit I enjoyed it.

Levi came by when we were done. "I picked this up for you today," he said.

I looked at the object in his outstretched hand. "A driver's manual." I flipped through the pages before smiling up at him. "Thanks!"

"I can take you to the DMV for your permit once you've studied."

A smile tugged at my lips. "That shouldn't take long."

He smiled back. "I didn't think so."

~~∿~~

On Sunday I decided to live dangerously.

"I'll see you after," I said as I walked with Jayne into the church foyer. "I'm going to go to the college group this morning."

"Oh," Jayne said, trying to cover her surprise and failing. "See you after, then."

I walked away, feeling my confidence fall away with every step. Determined, I reminded myself that I wore fashionable English clothes. I wore a little of my new makeup, and my hair—at least according to Jayne—looked artsy. I pushed through the heavy gym door with resolve.

Three steps inside, I wanted to run away. The people in front and behind me blocked my exit. It was crowded. Very crowded. The music was loud.

Just because the music was loud, I reasoned, didn't mean I couldn't meet people and hear a good message.

But…everyone stood in groups. They all seemed to know each other. One young man walked toward me and made eye contact. "Hi," he said, smiling.

Maybe everything would be okay. "Hi, I'm Sara." I offered my hand with only a slight hesitation.

He shook it. "Kyle. Want a program?" He offered me a bright blue piece of folded paper.

"Um…okay." I took it and examined each side. "Thanks."

But he was already five feet away, giving a program to someone else while another guy slapped him on the back.

Fine. I found a seat and studied the program. I could feel a headache gathering behind my eyebrows. The music was too much. The crowd of people was too much. It was so…rowdy. When everyone took their seats, no one sat near me.

What was wrong with me? My clothes were right, my hair was nice, I was clean and didn't smell…but no one spoke to me. Was I supposed to be more outgoing? Was I supposed to act differently?

Confused and frustrated, I slipped out the back ten minutes later. Jayne and Levi always sat in the same place in the sanctuary, so I knew I could find them. Maybe I would try the college group again later.

Maybe.

<hr />

I woke up extra early on Monday. I rose and showered as quietly as possible, trying not to wake Jayne.

Jayne is not a morning person, but I was raised to be awake before dawn. Sometimes she's not happy to wake up before dawn with me.

Okay. She's never happy waking up so early.

I toweled myself off and dressed in the outfit we'd picked the night before—the gray pants, paired with a graphic tee and the red blazer. Hip but relaxed and perfectly appropriate for a Portland bookstore. Both Jayne and Gemma agreed.

With great care, I smoothed the foundation onto my face the way I'd been shown and applied a light bit of blush, some brown eyeliner, and a tawny-red lipstick.

"I should have known you would get up this early," Jayne's voice crackled from the doorway.

I started, nearly marking my nose with lipstick. "I tried to be quiet."

"I know." She patted my arm, or tried to. She missed and made an awkward swipe at my elbow. "Hmm. Sorry. I'm hungry. Are you hungry?"

My stomach fluttered, but I'd never experienced success without a hearty breakfast. "Yes, I suppose."

"I'll make something. What do you want?"

What did I want? My mother's apple strudel sounded very good, or her autumn fruit coffee cake...For a moment I allowed myself to miss my mother so much I almost forgot my nervousness.

"An omelet, maybe?" I said, choosing something within Jayne's repertoire.

"Coming right up. Can I use the bathroom first?"

"Of course." I scooted out into the hallway.

Most of the time I tried not to think of the family I'd left behind. My parents, my oldest sister Rebecca, and my siblings at home—Amos, Elam, Sam, Leah, and young Elizabeth. Someday, Elizabeth would not be so young. Would she remember me?

Before I could stop myself, I called Levi.

"Is everything okay?" he asked, groggy. I must have woken him up. What time was it? I looked at the clock in the living room—5:30.

"I miss everybody back home," I said with a sigh.

"I know." There was a rustling—he must have rolled over. "At least I figured as much. You haven't talked about it since you left."

"What was it like for you?"

"Tough. My closest friends for a while were my academic advisors."

"That's 'cause you're smart."

"So are you."

"Thanks."

"Are you nervous about starting work today?"

"No," I lied, but then I thought better about it. "Maybe. Yes."

He chuckled. "I was terrified when I got my first job as an office assistant. I had only worked with my hands before."

"I should have looked for work with a seamstress doing something I knew. Or stayed home and made more quilts."

"It's good to learn new things."

I made a face. "I've learned so much these past months, I think my head will burst."

"You knew it wouldn't be easy."

"I know. I did." I exhaled. "But I didn't think I would miss everyone so much. Does it get better?"

"It gets…" I could hear Levi search for words. "Softer. I think of them, I pray for them. I miss them, and sometimes I get to see Mom or the younger ones or Grandma. But it will never be the way it was."

"No." I could feel tears gather behind my eyes despite my efforts to stop them. "It won't be."

"I'm okay with that. Life here is good—I love having freedom as a Christian. I love Jayne, I love my job. And the coffee's good, you know?"

"Yeah, I know." Levi may hold a job in economics, but he specialized in coffee.

"And I love having another family member around."

I smiled. "Thanks."

"You're welcome. You're going to be great today."

I closed the cell phone as Jayne exited the bathroom.

"Who are you talking to so early?" She asked.

"Levi."

"Was he awake?"

"Sort of."

Jayne tucked her lower lip between her teeth before moving on to the kitchen. I could tell she wanted to say something to me about not waking him so early.

We feasted on omelets and cocoa for breakfast. Jayne tried to chase me away from doing the dishes, but I found the mindless cleaning soothing. I cleaned until Jayne needed to leave for work. Then I checked my outfit one last time, and Jayne threw a scarf around my neck for good measure.

I needed to be at the bookstore by 8:45, but since Jayne needed to be at work sooner, she dropped me off at the coffee shop near the store. I sat at a table watching the morning crowd sift through while I nibbled at a scone.

At 8:39 I decided to leave for work. I stood, brushed crumbs from my coat, and walked out into the chilly December air.

I braced myself for a chillier greeting inside R.G. Cameron Books, but William the Crank was nowhere to be seen when I entered through the employee's door. I unwound the scarf from my neck and hung it on a hook by the door. Thoughts of calling out *hello* to the emptiness entered and exited my mind. If the Crank was just out of sight, I didn't feel like draw-ing attention to myself.

Instead, I stepped out into the main bookstore area and looked around. Most but not all of the lights were on.

I pushed a stray piece of hair behind my ear as I walked through the tall bookshelves. Logically, someone had to be here. The lights didn't turn themselves on.

"Hey, you're the new girl!"

I spun, startled. A grinning young man approached me with his hand outstretched, I presumed for a handshake. I offered my own hand silently, but rather than shaking it he slapped it.

I yanked my hand back.

"Great to meet you. I'm Zach. You're…"

"Sara. Um, Sara Burkholder."

"Awesome. First day of work. That's so cool."

In the face of Zach's exuberance, I hardly knew what to say. He was the opposite of William, that was certain. He dressed similarly, but his hair was cropped short and his eyes smiled. Zach was open where William was closed.

"I don't know exactly what I'm supposed to do," I admitted.

Zach clapped his hands and rubbed them together. "I work the register. 'I earned that territory with my talent.'"

I frowned. "You what?"

"Sorry. *Godfather III.*"

"Who?"

"The movie—*Godfather III.* It's a quote."

"Oh." I shifted my feet. "I haven't seen it."

"Really?"

Until recently, I'd never shared living space with a television or visited a movie theater. "Really. Sorry."

"No worries. Rich put you on inventory?"

"Yes." I tucked my hair behind my ear again. "Is he here on Tuesdays?"

"Rich? He's not here much. Usually Fridays, some Saturdays. He spends a lot of time at estate sales looking for first and second editions of old books."

"I heard about the *Anna Karenina.*"

"Yeah, he was real excited about that."

"*Real-ly,* excited, Zach. This is a bookstore. You need to speak as though you know how to read," William said as he walked through the front door, coffee in hand. "We're open for business, people."

I watched Zach's face for signs of intimidation or anxiety and found none. Fine, then. I faced William with resolve. "Where would you like me to work?"

"The workroom is fine."

"Aw, come on, Will," Zach interrupted. "Her first day, and you're going to shove her in the back? There's plenty of room behind the counter."

William looked back at me. "The back or the counter, it's your choice. You'll be doing inventory and shelving either way."

"If she's shelving, there's no point making her work in the back." Zach added. I just stood back and allowed them to argue. I didn't mind either way. I only wondered how long the argument would last. And why did William dislike me so much?

Chapter 3

Zach's stubbornness paid off in the end, and he brought me a chair from the back to sit on while I worked. I went through the books a stack at a time before finding their places on the shelves. William watched me like the hawks back home as I put each book in its place, but he didn't say a word.

Customers drifted in and out, some buying books and others not. Zach chatted with the potential buyers, asking what kind of read they were looking for and making suggestions.

I noticed that William looked at me differently than he did Saturday. He certainly wasn't any friendlier, but there was a little less disdain in his eyes. I filed that observation away as I finished out my workday.

※

I spent the next week reading my driver's manual. Levi offered to take me to the DMV on Tuesday morning to take the written test. Monday afternoon, I approached William, feeling a little nervous.

"I need to come late tomorrow," I said, reading his response.

His brows furrowed. "Why?"

"I have to go to the DMV."

"You don't drive."

"I want to."

"You mean you can't drive?"

"Without a license? Not legally. That's why I need to go tomorrow."

"You don't have your license?"

Was he deaf? "No."

My statement seemed to surprise him. "Oh. Late tomorrow is fine."

※

Thin beams of late-morning light speckled the sidewalk as we exited the DMV Tuesday morning. I studied my temporary permit as we walked. "So much work for such a plain piece of paper," I remarked.

"You'll feel better about it when you see the shiny one." Levi reached for his wallet and retrieved his license. "See?"

I held it up to the light and watched as the imprinted images turned colors. "Maybe I will feel better."

"You won't have your permit for long. I'll be teaching you how to drive."

"I hope I learn fast."

"You will." He shook his head. "You've picked everything else up with surprising speed."

"You think so?"

"Definitely."

Joely was visiting the apartment when I returned home from work. "Nice going, Ethel. Heard you got your permit today."

I couldn't stop my smile. "Levi's going to take me out to a parking lot later tonight." I smiled at Jayne. "Thanks for letting me learn in your car."

"No problem." Jayne slung her arm around my shoulders. "It is stick shift, but I've heard it's best to learn on stick anyway."

"Wait—Levi?" Joely made a face. "No offense to your brother, or"—she turned to Jayne—"your boyfriend, but he's a civilian driver."

My heart sank. "Is that bad?"

Jayne thumped Joely on the arm. "Don't scare her, Jo. That's just mean-spirited."

Joely put her hands in the air. "I wasn't trying to scare her, I was just trying to point out that you've got someone who drives for a living available for lessons."

I frowned. "Who?"

"Come on, me!" Joely shook her head. I can teach you performance driving."

"But I thought you were a police officer."

"I am. In a patrol car. It's my job to drive with impressive accuracy, and I'm willing to teach you."

"Wow, a little eager, are we?" Jayne teased.

"If she's going to learn to drive, she should do it right. There are enough bad drivers out there. You know, like the entire state of Washington."

"Talk about profiling."

Joely rolled her eyes. "I know. I feel horrible. If I tell you that Oregonians don't know how to merge, does that make you feel better?"

"Yes, actually." Jayne crossed her arms. "So, Sara, you've got your pick of driving instructors. Just be aware that one of them is armed."

—✴︎—

"The gas pedal is your friend," Joely said, tucking her arms behind her head two nights later. "If you press it down, we may go faster than five miles an hour."

I depressed the brake, maybe a bit too fast. We both lurched forward. "You want me to go faster?"

"Um, yes. Once we leave this parking lot, the suggested speed is thirty-five."

I sighed. "Oh."

"Think you can do it?"

"Until last spring, I rode in a car only a few times a year. Learning to drive one...it's difficult."

Joely patted my arm. "I know it may seem difficult. Driving is something you should take seriously. But it's not, like, heart surgery. Or nuclear engineering. There are idiots licensed to drive every day. You're not an idiot. That's how I know you can do this. I believe in your ability to drive the speed limit."

"Okay," I said, putting the car back in first gear. "I'll try again."

"Good girl. Just remember—clutch goes out *smoothly*."

—✴︎—

After we drove for another forty minutes, Joely decided we could call it a night. In the dark and the rain, she agreed to be the one to drive us back. I was relieved. I truly wanted to learn to drive, but the process was more difficult than I'd anticipated.

To add to that stress, there was work, with Zach's grins and Will's grunts, and the tiny little fact that I needed to apply to the Art Institute.

I could hear Jayne puttering in the kitchen. While she was occupied, I sat down with the laptop Levi gave me shortly after I moved in with Jayne. I looked up the Institute's website—it was beautiful, with pictures of people my age drawing things, images of designs...my heart beat faster just taking them in.

I looked to the top of the screen—there was a place to click that would open a live chat window. If I wanted, I could ask my questions about the program and admissions. I moved the cursor to hover over the chat button… and then moved it away.

Not yet. I couldn't bear it if I had come this far, leaving my family and my home, only to discover that I really wasn't good enough to design the clothes I'd dreamed of, to have the life I wanted. In the Amish world, everything revolved around hard work. Skill wasn't all that necessary—how much talent did it take to slop pigs? To tend a garden? To cook well enough to sustain a family?

But making clothes, that was different. I knew it was competitive. I knew there were girls who wanted to have that future, girls who grew up practicing, girls who were encouraged by their parents. If I came all this way to discover I had no talent—well, it would be difficult.

I closed my laptop and pushed away from my desk. Worrying about the Art Institute wouldn't help anything. I pulled out my sketchbook and began to think about fabrics and design. Maybe I didn't have the advantage of growing up English, but no one would be able to say I didn't work hard.

I had nearly finished my shelving stack when Richard entered the store.

He hadn't been in for nearly a week, and the last time had only been to ask William a few questions.

Richard carried a leather bag over his shoulder. A grin stretched across his face, and his breath was heavy from exertion. "Will!" he called as he entered. "I got it! Come see."

Richard saw me shelving and motioned for me to follow. "Kim said you liked clothes, right?"

I nodded, knowing I must have looked like an idiot. What did my taste for fashion matter?

"You'll want to see this too. Put the books down. They're not going anywhere."

I saw William open his mouth to protest, but he changed his mind as we followed Richard into the back workroom. I hadn't actually been in the room yet thanks to Zach's insistence that I work from behind the counter.

A small machine whirred in the corner, but I didn't want to ask what it was. There was a desk with a row of lights shining down on it. A cabinet full of large and small drawers filled the wall opposite the door. I looked around and took everything in, knowing that this would be the last time I'd be here if William had his way.

Richard reached into his bag and gently removed a wooden box. "I found this at an estate sale. I don't think the owner knew what he had—not really." He opened the lid to the box. Inside lay an old, leather-bound volume.

"This," he said, "is a collection of *Godey's Lady's Book* periodicals from 1834, bound together. And if you look at the January issue…"

"No. Really?" William's eyebrows rose. His eyes—did they sparkle? Was that possible?

"Look for yourself."

"Page 40?" Will reached into one of the desk drawers and removed two latex gloves. As he wriggled his hands into them without looking, his eyes never left the pages. With greatest care, he lifted the cover. "Overall text seems to be in good condition. Gilt stamped half burgundy leather. Brown cloth over boards—left board chipped. Some foxing at the edges. Pages are age toned, but not more than you'd expect for a text of this age." He stopped, with a sharp intake of breath. "There it is. 'The Visionary.'"

"What's special about it?" I asked, hoping my question didn't spark a tirade.

"'The Visionary' was later renamed 'The Assignation,'" William began.

"Not a change for the best, I'd say," Richard commented.

"I agree," William's eyes searched the page. "But regardless of the title and the fact that it was initially anonymous, it's the first published short story by Edgar Allan Poe."

"Really?" I peered over his shoulder. In truth, I hadn't read any of Poe's work. Jayne had a volume of his short stories, but his words were too frightening for my taste.

"He was friends with the editor, Sarah Josepha Hale, who, incidentally, also wrote 'Mary Had a Little Lamb' and convinced President Lincoln to make Thanksgiving a national holiday." William looked up at Richard. "How much did you pay for it?"

"Five hundred."

"No!"

"The guy had no idea what he had."

"So it's a collection of women's magazines?" I was still trying to wrap my head around the concept.

"Yes, but not women's magazines like we know them today. This edition is before Louis Godey purchased it, but historians often lump the two publications together. *Godey's Lady's Book* was part literary journal, part fashion magazine—that's what it's best known for. But it also had crafts, patterns, piano music, occasional medical advice…Nathaniel Hawthorne also published in *Godey's*."

"Now," Richard held up a finger. "This wasn't my only find."

William froze. "You have more? What else do you have in there?"

Richard patted his bag. "Its value is lower—at least to Poe enthusiasts—but to the right literature-reading bra-burner, it's worth quite a lot."

William waited in anticipation. I wondered about the sort of person who would burn bras.

Richard reached into his satchel again, this time retrieving a large yellow envelope. Inside the envelope was a clear plastic bag, the kind that fastened across the top. I could read the title of the magazine through the bag—it was a *Godey's*. A later issue, by my guess.

"Another issue? You'll have to tell me the significance of this one."

"January 1850—one of three issues written entirely by female contributors."

William tilted his head. "Huh."

Richard pulled the fragile magazine out and placed it onto the work desk with great care. "This copy is also completely intact." Richard turned to me. "This is why I thought you might be interested. Each issue included a hand-tinted illustration of women's dress near the front. Godey didn't tell his employees what colors to use—I could buy a dozen copies of the same issue, and they'd all look slightly different. People often rip out those illustrated pages. That's why it's so pleasing to find ones that are still all in one piece." He turned the pages until he reached the illustrated spread.

I stood on my tiptoes to see. The women pictured had round faces and tiny waists. Their dresses rounded out their shoulders and puffed at the sleeve. The skirts belled out from their waists and scraped the floor.

"I wonder how they walked through doors," I mused.

"Maybe they turned sideways," William suggested.

I looked at him in shock. Had cranky William just made a joke?

If he had, he recovered quickly. His expression turned serious again as he evaluated the manuscript. "Overall, good condition. Good finds."

"The 1834 volume, obviously, could use some gentle repair. What's your workload like this week?"

William shrugged. "About normal. I can have it ready to list shortly—unless you're wanting to keep it for your collection."

"Tempting, but I'm not a Poe fan. We'll list it. Have you shown Sara how to do the website inventory?"

William's usual sour expression returned. "No. I can do that this week."

I tucked my hair behind my ears casually. "Website inventory?"

"We list our rare books and manuscripts online. Collectors from all over the country order from us."

"Really." I could hardly believe people would buy things over the internet like that, even though Jayne did it herself from time to time. To have so many items available—and to not see them physically before buying—still seemed a little crazy to me.

I returned to work a few moments later, thinking again of the women in the magazine illustration. I knew what women wore today, but the idea of hundreds of years of fashion—that too astounded me. Amish women looked about the same now as they did when they arrived in the United States from Switzerland. There was so little change. But all around us, the world had transformed.

I only hoped I could somehow catch up.

Chapter 4

On Thursday night over dinner at DiGrassi & Elle with Levi, Kim, and Gemma, Jayne stopped eating and folded her hands.

"Sara."

I looked up from my ravioli. "Yes?"

"I believe I have been...remiss in your English education."

My eyebrows furrowed. "But I've read nearly all of your books."

"Not English as in literature, but English as in not-Amish. You've been so busy with studies, I haven't said anything..."

Levi lifted an eyebrow. "But now that she's working, learning to drive, and applying to school, it seems like the perfect time?"

"Shush. Sara, we haven't properly introduced you to movies, and I'm sorry."

"But we watched *Beauty and the Beast*."

"Yes, but—"

"And *Anne of Green Gables*."

"True."

"How many movies could there be?"

Jayne, Levi, Gemma, and Kim all exchanged glances. "A lot," Jayne answered.

"I mean"—I cut a ravioli in half with my fork and lifted it to my mouth— "filming has to be pretty expensive. There can't be *that* many, at least that many good ones, can there?"

"*Casablanca, Singin' in the Rain, La Jetée*..." Kim ticked the titles off her fingers.

"*A Night at the Opera, Amelie, Star Wars, Raiders of the Lost Ark*..." Gemma continued.

Jayne slapped the table with her palms. "*The Princess Bride*? Hello?"

Levi shrugged. "Good point."

"I've read the book," I pointed out. No one seemed to hear me though.

"She's going to start school, and she will not have seen *The Princess Bride*? I mean, I know it's a cliché, and every middle and high school in the country shows it because it's something they can show in the classroom without a permission slip, but I can't let her start without knowing about why the six-fingered man must prepare to die, alright?" Jayne folded her arms.

Kim leaned back in her chair. "You really should throw in a few early John Cusack films."

I took a sip of my iced tea. "Fine. There are lots of movies I need to watch."

"More than lots. Multitudes."

I rolled my eyes at Jayne. "Fine. Multitudes. Just tell me what to watch after I get off of work. Give me a list."

"You can't just watch them, Sara. Movies are a group activity. They're something people watch together, talk about together—it's a shared experience. I'm thinking we need to have a weekly movie night."

Gemma raised her hand. "I'm in. I'm single. I'll bring snacks."

"If I don't have work to do, I'll come—as long as Gemma's bringing snacks," Kim added as she snagged the last mozzarella stick. "Although I've never known Gemma to truly make snacks. They tend to be hors d'oeuvres or appetizers."

"Hmm…Yes, and they also tend to taste good, so that's enough out of you." Gemma turned to me. "So, now that your film education is planned, how are driving lessons going?"

I lifted a shoulder. "They're, um…slow."

Jayne stifled a giggle. "Literally."

Gemma patted my arm. "It's okay. Driving can be tough. Driving a stick is extra tough."

"The stick shift part is okay. I'm just…" I chewed on my lip. "Slow."

Gemma frowned. "As in learning?"

Jayne couldn't contain herself any longer. "As in, she can't get over twenty miles an hour. *That* kind of slow."

"In that case," Kim said, "maybe we should start with *The Fast and the Furious*."

Friday morning at the bookstore, William wore an expression of pained endurance.

"Are you ready to learn to maintain the Web catalog?" he asked, fidgeting with the edge of his sleeve as he did so.

I put down the books I was shelving. "Sure."

"If you're in the middle of something, it can wait."

"The books aren't going anywhere."

He sighed audibly. I ignored it and followed him to the computer in the back room, where I'd seen the antique collection of *Godey's Lady's Book* magazines. Now the book lay open on the desk, and a camera sat next to it.

"First step is to have some pictures of it. Generally, one shot of it open, one shot closed is sufficient. Sometimes a picture of the back cover. Generally, if a customer wants more pictures, we'll take more, but until then the two pictures are usually enough."

"So I take the pictures?"

"You take the pictures. This camera is a Canon, pretty simple to operate."

Easy enough for him to say.

"This top button opens the lens," he continued. "In here, with the lamps, you probably won't need the flash. I recommend putting it into macro mode, so you just move the camera to get the closeness you want."

"Macro mode?" What on earth was a macro? And how did I find it?

"Here." He thrust the camera under my nose. "Turn this, right to that symbol. Got it?"

"Okay."

He handed me the camera. "Good. So here's the book…go ahead and take some pictures."

"How do I take the picture?"

"Press the large button on the top."

"Oh." That made sense. The large button that sat beneath my index finger.

When the camera was turned on, it showed the image on the back. I waved the camera back and forth, trying to get the book to show up properly. When at last I had it, I pressed the top button. The camera whirred and clicked. A still image showed up on the back of the camera briefly and then disappeared. "Where did it go?"

"Oh, it's in there. You haven't used a digital camera before, have you?"

I shook my head.

"Were you, like, really sheltered?"

I only shrugged. William was the last person I wanted to know about my Amish upbringing.

After a few pictures of the cover, I reached for the front cover to open the book. Before my fingers could lift the cover, William's hand reached out to stop me.

"What are you doing?"

I yanked my hand away. "Opening the book. You said we needed a picture of the interior."

"Are your hands clean?"

I examined them. No dirt, no grime—they appeared clean to me. "Yes."

"Oils from your fingers can damage books. It's best to wash them just before handling a book, or to wear gloves."

"Oh. Fine. Shall I wear gloves then?"

He hesitated. "Don't worry about it. I'll open it."

I rested a hand on my hip. "I wasn't going to flip the cover open and start tearing through. I do know how to be careful with things."

William paused while retrieving gloves from the desk drawer. "Oh, all right. Put these on." He gave me the gloves. "When turning the pages, always turn from the top right-hand corner—least amount of strain on the leaf that way."

"Leaf?"

"The physical piece of paper. One leaf—two pages."

"Oh. Why are there spots on the paper?"

"It's called foxing. They show up on publications printed on paper milled in the eighteenth and nineteenth centuries. They're caused by impurities in the water."

"I see." How exactly *was* paper milled? I decided to look it up on Wikipedia when I got home. I had been spending a lot of time on Wikipedia lately.

William stepped back, and I took the interior pictures. "Good," he said when he looked at them on the tiny screen. Over the next few minutes, he showed me how to "upload" the pictures and enter his written description of the book into the online form. He crossed his arms when he finished. "So, do you have plans for the weekend?"

I nearly fell over from surprise. "Um, kind of. My roommate planned a movie night tonight with some friends."

"Nice. I'll let you get back to your work." He left the workroom without another word.

Hmm. Maybe Cranky William was starting to thaw.

~~✦~~

Jayne was practically buzzing when she picked me up from work. "So. We've got things all set. Kim and I agreed on a short list for movies tonight—"

"Movies? As in, more than one?"

"You've got a lot of catching up to do. Don't worry—we've decided to start with a short film and two feature films."

"And Gemma's bringing food?"

"Yes. She said something about goat-cheese stuffed mushrooms and endive spears with lobster, avocado, and grapefruit. I think it was grapefruit. I may have heard wrong."

I crossed my arms. "If we are sitting around, watching three films and eating Gemma's cooking, we will all grow fat."

The traffic light turned red, and Jayne stopped and turned to me. "Are you saying you don't want to do this? Everyone's all excited."

"I'm glad they're excited, but you never asked if I was interested in these films. Spending an entire evening watching the TV seems a little lazy and idle to me."

"You may see it as lazy, but think of it as education. These are films everyone at your school will have seen."

"I'm not in school."

"You will be."

I thought back to Zach and his quote from *The Grandfather* or *The God-father* or whatever it was called. Maybe Jayne was right. Maybe movies, for all their silliness, were important in this English world.

"Fine, I will watch the movies if you say it's that important."

A smile stretched across Jayne's face.

"Besides," I added, "Gemma's bringing food. How bad could it be?"

~~✦~~

"I don't show up for dinner, and y'all make decisions without me," Joely groused.

Jayne flicked her on the arm. "Shut up and eat a stuffed mushroom." She turned to me. "It really was grapefruit. Crazy, huh?"

"You say crazy, I say tasty. Never mind—I managed to get decent lobster in December," Gemma countered smugly.

"I suppose it doesn't hurt to have contacts with restaurant suppliers."

"Probably not." Gemma flicked her hair over her shoulder. "So—what's on the playbill for tonight?"

"*Steamboat Willie*, *The Princess Bride*, and *Casablanca*." Jayne snagged another mushroom. "Next week, I'm thinking *West Side Story*, *West Bank Story*, and *Toy Story*."

"*West Bank Story*?" Kim asked. "What's that?"

"Film short that places *West Wide Story* in the Middle East. Won an Oscar."

"Good pick then," Gemma nodded in appreciation.

We settled in for the evening, Jayne tucked under Levi's arm on the couch and the rest of us spread out on the remaining living room floor and furniture. I appreciated the early animation of *Steamboat Willie* and laughed with everyone else during *The Princess Bride*. I had difficulty hearing the words on occasion because everyone said them with the movie, but I was pleased at the end when Buttercup and Wesley rode into the sunset.

"You know, in the book," Kim said after the end credits, "Buttercup's horse throws a shoe and everything goes kind of haywire."

"True," I said. "I kind of liked that ending."

Everyone was quieter for *Casablanca*, especially since Jayne announced that there would be no breaks, no texting, and certainly no talking during the film.

I think Joely sneaked a text in anyway. For a cop, she certainly had a rebellious streak.

Of the three films, *Casablanca* was my favorite, although I felt a pang of guilt when Ingrid Bergman went back to her husband instead of staying with Humphrey Bogart. I certainly wanted her to be faithful to her husband, but a part of me felt a similarity between her situation and mine. Had I done the right thing by leaving my Amish past behind? I reminded myself that my family was in no way involved with the French Resistance, they were not an integral part of ending a war of any kind, and I had no husband.

When the TV silenced at last, the night hung heavy, and I could feel my mind and limbs grow sluggish. I said my goodbyes to everyone and headed for bed. I dreamed about my family and everyone I'd left behind.

—☆—

Saturday morning I rose, showered, and dressed, knowing what I had to do that day. The whole point of working at the bookstore was that it would be easy to schedule around my classes. Classes I was not yet enrolled in.

It was time. I sat at my computer and opened the Art Institute's website with its stylish designs and invitations to "chat" about the programs. This time, I clicked on the Request Info button and carefully entered my information.

I had to stop hiding.

Chapter 5

Rather than stay at the bookstore for lunch on Monday, I decided to wander. While driving to and from the store with Jayne, I'd seen a small fabric store a few blocks away.

I'd worked on one quilt project during my GED studies, but I hadn't done anything else. More specifically, I hadn't tried sewing anything English for myself.

A small bell jingled over the door as I entered. The shop lady waved before returning to a customer she had been helping.

There were bolts and bolts of fabric, and for the first time in my life, I could pick yardage from whichever one I chose. I could pick fabric with stripes or flowers or even small birds.

Some of the fabrics already had embroidery on them, others had sequins. I reached out to brush them with my fingers and feel the weight of the weaves. As I looked at the fabric, I envisioned different garments in my head. I thought of a skirt with the embroidered fabric, a fluttery blouse with the sequined fabric. I had a couple T-shirts in my closet I was already starting to be bored with…maybe appliqué some designs? Trim with lace?

Lace. I'd never used lace in my life. I walked over to where a stand of trims hung in spools. I fingered the holey strips and examined their patterns.

Near the lace I found bolts of fabric so sheer I could see through it. There were no holes like the lace—it had to be chiffon. I'd never actually seen chiffon, only read about it.

I wore my black hoodie that day, the one I thought was a little plain. What if I took the chiffon—which was also black—and used it to liven up my basic hoodie? I could tie a bow or fashion a rosette…

The edge of the fabric frayed and curled away—how did that happen? I liked the effect, especially against my hoodie, but I didn't imagine my scissors could produce such an effect.

I carried the bolt to the woman behind the measurements counter. "Excuse me," I said, proud of myself for using such an English expression. "I was wondering how you achieved the frayed edge here."

She tucked a piece of steely gray hair behind her ear. "I suspect it's just torn. Let's see." I watched as she made a one-inch snip at the top through the selvage edge, grasped the small tab of fabric, and rent the chiffon in one long tear.

She gave me the smaller piece for inspection. "Is that the finish you're looking for?"

I nodded.

I bought a yard of the chiffon and walked back to the bookstore, my mind full of ideas and inspiration.

※

After work, I positioned myself on the couch in front of the TV and the DVD of *Miss Pettigrew Lives for a Day*, one of the movies Gemma had loaned to me. I found that I kind of liked having something else to entertain me when I was working on a project. Miss Pettigrew reveled in a day of pampering while I tore my chiffon into strips of different widths.

Once I sat in the center of a pile of depressing black strips and self-doubt, I used my straight pins to tack the chiffon ribbons into shapes on my hoodie. At last I fashioned a sort of double bow for one side with the loops pinned apart and the tails looping down the front. I pinned two additional ribbons beneath it, tugging them up so they could trail along the back beneath the hood.

"How's your project coming?" Jayne asked after a couple hours.

"Fine," I said. I checked the pin placement and held it up to examine my work. "It looks...drab."

"It's black."

"Black is drab."

"Why did you pick out a black hoodie?"

"Because it will go with nearly everything. I think." My shoulders sagged. "I don't know anymore."

"I think it needs a bit of sparkle."

My eyes lit up. "Beads!" I could do a lot with beads. I could sew them on individually and give the front a light sprinkle of sparkle. Or...as I thought about it more, I remembered I was working with a hoodie. A lot of beads would be appropriate for cashmere—I supposed, I'd never felt cashmere—but not for something this casual. Maybe a gathering at the center of the bow? Like a brooch?

"There's a bead shop on Northwest Twenty-Third—Let it Bead, or something kitschy like that. You might look there."

I held the sweatshirt up again. Sparkle. What a strange new life I lived, one where a problem could be fixed with sparkle.

Having a clothes project to work on was fun. I could move on to other garments. "I wish I could have found a way to bring my sewing machine," I said. "It's probably best that my old one is home for Leah and Elizabeth to learn on, though." My chest clenched as I thought about my sisters, but I forced myself to remain calm.

"A sewing machine would be a clever thing to have around here," Jayne agreed. "With you going to art school soon and me with my stack of quilt squares…"

"How are those coming?"

"They're…you know, square."

"Oh. Good. Well, I can sew by hand for a while. Maybe I should start saving for a machine with my work money." I smiled, thinking about the things I could sew.

⁓∖⅍⁄⁓

On Wednesday night, I finally did it. I gathered the courage, applied to the Art Institute, and set a time for the personal interview. I felt proud.

I was terrified.

Completely terrified, because I couldn't prepare for the most basic part of all—what would I wear?

I cornered Jayne while she worked on her laptop. "What kinds of things are appropriate to wear to an interview?"

"Sounds like a Gemma question. I might send you out in overalls. Not that anyone but farmers wear overalls anymore."

"Come on," I said, sitting next to her. "You've interviewed for jobs, and I don't think you wore overalls."

"No, I didn't." She closed her laptop. "You know, something nice. Trouser pants. A skirt, if you're not me."

"You wear skirts."

"I wear skirts now. I didn't, not before Your Pickiness put my wardrobe in a chokehold."

"You're welcome."

Jayne tilted her head. "Are you thinking about your school interview?"

"Yes."

"Well, it's not like they've taught you to be all fashion artsy yet, so no pressure."

I sighed. "All the other students—they come from a different world. They get the in jokes, they know the songs that play at the mall, and they don't have to have someone explain what a cap sleeve is. I'm starting so far behind, I want to show the interviewer that I am willing to work hard."

"I think you mean that you have talent," Jayne observed. "It's still hard for you to see yourself as talented, isn't it."

"Maybe. Probably."

"Well, you got me wearing skirts, so there's some proof of your talent right there. You should tell your interviewer you're Amish up front. You might qualify for some sort of affirmative action thing. You know, keep their Amish quota up."

"I didn't understand any of that."

"Never mind, it was a terrible joke."

I sighed. "I'll never catch up."

"Yes you will. Friday night movie nights will help. And if you ask her, Kim will get you listening to all of the right hip indie musicians. Stop worrying. You'll be too cool for the rest of us in no time."

"I think I'll bake something."

"Sounds yummy. What's on the menu?"

I thought over my options. I liked my flourless chocolate cake, but it was eggy and airy enough to be a soufflé. I wanted something with more substance.

"The lemon chocolate tart. With candied lemon peel," I decided.

Ever since I left home, my baking had grown fancier and fancier along with me. I baked only when necessary before, but here I found myself trying increasingly elaborate desserts. Here, no one would raise an eyebrow if I made something extravagant. The bishop would not knock on our door. I could be as creative as I wanted to be.

Maybe I would make a skirt. It would take a while by hand, but I could certainly do it. I thought about skirt designs as I cut butter into the pastry dough.

⟶⟿

I left the bookshop on my lunch break again, this time to look for skirt fabric. William gave me a funny look as I left, but I'd already decided his face was stuck that way. Zach had already left, so I wasn't sure what William's problem was, aside from the fact that he was William.

Instead of looking over the sheer, frilly fabrics, I sought out the heavier ones that would stand up to a Portland winter. I looked at some corduroy but decided that sewing it by hand would be too hard on my fingers. The heavier cottons were...well, boring. And too prone to picking up lint. There were a few embroidered cottons, but I wanted something that could be both businesslike and artsy. Chain-embroidered flowers seemed neither.

I began to feel disheartened until I found the bolts of wool. There were nubby weaves—tweeds, I think they were called. One was in a plaid pattern in undesirable shades of cream, bright green, brown, and bright yellow. Another was brown, almost as uninspiring as black. But the green...it was a dark forest green, and even though it was heavier, it also had a nice drape. The weave could go either way, so I wouldn't have to buy extra to make allowances for a striped or plaid pattern. I liked the green. It made me think of trees and moss and, I supposed, forests. Probably why it was called forest green.

With that fabric in mind, I took a look at the pattern books.

So many of the styles were so ugly! If someone were to put the time into making clothes, why choose styles that were so out of style? Still, there were some classic cuts, and I found a basic pencil skirt that I liked.

The idea of a skirt that fit toward my body rather than away from it made me excited and nervous at the same time.

I liked the idea of a wool skirt. The fabric would be slow to dry if it got wet, but it would also be slow to soak if I got caught in the rain. Wool would be warm, and as long as I protected it from moths, it would last a long time.

As I looked at the photo in the pattern book, I began to think of things I could do to make it my own. I liked the idea of adding a three-dimensional cluster of flowers to one side.

Leaving enough time to eat some lunch, I purchased the necessary yardage of wool, matching thread, needles, and a zipper for the back. I couldn't hide my smile when I returned to the bookshop.

Zach and William were arguing in the back rooms. I couldn't help but hear their conversation as I put away my coat and fabric.

"I would have appreciated more notice," William said, clearly flustered.

"You've got about as much notice as I did, man. My mom only told me yesterday that she expected me home for the break. Said my grandmother's health is bad and if I don't go home, I may never see her alive again."

I walked through the short corridor and entered the room. "Is there a problem?"

William crossed his arms. "No."

Zach held out his hands in exasperation. "Are you kidding me? Whatever, man." He turned to face me. "I'm gonna be gone during the"—he shot a look at William—"*busy* holiday season, leaving him and Richard to be the only ones to work the register."

"Is that a problem?" I asked. "One person. One register—"

"Richard pulls out a second one during December so no one spends the day waiting in line. Hey…" Zach snapped his fingers. "You could teach Sara to use the register."

"Zach," William warned.

"Wow. Glad I thought of that."

I maintained an impassive expression. A smile at this time would not be wise. I could see William trying to think his way out of the predicament. And failing.

William looked to me. "Do you think you could learn the register?"

"Yes." I still refused to smile. And I didn't need to. Zach's grin nearly stretched off his face.

I was glad to finally have a chance to learn a new skill, but I wasn't sure how long I could survive without Zach around to smooth things out.

When Jayne picked me up, I asked if we could drive by the bead store she'd mentioned.

"Sure," she said, putting the car into reverse as she backed out of R.G. Cameron's tiny parking lot. "Have you practiced driving lately?"

"Not lately. Haven't had time."

"We'll have to fit something in soon. You should give Joely a call."

I winced. "Joely thinks I drive too slow."

"You do drive too slow."

I shrugged. "Faster than I used to."

"Not saying much."

Finding a parking space took a few moments, but once we were inside Let it Bead, I quickly found exactly what I wanted for the hoodie: five small Swarovski crystals with just a bit of smokiness to them and three dark grey Swarovski pearls.

They were all on sale. I loved sales.

After dinner I spread my materials out on the couch in such a messy way, I think I surprised myself. Jayne took a picture to document the event.

I threaded the needle through two beads at a time and worked until they formed the sort of cluster I was looking for—slightly off-kilter, but on purpose. I held it up to the light. "You're right, Jayne," I said. "The sparkle does make a difference."

She smiled. "I'm glad. Are you going to wear it to your interview?"

I set it into my lap. "You don't think it's too casual?"

"No. It's artsy, and really pretty dressy with those beads. But you might ask Gemma. She's the expert."

"I'm going to make myself a skirt to wear. I bought the yardage today—want to see?"

"What are you going to sew it with?"

"Oh, I'll sew it by hand."

"Seriously?"

"It's just a skirt."

"Sara…." Jayne took a slow breath. "Are you sure you don't want me to go to the farm and ask for a few of your things?"

"No." The word rushed out. "I can't go back."

"I wouldn't ask that of you. I'd go for you."

"Going back for my belongings would be close to going back altogether. I can't do it."

Jayne took a seat next to me on the couch, narrowly missing my threaded needle. "I just want you to know there are options."

"I know." I clasped my hands in my lap. "But having options means not going back."

Chapter 6

Wednesday morning, William showed me how to ring up a purchase. To William's consternation, I insisted on writing notes for myself as I learned how to do batches and get the little cash tray to pop out on purpose rather than by accident. By the end of the teaching session, I could run through a purchase, a return, an exchange, and even a gift card without a hitch. I think William was disappointed.

Trickier, though, was the fact that now I was working with the customers. Before, my work conversations were between me and stacks of books. Now, William wanted me to chat with people.

"If someone comes in and says they want something thoughtful, moving, and appropriate for a plane ride, what would you suggest?"

I hesitated. I'd never ridden on a plane. What sorts of books did people read when they traveled?

William shook his head. "No, you can't freeze up like that. Have you been keeping up with the new releases?"

"Not lately," I hedged. Between work and projects, I hadn't had much reading time lately.

"We'll have to fix that. I'll send you home with a stack to preview. You can't recommend books blind. Maybe they do that in larger stores, but not at Cameron's. If someone's looking for something to read on a trip, ask where she's going. Asia? Suggest *The Last Chinese Chef.* Or if she reads nonfiction only, as some people do, *Three Cups of Tea* is a solid suggestion."

"A clichéd suggestion." Zach called from across the room.

"People buy clichéd suggestions," William called back. "That's why Dan Brown has a job."

"Touché," Zach replied without looking up.

"No one expects you to have read everything in the bookstore," William began again.

"Except you," Zach threw over his shoulder. "Just saying."

William rolled his eyes. "It's smart to be versed in what we stock."

"I do read," I said, feeling the need to defend myself.

"I didn't say you didn't read. I just need you to read lots of different things. Books by someone besides Stephanie Meyer."

"Fine." I resisted the urge to cross my arms. It was just as well that I didn't know who Stephanie Meyer was. "Just give me a stack. I'll read whatever you want." Now that I had the power of the register, I wasn't going to let William's opinion of my reading habits stop me.

William didn't need any more encouragements. "Try this one," he said, grabbing a book from the front display table. "This one," he said as he chose another, "got a good review in *Publishers Weekly*, this one is being filmed, this one…" he flipped the book over and scanned the back. "Actually, I hated this one. Never mind. But this one," he picked up the one next to it. "This one wasn't bad. Actually pretty good, if you don't mind a bit of Nietzsche-esque fatalism."

I didn't know what to say to that. Instead, I nodded and reached out for the growing stack of volumes William held.

"Take a week for those," he said. "I'll give you another stack next week."

Could I finish a skirt by hand, read a stack of books, and sound like I knew what I was doing during my Art Institute interview, all in one week? Thank goodness I enjoyed a challenge.

※

"Is everything okay?" I asked Jayne as she drove me home.

"Hmm? Yeah. Fine. Everything's fine."

I lifted an eyebrow. "Oh?"

"Completely fine. Want to drive with Levi tonight? He's coming over for dinner."

"That sounds good. So…how are things with you? And Levi. Together." I winced. "My family dated by climbing through windows. I'm not very good at asking about relationships, but I've heard that English women talk about them a lot."

"If by English women, you mean Gemma, Kim, and Joely, then yes, we do like to talk about relationships. At least everyone else's." Jayne sighed. "There's something to be said for windows. Less of an audience, fewer people wanting to know every detail."

"But you and Levi are good?"

Jayne smiled. "Very good."

"Are you going to get married?"

I waited as Jayne inhaled and then exhaled.

"I want to be with Levi, get old and wrinkly with him, and get fat with his babies. We're engaged. I wear his ring. I love him, it's just…" she sighed. "The idea of marriage still terrifies me."

"Really?" The thought surprised me. But then, very few Amish girls *didn't* marry.

"Some days I'm fine. Other days…I spent most of my life never wanting to marry, barely able to have anything resembling a long-term relationship. Old habits die hard, you know?"

"You're not going to break up with him, are you?"

Jayne shook her head. "No. We tried not being together. Not fun." She shot me a smile. "It's a process. Don't worry about us."

How could I not be worried? Levi was the only sibling I saw anymore, and Jayne was my closest friend.

"Stop worrying," Jayne said.

I sat back into the seat and took deep breath. "I'll try."

My efforts continued until we reached the apartment.

Jayne pushed her key into the lock above the doorknob. "You're still worrying."

My shoulders slumped. "I'll try harder, really, I—"

I stopped talking. Levi stood at the kitchen table, grinning. His hands rested on an electric sewing machine.

"Surprise!" Jayne clapped me on the back. "Are you surprised?"

I had no words.

Jayne frowned. "Are you happy?"

"I think she's working on it," Levi said, coming around from the table to sling his arm over my shoulders. "What do you think?'

I patted his arm absently. "There's a sewing machine on the table."

"True."

"It's an electric machine."

"All the rage with the hep kids these days."

"And it's…" I tilted my head. "On the kitchen table."

Jayne gave a small smile. "We didn't know where you wanted it."

My head whipped around. "It's mine?"

"You didn't think I was really going to start sewing those quilt squares together, did you?" Jayne put a hand on her hip. "It's all yours. Don't you dare sew that skirt by hand."

"But…" I leaned over to examine the machine. It read Janome on the side. I looked at a switch on the side and flipped it without thinking. A small light bulb burst into life. I leapt back. "It has a light!"

Jayne swatted Levi on the chest. "You shouldn't have plugged it in."

"The light comes on only when it's plugged in. I thought she'd be impressed with it." Levi lifted an eyebrow and turned to me. "Are you impressed?"

Rather than respond, I crouched down and investigated the pedal. I figured that depressing the pedal would start up an electric machine just like it would a treadle machine. I gingerly reached out with a finger and…

The machine roared to life. The instantaneous reaction startled me so much I smacked my head against the table as I fell backward. "It's…alive!"

Jayne and Levi didn't stop laughing for twenty minutes.

———※———

"I'm serious," Jayne told everyone Friday night. "She said, 'it's alive!'"

I nodded. "After falling over."

"Your head feels fine now, right?"

"Oh, it's fine. You have to understand, treadle machines are very gentle." I looked around at everyone. "They're much slower."

Gemma rubbed my back. "You're adjusting so well. I'm glad you're laughing at yourself. And glad only Jayne and Levi were there to witness. If it were my family, the story would be told at every future birthday, your wedding, and at the birth of each of your children."

"The trade-off for eating well." Kim reached for one of Gemma's crostinis. "These are good, by the way."

"My brother gave me the idea. So, Jayne, you're the master of ceremonies—remind me what we're watching?"

"*West Side Story*, *West Bank Story*, and *Toy Story*. Next week, I'm thinking about a couple Pixar shorts, *White Christmas*, and *Elf*."

Kim frowned. "No *It's a Wonderful Life*?"

"We will, but I was saving it for Christmas Day."

Joely shook her head. "Can't believe it's the Christmas season already. Fall just flew by." She stretched her legs out and propped her arms behind her head. "I should probably think about my Christmas shopping."

I leaned forward. "Christmas shopping? How does that work?"

Everyone looked at each other. Gemma spoke first. "How do the Amish celebrate Christmas?"

"Well..." I had to think for a moment. How could I explain something I'd always taken for granted? "Christmas Day itself is very solemn I suppose, as we think about the birth of Christ. The day after is for visiting family, seeing friends...we eat a large meal and celebrate together."

"Do you exchange gifts on Christmas?" Jayne asked.

I nodded. "We do, but not until the day after Christmas. Small gifts, usually. Nothing fancy. It's a simple time," I said with a shrug. "Like everything else Amish. The children do have a school program that everyone enjoys. They give recitations, sing songs..." I felt pricks of tears sting my eyes. Leah, Samuel, and Elizabeth would be participating. For the first time, I wouldn't be there to see them. Did they miss me?

Gemma reached over and rubbed my back. I blinked back tears and looked away.

"So no Santa Claus?" Joely asked.

I shook my head. "Santa Claus is for *Englischers* who don't want to pay attention to the Christ child."

"And Christmas lights?"

"A little difficult without active electricity."

"Perfect!" Joely clapped her hands together. "Go get your coat—we're going for a ride."

"But...the movies..." Jayne looked around, bewildered.

"Hello? Christmas lights? We'll go near downtown, drive up Northwest Twenty-Third, look at the huge houses all lit up, hit Peacock Lane..."

Levi stood. "Sounds good. We can all fit in my truck."

"But..." Jayne's expression deflated. "The movies..."

"We'll watch them after. No reason we can't do both. And we can pick up hot chocolate on the way back." Levi retrieved his jacket from the coat closet. "Sounds like fun."

"Hot chocolate." Gemma's eyes glazed over. "Hot chocolate from Moonstruck."

I looked around for my shoes and found them under the couch. "Looks like we've got an itinerary," I said, though I would only admit to myself how uninterested I was. I may be fancy now, but I was raised to believe that Christmas was about the birth of Christ, not lights and decorations.

With a reluctant heart, I joined everyone as they piled into Levi's pickup. Jayne sat in the middle of the bench seat in the front, snuggled against Levi. Gemma sat next to her in the front, while Kim, Joely, and I squeezed into the backseat of the extended cab.

Jayne brought a Christmas CD from the apartment and fed it into the truck's CD player. Ella Fitzgerald—whose music I had learned about a few months prior—began singing about a sleigh ride, and everyone else sang along, even when Ella said "giddyap" and it made no sense to me.

I realized I was cranky.

I just wasn't sure what the fuss was about. I had seen some lights around town, lights strung in trees and around the edges of windows and rooflines. The logic of the lights eluded me. Some lights looked like icicles and blinked in spots. Didn't people know that icicles don't blink? Or they'd cover just the front of a house. That made no sense, because icicles grow from all sorts of ledges, all around homes and barns. When we visited our cousins in Ohio, I'd seen them.

I felt the same about blue icicle lights. Icicles weren't blue.

The other Christmas lights that didn't make sense were the deer-shaped things on people's roofs. How did the deer get on the roof? Why would they go on to a roof—it wasn't as if any sort of food was up there, unless putting food on the roof was some kind of odd English tradition.

I stopped paying attention to the view from the window, but when we approached Peacock Lane, I couldn't help but stare.

Kim tapped my arm. "This whole neighborhood has been decorating since the twenties. It's pretty famous. There is free cocoa, but Gemma's a cocoa snob."

"Hey!" Gemma protested.

"It's true." Joely patted Gemma's knee. "Just accept it."

"Horsies!" Gemma pointed out the window. "Let's go on one of the horse-drawn carriages!"

"We should! I did that a couple years ago when I had a boyfriend—I think the carriage was more fun than he was," Kim said.

"What's so fun about a carriage?" I asked.

Kim, Joely, and Gemma all looked at me blankly. "The horsies," Gemma repeated. "The whole experience, the romance of it, taking things at a slower pace…but I suppose they're not a novelty to you."

Looking at Gemma, I realized how much they wanted the experience to be fun for me, fun for everyone, and how easily I could ruin it with my attitude.

"I've never been in a…white buggy," I offered, observing the carriages that rattled by. "Let's try."

Gemma cheered as Levi parked and we prepared to walk toward the lights. I had to admit, they were beautiful. The houses were built in an older style, with pointed roofs and long lines. "What style of houses are they?" I asked Kim.

"Tudor," she answered. "It's a style of architecture based on the English Tudor period. It became popular again during the twenties."

"I like it."

"Me too."

There were people everywhere, laughing, walking, talking. I watched as they looked at the houses, each lit, most with additional decorations in the yard—nativity scenes, electric snowmen, and turning trees.

I hugged my arms to myself. I may have been raised plain, but I wondered how I could have missed out on something so beautiful.

"There's a carriage!" Jayne rapped on Levi's arm. "Run up and save it for us!"

Levi gave a goofy grin and jogged toward the carriage. Moments later, we all piled inside.

A horse was a horse, a carriage a carriage, but time with friends—I wouldn't want to be anywhere else.

Chapter 7

Movie night on Friday went very, very late.

So late that I fell asleep twenty minutes into *Toy Story*, much to Jayne's horror. But Levi wouldn't let her wake me up, and I promised the next morning to watch it over the weekend.

I would watch it while reading the stack of books William wanted me to read.

"Seriously?" Jayne said when she saw the stack. "Wow. If you need to cheat, let me know. I had a journalism class in college that taught how to skim books for research. I'm willing to share my wisdom come to that."

"It might," I said. William could boss me around all he wanted, but the fact of the matter was that I had two days off, and I had a skirt to make. Rather than experiment with my new machine using my nice wool, I used a few of Jayne's donated quilt squares. I practiced loading the bobbin, running a line of stitches, and backing up to secure the row.

The speed of the machine amazed me. Though my grandma was Mennonite and lived in a house with electricity, she used an old treadle machine. Said she liked the pace of it. Until now, I'd never even watched someone else use an electric machine. A part of me didn't think I'd like it, but now? I found it energizing. All I had to do was depress the pedal attached to the cord, and *whoosh!* The tricky part was getting the tension correct so the threads on the top and threads on the bottom matched, rather than looping or pulling so tight the fabric gathered.

As I cut the fabric pieces, I felt the familiar surge of anticipation. Starting new projects made me feel that anything was possible. Every length of fabric held so much potential. The wool I'd purchased could just as easily become something else—a jacket, a shift dress, even a children's toy.

I thought back to the *Godey's Lady's Book* sitting in the back room at work. It occurred to me that many of the subscribers were women who couldn't afford the designer gowns of the time and either made or designed most of their own garments. In a way, *Godey's Lady's Book* made it possible for women all over America to be fashionable. And not only fashionable, but well read. I determined to do more reading on *Godey's Lady's Book* and Sarah Josepha Hale.

But not until I'd finished William's books. Or the skirt that lay in pieces on Jayne's floor.

—✂—

Sunday morning before church dawned cold, dark, and drizzly. I rose early as usual and showered. Most days I would braid my long hair wet and wait for it to dry, but the idea of going outside with a head of wet hair held no appeal. I rooted around for Jayne's hairdryer and set about the dull task of drying my lengthy strands.

Long hair really was a pain.

During the church service I found myself eyeing Jayne's shorter hair. It hung just past her shoulders and probably took a fraction of the time to dry. I looked at the other women's hairstyles at the service. Some were short and puffy, others short and sleek. Other women wore their hair longer, but only one woman I saw had hair as long as mine. She wore a long, gauzy skirt with socks and odd-looking sandals. Not fashionable at all.

I turned my attention back to the pastor's words, guilt heavy in my heart. I was at church to hear about God. Hair would have to wait until later.

—✂—

"Do you think the other girls at the Art Institute will have short hair?" I asked Jayne on the way home from church.

Jayne's eyes widened like a trapped animal's. "Um, I guess. Probably. Most of them shorter than yours, but there may be an exception. You thinking about cutting yours?"

"It's long."

"True."

"And takes forever to dry."

"I imagine."

I leaned against the headrest. There were practical aspects to my thoughts of a haircut. The other fact was that I wanted to fit in with the other students. I didn't want to be "the Amish girl" or even "the ex-Amish girl." I didn't want my hair to set me apart for any reason. I told Jayne as much.

She shrugged. "Don't cut it unless you would really like it short though. You have lovely blond hair. Don't dye it brown because it sets you apart from a largely brunette class."

"I wouldn't do that. I don't know that I'd recognize myself if I had different-colored hair. I don't understand the people who change their hair color."

Jayne smirked. "That's because you grew up in a culture without much hairstyle change. I've had red tips on my hair and even blue tips for a bit. Liked the red better. Went blond for about two weeks in college. Used to highlight my hair before I got tired of paying for it. Now it's just brown, but I like it. Sometimes it's fun to look in the mirror and see something different—that's all I'm saying. I've had lots of friends cut their hair short after a bad breakup."

"Really? Over a boy?"

"Kim was in a two-year relationship with a guy. He dumped her three weeks before Valentine's day. She chopped it up to where it is now—used to be pretty long. Now she says the best two things she's ever done is to lose the guy *and* the hair." Jayne shifted down as she turned the car. "Hair's just hair, really. It grows. You can change it all you want, but it'll still grow back."

"True." I lifted a shoulder. "Not that I've ever tried to grow a hairstyle out."

"Well, if you'd like a cut, Gemma has a hair lady she swears by. I tend to walk into a salon whenever the urge strikes me and suffer the consequences. You probably want to listen to Gemma when it comes to hair. And clothes. And makeup…"

"Most things."

"Hey. I'm a killer feature writer. I make people cry with the power of my words."

I laughed. "I'm sorry. I didn't mean to sound the way I did. You're good at lots of things. You know things." I sobered. "You're English, you grew up English. You don't have to pretend that you understand what someone means when they talk about Barney the purple dinosaur." I shook my head. "Still makes no sense to me. Purple dinosaurs?"

"Children's TV show," Jayne supplied between chuckles. "Most people find it annoying, but after babysitting my niece, I can say that people who hate Barney have never watched Teletubbies. Anyway, back to hair. I'm all for letting go of deadweight. If you want a cut, go for it."

—✺—

Go for it. Go for it. I repeated Jayne's words in my head as I sat in the hairstylist's chair after work on Tuesday.

A lot of things had surprised me in the English world. Drive-through coffee. A different version of Santa Claus at every shopping mall. But nothing could have prepared me for the experience of being in a salon. The air smelled odd and tangy. Bottles of every color lined the walls. There were mirrors everywhere. Nearly all of the salon employees wore black. Several of them painted things onto their clients' heads. Others snipped at the ends of clients' hair, mouths moving just as fast as their hands.

My stomach clenched. I was terrified.

A strange woman named Stella ran her hands through my hair. I wanted to bat them away.

"Your hair is generally healthy, but there's breakage here." She indicated where my hair used to be pulled back. "What do you think about taking some of the weight off and giving you some volume?"

"That sounds…okay." Volume? Like, making my hair louder? As always, I didn't ask. I just pretended to understand.

"Did you have a length in mind?"

"Shorter." I gestured near my shoulders. It occurred to me that perhaps that wasn't the best indicator—I was so nervous, my shoulders were located somewhere near my ears.

"Shorter. I can do that. Let's get you washed up."

Was I dirty? Obediently, I followed Stella toward a row of sinks attached to chairs and sat when she told me to. My head landed in the sink. Stella turned on warm water; I jumped when it hit my scalp.

Never in my life had a stranger washed my hair, but here I was, with Stella's hands massaging my scalp and carrying on a one-sided conversation about the weather.

After a few moments, my hair was scrubbed clean, wrapped in a towel. She walked with me back to the chair in front of the mirror and then set about the painful process of brushing my wet hair out.

I closed my eyes and thought of clothes.

"Safe to open your eyes now," Stella said quite a while later. "Didn't want to ruin the surprise?"

Something like that. Dread curled around my stomach. Maybe if I told myself it would be awful, whatever my hair looked like, I'd like it when I saw it.

I opened my eyes. And blinked. My head looked…bigger.

Now that my hair wasn't three and a half feet long, it had a lot more puff to it. Not in an unworldly way, but it wasn't plastered down to my scalp anymore. The blond strands were still as straight as ever, but now they floated around my neck.

Stella ran her fingers though my dry hair, repositioning it this way and that. "I used a razor to give the ends texture. Had to go short because of the breakage. All of this…" She lifted my hair again. "Healthy hair. As long as you don't style it repetitively—ponytails all the time, that kind of thing, as you grow it, all you've got is strong hair."

"It's…short."

She frowned. "That's the length you showed me…"

I felt my eyes fill with tears. "Yes. It was." Because of my stupid tense shoulders.

Jayne and Gemma put down their magazines as I reentered the waiting area.

"You look so cute!" Gemma exclaimed. "Excellent job, Stella!"

"Sara?" Jayne's eyes narrowed.

"That's the length we talked about…" Stella's voice trailed off.

"It's perfect." Gemma jumped up and put her arm around me. I saw Jayne write a check out of the corner of my watery eye. Once Stella was paid, Gemma and Jayne shepherded me out of the salon.

"I'm sure it's a shock," Gemma said as we walked, my shorn head all but tucked under her arm. "But it's very, very cute. Very face flattering. Very modern…"

"Sara, take a deep breath," Jayne said in a stern voice, startling me with its severity. She pulled me away from Gemma and placed her hands on my shoulders. "This was your first haircut. No matter what, the change was probably going to shock you. Hair grows. Whether you have a good haircut or a bad haircut, it just keeps on growing. You need to take a deep breath and snap out of it!"

I stared at her as if she'd just slapped me.

"Wow. Quite the speech." Gemma said.

Jayne smiled. "Thanks. It's vintage—at least, the part about hair growing and deep breaths. I got a horrible cut in high school, and that's what my mom told me."

"And it worked?" Gemma asked.

"Perfectly. This was before I dyed my hair rodeo red. After that, no hair speeches for a while. So…" Jayne put her hands on her hips. "Who's up for cupcakes?"

———

I studied myself in the mirror. Like the trees outside, I felt I'd lost my foliage by cutting my hair.

"It dries fast. Remind yourself of that," Jayne called from the kitchen.

Levi came over for dinner shortly after. "I heard the haircut was a bit rough," he said, reaching out to fluff the ends. "I like it. You look English."

A smile stretched across my face. "Really?"

"Yup."

"For Pete's sake, she looked English before. Crescent roll from a tube?" Jayne offered. "They're hot."

"How's the skirt coming?" Levi asked.

He might have asked because fabric pieces and wads of thread covered a moderate portion of the kitchen table. Jayne's untidiness was rubbing off on me.

"Good," I said, snagging a crescent roll from the basket Jayne offered. "Hoping to be done with the skirt tonight."

I'd wanted to be done with it over the weekend, but I found myself wrapped up in reading. William hadn't asked about my progress. Yet. I stuck the roll in my mouth and examined the fabric pieces I'd assembled so far. Perfect.

———

On Wednesday morning, I walked into work feeling pretty good about myself. I wore my new skirt with the high-heeled tall boots, the ones I had finally figured out how to walk in. My hair…well, I was still getting used to it. But Jayne introduced me to the novelty of hair product. With my strands slightly stuck together in artful clumps, I rather liked my new look.

"Morning, William!" I called out as I entered.

"Mornin'," he said, with the look on his face that he got when he was about to say something critical. But he didn't. He looked up at me, and his mouth snapped shut.

Odd. But nice. I put my things down and set to work.

Chapter 8

"Sara, please, *please* calm down. You're scaring me."

I took a deep breath, but it didn't seem to help. I took another. And another.

And another. Not helping.

We were sitting, Jayne and I, in the lobby waiting area at the Art Institute. In five minutes or so, I would be interviewed for admission to the school.

Another deep breath. I began to feel light-headed.

"What if it goes bad?" I asked. "What then?"

"Then you'll go back and do it over."

"What if they refuse?"

"Then you'll find something else to do, something you'll love even more."

I shook my head. "I couldn't do something else. I left my home to do this! It has to work."

She patted my knee. "Everything works out. Sometimes not the way we'd like. I mean, I lost that Miami story that I wanted so bad, but then I went to Albany and met your brother. The person who went to Miami got a sunburn. I totally got the better end of the deal. Not that I'm comparing."

"You don't think I can do it."

"I think they're looking for determination, and you're certainly determined."

"How do you know that?"

"That you're determined?"

"No, about how that's what they're looking for?"

Jayne gave a wry smile. "I'm a journalist. I have a phone. I find out things."

"You might have told me that before."

"Didn't want to make you more nervous."

I didn't think it was possible to be more nervous—my stomach had passed butterflies hours ago and moved on to birds. Large, anxious birds.

"How do I look?" I smoothed my hair again.

"You look arty. You might not look arty anymore if you keep flattening your hair like that. Artists are supposed to be a bit messy. Like you only sleep when your muse is sleeping."

"My muse?"

"Your creative inspiration. I was making a joke."

"May I laugh when this is over?"

"Sure."

I smoothed my new skirt again. I'd paired it with the hoodie decorated with chiffon. I thought the combination looked dressy and edgy at the same time.

After three lifetimes of worry, my name was called. I stood, making an effort not to teeter in my heeled boots. Why did I wear heels today, anyway? I wore my first heels five months ago. Why wear them now, when my connection to the earth seemed so unstable?

It was too late to change my footwear.

I followed the admissions interviewer into the offices. The walls were painted in bright colors and covered in posters for school events. I think the idea was to help students feel welcome.

It wasn't working.

The interviewer introduced herself as Katrina and gave me a warm smile. "Tell me about yourself," she said.

"Um…" Every single intelligent answer I'd rehearsed flew out of my head. "I like clothes…"

※

"I like clothes? Was I *insane*?" I wailed on the car ride back to the apartment.

"Well…" Jayne paused. "It's true. You do like clothes."

"But I could barely tell her what *kinds* of clothes or my sewing background, or hardly anything of use."

"Did she ask about your GED?"

"She did."

"And…"

"I couldn't come up with anything evasive but truthful, so I told her everything. Told her I was Amish and dropped out of school like a good Amish daughter, but pursued my GED after leaving home to be a fashion designer."

"That's good! That shows you have drive."

I rolled my eyes. "It sounds like a bad movie on that channel on your television—Timelife, Lifetime, something like that. I'm sure she thinks I'm a freak. An ex-Amish freak."

Jayne reached out and ruffled my hair. "But we love our little ex-Amish freak."

I batted her hand away. "Thanks, I guess," I said. The thought of my upcoming driver's test loomed in my mind, but I kept those thoughts to myself.

※

For the second time in a week, I took a seat in absolute terror. This time, however, I was a bit lower to the ground and about to move.

"Tap your brakes for me," the DMV woman said.

I tapped. I also showed off my capabilities with my right *and* left turn signals.

Once she decided Jayne's car was fit to enter, the woman, whose name was Carol, joined me in the car and fastened her seatbelt with a decided click.

The next twenty-five minutes passed in a blur. At length, I pulled back into the parking lot and brought the car to a complete stop, perfectly spaced between the yellow lines.

Carol didn't say anything. Instead, she made a few marks to the paper on her clipboard. "You're a very cautious driver," she said at last. "You check your mirrors, drive defensively, signal ahead of time…my one question is if you maintained the posted speed throughout the test."

"I don't speed," I said, sure of myself. I knew I didn't.

"I didn't think you were speeding," Carol amended. "I wasn't certain if you were driving at the recommended speed. But again, I had difficulty telling, and you stayed within an acceptable limit of the traffic flow." She signed the bottom. "Eighty percent. You passed."

"Really?" I felt the knot in my stomach release a bit.

"Take this paper inside, and they'll prepare your license." Carol's lips tilted upward in what I expected was her version of a smile.

Levi waited inside. He stood and spread his arms wide when he saw me walk back in. "You look happy. Things go well?"

I showed him the paper. "I might have been going a bit slow, but she passed me."

"Might have?" His brows arched. "I'd say probably, but that's my humble opinion. Last I heard, Joely was ready to lace your shoes with lead."

I filled out the appropriate paperwork and got my picture taken. The DMV employee handed me yet another interim card. "I think I like this picture better than the one on my permit."

"It's the practice." Levi slung his arm around my shoulders. "Your student ID should be even better."

My shoulders drooped at the thought of my disastrous interview.

"You're not still worried about that, are you?"

"Why wouldn't I be?"

"Things are going to turn out, Sara. Maybe not the way you plan, but they will turn out. Think about it for a moment. What will you do if you don't get into the art program?"

"Work at the bookstore." I scratched my arm absently as we climbed into Jayne's car. "Figure something else out."

"Does that sound horrible?"

"I really want to design clothes."

"I'm not saying you can't. You could always apply again or ask for a second interview."

I wrinkled my nose. "You're so practical. You and Jayne. You're perfect for each other."

His mouth stretched into a boyish grin. "I think so."

"You guys going to get married anytime soon?"

"I thought I'd talk about that with Jayne first. Seemed fair."

"You're being evasive."

"Maybe."

I rested my head on his shoulder. "She's scared, you know."

Levi shrugged. "Aren't we all?"

⁓⁓

Things fell into an easy routine at work. William picked on me less. We didn't speak much except when he recommended one book or another that we'd chat about later. For work purposes.

Richard called and left a message on Thursday morning.

"He wants holiday decorations," William said, his voice strained.

"Okay," I answered. It seemed reasonable enough to me.

"Zach's gone. He always took care of that kind of stuff." William crossed his sweater-clad arms. "But you know how to decorate for Christmas, right?"

"Um…"

"You do, right?" His voice turned desperate.

I didn't have the heart to break it to him.

"You don't. You don't know how, do you."

I shook my head.

"But you're a girl!"

"A girl whose parents weren't into holiday decorating."

"Atheists, huh?"

"Nonmaterialists." I supposed that was the best way to describe them that didn't include the word *Amish*.

"But decorating now isn't, like, against your religious beliefs?"

"No," I said, letting a small smile creep out. "I've just never done it."

"Fine." He reached back and scratched the back of his neck. "The tree's in the back of the storeroom. To be honest with you, Zach usually puts it together. There are lights back there too, and Richard mentioned snowflakes in the window." He frowned. "Do you know how to make snowflakes?"

"Snowflakes I can do." Thanks to the Christmas program at the school, I had one skill to contribute. "Are there any pinecones?"

"Pinecones? I don't know. I thought your parents didn't decorate."

"They didn't, not like people around here do. But some pinecones and branches came inside, sometimes."

"That's something. Can you stay after hours today, help set things up?"

"Sure." I'd need to let Jayne know, but I knew it would be fine. I drove the car to and from work now. Jayne was back to riding her motorcycle even in the wettest weather and loving every moment of it.

The day proceeded like any other until closing. Then William closed up and disappeared. Rather than stare out the window, I tidied up the register and walked the shelves, making sure every volume was where it was supposed to be.

As I approached the door to the workroom, I felt the pull of the *Godey's Lady's Book*. I didn't know what it was, exactly, about those pages. I wanted to study the images and figure out how women could have worn floor-length, full skirts a hundred years ago and wear pants of indigo-dyed canvas with everything now.

It was true. I did love clothes. What would I do if I couldn't learn about them?

I could always do what Joely suggested—go rogue, I think it was. But I'd spent time teaching myself things, learning everything I could while hiding things under floorboards in my room. The floorboard life was no longer necessary, but I felt I'd come to the point where I needed someone else to teach me things, to tell me what was important to remember about fabric and fashion.

William was still far from hearing and sight. I reached for the workroom doorknob, and it twisted easily in my hand. I entered, holding my breath. I saw the book on the worktable, placed to the side. I could see where William was constructing a special box for it, lined with what looked like silk. I started to finger the material but then snatched my hand away. Instead, I reached for the gloves that lay beside the volume and carefully lifted the cover.

The illustrations were so detailed. I loved how the editor, Sarah Hale, had included instructions to her readership showing how to make and construct hats and capes and ornaments for gowns.

At the sound of a door elsewhere in the shop, I carefully closed the cover and put the gloves aside and stepped from the workroom on quick, light feet, remembering my days smuggling magazines into my room. By the time William fully reappeared, I saw he had his arms so full of boxes that he wouldn't have seen me anyway.

"Could you grab one of the top boxes, Sara? This tree box is killing me."

I rushed over and removed the cardboard boxes on top, revealing his face.

He looked away, shuffled a few more steps toward the front windows, and all but dumped the largest box on the ground. "Zach's a lot stronger than I gave him credit for. I may have to stop hassling him."

I chuckled and set my own boxes near the large box. "What's in here, anyway?"

"There's the tree, for starters."

"Um…" I looked down. I didn't see a tree. I saw a box. "Where's the tree?"

"In the box."

I tilted my head. "The tree is in a box."

"Right. We'll put it together. If that's okay—I ordered some takeout, thought this could take a while. You like Thai, right?"

"I'm not sure I've had Thai."

"Oh. Sorry, I should have checked with you. I can order something else—it's Richard's treat."

"I'll try it. One of my friends is a foodie, so I eat new stuff all the time." I looked down again at the box. I could only pretend I knew what I was doing for so long. This time, I wanted answers. "Now, tell me again," I said, "why there's a tree in a box, why it needs to be assembled, and if you want, tell me how it got in the box in the first place. Is it, like, preserved?"

William stared at me for a moment and then laughed. He actually laughed. "It's fake. You've never seen a fake Christmas tree?"

"Um, no. What's the purpose of a fake tree?"

"You decorate it like a real tree and then take it apart afterward. All the looks, none of the wildlife. Seriously, you've never seen a fake tree?"

I looked at the box yet again and shook my head. "Fake trees. You English people are crazy."

"What?"

"Nothing." I bit my lip. Oops. "So how do you put together a fake Christmas tree?"

William opened the box, revealing evergreen branches bundled together with zip ties. "There's a center piece…like a trunk. All the branches fit into slots. After that, I have no idea. This was Zach's thing. He's the only guy I know who can decorate a Christmas tree while impersonating Michael Corleone. If we get stuck, I've got his cell number."

"You'd call him at home?"

"The guy left us high, dry, and up to our armpits in tinsel. Yeah, I'd call him at home."

"What's tinsel?"

"Cheapo shiny stuff that melts in vacuum cleaners. You ready to start this?"

So we started. I got scissors from the office and cut the zip ties from the branches. "These are different sizes," I said as I made a pile of tie-free fake greenery.

William eyed the pile. "Big branches go on the bottom, right? Does that seem right to you?"

This side of William completely confused me. I was fairly certain he thought I was an idiot, and here he was asking my advice.

"Evergreens are shaped like this, right?" I made a tree-like triangle shape with my arms.

"Good call."

"Why don't we organize the branches by size?"

"Better call."

A buzzer sounded in the back. "That's food. I'll get it." William rose and jogged toward the back delivery door. He returned moments later with two plastic sacks full of white boxes.

"Obviously, the largest box held the tree," I said, clearing a place on the floor to eat. "What's in the others?"

"Lights for the windows and the tree, and some chintzy ornaments. I take it you don't do chopsticks?"

"No thanks."

"Whatever we don't finish tonight we can finish tomorrow, if that works for you. Do you have plans tomorrow?"

"Kind of," I said, thinking of Jayne's movie nights.

"Oh." He busied himself with opening the white boxes.

"I can probably…postpone it. It's a thing my roommate does."

"Okay. Whatever." He held out a box. "Panang Curry?"

Chapter 9

"There's a dark spot."

"No there's not," William said, not bothering to look.

I crossed my arms. "Yes there is. In the middle—there, to the left."

He turned, looked, and sighed. "I don't see it. There is no dark spot." He waved his hand in an odd, circular motion.

"What's with the hand?"

"*Star Wars.* 'These aren't the droids you're looking for.' You know."

"Haven't seen *Star Wars* yet."

"You really were sheltered." He ran a hand through his shaggy locks. "Do you think the spot's all that noticeable?"

"Moths will avoid it."

"Can you just scrunch the lights around a bit?"

I turned and reached for the tiny, electric lights. "I thought this would be easier."

"You and me both. I didn't know I'd need an engineering degree to put up Christmas decorations."

"Scrunching isn't working. I'm taking them off."

William sighed. I ignored him. "Go cut some snowflakes."

"Snowflakes?"

"We were making snowflakes, right?"

"You are."

I lowered the lights in my hands and looked at him incredulously. "You don't know how to make snowflakes?"

"My mom always did the Christmas decorating. It was a thing for her. When we were kids, we'd wake up on December first to find the whole house decorated."

"That must have been fun," I said, imagining what it must have been like to wake up to twinkle lights.

"I guess." William sounded less than excited.

"When I'm done with the lights, we'll have to find some paper. I'll show you how to make them." I got down on my hands and knees and took the lights around the tree twice, following the shape of the fake branches. "Does that look even?"

"It's fine."

In the next few moments I rewrapped the lights around the tree, and with William's assistance, placed every last ornament up.

"What's this one?" I pointed at one as we stood back to take account of our work.

"A dreidel—a Jewish children's toy. It's Richard's way of being multi-cultural."

"Ah." I clasped my hands together at my waist. "Do we have paper and scissors for snowflakes?"

"You still want to do those? It's getting late."

"At least a couple. I love snowflakes."

William went to the back to find me paper and scissors. When he returned, I took the top sheet of paper and started folding. "I make either twelve- or sixteen-point snowflakes. The number you come up with depends on how you fold it." I made the folds to produce a sixteen-point snowflake, making a square from the letter-sized paper and then folding it into increasingly smaller triangles.

"Whoa, slow down there," William protested.

I waved him off. "Don't worry, I'll do another. Look how I'm paying attention to the corners as I fold. They're nice and sharp." I raised the scissors and began to make a cut. "Ugh." I frowned, examining the scissor blades. "These are not."

"You need better ones?"

I handed him the dull pair. "Yes, please."

The second set was much better. I began cutting away various shapes along the folds. "Now," I said, "after I cut the larger pieces, I cut away smaller shapes around the larger ones. See this?" I pointed to the largest fold.

"Yeah."

"Never cut there. The whole thing will fall apart. Just cut away pieces."

I cut as I spoke, relaxing with the familiar feel of sharp scissors in my hands.

"I don't know about this…" William said, his voice filled with doubt.

"They're easy," I said with a shake of my head. "If I could teach Elizabeth to make them, you can learn too."

"Who?"

I froze. Had I...I replayed the last few moments in my mind.

"Who's Elizabeth?" William repeated.

I had. That's what became of me letting my guard down. "My sister," I said simply enough. "She's young."

"Oh."

Nothing more was said on the subject. I watched my words for the rest of the night.

⁓⁂⁓

By the end of that evening, we'd decorated the tree, taped a few snowflakes in the corner of the display window, laid out fake snow that William called "angel hair" on top of white lights, and placed Christmas books on stands on the display ledge.

"There's still work to be done," William said, surveying the progress. "We still need to put lights around the window and put dust-collecting decorations on the register counter."

"They'll look pretty," I said, covering a smile.

"They'll collect dust," he maintained.

"Your snowflakes look nice."

"Yes they do," he conceded. "I am a paper man though. Maybe tomorrow we'll have to make some others with better paper."

"Better?"

"I have some more finely milled paper that's thinner. It should be easier to cut."

"Sounds like fun," I said, picking up some of the boxes and mess from dinner.

"Don't worry about it," William waved me toward the door. "It's late, and you still need to show up tomorrow."

"So do you."

"I live upstairs." He pointed upward. "My commute's a bit shorter than yours."

I tilted my head. "Upstairs?"

"There's an apartment. Richard lets me rent it. The space is part of the bookstore's property."

"Oh." I hadn't thought about having an apartment above a store, much less that someone would be living in it.

"I'll walk you to your car."

He did. As I drove carefully away, I could still see his face in my rearview mirror, watching.

———※———

"So, how was decorating?" Jayne asked when I got home. She set her book aside. "And by 'How was decorating,' I mean, did Will behave himself?"

I laughed and almost regretted the way I must have described him earlier. "Decorating was fine. Will was fine. He's not a bad person, just…abrupt, I think. But I taught him to make snowflakes, so I think he'll grow up to be okay."

"You had a good time, then?"

"I did. It made me wonder—have you thought of putting decorations up in here?"

Jayne lifted an eyebrow. "I don't think I've decorated for Christmas here. Ever."

"Not ever?"

"Not ever. Never."

"Oh."

"You want to decorate in here? Since when are you into the holiday frivolity?"

"It looks pretty. Decorations are like clothes for your home."

Jayne sighed. "You would think of it like that."

———※———

I was a bit groggier than usual when I arrived for work on Friday morning. William didn't comment, but he did hand me a cup of coffee when he saw me. "Late night last night. Picked one up for myself and thought you might like one. It's Stumptown."

I knew from Levi that Stumptown was some of the best coffee in Portland. I lifted the coffee to my lips. It was strong and black and warmed me from the inside. "Thanks," I said.

"Are you able to finish things tonight?"

"I am."

"You said your roommate has a thing."

"She does, but she also said they'd wait for me."

"Who's 'they'?"

"My roommate, her friends—I suppose they're my friends too. And my brother. He's engaged to my roommate."

"Really?" William's brows arched. "How's that going?"

I gave a small smirk. "Harder for my brother than for Jayne."

"Jayne's your roommate?"

"Yes. He wants to set a date, she's…"

"Not interested?"

"She's interested. She's just…" I thought about it for a moment. "Confused."

William shook his head. "Women."

"You have a problem with women?"

He seemed to realize he was talking to one. A young one, but female all the same. "They're complicated. Sometimes too much so."

"Men are complicated too, just in a different way."

William shrugged. "I guess that's true. Well, let's get to work. Richard put a coupon in the Oregonian that starts today, so we'll have an onslaught of bargain shoppers to deal with."

I nodded and sipped my coffee, letting William's gruffness roll off of me. I was starting to get the feeling that he only acted that way when he didn't know what else to be.

―――――

"I think the window needs more twinkle lights," I said that night after we'd finished grazing on the pizza William had delivered.

William looked up from where he was cutting snowflakes, the designs becoming more and more complicated. "Sure. Just as long as there's still a clear view of the books inside."

"There will be," I assured him. I fastened the lights carefully down the windowpanes and checked my watch when I finished. "I should head out soon if that's alright." I paused for a moment and then blurted out what I'd planned to say. "You're welcome to join me, you know. Gemma brings lots of food every week. Jayne's picked out some Pixar shorts, *Elf*, and *White Christmas*, I think. She likes to hit a range of films, and with Christmas coming…"

"I hate Will Ferrell."

"Oh." I was lost, but that feeling certainly wasn't new.

"But thanks anyway."

"You're welcome," I said, confused but not surprised.

―――

To Jayne's annoyance, I wouldn't stop pestering her for our own Christmas tree. A real one, not plastic like the one at the shop.

Jayne called Levi, saying that if they were going to drive down to the Fred Meyer parking lot to pick out a living organism that had been severed from its root system in the earth, it may as well be transported in Levi's pickup.

Levi had other ideas though. "If I had my pick, I'd buy a Forest Service pass and hike around Mount Hood," he said when he arrived at the apartment Saturday morning.

Jayne's face contorted into an expression of frozen horror.

"But with the weather the way it's been, let's go to a tree farm. We won't need snowshoes that way."

"Snowshoes?" Jayne repeated, frozen.

"A tree farm...that sounds fun," I said. "I'll get my coat and shoes."

I turned and looked over my shoulder. Jayne remained rooted in place. I grabbed her hand and pulled her toward the coat closet. "Come on. It's just the outdoors. It won't hurt you."

―――

"My feet are cold."

"Walk faster." Levi swung Jayne's hand before tucking it in his pocket.

I smiled and looked away. "How big of a tree are we looking for?"

"Three feet," Jayne said.

"Seven feet," Levi said at the same time. "We're looking for a Christmas tree, not a Christmas bush."

"An *Abies procera* is an *Abies procera* regardless of the size."

I frowned. "*Abies procera*?"

"Noble fir. Jayne's getting in touch with the Latin within." Levi said. "If a tree's so small you could envision it on fire and talking to Moses, it's a bush. We're in the market for a tree."

I turned to Jayne. "You speak Latin?"

"Article on organic Christmas tree farming," she admitted.

"Which means she probably went to a Christmas tree farm and didn't whine the whole time." Levi nudged Jayne with his elbow.

She nudged back. "I interviewed the owner in his office, next to a blazing fire, thank you very much."

I rolled my eyes and pointed ahead to distract my chilly, irritable roommate. "What about that one?" I said, not really looking as I pointed.

"Scraggly," Jayne said. "Looks like the tree in *A Charlie Brown Christmas*."

I followed my own finger. The plant I'd indicated was at death's doorstep. "Oh. Maybe not that one then. Not that I know what the *Charlie Brown* tree looks like."

"We'll watch it next week," Jayne promised.

"Either way," Levi said, "that was a bush and not a tree." He raised his head and studied the trees coming into view. "I see some possibilities up ahead."

"How far ahead?" Jayne asked. "Just so I have a realistic view of my future."

I rolled my eyes. "If you're good and stop complaining, I'll make sugar cookies with lemon zest when we get back."

Jayne considered my offer, silently.

I sweetened the deal. "Peanut butter crinkles?"

"You're on." She gave a little skip. "I'll be good."

Levi shot me a conspiratorial look. "You know, I'm not sure there's going to be any good ones nearby. Might need to keep going for another mile or two. That's where they plant the better-looking trees."

Jayne opened her mouth to protest, thought for a moment, and then folded her arms. "Peanut butter crinkles?"

"With Dove chocolate rather than Hershey kisses."

She squared her shoulders. "See if you can keep up, Levi!"

Chapter 10

I t's leaning," Jayne said when Levi finally stood the Christmas tree upright. "And possibly crooked."

"It's nature. You want a straight tree, buy a fake one. Bet you it won't smell this good." Levi stepped back. "It looks green. Healthy. Needs decorations." He looked to Jayne. "You got lights?"

"Do you really want me to answer that question?" Jayne folded her arms.

"It would have been nice if you'd told me that while I was out for a tree stand." Levi studied her and shook his head. "I don't suppose lights and decorations were much on your radar."

"We need twinkle lights," I said. "And ornaments. And snowflakes."

"And peanut butter crinkles," Jayne added. "Just saying."

Levi ignored her. "We could string cranberries, hang tinsel..."

I wrinkled my nose. "The cheap shiny stuff that melts in vacuums?"

Suddenly I had Jayne and Levi's full attention. "When...what?" Jayne tilted her head. "When have you...come in contact with tinsel?"

"Um, William mentioned it at the store. That's what he said tinsel was." I sighed. I'd done it again. I watched as Jayne and Levi suppressed amused expressions.

"He's right," Jayne said. "Sorry. It was just funny hearing you say it. Absolutely right though, you and William. I would know. My mom went on a tinsel binge when I was eight. The vacuum had to be put down."

I clapped my hands. "Let's get decorations."

Levi patted my head. "I thought you saw Christmas decorations as frivolous."

I batted his hand away. "Some, yes. But just a little is okay. And they sparkle."

⁂

There was no mail Sunday, which was just as well. For the past week the only thing stopping me from going home every lunch break to check the mailbox was the thought of losing my parking space, even though it was tucked in the back. People in Portland were ruthless about spaces, and I wasn't going to take that chance.

By Monday though, I was getting anxious. Weeks had passed since my disastrous "I like clothes" interview, and I hadn't heard a word.

They would tell me one way or the other, wouldn't they? I knew I could ask nearly anyone, but I was too afraid and too tired of asking questions with answers obvious to everyone but me.

The shop was busy Monday. During a short lull, William shared with me his trick for getting rid of books that hadn't moved—he put them on the front display table with a sign that read "For Your Holiday Consideration, 30% Off Our Yuletide Picks."

"People come in looking for books," he said as I studied the display he'd put together.

I lifted one. "*Birds of the World*?"

"We've hardly sold any since we got them in two years ago. That's when Richard still did the ordering."

"He doesn't anymore?"

"Oh no. He knows I handle it better." He pointed at the book. "There are some very nice birds in there. Would work for coffee tables and bird lovers. And the cardinal on the front is festive."

"Festive?"

"It's red. Red like Christmas."

I put the book back. "Does this work?"

"Like magic. On the idiot shoppers, at least. Others are more discerning, but we have books for them too."

"Why wouldn't everyone be discerning? Wouldn't you want to find books for people that they'd actually enjoy?"

William snorted. "People should, but they don't. It's Christmas, you know?"

I didn't. But I didn't want to tell him that.

***

I hurried home after we locked up. Hurried as much as I could, anyway. Maybe three miles per hour over the limit. Maybe.

Jayne wasn't home yet, so I used my key to open the mailbox. Catalogs, a utility bill, and something that looked like a Christmas card from Jayne's sister, Beth. A Bed, Bath & Beyond coupon. And two letters addressed to me.

One bore the logo for the Art Institute. The other spelled my name out in familiar loops and lines. The name in the return address read "Rebecca Zook."

My sister.

———— ⟡ ————

Jayne came home to find me sitting at the table, both letters in front of me. "Mail? Did you get something from the art school?"

"I did," I said, still not able to wrap my mind around the situation. "I got a letter from my sister too."

"Oh." Jayne finished taking off her motorcycle gear and took a seat in the chair next to me. "Did you read it?"

"Not yet. How did she get this address?"

"Your mom has it."

"Did I know about that?"

Jayne placed her elbow on the table and rested her head in her open palm. "I don't know if we ever talked about it. But I called her a few days after you left."

"That wasn't any of your business!" I said, even though I knew it was stupid to even think such a thing. I lived in her home. She was engaged to my brother. It was completely her business.

She knew that too, I think. Instead of arguing, Jayne sighed and put her arm down. "You're not going to be happy with me, but there are other letters."

"What?"

"Levi calls it the mail brigade. For a year after he left, Rebecca sent letter after letter trying to get him to come back to the community."

"Rebecca's been sending me letters?" My head spun. I loved Rebecca, looked up to her. "For how long?"

"A while."

I felt my chest grow tight. "How long?" I demanded.

"They started after you'd been here all of a week."

"What did you do with them?"

"Levi was here when the first one came. He insisted I hold them aside.

He's got them if you want them. I didn't want to go through your mail, but I didn't want you part of a brainwashing effort either. None of it's true. It's all manipulation, trying to get you to come back. And it's not like I was spying on you—I can't read them. They're written in Pennsylvania Dutch."

Without waiting another moment, I opened the letter and scanned the contents.

> *We miss you so much…Mother cries every time she speaks of you…Father has grown so pale, I worry for his health…He has seen the chiropractor many times, but nothing seems to work…The children miss you…Leah looks so much like you these days, but sadder…*

I put the letter down. "Could it be true? Did I ruin my family?"

"Think about it. Rebecca wrote things just like that to Levi after he left, or so he's told me. What was it like after Levi left. Do you remember?"

"I was young," I said, "but I remember. It was very sad. But after a while, it got better. Levi sent letters. He visited, especially when the younger ones were born. We adjusted."

"See? You adjusted. Rebecca was trying to make things seem worse than they were."

"But Levi wrote letters and visited. I haven't. Now my parents have lost two children."

"Do you want to call your grandmother? Ida would be straight with you."

I thought about it and shook my head. "I can't go back. I can't call."

"Are you sure? It's only a phone call."

"No. It's contact. I can't."

"I'm sorry."

I knew she was. And I didn't blame her for keeping the letters away. I told her as much.

"Are you going to look at the other letter?" she asked.

My heart pounded as I looked at it, the narrow white envelope on the table. "What if they say no?"

"Then you will find work as an organic farmer. Farm woman. Farmstress."

I reached for the second letter, this time opening it with more care. I unfolded the enclosed paper and read.

"Oh."

"Oh?"

"They must not have thought I was a moron. They let me in." I looked up at Jayne. "They let me in?" I took a closer look at the letter. "Are they crazy?"

Jayne laughed out loud. "You did it! You don't have to be a farmette after all!"

We stood up in our chairs, hugged each other, and danced around the living room. I tried to fill my mind with thoughts of school and crowd out thoughts of home.

———

William squinted at me Tuesday morning. "You're smiling a lot."

"Am I?" I think I may have smiled when I said that.

"What's going on? New meds?"

I didn't know what he meant, but that was nothing new. "I got into the school I applied for."

"Oh yeah?" He paused with the box he was unloading. "What school?"

"The Art Institute." I couldn't help it. I beamed.

"So you're, like, an artist? I didn't know that. What's your medium?"

"Fabric, I guess. I want to go into..." I tried to remember what it was called officially. "Apparel design. You know, clothes."

"Congratulations," William said to my surprise. I had expected him to say something pointed or possibly show remorse for the holey flannel shirt he wore. "I hear that's a great program."

"Thank you," I said. Feeling bold, I asked where he went to college.

"William and Mary for my undergraduate degree. Colombia for my graduate work. Hated New York. Most of that time, I traveled back and forth to the American Academy of Bookbinding in Colorado to earn a diploma in binding and book conservation."

My mind tried to take it all in. "You attended two schools at once?"

"The Academy offers one-week classes a few times a year. It started out as a hobby and ended up as a profession."

"You went to school in three different places?"

"Yup."

"Wow." I couldn't imagine going to so many places, learning so much. "What did you study?"

"English literature at William and Mary, Russian literature at Colombia."

"So much literature," I said.

He shrugged. "I liked to read."

"If I make clothes with my design degree," I said, thinking as I spoke, "what do you do with literature degrees?"

"This and that." He gave an empty smile. "At least I'm not waiting tables."

"People wait tables with literature degrees?"

"Dirty secret of the academic world. When are you starting classes?"

"January eleventh. Although there's an orientation for new students on the seventh."

"Were you planning on working through school, or are you going to give notice to Richard?"

Was he trying to get rid of me? I shook my head. "I want to work. I need to work. I like being responsible for myself."

"That's always the goal," William said, with a bitter tinge to his voice. A customer stepped in before I could ask why.

⋙⋘

As elated as I felt over the acceptance to the school, Rebecca's letter weighed heavily on my mind. I called Levi over my lunch break, and he offered to bring dinner to the apartment that night.

Getting Levi to come to the apartment wasn't hard, considering his fiancée lived there. I wondered how long they would live in limbo before they married. I wondered where I would live when they did, but I stopped myself. I could only worry about one thing at a time.

"Is that Chinese takeout?" I asked Levi when I let him inside.

"It is."

"Buttering me up because you kept Rebecca's letters from me?"

"Felt like my sodium level was low, that's all. Jayne's not home yet?"

"She had a few projects to finish up at the paper."

"Sit down with me?"

"Okay." I followed him to the couch and seated myself next to him. "Were you ever going to tell me?"

"Honestly? No. There wasn't a good reason to. She's our sister, and I know we both love her, but Rebecca is a skilled manipulator when she wants to be. I didn't think you needed to be exposed to that."

"Manipulation or not, what did she say?"

"Everything she said to me when I left. How everyone was sad and miserable and crying in their pie slices at every chance. I've talked to Mom about it. She said it certainly wasn't easy, but it was never that bad."

"But you visited and wrote. I don't. What if it *is* that bad?"

"Then wait for it to come from someone who's still living at the family house. They have this address if they want to write. But I think Mom knows that you'll write or visit when you're ready. She told me once that she wasn't surprised that I left, that she could see my restless spirit outside my skin. She had hoped I might stay or even return, but she didn't expect me to do either. My guess is that it's the same with you. You've wanted this a long time."

I did—that was the crazy part. I wanted to be here so badly, and I now I felt torn between my life in Portland and my life at my parents' farm. Sometimes I felt as if I were splitting into two people, my Amish self and my new English self. I still knew how to be Amish, how to be plain, how to not say hello and goodbye because it was too fancy. But now there was my English self who watched films, baked fancy cookies, and dressed in clothes from Nordstrom's sale rack. Little wonder I had no friends outside of Jayne and Levi's circle—making friends with me had to be a confusing experience.

"The letters are in my truck if you want to see them," Levi said, his words interrupting my thoughts. "Although I really don't recommend it."

I sat up straighter. "But I could see them if I wanted?"

"Absolutely. You're an adult."

I lifted an eyebrow. "An adult whose mail you hid. In fact, I think that's actually illegal."

"Probably is. Want to give Joely a call?"

"She'd be more likely to get the police in Washington to make Rebecca stop—what's the word? *harassing?*—harassing me through mail."

"You're probably right."

We heard Jayne's footsteps as she came up the stairs. "So we're okay, you and I?" he asked. I could tell he was a bit worried.

I wrapped my arm around his back and gave him a hug. "We're okay."

The bolt on the door turned and Jayne stepped in. "Hi, guys. Chinese?

Everything good in here? 'Cause, you know, you have to tell me before you hitch a ride in the trunk of my car again."

We laughed together. The moment felt so much like home, like family. I blinked back tears without anyone seeing and went in search of clean plates for dinner.

awoke the next morning with a scratchy throat and eyelids that didn't want to open. Against my body's will, I pushed back my bed covers and sat up.

Every muscle ached. I couldn't breathe through my nose, and it felt three times its normal size. I rose and showered anyway and dressed in the most comfortable yet professional clothes I could find.

I shivered and reached for an extra cardigan, followed by a scarf. I skimped on makeup for the day, only using a bit of eyeliner, mascara, and lipstick. Maybe the bit of lipstick was a vanity, but at least it would help my lips from getting more chapped than they already were. I felt dried out.

Jayne stumbled out to the kitchen just as I'd finished preparing a corn syrup and warm water gargle. "Please tell me you're not putting that in your mouth," she said, her eyes glued to the cup I'd just poured the ingredients into.

"It's for my sore throat," I croaked. Ouch. That was the first time I'd tried to speak all morning, and it hurt!

"You have a sore throat? I'm so sorry! I have drugs—what do you want? Throat drops? Decongestants?"

I didn't know what any of those were. "Thanks. I'll just use this for now. It's what my mom always gave us."

Jayne wrinkled her nose. "Okay," she said, even though she clearly thought it was nasty.

I didn't think it was bad. But then I was raised on it.

As I drove to work, I noticed a lot of cars seemed to be passing me. Was I driving slower than usual? Hard to say. My nose started dripping then, and I fumbled with the glove compartment in search of something I could wipe my nose with that wasn't my coat sleeve.

Because that would be gross.

I finally found a Starbucks napkin just in time to catch the precipitation coming from my nostril.

I knew what Rebecca would say if she knew I was sick. She'd say it was because I wasn't outside and working hard. She'd blame it on my fancy living. And then she'd make me ginger tea.

Whatever. Rebecca wasn't here. I knew she got her own colds from time to time. It happened. It wasn't a punishment. But I began to feel it was a punishment as soon as I got out of the car and was faced a second time with the brisk Portland winter winds.

I didn't see Will when I stepped inside, so I unlocked the front door and got the computer and register running. When I heard the footfalls on the steps I knew he was on his way, remembering that he lived just upstairs.

"Oh, you're here," he said when he came in, looking around the store, likely making sure I hadn't damaged it in his absence. His eyes stopped when he saw me. "You look awful."

"Thanks," I said, and to make matters worse, I sneezed.

"I mean, you look fine, better than most people, actually..."

I barely paid attention to his words. My nose was running again, and I couldn't find where we kept the scratchy tissue. "Okay. I'm sick. I know. I'll be very careful to keep my hands washed."

Before I knew what he was doing, he reached out and touched my forehead. I would have jumped back about twenty feet if I could have moved at all. But I couldn't.

"You're warm," he said.

"No, I'm actually kind of cold."

"I mean, you're running a fever."

"Oh."

"I have some ibuprofen upstairs. It's a fever reducer. Want some?"

Instead of waiting for my reply, he put the Be Back in Ten sign in the door window and walked toward the stairs, clearly assuming I would follow. So I did. I followed him upstairs, my head growing stuffier with each step. William unlocked the door at the top and waited for me to finish my climb.

"Did you come down with this last night?"

"This morning."

He closed the door behind us. There was a kettle on the stove. He poured out the old water and filled it back up, replaced it, and turned on the burner. He reached into a cabinet and rifled through a shoebox he found inside.

Standing made me tired. I looked around the apartment.

It was basically two rooms—a kitchen, dining room, bedroom, and living space all out in the open, with what I assumed was a bathroom behind a partially open door. I blushed when I saw the bed. I'd never been in a man's home before, at least not one he didn't share with eight other family members. It didn't seem to bother William, who was still opening cabinets and rearranging his kitchen clutter, so I decided not to let it bother me. The table and chairs were close by, so I pulled out a chair and sat.

Then put my head down on the table.

And closed my eyes.

Moments later I heard the light tap of pills being placed inches from my nose and the faint ring of porcelain on wood. "Are you awake?"

I opened my eyes and sat up, slowly. "Yes, sorry. I was…resting my head."

"Here's some chamomile tea, two ibuprofen, and five hundred milligrams of vitamin C. The tea's not too hot, so you should be able to drink it okay."

A small wisp of steam rose from the mug. The mug looked like a William mug. Brown and sturdy, with crackles in the glaze. I shook my head. Illness made me think odd things. I tested the tea; William was right, it wasn't too hot. I lifted the pills to my lips and followed with the tea. William watched me until I finished the contents of the brown mug.

I set it down and stood to leave. William held out his hand.

"Honestly? I can't put you to work like this. You'll scare the customers. I'd send you home, but I don't trust you to drive. I saw you pull in." He nodded toward the window. I could see it overlooked the alleyway where I parked my car every day. "My grandmother drives faster than you were this morning."

I opened my mouth to say I always drove carefully, but I thought better of it as William continued. "I've got a couch, and it's comfortable. Why don't you lie down until the drugs kick in, and if you're feeling better and look less like a zombie you can work the register. If you don't, I'll call Richard and you can take a sick day. Sound okay?"

The couch sat against the wall. It didn't seem to be growing anything. In fact, the whole apartment seemed cleaner than I would have guessed. Rather than answer, I stood and felt my feet shuffle toward the couch.

Somewhere between the shuffling and laying down, a blanket appeared. I kicked off my shoes and pulled it over my chilly body.

I fell asleep within moments.

The light seemed different. My room never got so much light, at least not in the mornings.

But I didn't have heavy brown curtains.

I sat straight up and instantly regretted it. My congestion returned, accompanied by memories. William making me tea, giving me medicine to help my cold. I pushed the blanket away. I didn't feel feverish anymore, but my nose was so stuffed that my eyes watered from the pressure.

What time was it? I couldn't see a clock anywhere. Sitting up straighter, I saw numbers on William's oven. Surely it couldn't be right. I folded the blanket with some urgency, slipped my shoes back on, and began the descent to the bookstore.

"There you are," William said when he saw me. "How do you feel?"

"How long did I sleep?" Tension curled in my stomach.

"Three hours."

Then the oven was right. Horror washed over me. "Why didn't you wake me?"

"I tried. You hit me."

My horror tripled. I put my hand to my mouth. "I hit you?"

"Don't look like that. You're a bad shot when you're essentially unconscious. And your unconsciousness wanted to sleep longer."

"Has it been busy?" I looked around, spotting three customers from where I stood.

"Not enough to worry me. Richard's been here for two hours. Go home. Running yourself ragged won't make you any healthier."

I wanted to say thanks but sneezed instead. William took me by the shoulders, turned me around, and walked me toward the back door, where my coat and scarf waited. "Try to drive faster than my grandmother," he said in lieu of goodbye.

I really did try to drive home faster than I arrived, though I had no idea if I succeeded or not. The moment I got home, I shrugged out of my coat and went straight to bed.

When I awoke for the third time that day, the room was dark, and a faint savory scent made its way through my clogged sinuses.

I found Gemma and Jayne in the kitchen, chatting. Their conversation ended abruptly when I entered the room. "She's alive!" Jayne exclaimed, turning a bit on the barstool she sat perched on. "How are you feeling?"

"Better, I think."

"That's good. I've never seen you so down. Checked on you earlier, you were stone cold out of it. I called Gemma because I thought she might want to feed you."

"Chicken soup?" Gemma lifted a ladle from the Dutch oven on the stove.

"Is it French or Italian?" I asked.

"Neither. It just tastes good."

"Which is not to say there's not apple and Gruyere in there," Jayne said. "What Gemma means is that the soup is of indeterminate nationality."

"It tastes good. The soup does not need to be subjected to racial profiling. Sara, would you like some?"

I nodded, watching as Gemma poured a small amount into a bowl for me. "Finish that," she said, "and you can have more."

She watched as I lifted a spoonful to my mouth. My eyebrows lifted as the liquid hit my tongue.

"I can taste it," I said after swallowing. I smiled as Gemma gave a small victory dance. "It's very good. I'll have more in a moment."

"Would you like some toast with it? I brought some crusty herb bread with me."

I shook my head and patted my throat. "Too scratchy. Maybe tomorrow. You can leave the bread here."

Gemma waved her hand. "It won't be fresh tomorrow. I'll send Jayne home with a new loaf."

"This may horrify you," Jayne said as she faced Gemma, "but we have been known to eat day-old bread in this apartment. And lived to tell the tale."

"Of course you can eat it," Gemma countered. "The question is if you should, especially when you could have a fresh loaf."

"But we don't want to be wasteful with bread."

"Aha." Gemma lifted a finger. "And I bring the good news of great joy concerning the miracle of croutons. And bread crumbs. And Tuscan bread

soup. European cuisine doesn't recognize wastefulness. French cuisine was
based on using everything edible available. And I do mean everything."

I sat back and listened to them squabble amicably over bread as I sipped
at more soup. It really was very good, completely different from anything
I had grown up on.

Sometimes I felt as if instead of moving seventy-five miles north of home,
I'd actually changed planets. The food, the speech, the clothes—and even
though I didn't let my mind rest on it, even God seemed different.

The last point set my mind on edge every time I thought of it. I wished
that even though my world changed around me, the God I had been raised
to understand at a distance remained unchanged. But I knew it was not
the case. Jayne, Levi, and Gemma described a God very unlike the one I'd
been told about for eighteen years. I knew I needed to reintroduce myself
now that we were meeting under different circumstances. Maybe a part of
me was waiting for Him.

Chapter 12

The next two weeks flew by. I got over my cold and went back to work. Without help, I found and purchased presents for everyone, wrapped them, and placed them under the tree.

On Christmas Eve I took an extra bag of clothes to work, thinking I could change and head straight to the church service after I clocked out. But what I saw when I stepped inside the shop took me completely by surprise.

"Not a word," William said.

And that was just as well, because I had no words. Rather than his usual worn jeans and knit shirts, William wore black wool trousers—they had to be wool, their drape was so elegant—and a sky-blue cashmere sweater over a striped button-down shirt. His hair had been trimmed, and the ends no longer covered his ears. His face was clean shaven.

He looked miserable.

"Why would I say anything?" I said, innocently.

"My mom."

"What?"

"It's for my mom."

I could barely imagine William having a mother. But if she was responsible for his change in garments, she had good taste.

"We do a lot of things for our mothers," I said, speaking before thinking. The moment the words left my mouth, I thought of my own mother and how I'd all but abandoned her.

William harrumphed.

"Are you seeing your family for Christmas tonight?"

"And everything that entails."

I tilted my head. "Oh?"

"I said I didn't want to talk about it."

"No, you didn't."

"I did too. I told you, not a word."

"That was about your clothes, I assumed. I was asking about your Christmas. I don't know how I could have assumed about your Christmas earlier. You hadn't said anything about it."

"I don't want to talk about my Christmas either. Did you finish the reshelving pile last night?"

"Yes," I crossed my arms. "What else do you prefer I not ask about? Just so I know ahead of time."

"Fine. What do you want to know? Going to church with my parents, followed by their annual Christmas Eve party. I'm supposed to be presentable and talk to all of my dad's golf buddies and my brother's chums from his law firm, none of whom can manage to put together a sentence that doesn't involve excessive drinking, the state of the club's lawns, or whether the pinstripe suit sucks. Whole conversations about the choice of the pinstripe suit. I'd rather reorganize the entire shop alphabetically, but never mind. Oh, and my mom's friends will want me to meet their daughters, who will all be friendly until they find out that I work in a bookstore and have no aspirations to be CEO of anything and that my five-year plan doesn't include a trip to either law school or Biarritz."

"Whole conversations about a suit?"

"Whole conversations. Though that probably doesn't horrify you—you're a fashion person."

I shrugged. "A dress might warrant a conversation, but men's suits just don't seem that interesting."

"They're not, trust me."

"No one there will be interesting? No one who reads books, watches movies, and talks about them?"

"It's a dry, dry desert." He leaned against the counter. "You don't want to go, do you?"

"What?" Surely I'd misheard him.

"You're interesting to talk to. If you came, it might not be so bad. And the food is always good, it's just the people that are inane. You probably have plans though."

"I, um…" My hands flailed as I tried to put words together. I couldn't have been more surprised if he'd asked me to go skydiving.

"Don't worry about it. Just a harebrained thought," William pushed himself off the counter.

The bell over the door jangled as a customer walked in. William said hello and watched as the man began to browse the shelves.

I set myself up at the register. "I'll go," I said.

William's head snapped around. "What?"

"I said I'll go."

"You don't have plans?"

"I did, but they can be changed. I brought nice clothes with me to change into for church—why not just go to church with you?"

"Really? You would?"

"Sure."

"You know, you having plans is a great thing if you don't mind being a tad late. I can say I have to take you somewhere. It's a great out. And my mother will be thrilled…" His voice dropped off.

"She'll be thrilled?"

William spoke carefully. "She'll be glad I'm bringing…a friend."

"Oh. Good."

"What are your plans? While we're talking about them."

"My friend Gemma…her parents own DiGrassi & Elle." I shrugged. "I planned on going to their Christmas party tonight."

"You work there too?"

"No, but Gemma's a good friend, and her father likes to feed us. Thinks we're all too skinny. What time are you leaving here?"

"Shop closes at five—I was planning on being out of here shortly after."

"Okay."

His face opened into a rare grin. "Okay. Cool. Thanks—I really appreciate it."

William didn't know it, but I had a small wrapped gift for him in my bag. But I knew looking at his face that going with him tonight would mean so much more.

I called Jayne over my lunch break and announced my change of plans.

"William from the bookstore, really? Huh. You think you'll have a good time?"

"I do," I said, surprising myself as I admitted it.

"Cool. Well, we'll miss you at church, but we'll see you at the restaurant, right?"

"I'll be there."

"Good, because I'm counting on you. I want enough leftovers to make a meal for tomorrow. Think you can handle that?"

"I can cook for us, you know."

"I forgot about that. Don't worry about it though. There's no food at the apartment, and I wouldn't be so cruel as to send you to the grocery store on Christmas Eve."

"Thanks, I guess."

"You're welcome. See you later then. Levi will miss you, but I'll nurse him out of his depression."

"And I am coming to the restaurant."

"Very true. You're wearing that blue dress, right?"

"I was planning on it."

"You'll be a knockout. Be the belle of the ball—we'll see you later tonight."

⁓⁓⁓

Fifteen minutes before closing, William bumped me off the register. "You're a girl, right?"

"Um, yes."

"Then you probably need more than five minutes to get ready. My place is unlocked upstairs. You could get ready there if you want."

I tried not to show my relief. The employee restroom was tiny; I had no idea whether or not I could wrestle into a pair of nylons in such a small space without injuring myself.

Once upstairs in William's spacious bathroom, I wriggled into my nylons and slipped my dress on over my head. Of all the English items of clothing I found confusing, nylons topped the list. They were stockings not meant to look like stockings…I didn't understand. At least they kept my legs warm.

I'd found the dress on a sale rack while looking for Christmas presents. Made from midnight blue silk, it had a wrap-style bodice and an attached cami with lace the same color. The sleeves were short and puffy. The A-line skirt ended just past my knees, although it hadn't always been that way. I suspected the dress had been marked down because the skirt was cut to an awkward length, halfway past the calf.

Truly, about the length of my dresses back home.

But I bought it, took it home, and gave it a neat rolled hem with little effort. Paired with a black cardigan and black heels, I thought I looked very nice.

If my hair had been longer I might have tried to twist it up. Instead, I twisted back a few sections and pinned them back into a style I'd seen in a magazine once.

My mascara and blush were still fresh enough from the morning. I touched up my seashell-pink lipstick and dotted a bit of gloss on my lower lip the way the Sephora girl had shown me.

The last touch was a blue crystal beaded necklace. I knew earrings would look nice with this outfit, but I couldn't bring myself to punch holes in my ears just yet.

When I returned to the store, William had locked up and was finishing up closing the till. He looked up when I entered.

"You look nice," he said with a frown.

"Why does that seem to be a bad thing?"

"With my luck, my mom will probably like you. Ready to go?"

"I am."

"Great. Mind if we take my car?"

"Sure."

When he finished with the register, he unlocked a door I'd seen but never thought about. "Car's in here," he said, pushing open the door to reveal a small garage. He hit a button on the wall, and I watched in amazement as the back wall lifted up to reveal the alley I usually parked in.

"I had no idea the building had something like this," I said, trying and failing to sound as if I'd seen many mechanical walls before.

"Yeah, it's nice. Used to be a loading dock at one point. I don't drive my car much, so having it here means I don't have to worry about something happening to it."

The car was older, even I could tell that, but in very good condition. I looked at the front—Joely had been teaching me about car brands. A small logo read BMW. No wonder he didn't want to park this in the alley all the time.

He unlocked the passenger door and held it open for me. I stopped studying my surroundings long enough to climb inside, keeping my skirt clear of the doorway.

The inside of the car was clean, as I'd expected. A quick look over my shoulder revealed stacks of books on the backseat.

A moment of nervousness gripped me as William got in and started up the car. Was he a safe driver? Was he reckless?

Two moments in traffic with him, I realized I didn't need to worry. William used the same care with driving that he did when handling his rare books. He certainly drove faster than me, as most people did, but he was very careful and alert. In fact, driving with William was a lot like driving with Joely.

"The house is out in Lake Oswego," William said. "The church too. You attend church, right?"

"I do," I said, deciding not to elaborate. Elaborating might lead to explaining the type of church I attended for the first eighteen years of my life. Things with William and me were certainly easier than the day I first started work, but I wasn't ready for him to know about my Amish past.

Truly, William was the one person I spent quantities of time with who didn't know about my upbringing. To him, I was just sheltered and possibly quirky.

The Christmas Eve traffic heading out of town kept us from getting anywhere quickly. William sighed and tapped his fingers on the steering wheel. "We won't be late," he said, not that I was worried. This was his thing, not mine. "We just won't be there fifteen minutes early to meet and greet. In and of itself, not a bad thing. What CDs are in the glove compartment?"

I pushed the button and reached inside as asked. "There's…a Swell Season album, Andrew Osenga, The Shins…"

"Put in Swell Season."

I bit my lip as I studied the stereo system. I still had problems figuring out such things.

"Sorry, it's a bit tricky," William's fingers brushed mine as he found the right buttons. The current CD slid out. I pulled it out and replaced it with the new album. When the car filled with the sound of strumming guitar, I figured I'd gotten something right.

We listened without speaking for the rest of the drive.

—✦—

The church service was very different from the ones I'd attended with Jayne and Levi. William had been right—we arrived in just enough time to slide into the pew near his family before the lights dimmed and the service began.

The worship was…formal. That was the only word I could think of. I searched the attendees' expressions for any sense of joy but never found it. Maybe it was there, somewhere. I just couldn't see it, especially on William's face.

After the final *amen*, William leapt from his seat as if his life depended on it. "We'll see you guys at the house," he said, barely waving at the crowd of faces I'd yet to be introduced to.

I smiled my best smile and gave a short wave before turning to follow William.

Back again to the car, and more driving through tricky traffic.

"One of these years, I want to spend Christmas in a cabin somewhere," he said as we passed neighborhoods covered in tasteful white and colored lights.

"Oh?"

"None of the holiday craziness. None of the crowds of people standing in line to buy a Tickle Me Elmo, lines so long you can't buy cough syrup without being gone for an hour. America's too commercial. Too busy."

"Ah," I said. And that's all I said for the rest of the drive.

~～∥～~

"You want coffee?" William asked. "There's got to be a coffee place open somewhere. Atheists drink coffee."

"I don't really drink coffee."

"Hot chocolate? Chai? It's on me."

"Aren't we supposed to go to your house?"

"Yeah, but we left before everyone else. I mean, my mom's there—"

"Really? I thought she was sitting with your family."

William gave a wry smile. "Every year she sneaks out fifteen minutes early so she's home when everyone drives up. Didn't notice, did you. She's quick like that. Thing is, I like to wait until everyone's there. Disappear better, you know?"

No, I wouldn't know. I came from a family with eight children, and none of us were ever able to disappear. Not even Levi, when he left for good. Probably not even myself.

I rubbed my arms in an attempt to get my blood and my thoughts flowing in a different direction. "Cocoa's fine."

What was I doing? It was Christmas Eve. I was far from my family.

Instead of being near my brother, I was with this young man who had the uncanny ability to leave me in a state of complete confusion.

"Ha!" William cried out so loud I jumped. "There's a café with an open sign."

The car bumped and jostled over the curb in his enthusiasm to reach the coffee. "I'll run in," he said. "It's cold out."

I watched through the windows as he ordered, the bored barista barely acknowledging his existence. A few minutes later he returned, steaming cups in hand.

"Merry Christmas," he said, giving me a cup and one of his rare smiles.

I smiled back. "Thank you. So…is it always like this?"

"Christmas? Yeah. Less celebration, more production." He started the car again. "Whatever. It suits them, I guess. It's just not what I would pick. I started taking church more seriously when I was doing my graduate work in New York. There was a church start-up I loved, really loved. My family never understood, but that's not unusual. What about you? What do you think about spirituality?"

I struggled for words—no one had ever asked me that, at least not with those words. "I grew up in a very conservative church," I said, wrapping my hands around my cocoa cup. "My new church in Portland is very different. I've always considered myself a Christian, but I'm always surprised to find out the different ways that people follow Christ."

"Many ways," William agreed. "So you're a believer too?"

"I am."

He had the grace to look abashed. "I know…I know I haven't treated you very well. I'm sorry for how rude I've been."

"You're forgiven," I said easily. "Why were you such a pill, anyway?"

William sighed. "I wasn't happy that Richard hired you without my approval. I didn't think you were qualified at the time." He shook his head. "I was wrong. I should have apologized a long time ago. Forgive me?"

"Of course." I lifted up my cocoa in a toast. We clinked paper cups. "Merry Christmas, William."

Chapter 13

I had to admit, when we pulled up to William's parents' home, I thought it was lovely. Stately and large, the edges of the roofline were decorated with lit white icicles all the way around, with straight white lines of lights around the windows and doorways.

William took a brief look at it and shook his head. "Leave it to my parents to never do a little when they could do a lot."

Through the door a party was well underway, with tinkly piano music in the background and the sounds of chatter and laughter filling the space. Everyone was beautifully dressed. A quick glance around told me I'd chosen my ensemble well. I fit right in.

"William, there you are!"

My eyes followed the voice. The woman walking toward us had to be William's mother. With her brown eyes and dark hair, the resemblance was striking.

William's demeanor changed instantly. He stood taller. His shoulders straightened. "Mom. Hi."

"Merry Christmas!" She wrapped him in a warm hug, stepped back, and straightened his sweater. "Please introduce me to this young lady."

"Oh, yeah. Mom, this is Sara."

"Sara..."

"Burkholder," I filled in, as she shook my hand.

"Sara Burkholder. So nice to meet you. Call me Meredith."

"Absolutely," I said, trying to figure out what to say next. I had no practice at fancy social talk. "It's a lovely party. I'm so glad I could join William tonight."

Meredith grinned. "Oh, so am I."

⁓⋇⁓

I found myself paraded in front of William's family members for the next hour. His father, brother, aunts and uncles…everyone wanted to meet me. I shook hands and smiled, gave compliments and answered questions.

"Your dress was *how* marked down? What a find! To be able to alter things yourself—saves a fortune in seamstress fees," Meredith said when I answered her question about my dress.

"The Art Institute? Such ambition," William's father, Kip, said after I mentioned the start of classes to come. "Ambition is so important. Don't you think so, William?"

"Sure, Dad. I'm going to get some food. Sara? Want a bite?"

I assumed the food would have no questions, so I followed without argument. The buffet offerings really were tasty, but I grazed lightly, knowing I'd be heading to the restaurant.

"Ten minutes," William said. "Or two insults. Whichever comes first, we're heading out."

"Your dad…"

"He wants what's best for me, and he thinks the best way to get me there is by making thinly veiled verbal slights. Hasn't worked so far, but he's an incurable optimist."

"I'm sorry about that." I tried a stuffed mushroom. It was almost as good as one of Gemma's. "I had a great dad growing up."

"It's all about expectations, and I learned not to have any. Try the gray stuff—it's good."

I spooned some of the gray dip onto a cracker and took a bite. "You're right, it is good," I said after swallowing.

"I have no idea what it is, but Mom serves it every year. Oh, here we go," William said, patting my arm. "Uncle Louie's heading for the piano."

I turned and watched as a portly middle-aged man made a determined path toward the piano, which was already occupied by the professional musician, "Oh, does he play?"

"And sings. Does both very well when he's sober. In a moment, he'll start singing Christmas carols, but he'll get the lyrics mixed up as he goes."

"How do you know?"

"He does this every year. Probably my favorite Christmas tradition, and it's the one my parents don't pay for. Last year he sang about Rudolph nipping at boughs of holly. One of these days I need to find a way to record him. For posterity."

I watched as Louie began an opening roll of chords, each perfect until the last, where a finger slipped and sent the note awry. I looked around to see the reactions of the other guests. William's parents paid Louie no mind, not even glancing in his direction. Other guests looked over, expressions of confusion, amusement, and annoyance on their faces. William's face though, was my favorite, with its expression of complete contentment.

He shook his head. "Gotta love it. The night can only get worse now. Let's leave on a high note."

I lifted my eyebrows innocently. "But I haven't heard anyone speak of a pinstriped suit yet."

"Like I said, let's leave on a high note. We'll say goodbye to my parents. They'll probably offer to disown me and adopt you in my place."

—◊—

"I can't top your Uncle Louie, but you're welcome to come to the party at DiGrassi," I offered as William drove me back to my car. "Good food, no insults—at least, none directed at you. You might like it."

"Thanks, but I should get home," William's eyes didn't leave the road. "I have some book repair work to catch up on."

"On Christmas Eve?"

"Jesus' parents didn't take a night off for Christmas. Why should I?"

I opened my mouth and closed it again. "So you consider yourself a Christian?"

"I do, just not the way my parents might. My beliefs are very personal. My journey is my own, you know?"

"Do you attend church?"

"Every week. But I do it because I want to, not because people will think differently of me if I don't."

"Oh." I nodded, remembering a time where not attending church could have very serious ramifications.

"It's not something I talk about much."

Clearly, since this was the first time it had come up.

William sighed. "Next couple of weeks, things are really going to change."

I exhaled. The word *change* seemed like an understatement. "I start classes."

"Zach will be back."

Would we be able to continue in the friendlier pattern we'd found our-selves in? I hoped so. But I had no idea.

"You're sure you don't want to come?" I could see the alleyway where my car was parked.

William turned in, pressing the button that caused the wall to move upward, making a place for him to park. "Thanks for the offer. Maybe another time."

———※———

When I finally arrived at the restaurant, everyone was glad to see me, and I was pleased to see them. Music, louder and more joyful than the music at Meredith Blythe's, filled the air. Every flat surface seemed to be covered with platters of appetizers or with deep dishes heated underneath, full of lasagna and *boeuf bourguignonne*. Everyone talked, everyone ate, everyone talked some more.

Levi gave me a hug and told me he'd missed me. But by the way Jayne was curled up at his side, I knew he'd survived with little damage. "How was the party?" he asked.

"Fun," I said, leaving out the insults and inquisition. "William's family is very nice."

Nice, as long as they were talking to me and not William.

———※———

Levi joined us for Christmas breakfast the next morning and then helped pack the car as we readied for a trip to Lincoln City to visit Jayne's family.

"Seems a shame not to open gifts under our own tree," I remarked. I'd looked forward to that part of the English Christmas tradition.

"I have a gift for you in the truck," Levi said. "You can open it here if you want."

"Really?" I felt my face brighten.

"Sure. I'll get it. One less thing to pack."

I sat at the foot of the tree in anticipation. Levi returned and sat next to me, and Jayne joined us.

"I hope you enjoy it," Levi said, handing me a medium-sized square box.

Curious, I removed the wrapping paper, folded it, and set it aside before opening the box. I pulled apart the cardboard flaps to find objects wrapped in newsprint. "It's a set," Levi said. "You have to unwrap each of them."

So I did. One at a time, I lifted each piece from the box. A hand-carved sheep. A king. A cow. A tall simple man and a short simple man. A woman. A child in a manger.

"A nativity set!" I examined each piece. "Your carving is so beautiful."

Unlike the sets I'd seen on occasion as a child, every one of the pieces Levi carved had faces—beautiful, expressive faces.

Beneath the figures I found several round, flat pieces.

"The stable fits together. I know technically it was probably closer to a cave, but that's a bit more intensive when it comes to carving. With the wise men on the scene, we're obviously not going for historical accuracy."

"I love it. I do."

Before we left, I set up the whole scene on top of one of the living room bookcases. The last figure to place was the baby Jesus.

Maybe this Christmas would be a start. Maybe, if I could start fresh with the child in a manger, He and I could get to know each other all over again—slowly and truly this time.

─────※─────

Christmas in Lincoln City was better than I could have imagined. Jayne's mother, Kathy, welcomed me into her home and even had gifts beneath the tree with my name on them. Seeing Jayne's niece, Emilee, made me miss my sisters, but I enjoyed the feel of family, complete with mothers and children.

I was happy for my brother, glad he had Jayne and her family. And I wasn't the only one who was glad.

"So, when are you guys getting married?" Jayne's sister, Beth, asked after lunch.

Levi smiled. Jayne grimaced.

Kathy swatted Beth's shoulder. "Leave them alone. Let them have their privacy."

"What?" Beth protested. "I didn't ask when they were starting a family. We all know these two are engaged, and frankly, my calendar's filling up."

"Heaven help us if you have to cancel plans to attend your sister's wedding," Beth's husband, Gary, commented dryly.

At the mention of starting a family, Jayne's face flushed. "I'll keep you posted, Beth. I promise."

I shot a glance at Levi. I knew he'd marry Jayne over the weekend if she would consent, but Jayne wasn't about to rush into anything. Especially something as permanent and domestic as marriage.

"Sometimes you have to plan these things ahead. My bridesmaid dresses took four months to arrive, not that you'd remember."

I sat up a little straighter. Bridesmaid dresses. *Wedding* dresses. When Jayne and Levi finally got married—Beth was right, they would marry—Jayne would need dresses, lots of dresses. I wasn't deluded enough to think I'd be able to design a wedding dress while going to school, working at the bookstore, and quilting, but would Jayne let me suggest styles for her?

A thousand ideas flew through my head—fabrics, cuts, silhouettes…I knew Jayne wouldn't want anything fancy, though her tastes were more traditional than she'd admit. My sketchbook was in my luggage upstairs. I knew I couldn't bring it down to work out concepts without raising eyebrows. But if I had perfected one skill during my childhood, it was the ability to remember ideas and sketch them when no one was looking.

—※—

We opened gifts after the lunch dishes were cleared. Jayne gave Levi a beautiful merino wool sweater, and he gave her a cashmere hat and scarf set. I gave Jayne a hoodie I'd been working on, with an appliquéd pie on the front pocket and cherries near the heart. Kathy gave me a silk scarf that I wrapped around my neck the moment I lifted it from the box.

For Levi I'd made a simple yet oversized quilt from cozy flannel, something to keep him warm when he was home.

I loved watching Emilee open her gifts—every box and bag was a new, exciting discovery. I couldn't help but think of the Christmas a year before.

That year, few things had changed in our household. Levi had been gone several years, and Rebecca was married and in Washington with her own family. I hadn't met Jayne. I still kept my piles of secrets in my bedroom, tucked away from the eyes of my family. For Elizabeth, I'd made a cloth doll and an extra dress. I gave Leah a special set of grown-up soaps in a basket I'd lined for her.

My mother gave me a new dress, one I hadn't had to make for myself.

I felt Levi's hand on my shoulder before I realized there were tears in my eyes. "It's okay," he said, softly enough that no one else heard. "Want to step out for a moment?"

"No, it's fine." I dashed the tears from my eyes as quickly as they'd appeared. "Just a little homesick, that's all."

My thoughts were interrupted by Kathy's announcement of pumpkin pie. I followed everyone into the kitchen and tried not to think of home.

———※※———

The rest of our time away passed quickly. Before I knew it, I was back at work at the bookstore, noticing the other vehicle in the tiny employee parking area. In my space, actually.

"Hey!" Zach spread his arms open wide when he saw me. "How's it going?"

My brows lifted in surprise. "You're back! Good to see you. Thought you'd be out another week."

He shrugged. "Time to get out of the house, you know? So. What's changed since I've been gone?"

Chapter 14

With Christmas over, we undressed the tree and returned it to the back of Levi's pickup truck. I tried not to be depressed as the lights disappeared around town and winter's bleakness took over. I focused my thoughts as best I could on the beginning of classes.

I felt ready. At least, I thought I did. Gemma helped me shop for a proper shoulder bag that would carry my laptop as well as whatever sketch pads and pencils I might want to carry. We finally found a nylon waterproof bag in a sunny orange tone, which we agreed would be fashion-forward enough for me to carry with pride.

The days before classes were a blur. I rearranged my schedule to accommodate my recently released class schedule. The atmosphere at the shop was odd now that Zach was back, but no one was talking about it, and I didn't have time to answer Zach's questions or reassure William of...something. I just had no idea what.

New Year's passed without my noticing, as did Epiphany.

Sunday evening before my first day at school, I couldn't sit down, much to Jayne's frustration.

"If you lay out your outfit for the morning one more time, I'm going to tie you up and make you watch something really mind-numbing, like *Crouching Tiger, Hidden Dragon*. I know it's supposed to be a masterpiece or something, but a forty-minute flashback about a comb? Seriously?" Jayne propped a hand on her hip. "You're a princess. Buy a new comb."

"I'll take that one off my viewing list if you feel that way about it," I said.

"Sorry, don't know where that came from. That movie always bothered me. I like *House of Flying Daggers*. That's got to count for something. At least there aren't any self-indulgent comb-retrieval sequences."

"I want to start off right with everyone. I'd rather not be the outsider, at least not more than I already am," I said as a feeling of dread washed over me.

"If that's the case, the less thought you put into your clothes, the better. You don't want to look overprocessed. Really, you look great in everything you put on. Artlessly polished." Jayne crossed her arms. "If you don't stop worrying, I'll have Joely come over and give you a speech about saying no to drugs."

I giggled. I couldn't help myself.

"You think I'm joking," Jayne raised an eyebrow. "She'll make you wary of aspirin."

"I'm sure she would."

"Want to bake something?"

I took a deep breath. The kitchen. Oven-baked warmth. "That could be a good idea."

"Just don't take it out on the pastry."

"Scones then?"

Jayne snapped her fingers. "Good plan."

In a move that was less surprising than it would have been a month earlier, William had offered to let me park in my employee spot even when I was in class. I took him up on his offer without a second thought.

It felt odd, though, to pull up next to work and walk the opposite direction. The sky dumped heavy droplets of water. I walked quickly, my head and my bag tucked under my striped umbrella.

I arrived in my first class, Introduction to Apparel Design, damp but undamaged. I scanned the room for friendly faces. Most of the students were female, but there were a few young men in the class.

There was an empty seat near the window, so I claimed it. The girl next to me was still arranging her bags and belongings, and I watched as she pulled out a small bag of yarn and began to knit. I began to turn to introduce myself, but at that moment the instructor began to speak, and the class quieted.

The instructor discussed the contents of the class, passed out a syllabus, and gave a short lecture. I watched the girl next to me from the corner of one eye—she knitted all through class.

I was amazed. I could tell she was paying attention to the lecture because she only rarely looked down at her handiwork. Still, I admired the fluid motion of her fingers as they maneuvered the yarn around the needles.

"What are you making?" I asked when class finished.

She held it up. "It's a sweater," she said.

"It's lovely. May I touch it?"

"Go ahead," she said with a small laugh.

I reached out and touched the delicate, lacy fabric. "I'm assuming you knit each piece so it comes out the size and shape you want, correct? You don't cut it afterward?"

"Most of the time, no. There's a technique called steeking that involves running a couple lines of stitches before cutting between them. It's a traditional Scandinavian method—my grandmother used to do it on Fair Isle cardigans all the time."

"That's amazing." I offered my hand. "I'm Sara Burkholder."

"Britta Larson." She took it with a smile. "Are you fashion design track?"

"I am. Just started this term."

"Exciting. What class do you have next?"

"Garment Construction with Jacobson."

"Me too. The classroom's not far."

She pointed out the door and I followed, a little giddy at the thought that I may have made a friend.

～⊱⊰～

After class, Britta invited me to lunch with two other girls in the fashion program. The heavy rain had poured itself out and now fell in a lazy drizzle over the tops of our umbrellas.

Two girls waved when we walked into the P.F. Chang's across the street. The first was tall, blond, and striking. "Britta texted that you were coming," she said instead of an actual greeting. "I'm Sonnet Brooks. Sonnet like the poem." She shook my hand. "This is Megumi. We call her Meg."

I turned to smile at Meg. She was petite, Asian, and impeccably dressed. Instead of favoring the alternative styles many of the other students sported, Meg looked as though she'd stepped out of an Audrey Hepburn film.

"Nice to meet you both," I said. "Sonnet. That's an unusual name."

She rolled her eyes. "Yeah. Poetry-reading hippie parents. It could have been worse. If I were a boy, they would have named me after Jimi Hendrix."

I had no idea who that was, as usual, but the name sounded ghastly.

"Let's order—I'm starved." She eyed me up and down. "Nice bag."

Meg and Britta agreed, and the knots in my stomach began to release.

Over lunch I learned that Meg's family was Japanese, though she was born in Seattle and moved to Portland in the second grade. "My parents are very traditional," she told me as we ate our bowls of rice, vegetables, and garlicky chicken. "They didn't think the fashion program was a good business decision. It took two academic advisors explaining how the program prepares you for the real world to convince them to allow me to enroll. I think my mom is still hoping I'll marry a nice Japanese doctor."

I gave a wry laugh. "I completely understand."

Sonnet arched an eyebrow. "Parents not thrilled about the higher calling that is fashion?"

"They may never get over it," I hedged. "What about you? How does your family feel about you in the program?"

"I'm the responsible one in the family, since I've never dropped acid and don't do 'shrooms on the weekends." She shrugged. "I got my BFA at the U of O in the fiber arts program. Really enjoyed it. It's part of what brought me here. My parents are pretty sure I've gone corporate, but whatever. Someone has to support them in their old age."

"What about you?" I asked Britta.

"Oh, my parents are fine with it. All the women in the family are thrilled, actually. I want to design knitwear that's wearable, not bulky and frumpy. All the women and a few of the guys in my family knit, so they're all for new knitting patterns."

"You know guys who knit?" I tried to imagine any of my brothers knitting and failed.

"Once you get a man hooked on hand-knit socks, it's a slippery slope until he tries it out for himself."

"I'd love to learn," I said, remembering the project she'd worked on through class. "I've seen knitting before, but I've never known anyone who actually did it. Is there a book you'd recommend for it?"

Meg and Sonnet dissolved into laughter. Britta shook her head. "Oh, don't even try to teach yourself from a book. I'll show you."

"Of course she will! Britta's always looking for someone to bring into the fold." Sonnet's eyes glowed with humor. "She's fixed all of my bad habits. I used to throw—now I pick. Don't worry, that will make sense later. Britta holds the knitting wisdom of a dozen generations of Scandinavian women. They were probably all knitting as they give birth."

"I made a scarf," Meg admitted. "I should probably try another."

"You should," Britta agreed. "You should try *shibori*. It's Japanese, and it would complement your designs well."

"I'd love to see your designs," I said. "I've never been around other people who were…well, like me." Ever.

Meg pulled a scrap of paper from her bag. "This is one idea I'm working on. I like the idea of incorporating origami into my garments—the trick is making sure the folds and details don't add bulk."

"Right," I agreed as I studied her sketch. "I like what you've done with the lines."

"Just a thought…" Britta mused, "what if you paired your origami garments with something softer, more organic?"

Meg tilted her head, considering the idea. "Like a sweater?"

"I know I'm the knits proponent around here, but when it comes to layering textures…"

Meg sat back. "You have a point."

"Of course I do," Britta replied as she pulled out a sketchpad of her own. "See, if you do a horizontal rib, you can recreate the lines and make a mohair knit wrap for that dress you showed me last week."

I sat back and let myself absorb the conversation. I'd never known what it was like to be near people who thought like me, who loved clothes the way I did.

This was it. I'd made the right decision. There was no way I could ever go back.

I floated through my last class of the day. By the time Jayne came home from work, I had two pies cooling on a wire rack and sat in the middle of a pile of new sketches. Several of them were of wedding gowns for Jayne—I tucked them under my rear when she walked through the door.

Jayne didn't notice. "Someone's been busy," she said as she took a look around. "I'd say something about the place being trashed, but truth is, it's cleaner now than it ever was before you moved in. How was school?"

The words fell out of my mouth as I told her about Britta and her knitting, and how Sonnet got her name, and Meg's beautiful designs, and how for the first time, I'd experienced what it was like to meet people like me.

Jayne grinned. "I remember what it was like to be in my first journalism class. Everyone there—okay, not including sorority girls who just wanted to be on TV, but everyone else—cared about ethics in media and well-written leads. After growing up in a small town, finding people like me was…it was like breathing for the first time. I thought, *So this is what it's like.* I'll never forget it. I met Kim there too, you know."

"No, I didn't know."

"We didn't get to know each other and become friends until we got to the Oregonian, but we had several reporting classes together."

"What about Gemma? And Joely? I don't know that I've ever asked how you connected with them."

"Met Joely while I was doing a story. She cracked me up—and I didn't usually have that experience while interviewing officers. Gemma I met through the paper. She brought food to work."

I smiled. "And the rest was history?" I hoped I got that line right. It sounded right. "Like you and Levi?"

She crouched and found a seat next to me on the floor. "Like me and Levi. Sounds so cheesy, but I really am crazy about that man."

"You should let him marry you."

"I should." She sighed. "I know. And I will, when the time is right."

"What makes the time right?"

"He's just getting settled in at the firm—"

"It's been over six months."

"I don't know. Everything feels unsettled."

In that moment, I understood. Jayne and Levi weren't unsettled. *I* was unsettled.

I didn't say anything. I knew Jayne well enough to know that she'd deny it. But my heart began to pound as I realized that my lack of independence was keeping the two most important people in my world from starting a life together.

———

In the quiet of my room that night, I searched for apartment listings online. I had no idea renting an apartment could be so expensive! But I had financial aid and my job, and if I pieced a couple quilts in my evenings, I could sell them to put toward a deposit.

I was English now. I had to learn to take care of myself.

Chapter 15

Rather than continue to worry about my living situation, I decided not to think about it for my first week of class.

I wasn't particularly successful.

On Tuesday, I had only my Color Theory class before working for the rest of the day at the bookstore. I enjoyed the class and the opportunity to work with colors that the *Ordnung* didn't approve of, but I found myself sketching quilt concepts in the in-between moments.

"You seem worried today," Zach said Tuesday morning. "What's up?"

I put down the books I was scanning. "What do you mean, I look worried?"

"Your face is all scrunched up."

"I wasn't going to ask," William said from the opposite side of the store. "Nothing good can come of telling a girl her face looks like a crumpled paper bag."

My shoulders sank. "I need...I need to figure out a new living situation."

"You need a new place?" William walked over to join us.

"I don't know. I think so."

"Remind me—you're living where?"

"With my brother's fiancée. I think...well, I have a hunch..."

"Spit it out. I'm aging over here." William crossed his arms.

"I think they'd actually get married if it weren't for me."

"Oh." Zach winced.

"That's ridiculous. They're adults. You're an adult. They should be able to figure things out for themselves." William picked up a couple of the books and started scanning them for me.

"I don't think they believe I could take care of myself."

"Do you have a mental issue you haven't told us about?" William asked in disbelief. "You're just as capable as the rest of us."

I allowed myself a smile. "Thanks. It's just that I haven't lived in Portland that long." And I'd never lived by myself. Ever.

"You'll be fine," said William. "Seriously. Portland is not New York. It's not even San Francisco, as much as it wants to be. Sure, living costs aren't great. Have you checked Craigslist? Some of those listings are likely to be cheaper than ones offered by property management firms."

"No, I didn't know about Craig's list," I tilted my head. "He lists apartments in Portland?"

Zach and William chuckled, though William was less discreet about it. "Craig isn't a person. I mean, he may well have been at one point, but Craigslist.org is a website with all sorts of listings—real estate, furniture, pets, you name it."

"Sketchy personals…" Zach added.

"It's worth a look at the apartment listings. You might find something."

I could do this. I could be as independent as someone who grew up English.

───※───

Sonnet caught up to me in the hallway between classes. "Are you in or out?"

"Um…" I looked around. "Out of class?"

She patted my back. "You're very literal, aren't you."

"I am." Much to Jayne's frequent amusement.

"Fine. You're in. Meet us in the front at eleven?"

When eleven rolled around, I found everyone waiting inside near the doors. "Are you wearing good walking shoes?" Meg asked.

"Where are we going?"

"You'll like it a lot," Sonnet said.

───※───

The topic of discussion as we walked was vintage clothes. Sonnet had found a tiny shop tucked away in the Sellwood neighborhood that she wanted all of us to visit.

"Sure, you've got to do alterations. Not even Madonna wears pointy bras anymore. Being handy with warm water and a scoop of Biz doesn't hurt either. But there are some great clothes in there!"

Britta made a face. "I'm not sure. I mean, I'm sure the clothes are fine, but the *Mad Men* look isn't my thing. I can't pull off a sheath dress."

"She has a point," Meg said. "Sheath dresses are evil. They have to be perfectly tailored and belted before they're remotely flattering. Even then…"

"Even then they only work out for certain body types," Sonnet finished. "I'll give you that. But there are plenty of other silhouettes. It's worth trying, at least. You never know when you'll find an undervalued Pucci."

"Sounds like fun," I said. "I'll go with you sometime. My fashion history could stand to be strengthened."

"Excellent!" Sonnet's face broke out into a grin. "It's a date then."

"I hope they have the red velvet today," Britta said as we continued our walk. "I'm a little addicted to them."

The other girls agreed.

I figured we were headed to a dress or fabric shop of some kind, but Sonnet crossed Flanders and walked up some stairs and through a door marked Saint Cupcake.

"What is this?" I asked. "I've never been here before." And considering our frequent outings with Gemma, that was truly a surprise.

"A bakery, one that specializes in cupcakes."

"Oh." It looked like a bakery, with its pink-scalloped awning. "I just thought when you were talking about red velvet…"

Britta grasped my hand. "Let's find out," she said.

I followed her to the front display cases. I'd never seen so many types of cupcakes. Some chocolate, some vanilla, and some that were red and marked Red Velvet.

"Oh," I said. "It's a fabric *and* a flavor."

"And very good. I also like the toasted coconut cream. I'm usually a chocolate girl, but those are the two I pick up most often. It's a good thing we walk, or I'd have gone up a jean size."

Britta made her order. I waited while Sonnet and Meg ordered, and then I chose the Red Velvet, toasted coconut cream, carrot cake, and chocolate with vanilla buttercream.

"My roommate will want to try these. And our friend who works on the food section of the paper."

"Uh-huh," Sonnet said, sounding unconvinced. "Whatever. If you can share your cupcakes, you're a better woman than me."

〰️

Jayne shot an accusatory look at Gemma. "You've been holding out on me."

I tapped the corner of my upper lip. "You've got frosting there."

Jayne swabbed at the frosting remnant and licked it off her finger. "That is seriously good frosting. And I don't like frosting."

Gemma shrugged. "What can I say? When they opened, I didn't get the assignment. Never had the time to try it out afterward."

"Clearly, your time management skills could use a tune-up. Are you going to finish the rest of the carrot one?"

"Don't you even think about it," Gemma warned as she placed a protective hand between the remaining crumbs of carrot cupcake and Jayne. "Sara, all I can say is that you should be sainted for bringing these to our attention. Or knighted, if I had a tract of land to give you."

"Do they give land with knighthoods these days?" Jayne asked, collecting frosting from the cupcake wrapping with her finger.

"Ask Patrick Stewart. He was knighted not very long ago. You're the reporter. I'm just the food writer."

I sat up straight. "What movies are we going to watch tomorrow?"

"Trying to throw us off?" Jayne lifted an eyebrow. "It won't work."

"I think we should watch *Titanic*," Gemma suggested as she tucked a piece of her long, dark hair behind her ear.

"Ew, no!" Jayne's face scrunched up as if the frosting was suddenly wasabi flavored. "I thought you liked Sara. Why would you subject her to such dippy dialogue?"

"See?" Gemma looked to me. "It worked. Shall we watch *It Happened One Night* instead?"

"Anything but *Titanic*." Jayne's face hadn't returned to normal yet.

"I don't know," I said. "I was hoping to see *Crouching Tiger, Hidden Dragon* soon."

Jayne and Gemma looked at each other, looked at me, and looked at each other again.

"You're joking, right?" Jayne asked.

"Yes," I admitted with a small shrug.

"I'm so proud!" Jayne's arm wrapped around my shoulders. "Your first pop-culture joke!"

"First of many, I'm sure," Gemma said with a smile.

I gave a mock sigh. "I just wanted to see what happened to the comb."

I had an hour between classes on Friday, so I carried my things to the library, found a nearly cozy chair, and pulled out my sketchbook. I thought about Jayne's wedding dress. On the sketchpad, I played around with a few designs, making notes about my ideas of fabric, cut, and seaming.

"Whatcha working on?"

Startled, my pencil made an odd mark on the page before I could look up.

"Hey, sorry, didn't mean to scare you. I'm Arin. Arin Metz."

He was about my age, with hair even shaggier than William's and an easy smile. I put my pencil down and shook the hand he had offered. "Sara."

"I think you're in my Color Theory class."

"Oh," I said.

He sat next to me. "What program are you in?"

I held up my sketchbook. "Fashion."

"You wanna do wedding dresses and stuff?"

"This is for a friend."

"Right on." He slipped the strap of his bag over his head and set the bag down in the process. "I'm in the graphic design program."

"Oh," I said again. Maybe this was why I had trouble making friends. I was no good at English conversation. "Do you like it?"

"I do. It's my second year. It's been good."

"That's...nice."

Arin leaned forward. "You like the fashion program?"

"I do. I just started this term, but so far so good." I checked my watch. "My next class starts shortly," I said, gathering my things.

"Enjoy it," he said, standing. "See you around."

"Bye."

I watched him walk away.

That was...odd.

After class I walked to the bookstore, locked my school things into my car, and entered the shop. Richard was in the store today, explaining the finer points of a copy of Herman Melville's *The Confidence-Man* to a gentleman. A steady stream of customers milled through, so I made myself useful by taking over the register and shelving if someone didn't require my immediate attention. After the uncertainties of school, I enjoyed the structure of work at the bookstore. Before the sky had turned completely dark, I heard the jingle of the bell over the door and turned to see a familiar face.

"Levi!" I left my spot at the register to throw my arms around my older brother. "What are you doing here?"

"Thought I'd check in on where you worked. Haven't seen the place yet." He looked around. "It's nice."

"You're just here to take a look around? Your office certainly isn't that close."

Levi shrugged. "And Jayne's birthday is coming up next month. I'm collecting ideas. Thought she might like a first edition of something. Preferably something old."

"She'd like that. William knows what we have in the shop." I looked over my shoulder. "Zach? Could you handle the register for a little while?"

"Sure thing." Zach answered, watching us with curious eyes.

We found William in the workroom. I knocked on the open door so he could hear us.

He looked up, his gaze shifting from me to Levi. "What's up?"

"This is my brother, Levi. Levi, this is William," I said, performing introductions the way I'd been told the English did. If it wasn't right, neither Levi nor William said anything about it.

"You're the brother, huh? Nice to meet you," William said as he shook Levi's hand. "What brings you to the store?"

Levi explained. William nodded. "What is she interested in? We've got a wide selection. If she enjoys Poe, we're accepting offers for the *Godey Lady's Book* compilation with his first published short story."

I made a face. Levi shook his head. As much as I loved the *Godey's Lady's Book* volumes, I knew that Jayne wouldn't be interested in the Poe story or the fashion. It was sad, because if she was and Levi bought it, I'd at least be near it.

"She mentioned she enjoyed the L.M. Montgomery books when she was young, *Anne* and…oh, what's the other one…"

"*Emily of New Moon*? That's pretty rare. You're welcome to look over our collection and catalog—several of our titles aren't shelved." William reached up to scratch his head. "We do have a 1932 set of Jane Austen's novels. Red cloth binding, fairly clean boards—they would make a nice gift."

Levi brightened and looked to me. "Jane's books for Jayne? I think she'd like that." He turned to William. "How much?"

William named the price. I winced. Levi didn't.

"May I see them?" Levi asked. William led him to the correct shelf.

My lips set in a firm line. The sooner I moved out, the sooner Levi could put that sort of money toward their future together rather than buy a set of books Jayne would seldom read.

Though I knew she really would enjoy them.

I thought of the wedding dress sketches on the notepad in my car. I would check Craigslist when I got home from work.

meant to check Craigslist, but Jayne was on a rampage. She'd decided
to bake for everyone coming to the movie night later on. She'd chosen a
recipe for a plum galette, and in the oven it had practically glued itself to
the pan.

"I'm not emotionally invested in this," Jayne said, holding the baking
sheet with two oven-mitt-protected hands while I jabbed the wooden spatula
underneath. "I'm not. I followed the recipe exactly, and the filling ran over
anyway. I'd just like it to be edible. And for Gemma to eat it."

"Of course Gemma will eat it." Another jab.

"And like it."

"She loves plums."

"She'd also be too nice to tell me if she hates it."

"Sorry. I'll tell her to insult you if it will make you feel better. Stop worrying. Do you need to watch *Julie & Julia* again?"

Jayne wrinkled her nose. "Probably."

Two more fierce jabs and the galette came free, though a different shape
than it used to be.

Jayne's shoulder's drooped. "It's ruined."

"It's oval," I said. "And it will taste the same."

Crisis averted, I made a batch of buttery oatmeal cookies and helped
set up. Before I knew it, Joely was inside, taking off her jacket and casually
mentioning that she'd been shot at earlier in the day.

"The standoff this afternoon? That was you?" Jayne asked, incredulous.

"It was," Joely looked around. "Smells good in here. Hope it's not a scented
candle. I hate those candles that smell like cookies. Such a letdown."

"Don't worry, I made real cookies, and Jayne made a plum galette. Tell
us about what happened in the standoff. You weren't injured, I hope?"

"No, but my squad car has a few bullet holes."

"Oh. Well," Jayne said, "at least now you have street cred."

"Joely," I said, employing the voice I used on small children when babysitting and occasionally on Zach and William, "you can't have any cookies until you tell us what happened."

She spread her hands. "It wasn't a big deal. Basically what happened…" She eyed Jayne. "This is off record, right?"

"I'm off duty and Kim's not here, so you're safe."

"Good point. So a guy's locked himself in his house with a gun, and he's got a head wound, and according to the 911 call made by his neighbor, the wound was self-inflicted. A long story short, after two hours of nothing, we hear a shot. The SWAT guys decide to approach from the opposite side of the block in the armored vehicle and drive over the fence to get to the backyard. When the guy sees the SWAT vehicle driving over his fence, he goes ballistic. Literally. That's when he started shooting at anything he could see, which meant his flat-screen TV and my car. And me. But he was a really terrible shot. Probably why he's still alive after shooting himself."

"That's horrible!" Jayne clasped her hand over her mouth. But I could tell she was hiding a smile.

"Whatever. The guy grazed the top of my vest," Joely's finger brushed her shoulder. "I wouldn't have been able to tell, but it burnt through my uniform. Totally sucked, because I'd just washed and pressed it."

"I can see how that would upset you," Jayne said drily. "Just so you know? This story is not being repeated to Gemma. She'd cry. She'd hug you really tight. Then she'd bring you so much unpronounceable food that you wouldn't fit into your uniform—washed, pressed, or otherwise."

"She would. Well anyway, I was shot at, so I returned fire."

I could feel my eyes go wide. "You shot at somebody?" The idea filled me with horror. Violence and killing had no place in the Amish way of life. I couldn't wrap my mind around it. What had I gotten myself into, living in the English world?

"Self-defense," Joely said, her voice gentler. "He could very well have killed or injured me or one of my coworkers. Most of them are married with kids. I couldn't let that happen." She shrugged. "I actually hit his shoulder, shooting arm side. He dropped the gun, and the SWAT guys were able to enter and take him into medical custody."

"Wow." Jayne tilted her head toward me. "I think she can have a cookie now."

I nodded. "I think maybe two."

"Thanks." Joely took the few steps to the kitchen. She took three cookies, but neither Jayne nor I stopped her. "I'm on administrative leave for a few days, until they determine that it was a 'good shot.'"

"Forced vacation, huh? I know about those. I went to Amish country, and look what happened." Jayne winked at me.

"She's right," I said. "You never know who's going to jump in your trunk when you're on leave."

I took my laptop to work with me on Saturday, planning to use the next-door coffee shop's wireless connection to look at apartments during my lunch break. Book browsers came and went. When my break rolled around, I took my laptop to the back room and set myself up with my packed lunch. I heard the door open a few minutes later.

"Whatcha doin'?" William asked, his own lunch in hand.

"Checking Craigslist like you suggested," I said. "Is Zach still in the shop?"

"He is. Don't worry—it's my job to make sure there's someone running the register while the sign says Open. Any good listings?"

I shrugged. "I'm so new at this, I really don't know what to look for."

"Scoot over," he said. "Let's see. Are you looking for an apartment or a room? Or let me put it this way. How willing are you to live with crazies?"

I wrinkled my nose. "Um…"

"Indifferent. Okay. What areas are you looking at?"

"If it's cheaper to be a bit out of town, that's okay. But the commute shouldn't be too bad. I don't want to spend more on gas than I would on in-town rent. And I hate driving in traffic."

William snorted. "Me too. Why do you think I like living upstairs? Let's see. Here's an apartment downtown. Pricey, but utilities are included. Typical apartment appliances. If you wanted to rent a room…" he clicked a few times. "There are lots of options. A lot of them are significantly cheaper. Might be worth looking into if you don't have a roommate immediately in mind. See this one?" He pointed at the screen. "Easy freeway access, minutes from Trader Joe's—always a plus. Looking for clean, mature roommate. I think that's you—in spirit, not age."

I didn't say anything. I doubted William had any idea how young I really was.

With his help, I saved the links to several options. After work, I gave Joely a call.

"I'm thinking about looking for a place on my own," I said. "I don't know the good and bad areas of town like you do. Could I send you the links of some of the ones I'm looking at? I'd appreciate your input."

"You're moving? You didn't mention that the other night," Joely said. "But something tells me Jayne doesn't know about it."

I winced. Leave it to Joely to read me that well over the phone. "She doesn't," I said. "And I'd rather you not tell her."

"I've been known to keep a secret. Things not going well? Is she subjecting you to slave labor? Because I've got to tell you, that place wasn't so clean before you came. Now it's a level of clean that's, honestly, kinda creepy."

I laughed. "I like cleaning. It relaxes me. No, everything's fine between us. It's just time."

"Time. I only halfway believe you, but that's okay. Lucky for you, I'm on leave and bored. What are you doing now? I can meet you, pick you up, whatever you want. I'm even feeling generous enough to feed you, but it won't be as good as anything you'd get with Gemma."

"Fair enough," I checked my watch. "I could drive to your place. See you in a few minutes?"

<hr />

The Saturday afternoon traffic crawled, so I took more than a few minutes reaching Joely's. She had her shoes on and jacket nearby.

"I've got my laptop," I said, "I can look up phone numbers and addresses if I can hook up to your wireless."

"Look at you," Joely said, "hooking up to wireless connections. I'm so proud. Look up the listings. You call half, I'll call half. We'll line 'em up, make visits, be organized."

Over the next half-hour, Joely and I did just that, checking in with each other between calls to make sure neither of us made a promise I couldn't keep.

After all the calls had been made, we'd left four voice messages, made three appointments for that afternoon, and scheduled another two for Sunday after church.

"This one's not in a bad neighborhood," Joely said as we pulled up to the first one. "Not that I'd tempt fate—keep the face of your CD player in your purse when you're not in your car."

The place we were looking at was a room in an old Victorian. I'd have a bedroom and bathroom all to myself and share the kitchen and living room with three other girls.

The girl who opened the door introduced herself as Zoe. "Come on in and let me give you the tour," she said.

There were a lot of potted plants inside. Also bags of dried leaves and something else on a couple of the end tables in the living room. Interesting. One or more of them must study plants.

"Jen works downtown," Zoe said, showing us the kitchen. "None of us really cook, so if you do, you'll have the run of the kitchen. Just leave Bex's soy milk alone—she's prickly about that. She's a great person," Zoe amended. "It's just, you know, soy milk."

"Whose rooms are where?" Joely asked.

Zoe pointed down the hall. "Mine's there, to the left. Everyone else is upstairs."

"Oh. Sara has some things that need to be stored. Is that a storage room, to the right?"

I looked at the room Joely asked about. It seemed like a normal door, but an odd bluish light leaked through the cracks.

"No, that's for...something else," Zoe said. "One of the girls' projects. You know. Want to see the room upstairs?"

"Sure," Joely said. "Coming, Sara?"

"I am." I followed Joely and Zoe back down the hall and up the stairs. Joely struck up a conversation with Zoe about home décor and recipes for soy milk. The pitch of her voice even changed—she sounded girlier, softer. Odd, especially since Joely always made faces whenever the word *soy* turned up.

"This looks nice," she said as Zoe opened the door to the room that could be mine. "Great light. I like the paint color."

I lifted an eyebrow at her. Paint color?

"What do you think Sara?" She asked.

"I think it's—"

"Oh, hang on, my phone's buzzing. I'll be right back."

Joely left the house entirely. I could see her from the window, chatting away as if she were making coffee plans with a long-lost friend.

Zoe showed me the bathroom that would be mine. The pedestal sink provided little storage space, but I kept that observation to myself. In all honesty, something was a bit off about the whole situation. It reminded me of a time when I had gone to visit a friend and discovered she was hiding a boy in her room.

Joely returned while Zoe showed me the kitchen. "Sorry about that. Nice countertops. Thanks for taking the time, Zoe, we'll give you a call shortly."

We said our goodbyes and all but strolled out the door. Strange, because Joely almost always walked with a kind of eminent purpose.

Joely opened the car door for me, and I got in. As she climbed in herself, I noticed a patrol car pulling up behind us.

Joely waved at the driver, he waved back, and we drove off.

"What was that?"

Joely chuckled. "That's what I get for not running the numbers ahead of time. Zoe? There's been a warrant for her arrest for three weeks, but the narc unit's had a hard time tracking her down at the residence. It wasn't enough pot for an out and out manhunt, but enough that Steve owes me one."

"Steve? Pot? Like marijuana? There was marijuana in there?"

"Enough to induce a severe case of the munchies. That's what that blue light was for—they're growing it. Not uncommon, with the recession these days. I stepped outside and looked at their electric meter. Their energy use was...well, excessive. I made a call, and they took care of it. You didn't want to live there anyway. Smelled like mold."

I rested my head on the seatback. "Wow."

"We're going back to my place to do some background checks on the other places. I don't feel like touring a meth lab today, thanks. Speaking of the munchies, I'm hungry. Are you?"

"Sure," I said. "As long as it's got soy milk in it."

Chapter 17

Rather than worry about my inability to find an apartment without illegal substances, I decided to make sugar cookies. Since moving in, I'd started my own cookie cutter collection. The only type Jayne had was an overturned water glass.

With Christmas over, I chose a snowflake shape with light blue and white frosting and sparkling sugar on top.

While I waited for the frosting to set, I decided to send an email to Kim and Gemma.

> To: "Gemma DiGrassi" <mise.en.place@cmail.com>,
> "Kim Keiser" <k.keiser@cmail.com
>
> Subject: Apartments
>
> Gemma and Kim,
>
> I'm quietly looking for a new place to live, either by myself or
> with a roommate. Do you know anyone who might be looking
> for a roommate? Please understand that I love living with
> Jayne, but I think it might be best if I found another place.
> We can chat about it later.
>
> Sara

My phone rang four seconds later.

"You're looking at moving? Is everything okay?" Gemma's words came out in rush.

I suppressed a laugh. "Everything is fine. I just think it would be better if Jayne had more space."

"Has she complained?"

"No...I just don't want to be in the way."

"Does this have anything to do with Jayne and Levi?"

I couldn't help it. The breath I didn't know I'd been holding released. "Sort of. Yes."

Gemma giggled. "You're so funny. You're probably right though. Jayne's in full-on mother-hen mode. I've never seen her like this."

"It might be easier for her to watch over me than it is to think about marrying my brother."

"Could be. It's entirely possible. But she's a grown-up and responsible for herself. You don't need to move any more than she needs to mother you."

"It's just time," I said, though the very idea made my stomach churn. "I need to be independent."

"Don't let my parents hear you. In their perfect world, all of us would live with them until we married. They're very Old World. Probably not unlike your family in that respect." Gemma sighed. "Oh well. Anyway, I was also going to let you know that I have a friend who might be looking for a room-mate. She just finished a graduate program and is heading back to Portland. I know she wants to keep costs down, and sharing rent's a good way to do that. I'll chat with her and see what she says, 'kay?"

"I'd appreciate that. Really. I imagine she doesn't have any desire to grow and sell drugs illegally, does she?"

"She's looking at going to central Asia as a missionary. I'm not thinking she's much interested in the drug trade."

"Okay," I said, relieved. "Let me know if she's interested."

"I will. Don't stress about it."

"I won't."

I didn't think either of us believed me.

Monday morning arrived without my permission. I could feel the weariness to my soul, and the sky was so dark I never felt it was truly daytime.

All I wanted was to go back to bed and pull the covers far over my head. My desires aside, I had a day of classes and a few hours of work after. What had I become? I had been raised to work much and complain little. But after a few months of English living, I wanted to sleep the day away.

I didn't notice the empty chair next to me until it was no longer empty.

"How's it going?"

I looked up. It was the guy from the library. I vaguely remembered him saying we had a class together.

"Fine," I said, not knowing how else to answer. "Yours?"

"Not bad. I went to a great Indian restaurant I've never been to before. Do you like Indian?"

"I'm not sure that I've had Indian." I glanced around the room, looking for the instructor.

"Do you like spicy food?"

Wasn't class supposed to start sometime? "Sometimes." I checked my watch.

"Well, you should try it sometime. Are you doing anything Friday night?"

I wished class would start. The sooner it was over, the sooner I could move onto my next class. "I, uh, have movie night that night with my roommate and some friends."

"Right on. What about Saturday?"

I shook my head absently. "Nothing much."

"Then go get Indian with me."

"Oh, I, um…" I realized I was stuck. I couldn't say I was busy, because I'd just said I wasn't. "I suppose I could."

"Excellent."

The instructor chose that minute—a good five minutes past the time of usefulness—to begin class. Arin turned his attention to the color wheel while I tried to figure out what just happened.

He turned to me after class. "So can I pick you up? How does six thirty sound?"

"That's when I get off work," I said, hoping that might put an end to the evening.

"Where do you work?"

"R.G. Cameron Books."

"I'll pick you up there then."

"I…okay."

He grinned and walked away. I put my things away and started off for class.

And thought.

"I think I'm going on a date Saturday night." I admitted to Britta as we shopped for yarn after classes.

She lifted her eyebrow and a skein of mohair at the same time. "You think? What part are you not sure about?"

"I've never dated—not really," I said. I'd long acknowledged that my days of Amish courtship were over. Dating, the kind of dating I'd seen between Jayne and Levi, consisted of kinds of conversation and interaction that didn't happen among young Amish. I knew Levi took Jayne to restaurants, to movies, to concerts.

At home, dating didn't have an audience. If anyone else was around, it was other kids our age. But our parents didn't know, and our siblings couldn't tease us. Here, friends and strangers alike watched and observed as you potentially made an idiot of yourself with a member of the opposite gender. It made me nervous.

Britta shrugged. "I've dated some, though I'm not seeing anyone in particular at the moment. How well do you know the guy?"

"I've talked to him twice," I said, my voice dry. "He's in my Color Theory class."

"Is he cute?"

I frowned. "Um...I don't know."

"You don't know?" Britta laughed, put down the mohair, and picked up a ball of lambswool. "That's not a good sign."

"I just...don't know him. I don't know if he's a person of good character or if he's short-tempered. I guess I'm less interested in cute than I am in kind."

"I suppose you'll just have to go out with him to find out. But meet him there—that's safer."

"Oh." I winced. "He asked me if he could pick me up from work, and I said yes."

"Tell him you changed your mind. What do you think about this color?" She held up a skein of alpaca wool.

I wrinkled my nose. "Kind of washed out."

"That's what I thought. I just like the feel of it."

"Could you pair it with something else? Is that white one the same type of yarn?"

She held up the white yarn with the pale peach. "What do you think?"

"Hmm. Maybe with the brown? With your blonde hair?"

"And wear it with denim? Sold." She began to pull out skeins and placed them in her basket. "Make sure when you're buying yarn that all of your dye lot numbers match. I made a sweater once without checking, and the color changed right across the bust. Had to rip it back. It was pretty sad."

I walked around to the other side of the double-sided yarn display. "What do you think about this?" I asked, holding up a single-plied skein of magenta wool.

"Bright. Happy. And the single-ply will be easy for you to knit, just starting out."

"I'll take it, then."

"Good pick. When is this date, anyway?"

"Saturday. If I don't change my mind."

Britta grinned. "That's the attitude." She waved one of her skeins in the air. "Let's get out of here and play with this stuff."

⚡

I saw Arin between classes on Wednesday. "About Saturday," I said.

"Second thoughts?" He didn't look worried at all. "What's up?"

"Why don't I meet you at the restaurant." My words came out in a rush, and my heart raced. I felt so frustrated. This was so much easier back home, back when I knew the rules.

"Worried about my driving?" He smiled, a dimple showing in his cheek.

I looked at it in fascination. He had a dimple. And upon further analysis, I realized he had two, one on each side of his mouth. I studied his eyes. Were they kind eyes? Whether they were or not, he was waiting for an answer.

"Maybe," I said, deciding not to elaborate.

"You can stop worrying." I watched as his dimple deepened. "The restaurant is just down the street from your bookstore. I thought we'd walk."

"Oh." Now that I thought about it, I vaguely remembered an Indian restaurant near work. "Um, sure," I heard myself say. I only hoped I wouldn't regret it.

⚡

The week sped by. Friday night, we watched *It Happened One Night* while I worked on my knit hat the way Britta showed me. I dropped a couple stitches, but Britta had showed me how to pull them back up with a crochet hook. When I paused to examine my work, it looked perfect.

"That was fun," Jayne said after everyone but Levi had left. "What are you up to tomorrow night? I was thinking about hitting a couple shops. I've been feeling cold, and I'd like to pick up a couple new sweaters."

"I, um…" I hedged. I hadn't told anyone but Britta about Saturday.

"This should be good," Levi said, not bothering to hide his smile. "I know that face."

I crossed my arms. "I'm kind of going on a date. I think. A dinner date."

Jayne looked to Levi. "Is secret-keeping, like, genetic for you guys? Because this is the first we're hearing of Sara's first English date."

"I can't say," Levi answered.

Jayne swatted his arm.

"Who is he?" Levi asked as he picked up stray mugs from the living room.

I followed him into the kitchen. "A guy from school. My Color Theory class."

"Are you feeling okay about things?"

I shrugged. "I think so."

Jayne patted me on the back. "It's a date. It's not marriage—you'll be fine."

"That's rich, coming from you," Levi said. "You know how hard I worked to get you to go out with me?"

"I was dating Shane!" Jayne protested. "I was trying to be a good girl-friend, and you were trying to get me to go rogue, with your 'Hey, try some power tools in the shop with me' routine."

"You wanted to be with me rather than Shane, yet you put up such a fight," Levi said with the shake of his head. "Makes a guy wonder."

"Okay," I said, giving my brother a half-hug. "I'm going to bed."

I started off down the hall. When I looked over my shoulder, I saw Jayne lift her face to accept Levi's kiss.

I turned away with a small smile. I needed to move out soon. My brother had found love, and I didn't want to stand in the way.

I woke up Saturday morning to find Jayne sitting on the edge of my bed.

A feat, considering that Levi had set it up on a loft.

"Morning," I said, my voice scratchy.

"I wanted to check in with you about tonight." Jayne tucked a piece of hair behind her ear.

"You don't like it when I climb out of windows to court Amish boys, and you don't like it when I date an English boy that you've been informed of ahead of time," I pointed out, not bothering to lift my head from my pillow.

"Rule number one, don't drink anything he gives you. You open it yourself, you accept it from the wait staff, but nothing from him."

I didn't ask. "Okay. Is there any breakfast food? Did you get bread from the store?"

"Rule number two. Stay in lit, populated places."

"Okey dokey."

"Rule number three—trust your instincts. If you don't feel comfortable, call me. Or Levi. Or Joely—that'll give you the most bang for your buck."

"I will."

"And put a time limit on it. You have places to be, and it just so happens that you were able to fit him into your schedule."

"I promise," I said, sitting up, "that if he shows up wielding an axe that I will call you and sit in a public place until you arrive."

"Texting works too."

"Okay."

"Have you told William?"

"What? Why?"

"Levi just said…"

"What did he say?"

"It just sounded like William…might have an opinion."

I rolled my eyes. "Of course he'll have an opinion. He's William."

"Just saying. You might want to let him know."

I nodded noncommittally. I just couldn't think of a reason why William would want to know.

Chapter 18

I decided not to put too much effort into my clothing and makeup before I left for work. Instead, I focused on wearing layers so I'd stay warm through the walk but could lighten up after arrival if I wanted.

An embarrassing amount of vanity caused me to take the time to line my eyes and add a second layer of mascara to my eyelashes, but I didn't reach for my lipgloss.

It wouldn't have lasted through work anyway.

⚡

I began watching the clock—and the door—at 6:20 just in case Arin was early.

At 6:25 the shop was quiet. I'd already vacuumed the place and dusted the shelves. William had the till open and sat counting the cash with a careful eye.

"I'm off," Zach said, jacket and umbrella in hand. "If I leave now, I can get to the movie on time."

"Anything good?" William looked up for only the briefest moment.

"The new Scorcese pic."

"Nice and light, then. See you Monday."

I waved goodbye to Zach and resumed my dusting.

At 6:30 William finished his counting and started in on the Visa machine. "Plans tonight?" he asked, his voice oddly careful.

I opened my mouth to answer but heard the bell over the door chime.

"We're closed, man—you can come back in the morning." William almost sounded friendly.

"Not shopping, just here for Sara."

Willliam's face froze.

I turned to see Arin, dressed in what could be described as a cleaner version of his usual uniform of a layered graphic tee and jeans.

"Hi, Arin," I said, unsure of what exactly to do next.

"You look nice," he said with a smile. The dimples made a repeat appearance. "Are you about ready, or did I come at a bad time?"

"No, I'm finished up. I just need to put away this stuff"—I held up my rag and can of Pledge—"and get my coat."

"So, you're going on a date, huh?" William pasted a smile onto his face. "Cool. How do you guys know each other?"

I tucked the cleaning supplies into the cabinet beneath the register. "Class." I looked to Arin. "My coat's in the back."

"Class? So you're at the Art Institute?" I heard William ask—or maybe interrogate—as I exited for my coat and umbrella.

I hurried back.

"Ready!" I sounded annoyingly perky, but getting out of the shop as soon as possible seemed like a good idea.

"Nice talkin' to you, man," Arin gave a hand-up wave to William before opening the front door for me. We walked out together into the bracing cold.

"Nice out, isn't it?" Arin grinned up at the sky. "No rain."

I hoped the night wouldn't consist entirely of conversation about the weather. But then, I didn't know anything much about dating. Maybe a lot of weather conversation was normal. I knew I'd get bored with normal. "What made you decide to do Graphic Design?"

"It's Applied Arts." The air around us was so cold his breath steamed. "I love art, but it takes a lot of persistence and energy to make a career out of gallery showings. I also enjoy the interaction of art and text in graphic design. It's more creative than law school, that's for sure."

"Were you thinking about law?"

"Got through the first year before I decided it wasn't for me. What about you? What made you want to go into fashion?"

"I like clothes," I answered with a straight face, remembering my disastrous interview. "Honestly, I've always been fascinated with fabric and movement. I'm so blessed to be able to be in the program."

"Speaking of blessing," Arin said, pointing, "the restaurant's just up ahead. Their red curry is one of my favorites. I hope you like it."

≈≈≈

I discovered that I did, in fact, like curry. Arin ordered several dishes off the menu, encouraging me to try each one. I also enjoyed the *naan*, dipping it into various sauces and using it as a spoon with others. As I ate, Arin told funny stories about his family back home in Idaho and his current job working at a copy shop.

To my surprise, I found myself laughing and enjoying myself. Maybe dating wasn't so bad after all.

Arin offered to take me to dessert, but I was so full of food I couldn't imagine eating another course.

Instead, he walked me to my car, still parked behind the shop.

"Thank you for dinner," I said when the shop was within sight. "I like trying new foods."

"You're fun to feed," Arin said with a wink. "I think you ate more than I did."

I felt myself blush. "I'm sorry, I…"

"I'm glad you did. I would have felt bad if you'd hated it. Would have had to come up with a backup plan. Go to McMenamin's or something. Not that I have anything against the Captain Neon burger, but I like curry in the winter."

"I like curry in the winter too," I said with a rueful smile. "Apparently."

"Want to do it again sometime?"

I took a deep breath. Did I want to do this again? "Sure." I pulled out my keys. "I'm game," I said, repeating a phrase I'd heard Kim and Joely say.

"So am I." Again with the dimples. "See you in class?"

I nodded. "In class." I inserted my key into the door lock. Something above us caught my eye—light came from the window above, a window I knew to be William's. I thought I caught a glimpse of him, but I couldn't be sure.

≈≈≈

"I wasn't waiting up for you," Jayne said when I walked through the front door that night.

She sat cross-legged on the couch, holding a copy of *The Time Traveler's Wife*. I knew she'd gotten the book from the library the day before. But now she was two-thirds through the book, so I didn't believe a word she said.

"I'm home safe and sound. Feel better?"

She put the book down. "Much. How did it go?"

I shrugged out of my coat. "Better than I thought."

"With a review like that, it must be love."

"We can't all be you and Levi." I took a seat next to her on the couch. "Is there anything sweet? I didn't eat dessert."

"There's still ice cream in the freezer, but I'd appreciate it if you didn't finish off the gallon."

I rose and walked to the kitchen, intent on discovering exactly how much was left.

"Forgot to mention, there's a new episode of *Project Runway* on the DVR for you. We can watch it if you want. I haven't heard Marc Jacobs call something 'costumey' for a while."

"Yes, please." I peered into the ice cream carton. "This is still half full."

"And you've been known to polish off half of a carton."

"Not that much!"

"Um, yes that much. You're the Dyson of ice cream eaters."

"Because it's nighttime and I had a nice evening, I'm not going to Google that and be mad at you."

Jayne threw back her head and laughed.

I'd recently learned to start looking up things I didn't understand. Rather than stay confused, I did some research. I didn't always like what I found.

———— ⚜ ————

I looked up *Dyson* the next morning.

I threw open Jayne's bedroom door, not caring that she was still asleep. "You called me a *vacuum*?"

She groaned, just lifting her head enough to see her digital bedside clock. "It is 6:35."

I'd never been quite able to shake my Amish inclination to early mornings. "You called me a vacuum!"

"A Dyson is a very nice vacuum. A very expensive vacuum." She sighed. "I'm very sorry, I'll never do it again." A sleepy pause. "Or I might unplug your internet connection. I'll get back to you on my final decision in an hour and a half."

I rolled my eyes, closed the door, and let her go back to sleep. I heard her snores through the door within minutes. I'd occasionally wondered if I should warn Levi about Jayne's tendency to snore, but I decided I'd let him figure that out for himself.

~≈~

Rain fell hard and fast Monday morning on my drive to class. Or rather, my drive to the bookstore, since I still parked behind the shop before walking to the Art Institute.

I relaxed in the car, keeping a wary eye on the road while listening to a Norah Jones CD I'd borrowed from Jayne. I even started singing along and belted out a lyric about the spinning hour hand as I came to a perfect stop at the light a block before the shop, a foot before the pedestrian crossing line.

My eyes flew open at the impact. I felt the car, Jayne's car, lurch several feet forward, taking me with it. Before I could do anything, think anything, I found myself in the intersection, in front of a car that had been turning safely in front of me less than a second before. The second car clipped the front of mine. I could hear the shattering of the front light mixing with my own scream.

Heavenly Father, save me.

Horns honked. The car no longer moved. I sat frozen in the driver's seat, my hands shaking. My head hurt. I didn't know why.

I saw people out the window. A woman came up and knocked on the window, with her other arm crossed in front of her chest, protecting herself against the rain.

Her lips moved. I think she was asking if I was okay. It was hard to tell because my window was rolled all the way up. And of course it was—it was raining.

What was I doing before this happened, before everything literally spun out of control? I couldn't move, couldn't think. I wanted to pray, but the words were knocked out of me.

Suddenly William appeared outside my window. He knocked, his face stern. His face was almost always stern. Why was that?

William rapped again and pulled on the outside handle. When it didn't open, he gestured for me to unlock the door. Not knowing what else to do, I lifted the lock mechanism.

He pulled the door open in one swift movement. "Sara? Are you okay?"

I looked up at him. "I…I'm not sure."

"Your forehead, I think you hit it on the steering wheel."

I vaguely remembered such a thing. "Do you think so?" I said.

"Don't move," he ordered, taking his cell phone from his pocket.

Moments later flashing lights appeared—a lot of them. A car. An ambulance. William spoke to me calmly, holding my hand.

"I'm late for class," I said, still trying to wrap my mind around what had happened.

William moved aside but kept his grip on my hand as a man in a uniform looked over me, shined a light into my eyes, felt my limbs, and eventually helped me from the car. William left at that moment, and I felt lost. I watched him walk to the other side of the car, open the door, and reach into the glove compartment. I realized that he was getting the insurance and registration out of the car. He handed it to a uniformed police officer.

At the realization that the police had arrived, I searched wildly, hoping Joely would be among them. But she wasn't—all of the officers were male. If Joely were there, she would make everything better, but she wasn't. Neither was Levi, or Jayne, or Gemma, or Kim...or my mom. I wanted to hide in my mom's arms, but she didn't even know where I was, didn't know that anything had happened. She was so far away, and I was so alone and scared and wet that I began to cry, my tears mixing with the rain that fell on my face.

William returned to my side, shrugging his own rain jacket off, slipping my arms into it, and pulling the hood over my head. But the rain had already begun to soak through my clothes. I shivered.

William left again, this time to speak with one of the officers. William pointed toward me and back toward the shop, the front door of which I could see from where I stood. He came back a moment later. "Let's get you inside," he said, his arm secure around my shoulders.

I buried my head against the crook of his arm as he walked me to the shop.

Once inside, William flipped the Open sign to read Closed and locked the front door.

Zach rushed toward us. "What happened? What's going on?"

"That crash we heard? That was Sara's car. The cops are out there now. The idiot behind her was texting. I'm taking her upstairs. We're closing the shop until this has blown over, okay?"

"Do you need me to do something?"

"Call her brother—the number should be on her employee information sheet, 'kay?" He turned back to me. "Let's get you upstairs. Do you think you can make it?"

I nodded, still unable to find my words.

We took the stairs step-by-step. After a small lifetime, we reached the landing, and William shoved the door to his apartment open.

Inside, he led me to the couch and helped me out of my wet coat and cardigan. He tugged my socks off, left, and returned with a thick, woolen pair of socks that I imagined likely belonged to him.

Socks. Warm socks. My mom would have given me warm socks.

And with that, I collapsed into sobs on William's shoulder.

had hysterical hiccups when Levi arrived, looking ready to tear apart the driver who'd hit me…if the driver had been dumb enough to follow us to William's apartment, which he wasn't.

"I saw the car," he said, though I wasn't sure if he was speaking to me or to William. I couldn't see William's response because I hadn't moved from the crook of his arm since he brought me a thick sweatshirt to warm up in. The sobbing had ceased, but I hadn't come up with a good reason to move yet.

Levi crouched beside me. "How are you doing, hon?"

I nodded and hiccupped.

"Do you want some water?"

I shook my head and hiccupped.

"I tried," Will said, his voice dry.

"Where are your glasses?" Levi asked, looking around.

"Cupboard to the left of the sink."

Levi strode over to the kitchenette, found a glass, and filled it with water. He returned, holding the glass to my lips. "Drink."

I furrowed my brows at him—and hiccupped—but he furrowed his own brows right back at me. I drank, a droplet of water making its way down my chin and onto William's sweatshirt.

Oh well. I'd wash it for him later.

"You let the paramedics check you out, didn't you Sara?" Levi asked after I'd drunk enough water to make him happy.

"I think so," I said, trying out my voice to see if it still worked.

Levi studied my forehead. "I don't like that bruise."

"The paramedic said she had a slight concussion. They said if she gets worse or starts acting drunk to take her in."

"Is Jayne mad?" I asked the question that weighed on me most. "That I wrecked her car?"

"You didn't wreck her car. The driver behind you did. Jayne's crazy worried about you though."

I shook my head. "I'm fine," I said, knowing as I said so that my neck hurt and my voice was scratchy from crying.

On the other hand, my feet were toasty warm from Will's socks. These socks were very thick and very soft. Where did he buy such socks? I wanted a pair of my own. Or two. Or…if I wore them home and forgot to give them back, would he notice?

I immediately chastised myself for such a thought. I would never, could never steal. It was wrong. But for those socks, I would almost consider it.

※

The police came up to William's apartment to take my statement. By then, my hiccups had stopped, and I was mostly able to speak in complete sentences that didn't make me sound like a dumb blonde.

I told Officer McKinley how I had come to a slow stop, and after that didn't remember much. I did tell him I had been wearing a seatbelt, my headlights were on, and I had not been using drugs. I answered all of his questions without crying all over again.

Zach informed us when the tow truck came to cart the car away. I didn't feel the need to watch.

I tried to figure out why the experience shook me the way it had. After all, I wasn't seriously injured. I was insured. The police had even ensured consequences were in store for the other driver. And yet I was a shaking, weeping mess.

After the police left and Jayne's car was safely towed, I didn't have any good reasons to stay at William's apartment. With great reluctance, I began to tug off his socks.

"Don't worry about them," William said, catching me as I tried awkwardly to pull them off. "Your socks are still damp. You can bring those back later. The sweatshirt too."

"Tomorrow…" my voice dropped off, as I thought ahead to my morning work schedule.

William shook his head. "Don't worry about it. We'll see you when you're ready. Before you go though—" he held up a hand and left the apartment.

I heard his footfalls down the stairs.

Levi had my things gathered in his arms. "Where'd William go?"

"Um…" I took a few steps toward the door. "I'm not sure."

A pounding up the stairs, and William returned.

With books.

"Take these," he said, his voice only slightly wheezy. "And don't worry about bringing them back, you can have them."

I frowned, checking their spines for remainder marks, thinking he'd gone through the sale bin on my account.

No mark. He'd just plucked four new books off the shelf and run upstairs to give them to me.

"Thank you," I said, studying the titles. There was a lovely hardbound copy of C.S. Lewis's *The Horse and His Boy*, as well as *The Complete Works of Emily Dickinson*, Salmon Rushdie's *Haroun and the Sea of Stories,* and a copy of *Stuff White People Like.*

William looked down at me, holding my gaze. I couldn't understand the look in his eyes. Maybe that was just my headache.

"I'll see you later," I said, starting to feel unsettled.

William nodded. He looked miserable, even more miserable than when we'd gone to his parents' Christmas party. "Later," he echoed.

Levi thanked William, put his arm around my shoulders, and guided me down the stairs. "I guess I didn't need to worry," he said when we were outside. "You were well taken care of."

I thought about nodding, but my head pain was prohibitive. The Tylenol hadn't kicked in yet. "Um, yes."

"You doing okay?"

"I think so."

He patted my shoulder.

I followed him down to his truck, telling myself that I would be safe in Levi's truck, massive as it was. With its oversized tires and slight "lift," as Levi said it was called, we rode higher than most of the other traffic. Surely a car driving into the truck would only hit the tires, wouldn't it?

Still, I found myself cringing at every intersection, waiting for an impact. To distract myself, I found my phone and called Britta.

"Missed you in class today," she said, her voice playful. "But I understand. It *is* Monday."

"Well…" I played with my earlobe from beneath my phone, unsure of how to begin. "There was a car accident this morning." I paused. "I was kind of in the middle of it."

Britta gasped. "What happened? Are you okay?"

"I am now," I said, thinking of William's socks. "I do have a small concussion though. I was wondering if I might be able to borrow your notes from class today."

"Well, yeah, of course. Do you need me to go talk to your other instructors? I mean, if you've got a concussion, I doubt you'll make it to class tomorrow."

"I suppose you could. I don't know about tomorrow. I've never had a concussion before."

"I'll make the rounds, just in case. You've got Meyerson and Yates tomorrow, right?"

"Um…" If only remembering didn't hurt so much. I wondered if I'd smacked the remembering part of my brain. "I think so."

"Do you need anything? What are you doing this afternoon?"

"I'm not really sure." I chewed on my lip. Going home now, I had no idea what to do with myself. What did I do before I was in school full-time and working?

Right. Working full-time. And before that, studying for my GED. I hadn't experienced a lot of nonwork time during my existence as an English woman. Goodness knew I hadn't when I was Amish.

"What's your address?" Britta asked.

I answered without wondering why.

"Hope you feel better," she said. "Although I'm sure that's what everyone is telling you to do. So I guess I should just tell you to follow directions."

We laughed together before hanging up the phones.

I saw Jayne's motorcycle the minute the truck pulled in near the apartment. "Jayne's home?"

Levi smiled. "You're surprised? I called her on the way to the bookstore. It was all I could do to stop her from rushing straight over there."

Visions of Jayne storming in, asking questions, and having an overall moment of panic flooded my mind. They weren't entirely fair—when my father had his heart attack, she was the one who handled the situation. But I also had a hunch that where I was concerned, she might be a bit more animated.

Before Levi could knock on the door or I could pull out a key, the door swung open.

"Oh my goodness. I'm not freaking out, but oh my goodness." Jayne's hands fluttered. "Come in. Sit down. Or lay down, if you're supposed to lay down. I don't know what you're supposed to do about concussions, but they sound really scary on WebMD. Are you hungry? Do you want something?"

"Water?" Drinking water seemed to make Levi happy earlier. I hung up my jacket and reoriented myself.

I was home. I was safe. And I was still wearing William's socks and sweatshirt.

The Lord had taken care of me. Everything would be okay.

———※———

My eyelids fluttered open at the sound of the knock on the door. I heard Jayne's voice in the background. I guessed she was probably talking on her cell phone. The door opened—likely with Jayne's help—and I heard three familiar voices.

"We wanted to drop these off for Sara," Meg's voice said. "Really hope she's feeling better soon."

I forced my eyes open, sat up, and suddenly realized that sitting up was not a good idea. The blood in my head shifted in such a way as to remind me that it had been smacked around recently against its will.

"Hi," I said, aware that I sounded as if I had risen from the dead. "Come in, you guys. You're here, you may as well." I frowned. "Where's Levi?"

Jayne held the door while Meg, Sonnet, and Britta came in out of the rain, holding a pink box I had high hopes for. "He's picking up takeout for dinner. I'll have him pick up extra—you guys should stay for dinner. Y'all like Chinese, right?"

Dinner plans settled, Sonnet brought the pink box to the couch. "We thought we'd bring you Saint Cupcake. It was the least we could do." She lifted the lid so I could see the contents—a rainbow of cupcakes nestled inside looking beautiful and edible all at the same time. "It's possible one of us might have stuck her finger into the frosting though. Just warning you."

"That was Sonnet," Britta clarified. "Cream cheese frosting has that effect on her. She can't help it."

Sonnet shrugged. "It's an addiction."

Britta found the first season of *Pushing Daisies* in Jayne's DVD collection and suggested we watch, explaining how knitting's shining moment occurred in the second episode.

When Levi returned, he found the four of us squashed onto the couch with Jayne in the chair. Meg paused the DVD, and we broke only long enough to fill our plates and return to our seats.

Levi sat with his back against Jayne's chair, legs stretched out. Jayne twirled his hair between her fingers.

There was a lot of pie. I didn't get all of the jokes on the show, but I enjoyed laughing.

I liked having friends.

After four episodes, people began to trickle out. Under Jayne's watchful and worried eye, I readied for bed, reading *The Horse and His Boy* before falling asleep.

―※―

The next morning my head felt...worse.

Worse even than the day before.

I thought a shower might make me feel better, so I rose and headed for the bathroom. Inside the shower, I tried to raise my hands to shampoo my hair.

My hands, arms, and shoulders felt heavy, as if someone had tied weights to my muscles in my sleep. After ten minutes under the hot water, my muscles relaxed enough to allow me to shampoo and rinse. I was glad, in that moment, for my short hair. I couldn't imagine washing my old hair like that.

Another fifteen minutes, and I felt I was in decent enough shape to towel off with a moderate amount of efficiency.

Dressing was another matter, so I chose a simple outfit, a long-sleeved, waffle-knit tee in a pretty print, and jeans.

Jayne had breakfast going when I walked into the kitchen. "How are you feeling?"

"I think worse."

"Worse? Is that normal?"

"I'm not sure," I said. After all, I'd never had a concussion before. I didn't think my brothers back home—Elam, Amos, and Samuel—had either. Though while I'd been gone, that might have changed. I wouldn't know.

Rather than wonder, Jayne reached for her phone. "I'm calling Joely to find out. She's been shot at. She'd know about concussions."

"How is she, anyway? Is she back on active duty?"

"Slated to return tomorrow. It's killing her. She told me she actually bought a pair of shoes the other day out of sheer boredom. Now she's in a pattern of self-loathing because of it. Afraid she'll turn girly like I did."

I frowned. "Being girly means matching clothes?"

"I guess." Her expression changed the moment Joely answered.

Rather than listen in to a disjointed conversation, I sat at the kitchen table and read the front-page news, mainly because it didn't require any movement on my part.

The sound of a short vibration pulled my attention away from a piece about bridge construction. Jayne was speaking on her phone, so it had to be mine. With an impressive amount of resolve, I found my phone in the pocket of the jacket I'd been wearing the night before. Two new text messages. From William.

> *Hope you're doing okay.*

That was from last night

> *Hope your pain is better this morning. Let me know if you need anything.*

He'd sent the second just the moment before. I smiled and wrestled my fingers over the keys.

> *Am okay. May try to come in to work today. Thanks again for socks.*

My phone buzzed two minutes later.

> *Don't worry about it if you're not up to it. It's good for Zach to work hard. Keeps him humble. You're welcome for socks.*

"Well." Jayne put her phone on the counter. "According to Joely, you could have whiplash, and it's normally worse on the second and third day. So it sounds like you're normal so far. If it continues past that, we'll need to schedule you for a physical therapy visit. You can take some ibuprofen—it should help. I was thinking cinnamon rolls from a can sounded good. Are you game?"

"Sounds yummy," I said, knowing my mother could out-bake the Pillsbury Dough Boy any day of the week. The thought of a visit home to my mother's warm kitchen squeezed at my heart. But I pushed the thought aside and helped Jayne fit the rolls into a round cake pan.

Chapter 20

By the next morning, I was restless. I knew Jayne wouldn't want me to go to work. Period.

But I also knew I wasn't contagious in any way. And if I was going to feel bad, I could do that anywhere. And I was bored. Very bored.

So bored I thought about buying shoes, the way Joely had, except online shopping wouldn't result in something wearable for at least a week.

I thought about calling a taxi—we'd taken them from time to time back home, for doctors' visits and trips to see Rebecca and her family. But I didn't want to pay for the expense, and I figured that if I lived in a city with mass transit, I may as well figure out how to use it.

I looked up the MAX route, bundled up, and walked with careful steps to the bus stop. I prayed I hadn't gotten on the wrong bus and prayed I'd remember to get off at the right stop. Remembering seemed harder today than usual.

The man next to me flossed his teeth. Even his back molars. Combined with my headache, the sight made me nauseous.

When the buildings began to look familiar, I prepared to exit the train. The stop was six blocks from the bookstore. I held onto the strap of my messenger bag as I walked, thankful the day was overcast rather than rainy.

I walked past the spot where the accident had occurred. If I wasn't mistaken, I could still see pieces of shattered headlight on the road.

The bell over the door jangled as I walked in. William stood behind the register, but Zach was nowhere to be seen. One customer eyed the sale bin while another walked the shelves.

William's eyes widened when he saw me walk in. "What are you doing here?"

"I came in to work." I slid my bag off my shoulder.

He shook his head. "Sara..."

"Please." I spoke with my voice lowered, so as not to be overheard. "I just need to do *something*."

"How are you feeling?" He crossed his arms across his chest.

"Fine." Even as I said it, I knew I sounded defensive. Too defensive.

William's lips set into a firm line. He didn't want me there, and we both knew it.

"Please?" I asked, my eyes wide.

"I'd bet twenty bucks your brother doesn't want you working today."

I'd bet fifty he'd leave work and take me home if he knew. And I had a hunch William thought the same thing.

I crossed my own arms to match William. "I'm not contagious. According to Joely, who's a cop, what I'm experiencing is perfectly normal. There's nothing I can do to make myself worse. And I think I'll start with the shelving."

"You do?" William's lips quirked into a half-smile.

I squared my shoulders. Something about his expression made my face flush. "I do."

He sighed. "Just be careful, okay?

"Of course I'll be careful."

William rolled his eyes and didn't respond. Instead, he pointed at the book cart. "There they are. If you want to shelve that bad, shelve."

So I did. Out of self-preservation I separated out the books that I felt wouldn't require me to lift my hands any higher than my chest and started in on those first.

But then I realized I had trouble putting the books away. I couldn't remember what order the letters came in. Letters *E* through *V* were the worst, though when I thought about it I realized that pretty much meant the whole thing.

Rather than let William catch on, I struggled ahead.

Maybe he wouldn't notice that I spent about five minutes per book.

Zach did a double take when he returned to the shop from his break, Starbucks in hand. "What, you're back? That's hard core. If I'd known, I'd have gotten you coffee too."

"That's okay." I was pretty sure caffeine wouldn't do anything nice for my head.

"Feelin' better?"

"Yeah," I said, pasting a reassuring smile on my face.

William said something under his breath, but I ignored him.

~~~

After half an hour, I could barely see straight. Worse yet, I'd finished with the titles I could put away easily. All I had left were the books that belonged on the upper shelves.

I took a deep breath, planted my feet, made eye-contact with the target and lifted the book.

Or tried, actually. I stared at the hand holding the book and willed it to move.

My hand moved. But it moved down.

I tried again, taking a deep breath. I saw my hand go up, the pages of the book touching the shelf.

And then the world started to wobble, and I saw prickly black spots.

Before I knew what was happening or what was going on, William caught me from behind, steadying me.

"Don't forget to breathe," he said. "In and out. Repeat. Do you need to sit down?"

"Um…I'm not sure," I said. One of William's hands was on my back, the other on my arm. I felt even more disoriented than before.

"I'll take that as a yes. Let's go to the workroom, okay?"

Once my oxygen fully returned, I felt silly—and as steady as I had all day. But William didn't let go until we'd reached the workroom's studio chair.

I sat. He knelt next to me.

He gave a weary half-smile. "What am I going to do with you?"

I chose not to answer.

"Trouble lifting?"

"I can't raise my arms very far."

"That's whiplash for you. How's your head? And don't tell me you're fine. That bruise looks nasty."

"It hurts."

"On a scale of one to ten?"

I wrinkled my nose. "Seven?"

"That's what I thought." He moved into a sitting position on the floor, crossing his legs. "And you won't go home."

I bit my lip. The idea of maneuvering mass transit a second time sounded exhausting.

"Would you let me take you to a doctor? Just to be sure?"

"Joely said—"

He shook his head. "Joely's not a doctor."

"I can't afford a doctor. Not right now. I'm fine, really. I haven't had any symptoms of a more serious injury. All I really need is something to do."

William ran a hand through his hair. "Well, there's shredding to be done, but I don't trust you not to get your fingers caught. *But...*" he paused before presenting what I hoped to be another option. I hoped it didn't have to do with paper shredding. I liked my fingers. "We haven't done a new set of staff recommendations for a while. We also just got some new stock. Want to read some books and write up short reviews? I'll even take you home when you're done."

When he put it that way, of course I couldn't say no, especially considering I was of no use anywhere else. "I can do that," I said.

"Good." He stood and offered me a hand up before retrieving his keys from his pocket. "I'll even let you have my couch. Whatever you want, you can have it. Just don't fall over."

⁓∭⁓

William knocked before he entered his own apartment. "How's it going in here?"

I made a face and held up the book. "At this point, I think I've read enough to identify what I think you'd call 'strangled prose.'"

"Put it down, move on. We just recommend the good ones. There's no need to make disparaging comments about the bad. It's like telling people their babies are ugly."

I laughed. "I've never seen an ugly baby."

"That's because you've never seen my baby pictures. Hungry for lunch? It's one o'clock."

"Oh. Really?" I guess time flew while reading dull fiction.

"I was thinking of hitting Noah's Bagel."

I looked at William, and I looked at his apartment. "Why?"

"What do you mean, why? It's lunchtime. Noah's has lunch food."

"But...you live maybe thirty feet from your own kitchen. You could make yourself lunch."

"That's easy. I can't cook. And I can only eat so much canned soup before my ankles swell from the sodium."

I sighed. This was why, back home, young men lived at home until they married. I couldn't imagine any of my brothers, save Levi, trying to cook for themselves. I stood and walked toward William's kitchen.

He blocked my path. "Oh no, you don't. I know what that look means."

I lifted an eyebrow. "What does it mean?"

"It means you're going to raid my fridge and tell me what I could make with it."

I stood my ground. "Why not? You're not doing anything with it."

He smirked. "You can't lift your arms. I'm pretty sure you need them to cook."

"Don't be so smug."

"Sorry. Bagel?"

"I don't like bagels." I heard myself being difficult, but I didn't care. I was talking to William. As Jayne said, turnabout was fair play.

"They have paninis. Actually, I think *panini* is the plural and *panino* is the singular. The turkey club one is pretty good. They've got them, and that's the point. And soup. What do you want? My treat."

Soup with a straw sounded best, but I couldn't dream of asking anyone for that, especially not William. However...I could sip soup from the cup when no one was looking.

"Soup," I answered. "With a panino thing. Whatever you call it."

"You got it." He grabbed a jacket from the back of one of the kitchen chairs. "Don't cook anything while I'm gone." And then he winked. Winked and left.

Odd. Probably an eye twitch. Because he was hungry.

─── ⊰✧⊱ ───

William drove me back to the apartment before Jayne got home. "Thanks," I said as we pulled into the tiny parking lot. I pressed the button releasing my seatbelt. "Being out today was...nice."

"I don't understand it, but you're welcome." His voice softened. "I'm glad you're okay."

"Me too." I didn't want to think about how much worse it could have been.

"Before you try a stunt like you did today," he said, "just give me a call. I'll pick you up. Save you the pain."

"Okay." I suddenly felt shy.

"Go on in," he said, nodding toward the apartment complex. "Before you get in trouble."

I smiled. "Okay." And I winced on the inside over my sudden lack of vocabulary.

I hadn't thought it was possible to feel worse, but on Thursday morning I did. My headache had moved yet again. As hard as I tried, I couldn't come up with a good enough reason to get out of bed.

Jayne knocked and poked her head through the opened doorway. "You're not up? How are you feeling?"

I was feeling like I was tired of people wanting to know how I was feeling. And cranky. That too.

Jayne helped me out of bed so I could use the bathroom and then helped me back. After I was back in bed, she brought me breakfast and set up *The Young Victoria* for me to watch on my laptop.

I slept off and on throughout the day and soaked for an hour in the bathtub that night. As my eyes closed that evening, I prayed Friday would somehow be better.

Between prayer and another night's sleep, I found that waking on Friday was much more pleasant than the previous three days. I could wash my hair, dress, and feed myself with less pain.

As my pain abated, the complicated details of the aftermath surfaced. Jayne's insurance was liability only. Not only that, but the other driver was driving—illegally—with lapsed insurance. Jayne and Levi assured me that I had no need to contribute financially to the car repair costs, but the guilt weighed heavily on my heart.

Growing up Amish, I still couldn't make sense out of the whole idea of insurance.

In the end, things seemed to work out. Levi loaned his truck to Jayne so she could drive me places, and he insisted that taking the MAX saved him from filling his truck with gas so often.

My muscles were still sore as I walked the halls to my first class, but the pain wasn't debilitating.

"There you are!" I turned to see Sonnet walking behind me. "Glad you're back in the land of the living."

I shook my head. "Me too. I get bored when I'm not doing things."

"Ha! You and me both. But I'm sure that's not a surprise. It's sunny outside—Meg and I were talking about finding a place to eat lunch outside."

"Sounds like fun," I said, glad to be seeing a friend again.

"We thought so. Haven't seen Britta yet—let her know if you see her. Do you have any yarn with you? It's a good way to get her attention. I think she can smell it. Yarn is to Britta what people are to vampires. Sorry, terrible analogy," she said when she saw my face. "I'm reading the *Twilight* books at the moment. Have you read them?"

"Not yet," I said, visualizing William's face if he ever saw me reading them.

"They make me feel like I'm fifteen all over again, but they're amusing. My sister sent them to me in a care package. And I'm rambling. See you after class?"

"After class," I echoed.

I arrived early enough to check in with my instructor and explain my absence. One look at the bruise on my forehead though—which by now was starting to turn colors, despite my attempts to cover it up with cosmetics—and the instructor waved a hand and told me not to worry about it and that she was glad I hadn't been hurt worse.

It occurred to me in that moment that if I'd been in my family's buggy rather than my roommate's car, I probably would have been hurt much, much worse. There was something to be said for steel frames and seatbelts.

───※───

"The missing girl returns," Arin said as I entered Color Theory later that morning. "Thought something might have happened to you after dinner—maybe Indian didn't agree with you or something."

"No," I said with a soft laugh. "Indian was fine. I got into a car accident Monday morning." I pointed at the bruise on my forehead. "Concussion."

"That's too bad. I've had a couple of those—from snowboarding, not car accidents. You're safe with me behind the wheel."

I frowned. "The accident wasn't my fault. The guy behind me was texting."

"Didn't say it was...sorry, this isn't working out well. I was going to ask you—interested in going to the Art Museum with me? There's a new Warhol exhibit up. Do you like soup?"

"I like soup." But I didn't know how the two were linked.

"Perfect. Want to go?"

I didn't know much—yet—about Andy Warhol, but I did know that I'd been wanting to go to the Art Museum for months. "I'd love to," I answered honestly.

"Great." He grinned, his dimples making a repeat performance. They really were nice dimples. "It's a soup date."

I smiled but said nothing. I had no idea what he was talking about.

Chapter 21

I didn't have long to contemplate Arin's confusing comments about soup. During my walk from school to work, my phone rang.

I flipped it open as soon as I saw it was Gemma calling. "Remember the friend I told you about?" She said, sounding pleased with herself. "Well, she thinks it's a great idea—you guys rooming together—and thought the three of us should get coffee or something so you two can meet. What do you think?"

"Sure," I answered, my stomach performing handsprings without consulting me. Was I ready? I had to be ready. "What was her name again?"

"Olivia Cathen, but she goes by Livy. Great person, very quiet, very focused. She used to date my brother, about a million years ago. They broke up, but we stayed friends. She doesn't have pets—pretty much what everyone wants in a roommate. Everyone serious, I guess. I think it'll work perfectly for you guys."

"What coffee times work for you and Livy?"

"Not to rush you or anything, but could you do something after work today? Turns out Livy's anxious to find a place—she's done with school and not particularly interested in staying with her parents for very long."

"I'm off at six thirty," I offered.

"Six thirty? How about this—forget coffee, we'll do dinner. Well, if you want coffee with dinner, that's your prerogative, but we'll make sure there's a meal in there. I can pick you up if you want and take you back to Jayne's afterward."

My mouth went slightly dry as I tried to piece the evening together in my head. I wanted to meet Gemma's friend and a potential roommate, but I didn't want Jayne knowing what I was up to. Not yet. I told Gemma dinner was fine and that I'd see her after work. After I hung up with her, I called Jayne.

"I'm going to see Gemma for a bit tonight," I said, hoping Jayne wouldn't ask questions.

"Nice. Have a great time," Jayne said, not sounding the least bit suspicious. "I suppose I might be able to get your brother to hang out me."

"You might." The thought warmed me. I loved the two of them together. "Probably wouldn't take a lot of convincing."

"I didn't think so. You never know though, he's been pretty busy lately."

"Has he?" I wracked my memory, trying to think what would have made him so busy. Sure, he had work, but Levi wasn't the kind of person to let his job rule his life. "I guess I haven't talked to him for a few days." But then, I hadn't been much for phone calls lately.

"Well, I'll try my luck tonight. Maybe we'll see what Gemma's dad's got on the menu at DiGrassi these days."

I didn't know what to say. I wouldn't, couldn't lie to her, but neither did I want her a table away, listening to every other word of our conversation. Even at every other word, surely she'd be able to fill in the gaps for herself. But I couldn't say anything to dissuade her. "Good idea," I said, and we hung up.

I started praying that my brother would be desperately hungry for Mexican food.

※

My afternoon at work flew by. William was holed up in the workroom most of the day working on book repairs and a display box for one of Richard's favorite clients. Zach kept a running monologue during the slow times, regaling me with his impressions of Robert Duvall and Al Pacino. I'd never seen any of the *Godfather* movies, so I had no idea how accurate he was or wasn't, but I laughed and lauded him just the same.

However, he quieted down the moment Gemma walked in the room, standing taller and straightening his shoulders.

"Hi, Sara!" She said, sweeping in looking as gorgeous and put-together as usual in her long teal wool coat and matching navy hat and scarf set.

"Hi, Gemma." I gave the counter a final sweep with the dust rag before putting away my cleaning supplies. "I love your coat."

"I love your blazer," she said, smiling. "It's a good color for you."

"I'm Zach," Zach blurted, extending his hand.

I looked from Zach to Gemma and back again. I'd never seen Zach so red.

Gemma shook Zach's hand. "Hi Zach, I'm Gemma, Sara's friend."

"It's, I, um…nice to meet you. Gemma." Zach's gaze never left Gemma's face, despite his tongue-tied state.

"Very nice." Gemma shook Zach's hand a second time before removing her own. I noticed it seemed to take a bit of effort for her to retrieve it.

"I'll grab my coat," I said.

Gemma nodded. "I'll go with you."

———※———

"You're awfully twitchy tonight," Gemma remarked as we were escorted to our table.

"Jayne and Levi might be here tonight." I admitted. "I couldn't say anything."

"Don't worry," Gemma said with the toss of hair. "I'll shield you. If necessary, we can do an elegant, adult duck-and-crawl maneuver I perfected some time ago. There are windows in the pantry. We'll make it work."

"There's probably a back door, as well," I added.

"True. But why walk out a door when you can climb out of a window?"

"It's probably easier on your clothes to walk."

"Good point." Gemma checked her watch. "Livy should be here any time. I told her 6:45 and it's only 6:40." She folded her hands. "I could give a description of Jayne and Levi to the maître d'…make sure that if they come they're seated on the opposite side of the restaurant."

I looked around. The restaurant teemed with people, as it did every Friday night. "I'm not sure that opportunity would present itself. Don't worry about it."

"I won't if you won't—oh look, there's Livy!" Gemma stood and waved.

I stood myself. I'd learned in the last few months that I hated meeting people while sitting down.

Gemma performed the introductions, and Livy greeted me with a warm if distracted smile. I studied her as she and Gemma hugged.

Livy probably stood at about seven inches over five feet. Her fashion sense was nothing to remark about, and her strawberry-blond hair made her seem faded. But her smile was genuine and her eyes were kind. I could definitely live with her.

We sat back down at the table. Moments later, Gemma's father appeared. "Such beautiful ladies!" he said, his voice thick with the Italian accent of his home country. "Thank you for coming so I may feed you here tonight." With surprising ease he described the evening's specials. "The *Pollo Saltimbocca* is very nice tonight, very nice. The chicken has been pounded thin, thinner than my pinkie finger, floured, topped with paper thin prosciutto and sage. It's sautéed, topped with Fontina cheese, and served in a luscious white wine, sage, and butter roux." A brief pause for air. "The *saltimbocca* is served with a broccoli rabe, which will always, always be served hot, always hot. My sous-chef has a trick to keeping it hot. There is no cold broccoli in my restaurant. The broccoli rabe is accompanied by roasted fingerling potatoes, buttered and tossed with sage and lemon zest. I think there is a little white wine in there too."

"Sounds wonderful," Livy said.

That was good. If she'd said something about skipping the cheese and just a salad, thanks, I didn't think I could live with her.

Livy turned to me after we ordered. "Gemma tells me you're a student at the Art Institute. How are you liking it?"

I tried not to fuss with my napkin. "I've really enjoyed it. I'm very excited about the program."

"And you're in fashion?"

I nodded. "Fashion design."

"My first bachelor's was in art history, before I felt led to the mission field."

"Where exactly are you planning on going?" I asked before taking a sip of water.

"Kazakhstan." She laughed, seeing my frown. "Don't worry, a lot of people don't know where it is. It's Central Asia—south of Russia. Kazakhstan is one of the many ex–Soviet Union countries struggling to find its identity. Lots of people searching, looking for answers."

I couldn't imagine the country, much less a place so far away. The Amish had no missionaries. We expanded the church the old-fashioned way—by having babies and lots of them. "When do you expect to be there?"

Livy sighed, leaning back so the waiter could place the bread basket on the table as well as the dish of olive oil and balsamic vinegar. "Hard to say. There's support to raise, though I've been working two jobs to put a nest egg together. Well, my boyfriend and me. Clay and I are planning on eventually getting married, when we're ready, before going overseas. It'll be a while because Clay's still working on his studies. Don't worry—I won't be the roommate who's in one day and gone the next."

"How exciting for you," I said, at a loss. The whole process seemed so mysterious to me. "Are you two engaged?"

"No, not yet. We're waiting until we're closer to our departure date."

That made sense, I supposed. I hadn't thought to worry about what would happen if a roommate left. I'd have to go through the whole process all over again. The thought made me want to shudder, despite the fact that Livy had just told me I *wouldn't* have to worry about it, at least for a while.

But then, how long would I stay in Portland? Listening to my instructors, it seemed quite clear that anyone wanting a career in the kind of apparel I designed was unlikely to stay in the Pacific Northwest. The idea of moving so very far from those I knew terrified me, but I knew I had to be realistic. Being an English adult meant moving where the jobs were. I'd heard Britta talk about how her parents had recently relocated to Houston because her dad had been promoted.

I had several Amish friends and cousins whose families had moved at one time or another, but they certainly weren't in the majority. Most Amish preferred to stay in their community from cradle to grave, the way their parents had before them. Only things like scant farmland and poverty necessitated a move.

I pushed my thoughts aside. "If you're open to it, I'd love to room with you," I said. "How do you feel about it?"

"I'm game if you are," Livy said with a smile.

"Yay!" Gemma clapped her hands together. "I'm so glad."

"There's a unit I've been looking at." Livy swirled her bread in the oil and vinegar. "It's not great—no dishwasher, and could stand to be updated. But it's clean, cheap, and has a washer and dryer. Good freeway access without being too noisy."

"A washer and dryer would be great," I said, feeling myself relax. My sewing projects would be so much easier if I could rinse and tumble-dry cottons in the apartment. Jayne had laundry in her place, and the thought of going without troubled me. Ironic, considering that I'd never used a mechanical dryer until eight months ago.

"We can go look at it early next week. I'd be happy to meet you there."

I wrinkled my nose. "I wish I could. Maybe I could take the MAX there... the car I usually drive is in the shop."

"No problem. I can pick you up. Where are you living now?"

"Um…my work is probably more central," I hedged. "I'm off at six thirty most nights."

"That's fine," Livy said with the wave of a hand. "How's Monday?"

"Perfect," I said. And in that instant, I realized I had something I'd been looking for. A not-crazy roommate.

※

"So," Gemma asked on the drive home. "When are you going to tell them?"

I rested my head on the headrest. "Soon." I exhaled, knowing that wasn't right. "Tonight."

The conversation hung heavy in my heart as Gemma's car bumped into the driveway of the little apartment parking lot.

"Thanks again for dinner," I said. "And please tell your dad thanks. It was delicious."

"He loves feeding you. Says you have a good appetite."

I smiled. "It's an Amish thing."

"Keep me posted on things," she said, shifting the car into first gear. "Don't forget your leftovers."

"I think your dad gave me extra."

"He probably did. See you later!"

I waved as she drove away, watching her car disappear before walking up the stairs to Jayne's apartment.

Levi's truck stood guard, parked in the spot near the stairwell. Well, at least he'd keep things from getting too dramatic.

They were watching a movie when I walked in, Jayne snuggled against Levi's chest.

She blinked at me as though she'd been asleep. "Hi," she said, her voice fuzzy. "Gemma good?"

"She is." I put the leftovers in the refrigerator before joining them in the living room.

What do you think, Lord? I prayed. *What should I say?* I listened, hoping that one of these days I might hear something back.

"I'm moving out," I blurted. And winced. That wasn't at all what I'd thought about saying in my head.

"What?" Jayne sat straight up. "What did you say?"

I looked to Levi. His expression remained unchanged. "I'm moving out," I said, slower this time. "It's time."

"But…" Jayne was clearly searching for words. "Did I do something wrong? Is there something that would make it easier for you to stay here?"

"No…" I shook my head.

"I'll clean the ring out of the bathtub. And clean up the stray flour that's been on the counter for a week."

"It has nothing to do with the apartment or you as a roommate—not at all." I shifted in the chair, pulling my leg so it was under me while the other dangled. "I'm English now. I need to learn to be independent."

"How are you doing for money?" Levi asked

I swallowed. "I have some saved away…enough for a deposit and first and last month's rent. I'll be sharing the rent. My income is good at the bookstore. If I need extra, I'll make a quilt or two and sell them."

"You're a hard worker." Levi gave me a confident smile. "There's no doubt about that. I just hope you won't be so distracted that you'll struggle with school."

"My grades are good so far, and I've been working quite a lot. I can also use some of my financial aid to cover rent if I need to."

"But…" Jayne's face broke my heart. She looked completely forlorn.

Levi patted her head. "It's Sara's decision, and she's a good decision maker."

Jayne rested her head in Levi's hand.

"I'm moving in with Gemma's friend Livy," I said slowly. "She's very nice, very responsible, according to Gemma. I only met her briefly." I gave a small smile. "I think it will be good."

I watched them, hoping desperately in my heart that I'd made the right decision.

Chapter 22

Jayne was smart. She waited until Levi left to pepper me with questions.

"So—Gemma's friend Livy. I think I met her a long time ago. But you like her? You think it'll be a good fit?"

I walked to the kitchen and began to pull out butter, sugar, flour, salt, and eggs.

"What are you making?" Jayne asked.

"I have no idea. What sounds good? What do we have?" I pulled out a small bowl and cracked the eggs into it. Whatever I made, it would likely be something that didn't require separated egg whites.

"Oatmeal cookies?" Jayne suggested. "Do we have oats?"

I checked the cupboard to the side of the stove, retrieved the silo-shaped container of oats, and gave it a good shake. "Sounds like three cups, at least."

"Want me to mix the dry ingredients?"

"Sure." The vanilla was near the oats, so I pulled it out as well. Into the bowl with the eggs I added the white sugar, brown sugar, butter, and vanilla. "In answer to your questions," I said, emphasizing the s in questions, "I met Livy earlier this evening. And yes, I like her, and I'm fairly certain it'll be a good fit."

"Wow. You sure do play your cards close to your chest." Jayne stirred the flour, cinnamon, and rising agents with the whisk attachment belonging to the blender. "Though I shouldn't be surprised. Heaven help us if you take up poker."

"You're not mad?"

"Why would I be mad? The person who makes the yummy food and prevents me from being lost in a pile of clutter is moving out. Mad? No. Never."

I bumped her hip with my own. "I'm not far. It's just…something I needed to do."

"Don't worry, I get it, I really do. I moved two hours away from my parents at eighteen. I know I'm not family, but staying with me is only a baby step toward independence. I'm not mad because you're ready for a leap."

"I think I am."

"You are. Are we ready to mix? Because I'm dying for one of these cookies."

"One? I've never seen you only eat one." I straightened. "You're the Dyson of oatmeal cookies."

Jayne threw back her head and laughed. "I had that coming to me, didn't I."

"You did."

"I'll miss you."

I put my arm around her shoulders. "I know. I'll miss you too."

Arin had spoken so much about soup that I figured—as best I could—that he meant we would eat soup. He'd offered to pick me up from work again once my shift was over. That particular Saturday I got off at 1:30.

It made no sense to take my lunch break at 12:30 only to turn around and eat soup at 1:30, so I decided to work through lunch and snack on whole-grain crackers while Zach and William abandoned the shop in search of food.

I began to regret my decision when Arin picked me up.

"You look pretty," he said. "About ready to go?"

Before I could answer, my stomach made a noise. It was not a pretty noise.

And it was loud enough that William looked up. Or maybe he was already looking, but it was loud either way. "Yes," I said, folding my arms in front of my torso as if to muffle any further communication from that region.

I followed Arin outside. To my surprise, we stopped in front of a car.

"Are we driving?" I asked, eying the vehicle. I didn't know how I felt about driving with Arin.

"Yeah—the museum's a fair walk from here, and it's looks like it's gonna downpour at some point today. You okay?"

"Um…" My stomach gurgled in a definite *no* vote. "It's fine. It does look like rain, doesn't it." Of course, this was western Oregon. It looked like rain most of the time, most of the year.

Arin opened the car door for me, and I climbed in. The first thing I noticed was the peeling duct tape on the dash. What had I gotten myself into? I felt my hands start to shake. I could only hope Arin was a good driver.

Arin slung himself into the driver's seat and started the car. My right hand grasped the armrest as the car came to life, rumbling and making noises I didn't think cars could make.

At every stop, I pressed my foot down on an imaginary brake. At every lane change, I looked over my shoulder to check blind spots. By the time Arin parked outside of the stately museum, I had the urge to launch myself from the car, ground myself in the grass, and weave its blades between my fingers. I resisted, partly because it would have been weird and partly because the ground was wet and would have marked my trousers.

There were banners outside advertising the special exhibit within. Printed on them was a can of soup. Several cans of soup, actually. I began to get a bad feeling.

My stomach agreed.

≈≈≈

I wished I'd stashed some crackers in my purse. Arin bought the tickets for the exhibit, and we walked upstairs. "I love Warhol's style—so graphic, so *there*. No apologies, you know? More diverse than people give him credit for. He's got a portrait of Sarah Bernhardt that's gorgeous—makes you want to forget all about Marilyn, if that were possible."

Once we reached the exhibit, my first glance changed everything. My noisy, empty stomach receded into the background. The colors were incredible. I struggled to describe them in my head. *Saturated* was the only word that came close. They were so bright, so vivid, just looking at them warmed my soul.

Arin and I walked slowly through the gallery, studying each piece. We saw the Sarah Bernhardt and the wall of Marilyn Monroe, as well as Elizabeth Taylor, Ingrid Bergman, and Che Guevara. I knew who they were because of the little placards.

I loved the giant pictures of shoes and the way they sparkled. I told Arin so.

"Diamond dust," he said. "Not bad, huh?"

In another room we saw the 1979 BMW M1 Warhol had painted. "He meant it to look like speed," Arin explained. "Speed as in rapidity, not the drug. A car painted to look like an amphetamine wouldn't be that interesting."

"I like the yellow." I tilted my head as I studied it, throwing a glance at Arin.

He couldn't understand how yellow had been such a taboo color to wear back home, only worn on occasion by very young girls with mothers who didn't realize how badly it could stain. Here in Portland, with the English and their Shout sprays and Biz and Tide pens and washing machines that didn't rely on generators or car batteries, here I was free to love yellow. I loved the sunshine of it. Loved the brightness, the way it attracted attention without me worrying what the neighbors or the bishop thought.

How nice it was never to worry anymore about what the bishop thought! The sense of relief I felt at that moment overwhelmed me. I felt tears, once so unfamiliar and now so frequent, prick at the corner of my eyes.

I felt Arin's hand on my back. "What's the matter?" he asked.

I shook my head. There was truly no way he would understand.

～✺～

The last room to see made everything clear. Soup. As far as the eye could see.

My stomach rumbled again as if to greet the cans and cans of Campbell's soup. I wondered if there were any cans of Progresso when Warhol was working.

If there were, they didn't make it into his art.

We walked around the room, studying the pictures.

When we were near the door, my stomach made noise again. This time, it's wasn't a rumble or a gurgle. It was a roar.

Arin looked at me. "Are you hungry?"

I couldn't look at him. I could only nod.

He put his arm around my shoulders. "Well, let's get you something to eat."

～✺～

I waved goodbye to Arin as he dropped me off at the apartment. Not seeing anybody inside, I put my coat and purse away and walked down the hallway to my room.

My brother's voice came from nowhere. "Oh, it's you."

I shrieked and jumped, running into the wall in the process.

"Whoa, sorry. I didn't mean to startle you. I thought you were Jayne when you walked in."

"Where…" my eyes followed the sound of his voice. He was flat on the kitchen floor, head beneath the sink. I put my hands on my hips. "What exactly are you doing?"

"Garbage disposal's on the fritz."

"Where's Jayne?"

"Got a call—there's some huge breaking story. I offered to stay and fix the garbage disposal."

I walked over to inspect the sink. "What did she do to it?"

"Sometimes these things just break."

I was sure they sometimes did, but Jayne had a habit of sticking things she probably shouldn't down the disposal, like chicken bones and avocado pits. Not that I was well acquainted with the machine—I'd spent my entire life without one. Not even my Mennonite grandmother had one. But having been raised on a farm, I was familiar with machinery that ground things up and the kinds of things that made them unhappy. Like avocado pits.

"Glad I got to see you today. Saved me a phone call." Levi made a couple twists with his wrench. "Mind turning on the water?"

I lifted the faucet handle. Levi flipped the disposal's switch. The blades roared to life, rattling the countertop.

He switched it off. "Sounds about right. Enough about that." He sat up, resting his hands on his hips. "How are you?"

I took a seat on one of the counter stools. "Busy."

"Just a bit?" Levi looked me over, taking in the circles under my eyes and my badly styled hair. "Maybe a little stressed too?"

"Okay, a lot." I slumped over the counter.

"Thought so. Just so you know, I've been looking at buying a house."

"Oh?" I knew he'd been renting the last several months.

"One of the ones I'm looking at has a finished apartment in the downstairs. You could have that place to yourself, have lots of workspace, lots of privacy, but Jayne and I would be nearby."

I lifted an eyebrow. "You and Jayne?"

"The house would be for her and me."

"Does Jayne know about this?"

"Nope." Levi's eyes twinkled. "And don't you dare let on."

"Roger that," I said, repeating one of my new favorite phrases. "Thanks for the offer, but I'll have to pass. This is something I have to do."

"Don't work yourself too hard. Do you think you'd have space in your new place for a quilt frame?"

"Maybe. Maybe it could go under my lofted bed, if we were clever."

"Would that help with your quilting?"

"Definitely."

"I'll see if I can put one together for you then." He paused. "Are you sure I can't talk you into the downstairs apartment idea?"

I shook my head. "When you left, you made it work for yourself. I need to do the same thing."

"When I left, the economy was different."

"That doesn't make it less important to me. Richard pays me well at the shop, probably more than I deserve."

"Well, Kim visited the bookstore the other day—I think you were in class at the time. Said she's never seen it looking so sparkling clean and well organized."

I shrugged. "Dusting isn't something that much interests Zach or William. They weren't raised to be Amish women."

"No." Levi laughed. "Let me know when you decide to do the move. My truck is at your disposal."

"Yes. I suppose I'll actually have things to move this time. So…" I shifted on the stool. "How are…they?"

Levi gave a soft smile. "I won't lie and say they don't miss you. I think Mom…understands."

I didn't ask about my father. I knew he wouldn't talk to Levi and certainly wouldn't talk to him about me.

"It's also too early to say anything, but Amos is seeing a girl."

My eyes widened. "How do you know?"

"Elam's a blabbermouth. Having a sibling who's courting age too is dangerous."

I laughed. "Did he say who it was?"

"Rumor has it it's Miriam Beacher's Ella."

"Ella? Really?" Ella had been one of my best friends back home. If I were still there, we'd meet in the day, exchange stories, giggle, and plan our futures. Now my future couldn't be more different than Ella's. I wrinkled my nose. "I never would have seen Ella with Amos."

"From the amount of conversation about it, you're not alone. On another subject, Grandma would love to visit you. All she needs is a word, and she'll hop in that boat-like Buick of hers and voyage north."

My throat went dry at the thought. I rose from my spot at the counter and found a glass for myself, filled it with water, and drank. "I don't know," I said, swirling the water in the glass. "I really don't."

On one hand, I wanted to see her. Especially after the accident, I'd craved the warm arms of my mother, and Grandma would be similar. And yet she still represented my past, despite the fact that she'd left the Amish community to become Mennonite along with my grandfather. She'd always been a part of my Amish life.

I remembered my plans to quilt for additional income. Quilting was part of my past...why did I not struggle with it?

Unlike quilts, Grandma was real. She smelled of cinnamon. She held me as a baby. She was a living, breathing reminder of everything I couldn't have, everything I'd walked away from.

"I can't," I answered at last. Not yet." A part of me wondered if I ever could.

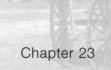

Chapter 23

Monday after work, Livy picked me up and drove us to the apartment complex she'd scouted. The manager walked with us to the open unit, carrying on a one-sided conversation about the episode of *24* slated to air later that night.

"Do you watch *24*?" he asked as he unlocked the door to apartment 22B.

"I'm more of a *What Not to Wear* fan," I answered.

He didn't say much after that. I guess he didn't know how to relate.

Livy walked in first. I followed.

The apartment was...stark. Even for a girl who was raised Amish.

Not only was the place devoid of furniture—as I expected—it was devoid of color. I felt like Dorothy stepping *out* of Technicolor. The carpet was somewhere between gray and beige, the linoleum white yet speckled with gray. The walls were white.

One thing was clear. I'd need to decorate. Or go a little crazy.

The bathroom was large, larger even than the bathroom at Jayne's, with a large closet equipped with doors that squeaked when they slid.

The bedrooms were small but only a bit smaller than Jayne's.

The kitchen was small and serviceable. Livy had mentioned the lack of a dishwasher, but that didn't bother me. I still preferred to wash dishes by hand anyway. Washing them before placing them in a machine to wash them again made no sense to me.

Livy and I picked up applications before leaving.

"I know its bare-bones," she said in the car, "but it is the cheapest non-scary place in the area."

"Cheap is good. I like to be frugal." I decided to address the question that had been bothering me. "Do you have...curtains?"

Livy laughed. "I have some, but you're welcome to make something you'd like better. I'm going to be working a lot, so I wouldn't be surprised if you're there more than I am. As long as the place doesn't look like a bordello, you can do what you'd like."

———✳———

I looked up *bordello* later. Oh. I didn't think I was likely to decorate a home to look like one.

———✳———

I used the bookstore's fax to send in my application for the apartment. "So, you're moving?" William asked, looking over my shoulder. "Found a place?"

"A place and a roommate," I said, unable to hide my satisfaction.

"Need help moving?"

The question caught me off guard. "Well, I..."

"You're moving?" Zach stuck his head into the office. "Cool. Need help?"

Amazing that these moments only seemed to happen when there were no customers desperately requiring assistance.

"I don't have that much to move, but I guess help would be good." Wouldn't it? At home, everyone pitched in for everything. Maybe the English and the Amish were more similar than I had thought.

———✳———

The next twenty-four hours sped by in a whirlwind of classes and work peppered with apartment paperwork. Livy and I decided she would cover the first month's rent and I would cover the last month. In an instant, I watched my savings take a significant dip.

There was no getting around it. If I wanted anything resembling a financial safety net—that didn't include my brother—I needed to get quilting.

Kim called me on Thursday. "I know it's been a while," she said. "The job's still good, right?"

"I enjoy it," I said, thinking of Zach and William and the many, many books I got to watch over.

"Cool. Well, I heard through the grapevine that you're moving out with a friend of Gemma's. I think it's great—really. Should help get Jayne down the aisle and marry that man before I steal him away."

I did not mention that I didn't think Kim was Levi's type. "Mm-hm."

"Anyway, what I was going to say is that since you need transportation, and the weather's not crazy freezing anymore, I thought you might be interested in my old bike. Oh, and by *bike* I mean bicycle. Not a motorcycle like Jayne's. I don't ride it anymore, and you're welcome to it."

"That's a great offer." I hesitated, searching for words. "I, um, actually don't know how to ride a bike."

"Really?" I could hear the shock in Kim's voice. "But…it's not a car. And it's not electric in any way."

"But it's tricky to ride in a skirt," I explained. "The Amish are more likely to use roller skates for that reason."

"There you go, then. You can roller skate to work."

I shuddered thinking of it. "No thank you. I'd be open to learning to ride a bike someday, but I'm frightened enough driving around the bikers. I think I'd be too terrified to bike around the drivers."

"Fair enough."

"I'm thinking of buying a car," I admitted. "I don't know anything about cars though."

"Expect to pay between two and three thousand for something that runs well and doesn't need constant repair."

I processed the amount. "Good to know." I could sell a quilt for somewhere around that if it were well detailed and of good size. It wasn't an unattainable goal, and that way all of my financial aid would go straight to school and living expenses.

A part of me began to panic as the sheer amount of work in my future took shape in my head. I shoved the desperate thoughts aside. As much as I wanted to pretend I wasn't raised Amish, nothing would ever change the fact that I was raised to work hard. I was no stranger to long hours and manual labor. Quilting wasn't brick laying, but it was a lot of labor.

"Let me know when you move," Kim said, interrupting my thought process. "I'll come over and help."

I doubted I'd need the assistance of—five people, was it now? But if Kim wanted to help…"Absolutely," I heard myself say. What was that phrase Jayne used? The more the merrier? I supposed it would be a very merry move.

The week of the move, it rained like crazy. Making matters worse, every forecast agreed the rain would only continue.

I loved weather forecasts. Did English people realize how wondrous it was to be able to know what the weather would be like ahead of time? Granted, I knew how to read clouds better than Jayne, but I liked having an idea in the morning exactly how cold it would be in the afternoon.

Keeping the forecast in mind, Levi suggested renting a small moving truck to move my things rather than filling the back of his truck and suffering potential water damage.

I agreed. Levi made the arrangements.

———※———

As it turned out, Meg, Britta, Sonnet, and I all had sewing projects for school that week. We piled into Meg's Camry—the cleanest car I had ever seen—and drove to Bolt together. During the drive I happened to mention that I'd be moving to a new apartment.

"I'd love to help," Britta said while fingering a white dotted swiss. "You're moving Saturday?"

"Saturday," I confirmed.

"How much of a cliché is red satin?" Sonnet asked.

Meg shook her head. "Too much. Back away from the red satin. Think olive or aubergine if you're committed to satin." She tapped my hand. "I'm mostly free Saturday. I can help too."

"Yeah, me too," Sonnet added. "What if I used the red satin ironically?"

Britta rolled her eyes. "Get over the red satin already. What time Saturday?"

"Around ten or so," I said. "I thought it might be nice to get it over and done with."

"Cool. Well, I'll be there. How's the knitting coming?"

"Slowly," I admitted. "I like it, but I haven't had much time lately, and I'm not quite good enough to knit in class without being distracted."

"I understand. Life is busy. Don't worry about it." She smiled. "We all go through seasons."

I hoped this was only a season. Personally, I was done with it.

———※———

Gemma called the morning of the move, letting me know she'd be there to help and was bringing, naturally, quite a lot of food for everyone to eat afterward.

Joely called shortly after, saying she'd been able to rearrange her shift and would be able to carry as many boxes as I needed. All told, that meant that ten people, not including myself, were helping me move. I told Jayne as much as we shared the bathroom mirror, each of us putting on makeup for the day.

She paused and slung her arm around my shoulder. "The Amish have barn raisings. The English help move people from one part of town to another. We could have a conversation about how the Amish help people stay in one place, and the English help each other go away, but it's best to enjoy it for what it is—free manual labor. You know, some people actually pay for movers."

I wrinkled my nose. "Really?"

"I kid you not." Jayne dusted her cheekbones with blush. "And they're famous for dropping pianos from high-rises."

"Interesting. Should I warn Gemma how many people will be there? So she brings enough food?"

"You could, but it's Gemma. When doesn't she bring too much food?"

"Good point." I fished through my makeup bag for the right lipstick.

"So who else is coming? I'm guessing Britta, Meg…the one with the cool name, what is it?"

"Sonnet." I finished. "Zach and William are coming too."

"Really?" Jayne put her mascara down. "Who's running the bookstore?"

I hadn't thought of that somehow. "I have no idea."

The crowd started showing up at 9:45, starting with Zach and William.

"Who's at the store?" I asked as they came in and wiped their feet.

William smirked. "Richard is. He'll be there by himself, but it's good for him. Helps him stay in touch with the little guy."

"Oh." I couldn't imagine informing my boss that his schedule was changing. It didn't seem to intimidate William in the slightest.

Meg and Britta showed up moments later. "Sonnet's on her way," Meg explained. "She's running a bit late."

"Missed her alarm." Britta clarified. "She's not much of a morning person."

I had almost finished introducing everyone when another knock sounded at the door.

I opened the door to find Gemma. "It's just me!" She gave me a hug as she came inside. "Are you excited?"

I nodded, and I couldn't help but notice that Zach had turned Roma tomato red.

"The food's in the car, in the cooler. I figured I'd pop it into your new oven when we made the first trip over. I've even got plates, cups, silverware, and napkins, so don't worry about a thing."

My stomach lurched. Silverware, plates, cups—I didn't have any of those things. I hadn't even thought about it, with the craziness of packing things up. Oh my goodness. How would I cook, much less eat? What if Livy didn't have a frying pan? Or a soup pot? Or a *rolling pin*?

The only thing I could think at that moment was that if I were still Amish, this wouldn't be a problem. Moving out would mean I was getting married, and getting married meant that my new husband and I would be provided for with practical gifts to start our lives together and would travel every weekend to visit relatives and receive yet more gifts. I wouldn't have to worry about whether I would have a pie pan to my name. It would be taken care of.

Jayne must have noticed my face. "What's wrong?"

"Spoons," I said. "I don't have any. I didn't even think about it. I don't have spoons or forks even. Or glasses or pots or ladles or—I don't even have bath towels!"

As soon as the words left my mouth, I felt my face flush. I couldn't believe I'd just mentioned bath towels in front of my coworkers. My male coworkers.

"I picked up extra towels when you moved in," she reassured me, "and I assumed you'd take them with you. As far as kitchen things, don't worry about it."

"But I—"

Jayne grasped my shoulders just as the door opened again. "Don't worry about it," she repeated.

"Put her in a headlock, that always convinces me," said Joely, looking around the now crowded room. "Everyone here helping move? Good times.'"

I forced myself to calm down.

Levi arrived several moments later with Sonnet just behind him. "Good crowd," he said, nodding to everyone. That was my brother. He always knew the right things to say. Unlike me, who had meltdowns about spoons and towels in what Jayne called "mixed company."

"This should go quickly," he added, taking the lead. He reintroduced himself to Zach, whom he'd met briefly after my car accident, and shook William's hand. "The three of us should be able to handle the heavy stuff. I've got a quilt frame in the back of my pickup that will have to be moved in at the end, and there's Sara's bed, the desk, and a small bookcase." He glanced at me. "There may also be a tall bookcase in the back of the pickup as well. I might have had it made and driven up from the shop."

I smiled, thinking of the shop he used to own and run in Albany. "There may be?"

"It's possible," he said. "And don't worry, they're well secured and very dry. The ladies," he added, looking at Jayne, Gemma, Joely, Sonnet, Meg, Britta, and myself, "can handle the boxes, giving them to the men to take down. Where's Kim?"

Yet another knock at the door. "I'm here!" Kim announced, lowering the hood of her rain slicker as she stepped in. "Sorry I'm late. Are we moving Sara, or is this a political rally of some sort?" She raised her fist. "Votes for women!"

Gemma patted her shoulder. "Up late last night, sister suffragette?"

"The newspaper biz is a cruel mistress. Or mister. Whatever." Kim tugged off her jacket. "Am I that loopy?"

"Not in the slightest, Mrs. Pankhurst," Jayne reassured her. "Let me give you the roll call."

Jayne listed the names of everyone present, pointing as she went. "Got that?"

Levi didn't wait for a reply, giving everyone marching orders instead. It was official then. I was moving out.

Chapter 24

I may not have contemplated how I would dry off after a shower in my new apartment, but I had been packing with meticulous precision for the last week.

All of my desk items had been sorted and boxed, as well as my sewing machine, fabric, and notions. My sketches were carefully tucked away into a plastic accordion file. The sketchbooks were packed along with my books.

My clothes were carefully folded and boxed. Knowing others would assist with the move, I'd packed my underthings between my knit tops and jeans.

Earlier in the morning, Jayne had helped me roll up my comforter and stuff it with my pillows and sheets into an oversized garbage sack. In an uncharacteristic move, Jayne insisted on making sure each box and bag was marked and labeled with a fat sharpie pen.

Now that everyone was here—and frankly, making it difficult to move around—the time had come to get everything out. I felt bad I didn't have more stuff to move.

Meg, Kim, and Joely handled the boxes of books. Gemma and Sonnet carried the clothes boxes while Jayne wrestled the bedding bag to the door. Britta took my bath things out, including the towels Jayne let me keep. I moved my sewing things.

Once the smaller things were out, Levi, William, and Zach began the truly heavy lifting, dismantling my bed and loading each piece into the moving van Jayne had picked up. Next came the small bookcase, and finally the desk.

Looking around, it seemed as if my world had collided and emptied, all at the same time. Jayne's apartment no longer contained any of my belongings or any other sign of my presence other than the overall lack of dust. However, my friends through Jayne, my brother, my friends from school, my coworkers—everyone mingled in the living room in one large, odd mix.

Levi clapped his hands together. "So, we're all loaded and ready to go. If you'd like to follow us over, we can unload. Gemma's got lunch for everybody."

Zach gave a cheer at the announcement of food. The fact that it was Gemma's food probably added to his excitement.

Levi announced that he and Jayne would be going in his pickup. Zach and William spent the next ten minutes arguing over who would drive the moving van. William won.

"Why don't you go with them?" Levi suggested, nodding to me. "You know the way, and you can help tell them where things go when you get there. You have your apartment key?"

"I do."

As everyone else negotiated their own rides, I followed William and Zach out to the van. I tensed as I realized that the van only had one bench seat across for the three of us. The drive would be very, very close.

"Why don't you take the middle?" Zach said, holding the door open. "You're the smallest."

I opened and closed my mouth. "Oh...um, okay."

"Sure you don't want me to drive?" Zach asked William, his eyes hopeful.

"I'm sure. Stop whining and get in."

"I'm waiting for Sara."

I climbed in quickly so he would wouldn't have that excuse anymore. Zach hopped in after me, complicating things as I tried to buckle the middle seat belt without touching anyone else.

William slid in on my left a moment later. "Sure you got everything?" he asked. I found myself distracted by William's attempt to buckle his seatbelt, his hands close to my hip.

"Leave the gun. Take the cannoli," Zach said when I didn't respond.

"What?" My head shot up. "I don't own a gun."

"No, it's a quote..." Zach corrected.

William shook his head, closed the van door, and started the ignition. "You know, Zach, not everyone knows *The Godfather* the way you do."

"I've never seen *The Godfather*," I pointed out as we pulled out of the complex driveway. "I'd never even heard of it until I started working at the bookstore."

Zach frowned in disbelief. "Come on, never?"

"Never," I repeated, folding my arms for a lack of a better idea of where to put them. William smelled good, like pine needles and spice. How had I never noticed before?

"I can't believe that." By now, Zach was nearly bouncing in his seat, unable to contain himself. "*The Godfather* is an American icon. It's like *Star Wars*, with less merchandising. And you'd never heard of it? What are you, Amish?"

"Well…" I couldn't lie, and keeping up the pretense was getting to be exhausting. "Yes, actually."

"Huh?" Zach looked at me blankly.

William didn't take his eyes off the road. "I thought so."

"How—really?" I turned to him, my expression quizzical.

"I just put the pieces together," he said.

"You're serious?" Zach's voice, if possible, had gotten louder in the last three minutes. "Like, Amish Amish? Amish with the buggies and the funny beards Amish?"

I lifted an eyebrow. "I don't have a funny beard."

"No, I mean the men have funny beards. I'm confused."

"I thought so," I retorted. Coming clean may have given me an attitude.

William smiled.

"But don't Amish people speak a different language?" Zach asked.

"You hear me speaking English, don't you? We speak both English and Pennsylvania Dutch. And High German too, actually, but only at some church functions."

"Pennsylvania Dutch? Wait—I think I've heard about this. They migrated to the U.S., and everyone thought they were Dutch when they were saying, like, *Deutsch* for Germany, right?"

"Pretty much." I leaned back as far as I could, wedged between the two of them. "The Amish were actually mostly Swiss. The Pennsylvania Dutch as a people—not just language—included several groups. The Amish were just one of them."

Zach wasn't through asking questions. "How'd you wind up here? In Portland, I mean."

"You know, directions at some point wouldn't be a bad thing," William interrupted. "Or I could just drive in circles. Whatever you want, we've got a full tank of gas in this thing."

"Make a right on MacAdam." I turned back to Zach. "I'm in Portland because I ran away from home."

"I thought you were over eighteen."

"I am."

"So…you're legal. You're not a runaway."

William rolled his eyes. "Zach, get a clue. In families like Sara's, you don't get a nice send-off party. It's not like moving out for college—your parents are not going to drive you there."

"No," I agreed. "Jayne did. She just didn't know it."

William chuckled. "This I might have to hear."

"Jayne was staying with my family while working on a story. Right before she left, I snuck into the trunk of her car." Enough time had passed that I now understood why Jayne had been so horrified. I had experienced what happened when things went wrong on the road. I made a mental note to apologize to Jayne for scaring her so badly. The English were crazy for car safety, and now I knew why.

"I'm guessing," William said, "that not a lot of people know about your background."

I sighed. "No."

"Hear that, Zach?" William raised his voice to be heard over the rumble of traffic noise. "Are you going to be able to keep your mouth shut?"

"I'm Amish, guys," I said, as realization sunk in. "I'm not running from the law. There's no reason people shouldn't know."

"But there's a reason you didn't want people knowing," William shifted down as he got ready to turn. "Something held you back. Whether you decide to tell everyone else is up to you, not Zach's oversized mouth. Right Zach?"

"Huh? I wasn't going to say anything." Zach protested.

The truth was, though, that everyone helping with the move deserved to know. Sure, Jayne, Gemma, Kim, and Joely knew, but it was time for Sonnet, Britta, and Meg to know too. They were my friends. And Livy, when I saw her next. I knew she'd moved her things in already but was at a missions conference.

"I'll tell them," I said softly. "I'll tell them myself."

We sat in silence the rest of the drive except when I gave William directions.

I pulled my jacket hood over my head when we turned into the driveway of the new complex parking area. The rain had slowed but hadn't ceased. We would all be damp at the end of the day.

I climbed the stairs and unlocked the door while Zach and William opened the back of the van.

Inside it was just as I remembered, though a bit less sparse. Livy's things were inside, and I was glad to see she had brought a table with three chairs, a couch, a recliner, and two end tables. A TV on a small stand had been placed in the corner of the living room. In the kitchen I saw a microwave and some cookware, and when I opened the cupboard I nearly wept in relief.

Drinking glasses. Eight of them.

In anticipation of Gemma's arrival, I turned the oven on to 350 degrees, figuring whatever Gemma had brought would require at least that temperature to warm.

The knock on the door interrupted my preparations. I opened it to find Zach and William with a piece of my bed in their arms. "Hold the door, maybe?" William asked, voice tight.

"Sorry!" I held the door open for them before they dropped the heavy wood frame back down the stairs. From the corner of my eye I saw Levi and Jayne pull up in Levi's truck. I waved, making sure I kept the door open wide enough.

Everyone else arrived in the next ten minutes, including Gemma with something that could only be wonderful.

"It's rosemary chicken lasagna with spring vegetables—it may not be spring yet, but everything's in season in the freezer section. If anyone has a question about the veggies, I'll just tell them about the béchamel. It's that good. I also brought a tossed salad and two loaves of bread—rosemary focaccia and crusty sourdough," Gemma explained as she busied herself in my kitchen. "I brought enough for twenty so you'd have leftovers. If you want, you can freeze any leftover lasagna. The rosemary focaccia makes great breadcrumbs, and the crusty sourdough could be used with a bread pudding so nothing goes to waste."

I doubted there would be enough food left over that I'd worry about waste, but I let Gemma plan anyway.

While Gemma got the food ready, the rest of us moved my things from the van into the apartment. William proved to be handy with a screwdriver as he and Levi reassembled my bed. Sonnet and Britta argued in the bathroom over how my toiletries should be stored best. Meg and Joely arranged my clothes and closet in a complicated scheme involving sleeve length and color while Jayne made up my bed. I set up my sewing station before moving my books into the new bookcase Levi had brought for me.

I used to have books stacked on top of each other, two deep, but now I had room to spare in my new shelves. On my old shelf I organized my fabrics and scraps.

When Gemma called that the food was ready, I half expected people to get wedged in the hallway in their haste to reach the kitchen. For the past thirty minutes, the scent of warm bread and cheesy rosemary had filled the air with a perfume that was especially intoxicating because we were all hungry.

"Before we eat, I have something special for Sara," Gemma announced.

I watched in amazement as she presented me a cupcake with a lit candle in the center. "Happy first apartment!"

My brows knit together in confusion. "But…I'm sharing it with Livy."

"That's okay," Levi said with a chuckle. "It's a housewarming…an apartment-warming…whatever. We're all for a reason to celebrate anyway."

Not knowing what else to do, I blew out the candle. "I'll eat the cupcake after lunch," I promised.

Gemma waved a hand. "I figured you would, don't worry about it. Would you rather start with some lasagna?"

I let her serve me lasagna—she wouldn't let me help serve anyone else. I had nothing to do but go to the living room with my food. Eating on Livy's furniture made me nervous, so I sat against the sliding door to the deck, the glass cool against my back.

William joined me a moment later, setting his food down before sitting next to me. "I think Zach wants to marry your friend Gemma, eat her food, and father her children."

I looked up to see Gemma serving Zach lunch. The expression on Zach's face could only be described as cow eyes. "Oh dear."

"Oh dear is right." He took a bite of the lasagna. "This is really good." He took another bite before lowering his plate. "Are you…you know, doing okay? With the move and everything? It's got to be a lot of change for you."

I shrugged. "I guess so." In truth, nothing had sunk in yet, but a small piece of me had begun to panic. I wasn't going to tell him that though.

"If you need anything, you can always, you know, call me," he said, not quite looking me in the eye. "I know you've got your brother and Jayne and everybody, but sometimes people are busy or they don't hear their phones. The store's not that far away."

"Thanks. And, um, thanks again for the books. I don't know if I said thank you properly after you gave them to me. And your socks are around here somewhere, clean."

"You can look for them some other time. It's your birthday party. Early." He smiled one of his rare, crooked smiles.

"I really will give them back to you."

He smiled again. "I believe you."

How did he do that? How did he make the fact that it was nearly my birthday and I was nowhere near home—how did he make everything seem like it would be okay?

Chapter 25

My back must have been turned. Maybe Sonnet was standing in the way. All I knew was that one moment, I was talking to William, and the next, there were wrapped gifts in the middle of the living room.

I began shaking my head. "This...this is too much."

Jayne shrugged. "Maybe. Maybe not. They're just going to take up room on your floor unless you open them."

William tapped my knee. "You heard her. Tear some paper for me."

I followed instructions for once and knelt in front of the pile. From the corner of my eye, I could see Gemma passing out cupcakes. Zach helped.

The tag on the first gift read, "To Sara from Joely."

Gifts from Jayne and Levi, that was one thing. A part of me wanted to tell everyone else that it was really, truly okay, I didn't need anything—but I knew that particular conversation would be as fruitless as an apple tree in January.

Inside the bag, wrapped in tissue paper, I found pepper spray, a whistle, and a very heavy flashlight.

"It's a Maglite," Joely explained, looking satisfied with herself. "Part flashlight, part heavy object. Every woman should have one."

"Thank you," I said, wondering what she intended me to do with it. For better or for worse, I had been raised a pacifist. I wasn't accustomed to hitting potential assailants with heavy objects. If that's what she intended. Maybe it was supposed to be a paper weight or a doorstop. A doorstop that rolled.

I moved on to a large box with a tag that said it was from Gemma. I moved aside packaging peanuts to find a large stock pot, complete with fitted lid, a copper-bottomed frying pan with a lid, and a three-quart saucepan. I stared at them in disbelief.

"Before you get worried," Gemma said, "remember that I can order kitchen

177

things through the restaurant at a discount. I know Livy has a fair amount of her own kitchen things, but I thought you'd enjoy having your own proper kitchenware."

I felt my eyes grow wet with tears but willed them away, partly because I didn't want Joely to see me cry over Gemma's gift when I hadn't cried over hers.

A box from Kim revealed a Corningware baking dish set of a variety of sizes. "I don't cook—you know that—but I've heard they're really great for baking and casseroles and stuff," she said, by way of explanation. "And I thought the white was nice."

From Jayne, a large box and a gift bag. Inside the bag I found a boxed set of silverware, two more bath towels, two Pyrex measuring cups, and a set of baking measuring cups. "I need to know you're eating," she said with a smile.

"Though it's probably Jayne we should be worried about," Gemma said.

"Hey," Jayne protested, eyebrow raised. "I can boil pasta with the best of them. Don't slow down, Sara, you've still got some to go."

I opened Jayne's box to find a 30-piece set of dishes. "They're from Fred Meyer. Nothing fancy, but I thought you'd like the pattern," Jayne said.

I nodded, studying the picture on the box. The dishes were a creamy white with a lacy, scalloped pattern around the edge. Simple, but definitely not plain. "They're beautiful," I told her, humbled I had a friend, roommate, and future sister-in-law who, let's face it, had friends who knew my taste and wanted to make sure I would go into the world prepared. "I can't wait to eat off of them."

"Last gift's mine." Levi took a huge bite of his cupcake. "These are good, Gemma."

"You already brought me a quilt frame and a bookcase," I protested, sitting back on my knees. "You should probably stop giving me things at some point."

Levi couldn't contain his smile. "I should. I'm mostly done—don't worry."

I reached into the oversized gift bag and began to pull out items. I found two baking sheets, and between them sat a rolling pin, a pin cover, a pastry cloth…The last bits I had difficulty grasping. I giggled when I realized what they were. "Pie and tart pans," I said, holding one of each up for everyone to see. "A ceramic pie pan, a deep-dish glass pan, and a tart pan with a removable bottom."

"A who what?" Zach asked. "That just sounds...wrong."

"A tart. Pastry without a top, baked in a pan that serves as a mold. You can get the pastry out without destroying the shape if you use one with a removable bottom. I like to set a baked tart on top of a glass bowl that's a bit smaller and work the edge part off. Does that make sense?"

A look at Zach's face told me no.

"Don't worry," I said. "I'll bring one into work sometime." I looked to Gemma, Joely, Kim, and Jayne, and my brother. "Thank you," I said, fearing my words were too simple.

Simple was all I had though. My heart was too full to say anything else.

After the gifts were opened and the food was eaten, people left in small groups as they moved on with their Saturday. Sonnet, Meg, and Britta left to work on their design projects, and I needed to work on mine as well. Kim, Gemma, and Joely left, and Zach rode with them in Kim's car back to Jayne's apartment.

"We should get the van back," Levi said after my new home goods had been put away.

One glance at his expression told me he wanted Jayne with him. I didn't blame him. I gave her a hug and thanked her yet again for my gifts, gratified when she gathered up her jacket and purse to leave with my brother.

Mission accomplished.

William gave me a look I couldn't read and said he should leave as well, and he offered to drive the van back to Jayne's apartment. With a strange reluctance I said goodbye to him as well, giving an awkward wave as the three drove off, Levi and Jayne in the truck and William in the van.

I watched from the window as the three drove away.

When I turned around, I fought the urge to run down the street after them. I was alone in the apartment.

I'd been alone before. I had. But I always knew that Jayne would be home—or I could drive somewhere, not that I did very often. But I didn't have a car, and though I was trying to use MAX more often, the truth was that public transportation terrified me. I was happy to walk places, but aside from a small grocery store and a coffee shop, there wasn't much to walk to.

More specifically, I think, there wasn't anyone for me to walk toward. Jayne, Britta, Meg, Sonnet, Levi, everyone at the bookstore…They were only within walking distance if I didn't mind walking for a very, very long time. And my family—well, I couldn't even think about that.

One thing was certain though. If I didn't want to sit around alone all of the time, I'd need a car. And before I could buy a car, I needed money.

Between class and making quilts to sell, I had a lot of sewing to do. Maybe I was alone, but there was work to be done.

Over the next several hours, I made all of my plans for my assignment and drew up a quilt design. The quilt was unlike something I would have necessarily made at home and closer to what English people expected Amish quilts to look like. Solid, bold colors, despite the fact that most everyone I knew at home enjoyed quilting with prints.

Whatever. I needed the quilt to sell, and sell fast. If quilting more "Amish" would make it sell, that's what I was going to do.

I took a break for dinner, enjoying leftover lasagna, salad, and toast with butter. None of Livy's things in the kitchen looked like a toaster, so I made the toast in the oven.

I tried watching Livy's television but couldn't figure out how to get the sound to come through. Rather than calling Levi to ask his advice, I put the remote down and went back to work, adding the details to my quilt design. After I bought fabric, I could complete the project without stopping to make adjustments.

I already had the fabric for my class project—a skirt with unique detail. I started in on the construction, making sure my edges and technique were perfect.

The sky grew dark as I worked. Unsatisfied with a seam, I ripped it back and meticulously did it over, pinning and pressing it before running a new line of stitches.

To my horror, I watched as the thread bunched up six inches in. I blinked, realizing my eyes were dry. I looked at my watch. It read 11:35.

How had it gotten so late? I removed the nearly mangled fabric and turned off the sewing machine before washing my face and preparing for bed. Levi had offered to pick me up for church the next morning.

I crawled into bed in my new room, turned off my bedside lamp, and waited for sleep to come.

It didn't. Rather than sleep, I could only think about how I had never spent the night in a house or apartment alone. Every nighttime noise intensified. The apartment creaked as it cooled, sending my nerves on edge. I heard footsteps on the stairs and my neighbors' doors slamming shut. An ambulance siren blared nearby and faded as quickly as it had come.

I turned over.

I was fine. I was safe. The door was locked and bolted

Maybe things would be better if I had a dog. I'd never had a dog, at least not one indoors with me. But I'd read books with female characters who had dogs, and Joely had told stories about women whose dogs had protected them until the police arrived. It seemed like something to consider, if only I lived in a place appropriate for a dog that would surely need exercise and a place to do its business.

I tried to pray. God seemed so quiet lately. I recited a Dutch prayer in my head before moving on to an awkward English prayer of my own.

I was cold. I thought about turning on the heater, but it was the kind that would continue to heat the room until I turned it off. I didn't relish the idea of finally falling asleep and then waking up covered in sweat.

The thought of socks occurred to me, and with that thought a stray memory that maybe William's socks just might be in one of the boxes we'd temporarily stored in my closet.

I switched on my lamp, climbed down from my lofted bed, and stumbled snoozily to my closet.

Nothing in the first box.

Nothing in the second box.

In the third box I found my old clothes, the ones I'd come to Portland in, a GED study guide, and finally, William's socks.

He wouldn't mind if I wore them again, I knew he wouldn't. I could wash them again. I worried for a brief moment about overwashing and the knit fabric becoming threadbare before its time, but I reasoned that William was a bachelor and probably had plenty of socks so he wouldn't have to do laundry too often.

I tugged the socks over my feet and padded back to bed.

The socks protected my toes from the chill, but I couldn't stop hearing every noise that came from inside and out of the apartment. Had Jayne's place been this noisy? Had I not paid attention because I knew she was nearby? I thought of the time she'd stormed into my room back home about a year ago. Had it really been so little time? A young man had been at my window, and I'd been preparing to leave with him. That was the way things worked in the Amish community.

But Jayne hadn't known that, storming into my room in her nightclothes, armed with a shoe. I think it was a shoe. At any rate, the young man fled, fast. I felt bad for him, but in that moment I decided I truly liked Jayne, even if she was awkward and completely out of place in our plain world.

About as out of place as I was in her fancy one.

I snuggled deeper into the covers. Being English meant being independent. Being independent meant being able to be alone and get sleep at the same time. I closed my eyes and breathed deeply.

And jumped when another siren roared by.

My phone was on the shelf next to my bed. I reached for it and dialed Levi's number.

It didn't even ring, but went straight to voicemail. I tried again, waiting until I heard his voice again reminding me to leave my number.

I didn't. There wasn't a reason to. He'd probably realize in the morning that his phone battery had died overnight.

My heart beat faster as I began to panic. I needed to hear someone's voice.

My bedside clock glowed 12:16.

Before I realized what I was doing, I called William.

Chapter 26

Hello? Sara? Are you okay?"

I breathed a sigh of relief at the sound of William's voice. "Are you… awake?" I asked, belatedly realizing it was a silly question to ask someone who had pushed buttons on a phone before speaking into it.

He chuckled. At least he thought it was funny. "Yeah, I'm awake. What's up?"

"Oh, um…" I felt myself grow inexplicably shy. "Not very much, I guess."

"Can't sleep?"

"It's noisy."

"You've never lived alone, have you?"

I made a face. Leave it to William to get right to the point. "I do have a roommate…"

"But she's not there. You know what I mean. It's nothing to be embarrassed about, Sara." He paused. I saw him in my mind sitting up, leaning forward the way he did when he was thinking something. "When I moved out, I moved across the country. I'd waited months to get out, and all I could think of that first night was how far from home I was."

"It must have gotten better."

"It did. Maybe I got too used to it. I doubt you'll have that problem though."

"No?"

"Everyone short of the mayor turned up to help you move today. You're special to a lot of people."

"Thanks."

"You're welcome," he answered, his voice gruff. "So, what are you reading these days?"

"*The Horse and His Boy*, actually."

"The copy I gave you?"

"The copy you gave me. I've read it before, but it's probably my favorite." I rolled onto my side, facing the wall, the phone in my right hand, covers pulled snug over my shoulder.

"What do you like about it?"

"It's like a fairy tale. A boy is lost and displaced but finds where he's supposed to be. I like Aravis and her snotty little tantrums. She reminds me a bit of my niece. And maybe of me, if I were honest."

"Only if you want to be."

I smiled and closed my eyes. "You're funny. Fine. I'll be honest—I have snotty tantrums sometimes."

"I can't imagine."

"Really?" I yawned. "Sometimes I think I took the job at the shop just to spite you."

William's laughter warmed my ear. "Somehow, that doesn't surprise me."

"No?"

"Well, let's just say I probably had it coming."

"True."

"Getting sleepy?"

"Maybe." The drowsiness was undeniable, but the idea of hanging up terrified me.

"How about this," he proposed. "Where are you in the book?"

"I think I just finished chapter nine."

"Chapter ten, then. Hold on a moment." A long pause, some fumbling. "You still there?"

Because I was too afraid to hang up? "Yes."

"Okay. *The Horse and His Boy*, chapter 10. 'After they had ridden for several hours…'" he began.

I kept my eyes closed and thought of Shasta and Aravis riding toward Archenland on the backs of talking horses.

When I opened my eyes, my phone had fallen to the floor. It was morning.

─❦─

Levi came to pick me up an hour and a half later. "Everything okay in your new apartment?" he asked as I pulled on my coat.

"Um…did your phone battery die?"

Levi frowned. "It did. Did you try to call last night?"

"I did. It wasn't a big deal—" I assured him. "Everything was fine."

"Really?" He arched an eyebrow. "You're not just telling me that to make me feel better?"

"I couldn't sleep. Nothing earth-shattering. I'm just not used to being alone."

"But you're okay? You look well rested."

"Yeah, I'm fine."

"Did you call Jayne?"

"No. I, um…" I shifted my feet. "I called William."

"Oh." Levi put his hands on his hips. "Huh. Alright then. I've got some mail for you from yesterday."

"I'll look through it later," I said, placing the items on the kitchen counter. Shall we leave?"

"After you, then," he said, opening the door for me.

The morning, just as every other Sunday morning, left me with more to think about than I thought my mind could handle. The stern, unbending God I grew up with who demanded obedience from His children seemed so different from the God present at Jayne and Livy's church. Their God was stern yet loving, unyielding in faithfulness, slow to anger, and quick to love.

I wanted to mull it all over, to spend time making everything reconcile in my head, but I couldn't. I had quilts to make, projects to complete, and classes to attend. I had work. I had a brother to marry off.

Would God wait for me to get my heart straight? Was it fair for me to hope He would?

After church and lunch at Jayne's, Levi took me home. As I tucked my gloves and scarf away, my eyes fell on my mail. There was an Anthropologie catalog, a mailing from the Art Institute about an upcoming art show, and a white envelope with my name on it.

I opened the white envelope and studied the contents. It was a bill for the ambulance—$783.24.

I sat down on the floor and reread the bill. It was true. As was the fact that I didn't have $783.24. I thought about my options.

I could ask Levi for help, but it was a lot of money. I couldn't ask for that much money, and the whole point was that I was independent. I had to start figuring things out on my own.

Neither did I want to use a credit card. My family never used them, and I didn't trust them.

I had planned to make quilts to create some financial stability for myself. Rather than go toward a car and a nest egg, some of the profits would have to go to this bill. I had already planned to be sewing quilts. Nothing had changed aside from the time when I needed the first to be completed.

The due date on the notice gave me three weeks.

I rose, tucked the bill away and headed for my fabric stash. It was time to get to work.

〜〜

Glancing at the calendar on Tuesday, I noticed it was the sixteenth—and then I did a double take. Shrove Tuesday. The day before Lent.

I hadn't observed Epiphany. I didn't want Shrove Tuesday to pass without *fastnacht kuecheles*. In a moment of courage, I called Britta, Meg, and Sonnet to see if they wanted to come over to the apartment and eat them with me.

"You're baking? I love baking. Want company?" Britta asked. "I need to get out of here for a while anyway."

Meg said she really wanted to come but had too many things to do.

My conversation with Sonnet was short. "I'll be there," she said the second after the words *deep fried* left my mouth.

While I waited, I started the dough. After donning an apron, I added the sugar to warm water and stirred in the yeast. As the yeast proofed, I creamed the butter with the sugar.

When the bolt on the door slid back, I jumped.

"Hey, sorry, did I scare you?" Livy smiled and gave a small wave. "It's just me." She closed the front door after herself. "What are you up to?"

"I'm making *fastnachts* for Shrove Tuesday." I wiped my hands on the front of my apron. "They're a family tradition."

Livy frowned. "Looks like your yeast isn't doing so well."

I turned to check on it. It was foaming, but only a little. "I only just put it in—" I said, but my words were cut off by the sight of Livy sticking her finger in the yeast bowl.

"The water is fifteen degrees too cold." She shook her finger over the sink.

"Optimal proofing temperature is around 110 degrees. Hang on." She sorted through one of the drawers and retrieved a long, skinny instrument with a dial face on top. "Here's my thermometer. You're free to use it."

I examined the tool. "Wow. I never thought to take the water's temperature before. And I've been working with yeast for years."

"Well…I actually have a baking and pastry certificate."

"Really?" I dumped out the existing yeast water and made a new batch, this time making sure the water was the correct temperature.

"It was a lifetime ago." Livy explained. "I was—well, about your age. I loved baking and thought I'd enjoy doing it professionally. It turned out to be a small step in a longer journey to figuring out what I wanted to do with my life, but I learned a lot. And I met Gemma."

"You dated her brother, right?"

"Niko, yeah. Sweet guy, big personality…a little too big for me. He was in the culinary program as well. But Gemma and I have kept in touch, so that's been nice." She looked around the kitchen. "So. Do you want a hand? Have you scalded the milk yet?"

"Not yet." I pulled a liquid measuring cup from the cupboard. "I've always wondered why the milk had to be scalded."

Livy reached into the fridge and handed me the jug of milk. "The non-technical answer is that the dough won't raise as much if it isn't. The more technical answer is that there's a protein in the whey that interferes with the raising unless the milk has been held to about 185 degrees for a while without boiling."

"Interesting."

"That's sweet of you to say." She glanced at the new yeast mixture. "That looks nice and foamy. Perfect." A buzzing noise distracted us both from the chemistry discussion. "That's my phone. It's probably Clay. I'll be a while—have fun," she said as she took her phone back to her bedroom.

Britta arrived a moment later, followed shortly by Sonnet, with Meg in tow.

"I made her come," Sonnet explained, still hanging onto Meg's wrist. "Girl works too hard. Needs to make time for deep-fried goodness."

We laughed and set to work together as I shared the instructions for the *fastnachts*.

Britta tucked a hand towel into the waist of her jeans. "So…what are we making, exactly?

I remembered my conversation with William and Zach in the moving van. I knew it was time to be open, time to be honest, but there was no reason to blurt it out.

"They're basically doughnuts," I said, not choosing to elaborate.

After we combined all of the ingredients and set the dough to raise for an hour, we moved to the living room.

As the subject of conversation turned to spring break plans, I realized the opportunity to share my background might present itself sooner than I expected.

"Stephanie Pearl-McPhee is going to be speaking in Seattle," Britta explained, her eyes bright. "We're all going to drive up for a few days over the break—my mom, my sister, my grandma, and me. Make a trip to Weaving Works and the Fiber Gallery."

"Sounds like fun." Meg folded her arms. "My parents aren't much for breaks or vacations unless it means going back to Japan to visit family. Which is fun, you know, if you don't mind plane travel."

"You should think about some kind of adult Space Camp," Sonnet suggested. "Maybe the flight simulator things would help the friendly skies seem a little friendlier.

"I like boats," Meg offered.

"So, Sara, what are you doing over break?" Sonnet leaned back and stretched. "Seeing family? They're not in town, are they?"

I was hoping for an opportunity but didn't expect one to smack me between the eyes like that.

"No, they're south of here, outside of Albany," I said. "I don't suppose I have many plans. I'll probably be working a lot." I took a deep breath, hoping to steady myself. It didn't particularly work, but I pressed on anyway. "I haven't seen them since I moved here. See…my family is Amish." The words came out in a rush, but they must have been understandable from the looks of surprise on my friends' faces. "I left home and came here. My brother had already left, so he's my family. But everyone else…Well, I can't really go back."

"Oh." Britta tilted her head. "Wow, so…Amish?"

I nodded.

"You grew up Amish and got into design school?" Sonnet lifted a hand. "Props. Does anyone say *props* anymore?"

"I never know what anyone's saying anymore," Meg admitted. "Though

I'd be more likely to say something about how it's an impressive achievement or something like that." She smiled at me. "Which it is."

"So how did you do it?" Britta asked. "You have such a great design aesthetic, but…"

"But you don't imagine my family was all that fashionable?" I filled in what she wouldn't say with a laugh. "No, but we would go to town, and I'd see beautiful clothes and others much less so. I smuggled magazines and catalogs home and hid them under the floorboards."

"You too?" Meg laughed, covering her mouth as she did so. "My parents would have been horrified to know I was studying the—how did my mother put it once?—oh yeah, the ostentatious clothing of vapid women."

"Then there's *my* mother, the not-quite-ex-hippie," Sonnet crossed her arms across her lap. "She'd look at shots from fashion week and tell me who's high in each picture." She held up her hands. "It didn't work, but mama tried."

"I've always wondered," Britta said, picking up a throw pillow on the couch and hugging it to herself, "if Amish people really made Amish friendship bread."

"Gemma asked me that once." I shook my head. "We bake with sourdough starters a lot—we're all for things that don't require refrigeration. But we don't call anything Amish friendship bread or even just friendship bread for that matter. At least, not where I live."

Britta stretched, arching her back. "Cool. Good to know. So how's your project coming?"

And that was it. What had I been afraid of this whole time? What had held me back?

After the dough finished rising, I rolled it out, and the four of us took turns cutting out circles with overturned drinking glasses and mugs. Sonnet readied the oil, and after thinning out the insides with our fingers, we dropped each one in. Meg used tongs to pull them out and placed them on top of paper lunch sacks to blot off the excess oil. When they had cooled enough to touch, we dredged them in granulated sugar, though Britta suggested a spiced sugar variation that included cinnamon and a hint of cardamom.

"This is good," Sonnet announced around bites. "Like, really good. I'm glad you grew up Amish, if only to bring these into our lives."

I laughed, relief washing over me. "You're welcome. Glad I could oblige."

The store was unusually busy Wednesday afternoon.

Not that I minded. A part of me was still a little mortified about calling William Saturday night, even three days into my workweek. Mortified and something else, not that I could quite identify the feeling. Nervous? Overwhelmed? A thousand reactions battled for supremacy in my head, and they didn't fight fair.

The crowds started to thin out around five. I watched William's placement in the store out of the corner of my eye, despite my intentions not to. However, he retreated to the workroom for a rebinding project, leaving Zach and me to check over the shelves and put away everything customers had pulled out.

I was on the phone with a customer trying to find a first printing of A.A. Milne's *And Now We Are Six* when the bell over the door rang. I didn't even turn to look, assuming Zach would handle that particular visitor.

"That's alright, I'll wait," said a familiar voice.

I took down a message and double-checked the number before hanging up and turning around.

And finding Arin at the counter, waiting for me.

"Hi," I said, sounding much more breathless than I would have liked.

"Hi. I missed you. Are you getting off work anytime soon? I thought you might let me feed you."

I tucked a stray piece of hair behind my ear. "I'm not off for another half hour, but after that? I like food."

"I can hang out for half an hour. It's a cool place. I like the ladder. You've got that chair in the corner—can you recommend a read?"

I studied him for a moment. "Hmm. Well…have you read Jared Diamond's *Guns, Germs, and Steel* yet?"

Arin winced. "Sounds a little too…confrontational for my taste."

I walked to study our display table in the center of the store. Arin followed, eying the selection. "*Birds of the World*. That sounds interesting." He lifted the book and flipped through the pages.

I struggled for words. "You like birds?"

"Everyone likes birds." He closed the book. "I'll take it."

"You don't have to—"

"It's on sale—thirty percent off. I also don't want to be the guy who reads a book in a bookstore for half an hour before putting it back on the shelf…or table, I guess."

"Okay." What was I going to do, talk him out of buying a book?

William came out of the workroom while I was ringing up Arin.

"Hello, sir." Surprised, I watched as he came and leaned on the part of the counter next to Arin. Friendliness was not a characteristic of William's that showed up much, particularly where Arin was concerned.

"Hello back," Arin answered with the same nonchalant, hip attitude.

So hip I didn't feel qualified to be in the room. I swiped Arin's card anyway.

"So. Birds." William said.

Arin nodded. "I like birds."

"Good book for you then. How are things?"

"Not bad. Gonna take Sara for some dinner when she's off."

I ripped off the first receipt from the Visa machine and pushed it toward Arin. "Want to sign this?"

"Got a pen?"

William reached into his pocket. "Here's one." Never mind there were a dozen on the counter.

"Thanks, man." Arin signed and handed me back the copy before turning to William. "Things good for you?"

"Good. Can't complain. Hey—have you seen Sara's new place yet?"

I really wished Sonnet was here, watching this. At the very least she'd be able to fully tell me what was going on. To say there was a weird vibe was a complete understatement.

"No," said Arin, standing taller. "I haven't. Sara—did I know you were moving?"

"I don't remember," I answered honestly.

"Yeah, well, it's nice," William said.

The customer copy of the receipt printed a moment later. I tore it off too and all but shoved it in Arin's direction. "I'm going to dust the counter," I said. "You both need to scoot."

I reached under the counter and pulled out my can of Pledge, spraying a line right in front of them.

They both jumped back, and I swiped at the counter with my dusting cloth. Much better.

Arin retreated with his albatross of a bird book to the chair while William busied himself with the shelving out of my view.

William returned to the counter twenty minutes later. "Take off early." He rapped his knuckles against the wood. "Have a good time. See you tomorrow?"

"Tomorrow," I echoed.

I left work shaking my head. I didn't understand men.

—※—

Sitting across the table from Arin, separated by bowls of pho, I decided to be a bit more direct than I had earlier in the day. "I just thought you should know," I began, pushing my noodles around with my chopsticks while watching his face, "I mean, since I've been telling my friends lately... well, I'm Amish. I mean, my family's Amish. I'm not anymore," I rushed to add. This wasn't going well. "But I was raised Amish. I was kind of keeping it secret for a while, and I decided not to anymore."

Arin's stunned expression reminded me why I'd been so hesitant to tell people in the first place. I think he even scooted farther back in his chair before sitting up straighter. "Amish? Really?"

Hadn't I just said so, repeatedly? "Yes."

"Huh. Is this," he sputtered as he gestured around the tiny restaurant, "okay? Do you have, like, dietary restrictions? I mean, you eat beef, right?"

"Um..." I frowned, unsure of how to respond. "My family farms. We raise livestock, among other things. We're not vegetarians."

"Oh. Right on."

I looked down at my noodles before taking another bite. This would be a long meal.

Chapter 27

Sorry, one more time—" Britta asked as the four of us worked on our projects on my living room floor later that night. "He asked you if Amish people had birthdays?"

"He did." I wrinkled my nose as if the memory had left an unpleasant smell. "I didn't know what to say. I just looked at him and said, 'Well, we were all born, obviously.'"

Sonnet nodded. "Good answer."

"Thank you. He didn't know what to say for the rest of dinner."

"What do you think?" Meg held up her project, the front panel of a pencil skirt with origami-like tucks and pleats down the side.

"I like it," I said, studying it. "Very sculptural. Is any of the detailing going around to the back?"

"I haven't decided yet." Meg set the piece down and picked up her sketchbook. "I'm trying something new, trying to improvise a bit."

"How's the CAD class going?" Sonnet asked her. "I'm taking that next term. I hate computers."

"You may have to get over that." Britta nodded toward Meg's skirt in progress. "I still think something knit with that would be perfect. Even if it's not hand-knit."

"I was thinking maybe something out of a watercolor-print jersey. Flutter sleeves to balance out the architectural quality of the skirt." Meg held out her sketchbook.

I studied the sketch. "What about a wide leather belt? Mix up the textures a bit more."

Meg grabbed a brown colored pencil from her pile and added it to her design. "Oh."

Sonnet leaned over to look. "I would wear that. And I don't say that lightly, since I only wear skirts about twice a year." She tapped my knee. "So tell us about the guys who helped you move. What's the story there?"

"Oh." I shifted off my knees and crossed my legs. "I work with them, and you know, they're friends."

"The blond guy was…" Sonnet probed, leaning forward.

"Zach. Zach is the blond. William's the one with the dark hair."

"Well, I'll just put it out there that Zach the blond is not bad looking."

"Not bad looking and totally gone on Gemma," Britta observed. "Not that I blame him. That lasagna was a religious experience. With cheese."

"I love cheese," Sonnet flopped back onto the floor. "I think I'm addicted to cheese."

Britta lifted her finger to the air. "Here here."

"Seriously," Sonnet said. "For every food in existence, there is a cheese I would put on it."

I wrinkled my nose. "Really? What about chocolate?"

"Mascarpone," she answered.

Meg lifted her chin. "Sushi?"

"Cream cheese. Or provolone, honestly, because I'm weird like that."

"Green beans?" I asked.

"Pecorino Romano. Or else Parmesan—one of the hard, sharp Italian cheeses."

"This is illuminating," Britta said. "Sonnet, I think I understand you better knowing this about you. In fact, I think you should design a cheese-inspired line. Whites and creams—white shot through with blue. Some saturated yellow-oranges. I think it could really work."

"Huh. I'll have to think about that. If I do a cheese-inspired line, Sara has to do a cupcake-inspired line. Meg has to do sashimi, and you—" Sonnet pointed at Britta, "you should do a latke line. Because nothing says fashion like potatoes."

"Or raw fish," Meg said with a smile.

"What about William, anyway?" Britta asked. "Kind of serious, but…"

"Hot," Sonnet finished.

I clasped my hand over my mouth.

"Sonnet!" Meg's brows flew upward.

"What? Deny it. Sara?"

My hand was still over my mouth. William? Handsome—hot, even?

"I—I don't think about him like that," I said, embarrassed by my stutter. "I was raised to think of only Amish boys like that."

"You were raised to wear pinafores, but that didn't stick." Sonnet raised her eyebrow. "You think maybe the guy thing might be a bit flexible? Because us English girls think he's a catch, but he wouldn't give any of us a second look."

Britta shook her head. "Nope. Maybe you should picture him in one of those hats the Amish men wear, see if that changes anything for you. Sonnet's right. He is good looking. "

I looked away, pretending to be very busy with my hand-stitching. Trouble was, I knew by the way my heart fluttered that it was true.

‒‒‒

The fluttering hadn't quite stopped by the time I arrived for work on Thursday.

I had to admit, being at work these days felt increasingly awkward.

William joined me behind the counter. "So. How was dinner with Arin last night?"

"You really want to know?" I asked. In fact, I think I sounded down-right flirty.

He put a hand on his hip; the other held a cup of coffee. "Sure."

"He took me out for Vietnamese."

"What did you think about cold noodles?"

"They weren't bad. I liked the pho." I tucked a piece of hair behind my ear. "I told him I grew up Amish."

William set his coffee down, braced his hands against the counter before lifting himself up to sit on it. "Yeah? How did Arin feel about that?"

I watched as he took a sip of coffee. "He asked, among other things, if I had an Amish passport."

William choked on his coffee. "You're joking."

I rolled my eyes. "If only I were creative enough to make up such a response."

"That's amazing."

"Sure, amazing. Or horrifying. That's the one I'm going with." I wrapped my arms around myself. "The reason I didn't want to tell anyone was that I didn't want to feel any more like an outsider than I already did. I told my friends from the Art Institute—you met them when we were moving. It wasn't a big deal. But Arin?" I shook my head. "It was awkward."

"He might need time," William offered.

I snorted. "To give him time would mean being generous. I don't feel like being generous, not when I was treated like a two-headed sheep."

"Understandable."

"I've seen one, you know."

"Fascinating. And speaking of two-headed sheep, I had something to ask of you."

"Oh?"

"And you can say no—I want you to know that ahead of time."

I waited.

"My mom's having a birthday party. This weekend. And she wants me to bring you."

Didn't expect that. "Your mom, birthday, me...she wants me? I mean, she wants you to bring me?" I frowned. "What does that have to do with deformed sheep?"

"Nothing. I was making a joke. But yes. Seems you made a big impression over Christmas."

"But...that was a long time ago."

"She's got the memory of an elephant when it comes to...certain things."

"Certain things?" I waved at a customer who'd just walked in. "Let me know if you need help finding anything." I turned back to William. "You were saying?"

"I was saying she liked you, and she remembers people she likes. Saturday night? Are you free? Or are you fielding more questions about whether or not Amish people can read?"

I giggled. "I think I'm free."

"Yeah?"

"What should I wear?"

"Dress is probably about the same as the Christmas party, without the Christmas."

"Do they—did you tell them? About me being Amish?"

William shook his head. "I figured that was your piece of information to share if you wanted to—or not. I honestly don't think they'd care much. Might ask you about how the Amish feel about legal representation, something silly like that."

I smiled and shifted the subject. "What are you taking as a gift?"

"Probably a book." He shrugged. "I'm original like that."

"Does your mom read much?" I asked.

"Well…not really."

"Oh. Well. I'm sure she'll love it."

"You're being sarcastic."

I thought about it for a moment. "I suppose I am." I guess Jayne had rubbed off on me. Anytime now, I supposed I would start leaving my things everywhere and ordering Chinese every other night. "If she doesn't really read books, why do you buy her books?"

William shrugged and hopped down from the counter's ledge. "I guess it's the only thing I know how to buy. Books and supplies related to books. Book repair tools. Bookmarks. Book lights."

"Do you want help?"

"Help? As in, help finding a birthday gift for my mom? You'd do that?"

I guess I would, since I'd just nominated myself. "Sure."

"Friday, then? I'll drive and pay, you just tell me where you want to go. For the trouble, I'll buy you dinner."

Suddenly, everything seemed to change. Was it the specter of dinner? My thoughts tangled in my head.

William noticed my hesitation. "We don't have to—"

"No, it's okay. Friday is free." Actually, it wasn't. For one thing, I had twenty-seven magenta triangles to cut out. Even more than that, Friday was movie night. Movie night and lots of questions about how I was doing and if I was seeing anyone. If I didn't attend though, I imagined some of those questions would answer themselves.

Things seemed so much easier when I could just climb out the window to have a social life.

"You're working Friday afternoon and early evening, aren't you?" William reached for the schedule under the counter.

I nodded. Then I remembered his back was turned. "Yes."

The customer—whom I had entirely forgotten about—came up to the counter, book and credit card in hand.

"Did you find everything you needed?" I asked, switching back into employee mode.

"If you're going to be here until closing Friday, want to leave from work? I can drive you back home afterward," William offered, completely ignoring the man whose credit card I had just finished swiping through the Visa machine.

"Um, sure," I said. "After work on Friday is fine."

I finished up with the receipts and gave the store copy to the customer to sign before putting his book in a bag along with the second receipt. "Have a nice day," I said, trying to feel as if all of my secrets weren't out in the open.

"You too," the customer replied. He looked at William before looking back at me with a wink and walking away.

The store was empty again. "Sleeping better?" William asked.

It was my turn to blush. "Yes."

"That's good."

"I've been reading at night," I said. "It helps."

I wasn't going to tell him the whole truth. I was reading, yes. But instead of *my* voice in my head, or the characters' voices, I heard William reading to me, reading the way he had that late Saturday night.

I wasn't about to tell him.

⁓⁕⁓

The next day, William brought me coffee. Caramel-flavored coffee.

Later that afternoon, two new boxes of books arrived from two different publishing houses. William offered to sort them out with me while Zach watched the front.

Friday morning I felt jittery as I got ready for my day at class and work. I had no idea what to wear—so much so that I was late to my first class of the day.

I may have been late, but I knew I looked nice. I'd finally paired a printed Weston Wear mesh top with my red corduroy blazer and worn my winter overcoat over the top to keep me warm. My makeup had been minimal that morning, but I knew I had a few moments between class and work to add some shimmery eye shadow and a touch of eyeliner.

I liked to look nice for work. It was more professional that way.

"Looking fancy," Zach commented when I arrived that afternoon.

I looked around, making sure William was still in the workroom. "I look normal," I protested.

"But you really match today," Zach said. "And your eyes are all shimmery. It looks good."

"I wear eye shadow often," I protested.

"You're bad with compliments." Zach shook his head, smiling. "I'm just saying you look especially nice today. Do you have plans after work?"

"Kind of." I really didn't want to answer that question. Not for Zach. "How much filing is left after yesterday?"

"Lots." Zach winced. "I hate filing."

"I'll do it."

"Really?"

Filing meant working in the back office, out of sight. I gave a genuine smile. "Really."

I settled in on the filing, making piles of the invoices and receipts. I heard a knock on the open office door a couple hours later. I looked up to see William, a sideways smile on his face. "Hi," I said, sounding just as awkward as I felt.

"There you are," he said, leaning against the doorframe. "You're not hiding, are you?"

"No," I said. My answer probably would have been more believable if it hadn't come out in a squeak. "Just filing. Is Zach still out front?"

"He is. Are we still on for tonight?"

"Yes."

"Because if you're too busy, I can always buy my mom another book. Maybe *Birds of the World*."

A giggle escaped. "No, don't do that. I'm free." And now that I thought about it, I realized I'd forgotten to tell Jayne I wouldn't be there. I'd make that phone call a little later.

※

I touched up my makeup one last time before getting my coat and gathering my things at the end of the day. William was at the counter, closing the till. "You ready?" he asked.

"I am."

"You look nice."

I smiled. "Thanks."

Zach returned, putting the cleaning supplies back below the counter. "So glad it's Friday. Either of you guys free tonight? Want to catch a movie?"

I froze.

"Thanks," William said, closing the cash drawer. "Maybe another time. Sara and I have plans."

"So you..." Zach looked at William. He looked at me. "Oh. Huh." He looked back at William. "Really?"

I sneaked my own look at Will. Will's face wasn't giving anything away. "Really," he said. "But you have a good night. Don't be out too late—you're working tomorrow, remember?"

Zach shrugged. "Yes, sir. I must accept my age and grow my olives and tomatoes."

"*Godfather* quote," William said before I could ask.

I nodded.

"My coat's upstairs," William said after Zach exited. "And my keys, come to think of it."

"It must be nice to live so close to work."

"I like it. Ready to go?"

I knew I was, on a practical level. I had my coat and purse, my phone and keys. But anything else?

Windows were so much easier to deal with. Amish boys were so much easier—I knew exactly what they wanted. I doubted William was looking for someone to cook and clean for him, someone to raise his children and make his parents happy. What did he want? Was I ready to find out?

"Sara?"

I pasted a smile on my face. "I'm ready," I said.

I hoped I was telling the truth.

Chapter 28

Seated in Will's car, I found myself crossing my ankles primly. I don't know why.

"Where to?" he asked.

"TJ Maxx," I told him. "The one in Beaverton."

At least I knew that much. Over the last several months, TJ Maxx had become my favorite place to go for any sort of gifts. Or nongifts—I'd found a very nice pair of leather gloves for myself a few weeks before on clearance.

"Are we looking for anything in particular? Because I'll tell you, my mom is picky."

I wasn't worried. I'd been in her home, and finding something to fit her taste wouldn't be difficult. The fact that I was female probably helped as well.

I expected the drive to be awkward. Difficult, even. But it wasn't. Will kept talking about books and movies and the shop so much that I had forgotten our destination until we pulled into the parking lot.

"You should know," Will said as he pulled the parking break up, "I hate shopping."

"It's probably your own fault." I unhooked my seatbelt.

"What?"

I met his eyes. "I said it's probably your own fault. I find that most people who hate shopping do it all wrong and get angry when it doesn't turn out."

"Okay." He climbed out of the aged BMW and slammed the door shut. "What's the wrong way to shop?"

I stood and closed my own car door. "Shop hungry, shop dehydrated. Shop without knowing where the restrooms are. Don't try on things, or try on things in the wrong size. Go to the wrong stores."

"I would say most stores are the wrong stores. But I'm sure you have a better definition."

"Sure." I thought about it for a moment. "Say you're looking for a book. It's been released recently, but not a huge print run. Where would you look for it if you wanted to buy it in a store?"

"R.G. Cameron. Powell's. Barnes & Noble."

"Exactly. You'd go to the stores with wider selections. You wouldn't go to Fred Meyer or Target. Similarly, if I wanted to buy a skirt, I'd be better off going to, say, Ann Taylor than REI. Sure, REI has some skirts, but Ann Taylor would be more likely to stock what I'm looking for. There's no sense in going to the wrong stores looking for things because you're only going to be frustrated."

"Shopping was a big deal to my mom. I guess that doesn't come as a huge surprise. We'd spend a whole day looking for school clothes. And she didn't like breaks."

"See?" I felt pleased he'd proved my theory. "You were probably hungry and dehydrated. And tired. There's no sense in looking for things while you're uncomfortable and miserable. Shopping like that on your own, you'll probably buy the first thing you see and hate it forever after."

"Huh. Well, we're here and we're not looking for clothes. What do we do, sensei?"

I looked around at the store and oriented myself. "Home décor."

"Are you sure? My mom's house is pretty decorated."

"Exactly. Does she change things around a lot?"

"Yeah." Will thought about that for a moment before shoving his hands into his pockets. "Okay. Good point."

I looked through the dishes but didn't see anything. I found table linens too personal to buy for other people, so I avoided that section all together. But glassware...I took my time. I knew Meredith, William's mother, liked jewel tones a lot. My eyes fell on a fused glass plate. It was about fifteen inches across with clear sections accented by shades of blue and green.

I pointed it out to William. "What do you think?"

He crossed his arms. "How did you do that?"

"What?"

"I keep looking around and nothing looks right. But that—it's perfect."

I smiled and picked it up. "It's perfect—and $24.99."

"You're kidding."

"I never kid about sales."

"Think she'll like it better than *Birds of the World*?"

I laughed. "Maybe. Just a little bit."

—※—

"That was...surprisingly painless," William said as he opened my car door.

I beamed up at him. "I suppose it would be rude to say I told you so."

He closed the door, walked around, and climbed into the driver's seat. "It might be, if it weren't true. Are you hungry?"

I suddenly felt shy. "Yes, actually."

"What sounds good to you?"

"Pasta," I said, telling myself the shyness was ridiculous. "Italian pasta."

He nodded and pulled out his phone. "Italian pasta. Sounds good. Give me a minute?" He climbed back out, ignoring the cold mist that filled the air. He was speaking on his cell phone, but I couldn't hear a word.

Not that I was trying to eavesdrop.

Moments later he got back into the car, buckled his seatbelt, and headed back toward town. I had no idea where we were going, but I knew William did. That was all that mattered to me.

I watched out the window as we drove. I had lived in Portland for nearly nine months, and I never tired of looking at the lights. I loved the lights over the streets and the way streams of traffic formed light patterns.

Though to be honest, I also missed the stars. The stars back home were so much brighter with so much less artificial light to drown them out. Was it a fair trade-off? I wasn't sure.

The car came to a stop on Southwest Second Avenue, near the river. We were so close to the entrance of the Morrison Bridge, I could hear the cars roar as they ascended. I looked up at the restaurant sign. Mamma Mia Trattoria.

The inside was crowded, but not so crowded I wanted to run away. Chandeliers hung from the ceiling. Gilded mirrors lined the walls, making the space feel much larger than it actually was. The hum of happy chatter and clinking glasses filled the air.

We were seated and given menus within a few moments. I ordered water. William ordered tea.

We looked over the menus. The prices on many of the entrees worried me. I supposed they were the same as DiGrassi's, but Gemma's father never let us pay full price if he let us pay at all.

I was still trying to make a decision when William put menu his down. "I don't want you to feel stressed about what you order, and I know you well enough to know that you're going to worry about how much your dinner will cost."

I didn't say anything.

"To make things easier on you," William continued, "I'm going to order the veal parmigiana because it's good, and it's the second-most expensive item on the menu. I'm not a big enough man to order the most expensive item because I don't like mussels, and the thought of them in a stew makes me want to hurl. If mussels are your thing, by all means, order away. I'm sure it's good. I want you to order whatever you want because it's my treat and you found a gift that my mom might actually like for a change. She might even like it enough to overlook the fact that I won't be wearing a tie tomorrow night."

"No tie?"

"I wear ties for Christmas, Easter, funerals, and interviews. Tomorrow is not Christmas, it's not Easter, no one's dead, and no one's hiring, so no tie."

I giggled. I couldn't help it—he made me laugh.

When the waiter returned I ordered the penne à la vodka, adding the Italian sausage and a bowl of soup. The garlic bread arrived shortly after with the cups of soup, and I followed William's lead as he dipped his bread into the soup, allowing the rich tomato flavor to soak into the bread.

"Tell me about how your classes are going," Will said after he finished swallowing his bite. He looked around. "I don't know how you feel about it, but I like having a conversation without worrying about customers over-hearing."

"Or Zach."

Will laughed. "That too."

"Classes are good. They're certainly challenging, but I like being pushed. It helps having friends who I can bounce ideas off of and who know the current trends and fashion history that I missed growing up the way I did."

"But you feel like you can keep up?"

I nodded. "I can. I work hard, probably harder than everyone else. But my grades have been good so far, and my instructors have been encouraging. Part of the process starting out is to begin developing the fashion line that I'll complete at the end of the program. I'm having a hard time getting going on it though."

"Yeah?"

I shrugged. "Maybe my problem is that I have too many ideas, and there isn't one that I love enough to make a cohesive line out of. I want to try everything, experiment with everything. But if I do that with this line, it'll be disjointed and unfocused."

"I can understand that. It's like picking a topic for a thesis."

"Exactly. I'm just doing it visually instead of choosing words." I sighed. "Sometimes I wish it were words. Sometimes I think they're easier."

"Everything but what you're working on is easier," Will said before sipping his tea. "Trust me. My master's thesis was on the roots of Bolshevism in nineteenth-century Russian literature. I knew the material as well as anyone could, but I dug my heels in doing the work. That's about when I started looking into the book conservation programs—I wanted to be doing anything other than what I was doing at the time."

"And when you were doing the conservation program?"

"I got nostalgic about the simplicity of writing papers." He shook his head. "It was sick. And I don't mean that in a hip way."

I wrinkled my nose. "*Sick* as slang makes no sense to me." I took another bite of soup-drenched bread. "But then, most English slang makes no sense to me."

"Do you miss home?"

Another bite. "Yes. I think I may always miss it. I wanted to be here when I was there, but now that I'm here, I can't stop thinking about home, no matter how much I try."

"Do you think about going back?"

The waiter appeared with our food. The vodka sauce looked and smelled divine. When we were alone again, I answered. "I think about it. It's not an option though. It would never be the same."

"I hear that. Want to pray before we eat?"

I consented, bowing my head. Will must have done the same. We sat in silence for a few moments before lifting our heads and then our forks.

The silent prayers again reminded me of home. This time it wasn't an aching reminder. Instead, more of a friendly memory stopping by for a visit.

My first bite of pasta tasted even better than it smelled. The creamy tomato flavor made me smile. I looked up to see Will smiling at me.

The perfect moment shattered the second I felt my phone vibrate in my jacket pocket. "Oh, I'm sorry," I said, reaching for it. "I'll turn it off."

"If you need to take a call, I understand," Will said. "I don't mind."

I checked the caller ID. Oops.

"Sara?" Jayne's voice filled my ear, loud and clear. "Where are you? We're about to start the next Pixar short before putting on *The Band Wagon*. Everyone's here. Are you coming?"

Oh dear. "I forgot. I'm so sorry."

"That's okay. Do you need me to come pick you up? Sorry, I didn't even think of it."

"I, um…I'm not home."

"Are you working late?" Jayne asked.

There was no getting around it. "I'm eating dinner. With Will."

"Oh."

That single syllable communicated so much. But she wasn't done. "Really? Will? I—huh. How did—well, I guess you can't talk about it. He's probably right there, isn't he."

"Um, yes."

"Right. Have a great time. A really great time. Wow. Will." I could hear Levi in the background, telling her to leave me alone. "I'm hanging up, right now, relax, hon. Sara? Sorry. Anyway, have a great time. If you want to come by, you can absolutely bring him. I'll even tell Joely to keep her gun and nightstick out of sight." Now there was input from Joely that I couldn't make out.

"I'm going to finish my dinner," I said. "I'll talk to you later."

"Yes! Because I want to hear all about it. I'm hanging up, or your brother's going to do it for me."

Then the call ended. I had a hunch my brother had a hand in that.

I put the phone on the table. "That was Jayne. Sorry. Tonight's movie night. I forgot to call her and let her know I wouldn't be there."

"Nice. What movie?"

"A Pixar short to start, followed by *The Band Wagon*."

Will laughed. Actually laughed. "Great movie! Have you seen it?"

I shook my head. "The movie nights started as a way to educate me in film."

"I hate to get in the way of your education. Want to go after dinner?"

"What?"

"Do you want to go and watch it at Jayne's?" he repeated. "It's a great movie—a total satire about the theater trends at the time, *Faust* as a musical." He chuckled again.

Amazing, to hear William laughing twice in one night. It occurred to me that if we watched *The Band Wagon* together, I might get to hear him laugh more. And I really enjoyed hearing him laugh.

"Sure," I said, trying not to think about the reactions from everyone when they saw I'd brought him. "They usually take a while to get from one film to another, so we probably wouldn't miss much at all."

"If you're worried, we could always take dessert to go. I wouldn't take dinner though—you want to eat it while it's fresh and hot."

"You'd do that?"

"Why not? Just don't rush through your pasta. My mom, the plate—you deserve to enjoy your food."

I ate—at a mostly leisurely pace—as much pasta as I could eat until I knew I'd feel ill if I continued. Will had the waiter box the leftovers and then rose to visit the restroom. At least that's what I assumed. When he returned, he was carrying a large box. "What's that?"

"An amaretto cheesecake." He frowned. "You like cheesecake, right?"

I nodded, once again speechless.

His face relaxed. "Good. I thought we'd take a whole one to share rather than eat our dessert in front of everyone."

"There's food there…"

Will shrugged. "Then they'll just have another option. Cheesecake freezes. Are you ready to go?"

Again with the readiness. Was I ready to bring a boy with me to Jayne's apartment? I reminded myself of the sound of Will's relaxed laughter. "I'm ready."

Chapter 29

The opening titles of *The Band Wagon* still rang out when Jayne opened the door to her apartment for us. "You're here! You made it!" She looked over my shoulder at William in surprise. "And you brought a friend."

From the corner of my eye I saw William lift the dessert box. "And the friend brought cheesecake," he said.

Jayne's jaw literally dropped. "You're *really* welcome. Come on in! It looks like it's drizzling outside." She stepped back to allow us to enter. "William, right? Do you remember everyone?" She took a moment to repeat everyone's names. William nodded and responded in a very friendly, pleasant manner.

I was amazed.

Gemma wasn't the least bit put out that William brought cheesecake. In fact, she was first in line for a slice herself, saying how much the creaminess of the cheesecake complemented the cheese and polenta stuffed baby red peppers.

When it came time to actually watch the movie, Kim and Joely moved off the couch to make room for Will and me. Which meant we were sitting quite close together.

Will didn't say anything. I couldn't say anything, but I knew my face was beet red. I sat and ate my slice of cheesecake, trying to pay attention to Fred Astaire's hoofing around an arcade rather than the fact that I could feel Will's arm against mine.

"I had a good time," Will said as he walked me up the steps to my apartment. "Your friends can sure eat a lot of cheesecake."

"That they can," I agreed, retrieving my keys from my pocket. "Thanks for coming and watching the movie with us."

Will shrugged. "It was a good movie. We should do it again sometime. You're still on for tomorrow, right? Because you should be there to help present the plate."

I smiled. "I'll be there."

"I'll pick you up at six thirty—does that work for you?"

"It does," I said, my mind racing. I still hadn't decided what to wear.

We waved goodbye and I stepped into my apartment.

I was still alone. Livy wouldn't return from her missions conference until Sunday afternoon. I sighed and took my coat off. It was late—the clock read 11:34. Despite the hour, I had work to do. The ambulance bill from the stupid accident was tucked away in my desk. There were many, many quilt pieces to cut before I could start the piecework. Despite my sagging eyelids, I turned on the coffeepot and went in search of my scissors.

———※———

Saturday morning arrived too early. My eyes felt as if they had coffee grounds rubbed into them. I stumbled down from my bed, waddled into the bathroom, and surveyed the damage in the mirror.

Bags under my eyes. Icky, dehydrated skin. I started wishing for home— no mirrors. Wood walls kept excellent secrets.

Following a suggestion I'd remembered Meg talking about, I dampened a washcloth with very hot water and laid it over my face for a few moments before giving my face a good rub with the terrycloth.

In the kitchen, I cracked an egg and separated the white from the yolk. The yolk I put back in the fridge to be used in scrambled eggs later. The white I slathered onto my face, cold and slimy, all over my cheeks and just under my eyes. I let it dry and then stepped into the shower.

As good as the hot water felt, I didn't have time to linger. I washed the egg from my face and lathered my hair with shampoo. Afterward I slathered on the moisturizer and examined my face again, gratified to see that my skin looked refreshed and I almost looked rested.

I dressed without putting much thought into my outfit. I had food in the house, so there was no reason to dress to make a good impression until the evening. After all, it would just be me and the fabric.

The hours passed quickly. I had the place to myself, so I began to lay my quilt pieces out on the floor half an inch apart.

I tried cutting on the floor, but my legs cramped up. I moved to the couch until my back got sore and my stomach started to make anarchistic noises.

Livy's wall clock read 1:30. I stretched and cobbled a lunch together before returning to work, this time at the tiny dining room table.

At four o'clock I switched projects, shifting to the garment that was due Monday. In a moment of whimsy after completing the hem, I decided to pull out my needle and thread and revisit my embroidery skills. I found a lightly contrasting thread and a passage from an Emily Dickinson poem and embroidered the passage onto the hem. From afar, it looked like an interesting color detail. From close up, it was a tiny but legible line of poetry.

I liked the idea of a garment containing a secret.

The skirt had pockets, and I decided to do the same along the edge of the pocket openings. I loved the look. But it was completely time consuming—after an hour, I'd completed only half of the hem work. With a jolt, I realized I might want to start thinking about what I'd wear to Will's mother's birthday party.

I examined the contents of my wardrobe. With the weather the way it was, I didn't relish the idea of wearing heels. Boots would protect both my legs and my toes. But my green wool pencil skirt wasn't festive enough. I'd already worn my good blue silk dress to the Blythes' residence. My selection of dressy clothes was limited.

I called Gemma and explained the problem. "That is tricky," she agreed. "What about that periwinkle blouse with the peplum?"

I chewed on my lip, thinking. "I usually wear that with dark jeans."

"I can bring a few pieces over, but you're more petite than I am. I've got a skirt...Listen, I'll just be over in a little bit, okay?"

I pulled out the periwinkle blouse while I waited for Gemma's arrival. It buttoned down the front and had narrow tucks down the bodice. The peplum hit right at my waist, making it appear even smaller. The capped sleeves were short and puffy with a little blue pearl button on each side.

Looking at the blouse, I realized I could dress it up with a sash at the waist. Taking the blouse with me, I dug through my ribbon bin. At the bottom I found a wide black satin ribbon, just long enough to tie around my waist and still have enough left to leave nice tails on a bow.

I tugged off my thermal knit shirt and tried on the look in the mirror. With a little work, I got the bow the size I wanted, deciding it would probably lay better if I pressed it. Though how to press it presented a problem. But if I tugged the sash until it was roomier, turned it, and made a snip down the back…

Perfect. I hemmed each raw edge of the ribbon where I'd cut it and sewed on two sets of hooks and eyes so I could reattach the sash.

Gemma's knock sounded just as I finished pressing the bow. I hooked it quickly around my waist before opening the door.

"Look at you!" She said as she walked in. "Glad the blouse is what's working out for you, because I brought you stuff to coordinate with it." She set the garment bag of clothes down on the couch. "I know there's not tons of time, but I thought my black satin pencil skirt could work for you. It's short on me, so if it fits you can keep it. My younger sister wouldn't be caught dead in something that won't twirl, so it's up for grabs. And if that works, I thought you might want a sweater over it. I know you've got a black cardigan, but I thought this might be fun too."

I watched as she unfolded a sweater that looked like it might float away of its own accord. "What is it?"

"Mohair and silk. I close it with a shawl pin, so I figured fit wouldn't be as much of an issue because you can just pin it tighter. And if the sleeves are long, you can roll them up and it'll look like a cuff. Though personally, I think very long sleeves are very pretty and old-fashioned looking as long as the torso fits properly. I also thought the periwinkle would show through the knit really prettily."

I tried on both pieces to discover Gemma was absolutely right. The skirt fit perfectly, falling just below my knee. The peplum of the blouse flared over the skirt just right, and the sweater was surprisingly warm considering how airy it was. I pinned the sweater just under my bust so the sash on the blouse could be seen. As a final touch, I added the blue crystal necklace I'd worn for Christmas.

"That looks amazing." Gemma crossed her arms as she looked over the ensemble. "I thought it would work, but I had no idea it would look *that* good. When does Will come to pick you up?"

"Six thirty," I answered.

"Well, that's swiftly approaching. I'll take off. Let me know how it goes, okay?"

I gave her a hug. "Thank you for coming over. You're like my personal fairy godmother."

Gemma laughed and hugged me back. "You're welcome. I'm happy to share—it validates the size of my closet."

I walked her to the door and waved goodbye.

Now that I was dressed, I headed to the bathroom to finish my hair and makeup. I touched up the makeup I'd applied earlier in the day, adding a shimmery neutral shadow and blush. I carefully lined my lips with a light pink lip liner and then applied a cheery red lipstick with a lip brush, blotting at the end so the pigment wouldn't wind up traveling to my teeth or chin.

I added a bit of eyeliner to my eyes while the curling iron heated. Once it was hot, I curled the ends of my hair, including the shorter top layers, in different directions to create a tousled, curly look. The strands weren't as short as they had been a few months ago. I supposed it was probably time to get it trimmed, though the concept was foreign to me. I knew Gemma and Meg got their hair trimmed every six weeks to the day. Maybe I needed to at least consider doing the same.

I gave my hair a good coat of hair spray, but I was realistic. I knew there was a high likelihood it would go flat the moment a bit of damp air touched it. At least it would look cute for ten minutes or so. I was optimistic and hoped it might last half of the evening.

I stood back to take in the complete look. I had to admit, I loved it.

There was a brusque knock at the door. I jumped and stopped my vain primping. And took a deep breath.

―――❊―――

Meredith Blythe's "small" family gathering consisted of her husband Kip, Will's brother Carter, Carter's girlfriend Allison, and a smattering of aunts, uncles, and cousins whose names I couldn't remember.

Meredith greeted Will and me at the door. "Sara! So glad you could make it! You look lovely—let me take your coat for you. William, thank you for bringing her."

I shot a quick glance at Will. He gave a rueful smile. Meredith sounded happier to see me than Will, but it didn't seem to bother him. We followed her inside to a table in the entryway that seemed to be allocated for gifts. Will put his own gift with the others.

This type of family gathering should have been familiar to me. After all, I'd been raised in a large family. This was different though. Shinier. Harder. Less sincere.

Will stuck close throughout the evening. He hadn't said much since he'd arrived to pick me up, other than to tell me that I looked very nice. I must have looked better than that though because he couldn't seem to stop looking at me.

Meredith was usually nearby as well, asking questions about how my studies were going and how I was enjoying Portland. Will had explained I'd recently moved to the area.

A buffet was laid out. In the corner I could see a fondant-covered cake with a small flowering dogwood tree growing from the center.

Built-in bookshelves held hundreds of framed photos of friends and family. Will and Carter as babies, Will and Carter as toddlers dressed in miniature tuxedos, Carter wielding a tennis racket, Will…

That couldn't be right. I picked up the picture in question. "Um, what's this?"

Admittedly, both Will and I had been doing our fair share of blushing lately. This particular flush might have been the brightest. He snatched the frame from my hands. "That shouldn't be out."

"But it…"

"Forget about it."

I crossed my arms. "It looked like you. As a kid. Ice skating, wearing a special suit. With your arms in the air and a medal around your neck. So I know what it looks like, but I wondered if you had any input in case it's not you twirling on ice, wearing a full-body leotard."

"My mom had me doing it, okay? It was exercise, and I didn't like soccer, and the local swimming pool made me break out into a rash."

"You ice skated competitively."

"I…did."

"Okay, just so I've got it straight." I turned my attention to my plate. "Do you like the meatballs?"

"How do you know about ice skating anyway?"

"I caught *Cutting Edge* on TV earlier this week. And Jayne's secretly a fan."

"Does it change how you think of me?"

I shook my head. "I suppose you have a better sense of balance than I thought. But otherwise, no."

He chuckled. I took the picture from his hands and replaced it on the shelf.

—\\//—

After everyone had finished eating, we gathered in the formal living room. The gifts were waiting, having magically moved from the entryway to a glass-topped coffee table in the center of the room. Kip handed his wife each gift, and Meredith began to open them while everyone looked on.

She received earrings from Kip and a cookbook from Carter. Allison provided a small box with a hand-beaded crystal bracelet. When Meredith came to the flat box containing the glass plate, she gave Will a smile of excitement that even I could tell was feigned.

Poor Meredith. She probably had a stack of books on string theory from Will that she'd never read. As much as I liked Will and had difficulty understanding his family, there was no excuse for ill-chosen presents, not for an immediate family member.

As Meredith lifted the lid and brushed away the protective tissue paper though, her face changed. "Oh, my goodness! It's beautiful!" She lifted it from the box, inspecting it closer from the front and back. "I love the colors! Honey, look," she presented it to Kip, who gave a nod of approval. "I know exactly where I'll put it too—oh, but as a serving plate…" She turned it over on its back again. "This is Cyprus Glass—that's a really good glassmaker. They're out of Louisiana. Remember, honey, when we visited their headquarters? Just beautiful." She pressed the plate to her breastbone. "I love it! Thank you, William!"

I turned just in time to see the look of surprised wonder on William's face.

Chapter 30

William held the car door open for me. I slid in, looking up to see Will waving goodbye to the other family members departing at the same time. He closed the car door, walked around to the drivers' side, waved again—not unlike the pope, I thought—before climbing in beside me. And exhaling. "Wow."

"Are you okay?" I resisted the urge to place a reassuring hand on his leg.

"Did you see that? My mom? That was amazing. How did you do that? She loved it. I've *never* seen her like something I've given her that much." He shook his head, his features easy to read because he'd shaved within the past twenty-four hours. "That's…Wow."

"She more than liked it—she loved it." I clicked my seatbelt into place. "I wouldn't be surprised if she sleeps with it under her pillow."

"How did you know she'd like it? Sorry—love it?"

I shrugged. "I was at her house. I saw the colors and things she liked to decorate with. The plate fit. Gifts…" I said, trying to phrase my words delicately, "are about paying attention. That's all."

"Whatever it was, it was amazing. You're amazing."

The warm words took me by surprise. From the way Will suddenly focused his attention on exiting his parents' driveway, I guessed the words took him by surprise as well.

I let it go and decided to change the subject.

"How did you know about me?" I crossed my arms. "When I told you and Zach about how I grew up Amish, you said you put the pieces together. How?"

Will ran a hand through his hair before shifting his car into third gear. "It was a lot of little pieces. Your complete lack of knowledge of any kind of pop culture or current idioms meant that you grew up separated from those things. You said your parents were nonmaterialists. I figured you hadn't grown up abroad because several kinds of ethnic foods were new to you. You mentioned once that you grew up on a farm, and it seemed like your family was pretty large."

He shifted again as he led the car onto Highway 217 North, back toward my apartment. "Most isolated farming families are either true-blue hippies— which you're obviously not—or part of a very conservative, very religious community. There are Amish and Mennonite communities in Albany and Washington. It made the most sense."

I suppressed a smile. "You paid attention."

"Yeah, well…you were a mystery."

"You paid better attention than Zach."

"I've spent more time with you. And, let's face it, Zach's a great guy but not the most observant. At least, not when non-Corleones are on the line."

I opened my mouth to say something when I felt my phone vibrate in my tiny clutch purse. That was odd—few people called my phone, especially on a Saturday night. "Hang on, my phone's ringing." I pulled it out to see it was my brother calling. "Do you mind if I take this? I want to make sure everything's okay."

"Go ahead."

I slid the phone open. "Hello?"

"Sara? It's Levi."

"And Jayne!" A second voice squealed. Was that really Jayne? I didn't think her voice went up that high.

"We're here together," Levi said. "We're on speakerphone."

"We've set a date!" Jayne's voice was so loud the tiny phone speaker crackled. "We're getting married!"

"When?" I asked, holding my palm to my forehead.

"April 17. That's the day, and I'm sticking by it. Like glue. Like duct tape. Like…um…"

"Postage stamps," I offered.

"Right!" Jayne released another giggle. "Like postage stamps. And peanut butter."

"We wanted you to be the first to know," Levi said, interrupting the name-the-sticky-things game. "We were hoping you would be Jayne's bridesmaid."

"Hey!" Jayne interrupted Levi right back. "I was going to ask her! The girl's supposed to ask. The girl bride, I mean. 'Cause I'm the bride. I'm the bri-i-ide. Wow." Jayne gave a nervous chuckle. "I'm a little loopy."

"Just a little," Levi agreed. "So April 17, okay? Mark your calendar?"

"I will," I said. "Congratulations. I'm *so* excited for both of you."

"Thanks, hon. We'll see you for church tomorrow."

We hung up, and I put the phone back in my clutch. "Well, my brother's officially getting married."

Will shot a quick glance at me. "I thought you said he was already engaged."

"Oh, he was. Jayne just needed an extra push to set the date and move forward with plans."

An extra push, like me move out. Suddenly the air seemed lighter, warmer. I'd done the right thing, as difficult as it had been. My older brother and my best friend would finally start a long, happy life together.

I shook my head. "They're really getting married." I couldn't stop the grin from spreading across my face. "I need to make them a pie," I announced. "They need a date-setting pie. A date-setting engagement pie."

"Why do I get the feeling Marie Calendar's has nothing to do with this?"

"Who?"

"Never mind. I assume you're going to bake when you get home?"

I pressed my hands into my lap. "I am."

He changed lanes, his movements so subtle I didn't tense up in the slightest. In fact, I noticed that I never felt uncomfortable riding with Will. I didn't feel as if we were going to crash and die if he didn't brake at a stoplight a certain way.

"Want help?"

"What?" I redirected my attention away from the experience of driving with Will.

"Do you want help? Baking your pie? Sorry—your brother's pie."

"Well, his and Jayne's. They're supposed to share," I said primly. "Sure, if you want to help."

"Do you need to pick up ingredients?"

I hadn't thought about that. "I guess I do. I don't have much to make a pie with, aside from milk and flour and eggs and butter."

"Respectable ingredients. I've never made a pie, but I thought they tended to have fruit and stuff in them."

"Not much is in season right now." I ran through the options in my head. "We could do pumpkin, pecan…apples are easy enough to get. We could use frozen fruit, but it would take a while to bake."

"Because it's frozen?"

"Yes." I frowned. The reasoning seemed simple enough.

"Why not thaw the fruit before you bake it?"

"Oh." I hadn't thought of that. "True."

"Just a thought. It's entirely up to you, you're the baker."

I thought. And thought. "Apple pie is reliable, and unlike a pecan or pumpkin pie, it has a top crust that can have a message carved into it."

"Sounds like a plan."

William pulled into a Fred Meyer that was just a few miles from my apartment. Picking up one of the hand baskets by the door, he said, "Produce is over here," and pointed toward the right. "What all do you need?"

"Granny Smith apples to start." I surveyed the displays of shiny, waxed fruit. "Maybe some Galas to mix it up. A couple lemons for their zest. I've got flour, sugar, and spices. Oh!" A new thought ran through my head. "We could do an apple *custard* pie. It's a little more special, a little more wintry."

"Sounds good to me. What do you need for that?"

"Buttermilk and eggs. The eggs I've already got. The prep takes a little longer, but it also doesn't bake as long."

That decided, we chose the apples, avoided the lemons since we were doing a custard, and found a carton of buttermilk. Will also picked up a separate carton of eggs. "Just to make sure there's enough."

I didn't argue.

─※─

At the apartment, Will rolled up the sleeves of his dress shirt and washed the apples. "I don't know if I mentioned this earlier," he said, "but you look beautiful tonight."

My hand paused on the oven dial. "Really?" I didn't think a young man had ever called me beautiful before. "Thanks."

After turning on the oven, I showed him the best technique to core and peel the apples. He worked with them while I prepared the crust.

"I know I said something a while ago," Will said, clearing his throat, "but I want to tell you again that I'm sorry." He sliced a brightly colored Gala. "I know I didn't treat you very well when you first came to the shop.

I—I shouldn't have been rude. You're a good person, smart and kind. You didn't deserve that."

I paused in the mixing of the dry ingredients. "You're forgiven, just so you know. I forgave you a long time ago."

"Yeah?"

"And all but forgotten by the time you gave me the wooly socks." I cut the shortening in. "They're very impressive socks."

"Glad my footwear could speak so well for me. I wanted to make sure, though. You deserve it."

"Thanks." I didn't know what else to say. I bit my lip. "I'd give you your socks back, but I wore them the other night—the night I called you—and I haven't done any laundry recently." I reached for the ice water, adding the liquid until I had the consistency I was looking for.

"You can keep the socks," Will said, smiling. "I've got lots."

I smiled back. He had such nice, warm eyes.

Will broke the moment, pointing at the bowl of cut fruit. "That's a lot of apples."

"Oh." I stepped back and looked back at the bowl. "You're right." If the pie was too full, the custard wouldn't lay right. "I've got a six-inch pie pan. Want to make a smaller pie for us? It'll bake in less time and cool faster too."

"You'd share a pie with me?"

I couldn't hide my grin. "I would."

I rolled out the first crust and placed it in the large pie pan before looking for the smaller pie pan in the cupboard. Within moments I'd made a second, smaller batch of piecrust while the first chilled in the fridge. The technique worked well because the first crust needed to chill anyway to keep the pastry flaky.

"I'm sorry about how things worked out with that Arin guy," Will said as he watched me work. "I hope you weren't...disappointed."

I dropped half of a stick of butter into my large skillet, turned on the heat, and waited for it to melt. "How so?" I asked.

He watched as I added the sugar, cinnamon, and the apples to the pan. "I didn't know if you...if you and he..." He exhaled. "If the two of you were romantically involved." The last words came out in a rush.

I shook my head. "We weren't. I wasn't disappointed, not that way."

"Oh." Will measured out the custard ingredients. "That's good."

I set the apples aside when they were done and focused on the buttermilk, eggs, and sugar. "I'm glad things went so well at your mom's party," I said as I whipped the remaining half of the butter stick with the sugar.

Will cracked the first egg into the mixture. "I still can't believe it. She likes you a lot."

"Really? That's sweet." I waited while Will cracked the rest of the eggs in, waiting for each one to blend before adding another. The tablespoons of flour came next, followed by the vanilla and then the buttermilk. "I miss my mom a lot," I said. "It's nice seeing other people's moms, even if they're completely different from mine."

"I imagine our mothers don't have much in common."

I poured most of the apple mixture into the main pie pan, leaving just enough for the smaller one. "No. But they're both women who love their kids. That's the same."

Will poured the custard over the top of each pie. I fit the crusts onto both, cutting a heart-shaped hole in the center of Jayne and Levi's pie to keep the custard from bubbling out the edges and adding vents around the edge. With the scraps, I fashioned two letters—an *L* and a *J*—and placed them with a dab of water on either side of the center heart.

We leaned against the counters after putting the pies in the oven. I suddenly felt awkward.

Will broke the silence first. "I'm going to be honest with you, and I'm going to just throw this out there." He lifted a hand. "When you were in that car crash, it scared me. I know it's a cliché, but I realized that you'd become...a very important person to me. You make me see the world differently. You're beautiful in a way that I don't think you understand, but it blows me away. You have an incredible amount of courage, and that makes me want to reevaluate my life." He ran his hand through his shaggy hair and took a step nearer. "And...I just like being with you. That's why...I think we should date."

—you—what?" I stuttered. I thought I heard…I wondered if he meant… not growing up English was so hard sometimes! I crossed my arms. "I'm sorry, I don't know that I understood you quite right."

"I think we should date," Will repeated, taking yet another step closer. "I think we should spend time together doing various activities and getting to know each other better."

"Various activities," I echoed.

"Right."

"And we would be doing this because…"

Will's gaze captured mine. "I think I'm falling in love with you, Sara."

"Oh." I took a step closer to him without thinking. "Really?"

He nodded. "Really. Have been for a while."

I gave a small smile. "That's…nice."

"Nice?" He lifted an eyebrow. "Just nice?" He brushed a piece of hair from my face.

I could never have expected my response in that moment. Will and I had touched before, but the contact had never been intentional. This time was more than different. Will's hand in my hair was an epiphany. My eyes closed as memories flooded through my mind. Will and I decorating the shop for Christmas, Will helping me back to the shop after the accident and letting me wear his socks and cry into his shoulder. Will there helping me move, taking the news of my background with a surprising calm.

I flashed on memories of the way Will responded whenever Arin was in the shop. The way Will read to me until I fell asleep. The way he brought me coffee at work. So many little pieces, adding up to something so big, so important. In that moment, I knew. I understood. Will was falling in love with me.

And I was falling in love with him.

I raised my hand and stroked a piece of his hair, near his ear. It was as soft as I'd expected, so dark, with a touch of curl to it. I traced the line of his eyebrow, the one that arched and quirked and showed on the outside what he was thinking on the inside.

"Sara?" Will's eyes were dark and serious.

"Yes?" My hand had moved to the back of his head; I fingered the hair that liked to brush against his collar.

"If you don't want me to kiss you, you should probably take a step back."

My gaze held his. I don't know where my boldness came from, but I inched forward.

Inched, because we were toe-to-toe as it was.

His breathing grew husky. His hand stroked my cheek, my chin, the back of my neck. My eyes fluttered closed.

He kissed my lips with incredible gentleness, greeting them softly before weaving his hand into my hair and making a more thorough introduction.

I kissed him back. My movements were careful, unpracticed, but I wanted him to know I was with him. I trusted him. I was falling for him just as readily as he for me.

Will ended the kiss, pulling back ever so slightly, leaving a tiny kiss on my cheekbone that made me shiver. He tucked another piece of hair behind my ear. "I hope that means you'll go out with me."

I giggled. "Yes. I will." I tilted my head. "But you should know I've never dated the way English people date."

"You went on dates with Arin," he pointed out.

I shook my head. "But I was never interested in Arin. I never thought of it that way."

He took my hand, leading me to the living room.

And stopped. I followed his gaze. Oh, that...

"What is that?" he asked, pointing at the gigantic colored mass that had taken up the living room floor.

"My quilt." I took a seat on the couch, sitting cross-legged against the arm.

"Wow. Did you get tired of your bedspread or something?"

"Something like that," I hedged.

The answer must have satisfied Will, because he sat on the couch near me.

"What were we talking about? Dating?" he asked, folding his own limbs until he looked comfortable. "Tell me about it."

"Well," I started, "first off, all courting is a secret from the family. At least, mostly a secret. Everyone pretends it is, at least. After everyone goes to bed, the young men go courting. They go to the girls' windows, the girls climb out, and they go driving. Sometimes they drive into town—if the boy has a car—and walk around Walmart. Other times, the boy comes over and the couple sits and talks in the living room for most of the night."

"While everyone's asleep?"

"Yup. I know—it sounds weird. Jayne was shocked when she found out. The first night Jayne stayed at our house, she rushed into my room and tried to protect me from the shyest boy in town." I smiled at the memory. "She was going to protect me with a shoe."

"I can believe it. So your parents, who I imagine are conservative people, were okay with you sneaking out at night?"

"That's how they courted."

"I guess…that makes sense. Huh. How familiar are you with English dating habits?"

"A little." I folded my hands in my lap. "I've watched Jayne and Levi, after all. I know there's a lot of food involved. And gifts—Levi likes to give Jayne gifts. I've heard Kim talk about how the guy is supposed to call within a week after a date, and that means the guy still likes the girl, or something. But that a text doesn't always count, and especially not if the text is just smiley faces and not actual words." I sighed. "It just seems so complicated. She had something to say about email too, but my head hurt too much. When I was Amish, sometimes we left notes for each other. But there were no smiley faces and certainly no emails." I rested my head against the back of the couch. "Things were much simpler back then, in many ways."

Will stroked my knee with his finger. "You told me once that you didn't want to go back. Is that still true?"

"There's nothing there for me," I told him, my heart aching with the words. "I hid my things from my family. They thought I was happy, and I wasn't. I lied to them. I know that I would have left even if I had told the truth, but still, I don't like that I deceived my parents." I shrugged a shoulder. "I'm here now."

"Think about it all the time, huh?"

I could only tell him the truth. "Yes." I looked away. "But it's not an option." I jumped when the timer for the miniature pie beeped in the kitchen. "Our pie's done!" I said. A look in the oven confirmed my suspicion. I pulled it out and inspected it for doneness. The crust was golden brown. I poked a knife through the hole to find that the custard had firmed. Rather than let it cool and set, I scooped generous portions onto dessert plates.

"You're serving it up now? It doesn't have to rest or anything?" Will rose from the couch. "Let me give you a hand. Do you want something to drink with that?"

I put a hand on my hip. "I'm the hostess here! That's my line."

"I wanted to help out." He gently moved my hand from its position, propped on my hip. "At ease, soldier."

I shivered when he ran a light hand down my shoulder blade.

"Do you want anything to drink?" he repeated.

"Milk."

I watched, transfixed, as he poured me a glass and handed it to me before pouring one for himself.

"So what about you," I asked as we walked back to the living room with our food. "I assume you've dated lots of girls."

"Never."

"Never?"

"I never met a girl who surprised me." He looked up from his pie. "Not like you."

❧

Will and I talked and laughed until I began to replace talking with yawning.

He gave me a lazy grin. "You're tired, aren't you."

I yawned again. "Maybe." I smiled. "It's been a busy day. But a fun day."

"Yeah? So, since we're dating, I should probably ask you out on a date."

"Something that doesn't involve going to your parents' house?" I stretched an arm in the air.

"Preferably not. I know you've got movie nights on Fridays. Saturday then? Are you free?"

I hesitated, but only for a short moment. I realized that dating Will meant less time not only for school but also for the quilts I needed to make to pay my bills. Could I afford the time?

Could I afford *not* to? I looked at William sitting in front of me. His body was relaxed, his eyes kind. The time? I would make it work. "I'm free Saturday," I said.

His face opened into the most beautiful smile I'd ever seen.

I knew I'd made the right choice.

⁓⁓

Working around the clock, I finished the first quilt that week. I celebrated the final stitch by splurging on a sweet latte.

Not that it helped—I also fell asleep in class twice. Britta woke me up before the instructor had a chance to notice.

At the shop, Will commented on my lack of energy. "Are you doing okay these days?"

"I've had a lot of projects lately," I hedged.

"But everything's fine with school?" He leaned in closer and put an arm around me. "I'm a little worried about you."

"What is *with* you guys lately?" Zach's voice came from behind.

We turned around. Zach stood with his hands on his hips, studying us. "Will? What do you have to say for yourself?"

"I thought he was still on break," Will said under his voice. He grabbed my hand. "Sara and I are seeing each other."

I looked up at Will in surprise.

"He was going to figure it out sometime," he told me. "I thought he'd be more subtle about it."

"Zach? Subtle? Really?"

"You guys know I'm still here, right?" Zach asked. "I mean, I kind of figured things were going, you know, that way. I mean, Will's been making googly eyes at you for a while. A long while. But, man," he placed his hand over his heart. "I'm hurt you didn't tell me."

Will wasn't about to be pulled into Zach's melodrama. "I just told you."

"But, I mean…"

Will stepped forward and gave Zach a slap on the back. "It was on a need-to-know basis."

"Glad I know now, at least. It would have been awkward to find out on your wedding day."

I froze. Will didn't—he just told Zach to stop wasting his time while he was on the clock.

He turned back to me and placed a kiss on my cheek. "In all fairness, we should go back to work too. Promise you're okay?"

I pasted a calm expression on my face. "I'm fine. Everything's okay."

＝＝＝

With the aid of Sonnet's camera, I uploaded pictures of the finished quilt and posted it on eBay for a starting bid of $1,750. I prayed it would sell quickly at a high price. Livy had graciously covered my share of the deposit on the apartment, saying she had the cash and knew I'd pay her back.

Between that and living expenses, the ambulance bill, and the growing realization that I needed a car, I awaited the sale of the first quilt with anticipation.

I had a window in my schedule on Friday, so when Levi called early in the day and asked if I wanted to meet him for lunch, I agreed.

"Noah's Bagel okay with you?" he asked. "I think that's pretty central for both of us."

"Perfect," I told him, excited about seeing my older brother.

He was waiting for me inside when I arrived. "Good to see you!" he said before enveloping me in a warm hug.

I hugged him back. "Congratulations again. I know I said that on Saturday, but I'm so excited I thought it could be repeated."

Levi was excited—I could tell. His eyes were bright, his smile unwavering. We ordered and sat down with our drinks.

"Tell me how classes and work are going," Levi said as he leaned forward. "And Will, if you're willing to share."

I couldn't stop a goofy smile from spreading across my face. "Will and I are dating. I…we…we're really happy."

"Yeah?"

I nodded.

"Good. Classes? You look tired."

"I've been quilting." I propped my head up with my hand. "Quilting and doing class assignments. And working. It's been a lot, but the first quilt's done and up for auction, and the second one is halfway through."

"That's part of what I wanted to talk to you about. I wanted to let you know that I got a letter from mom yesterday."

I straightened. "Oh?"

"They're fine. Dad's in good health. He's apparently started drinking green tea. Anyway, she sent some cash for you." He rose to get our sandwiches.

I was still frozen when he returned. "She what?"

"She wrote a note about it. Her reasoning is that if you'd left home because you'd married, you would have received enough in gifts to set up your household. Since you're not likely to go home and marry an Amish man, she sent some money to you to help defray the costs of living. How did she put it? 'Living in the English city of Portland.'" Levi held up a hand. "I realize you may not want to accept the money, and that's your choice. But I want you to know that it's there."

"How much?" I asked, my voice barely audible.

Levi tented his fingers. "One thousand."

My eyebrows flew up. "Dollars?"

"Yes."

I put my sandwich down. "Oh my goodness." I tilted my head. "Oh my goodness."

"Like I said, what you do about it is entirely up to you."

I sighed. "It seems like no matter what I do, my Amishness keeps creeping in. Money from home. Money from quilting. I came here wanting to be an *Englischer*, and yet I keep going back to my background to support myself."

Levi shrugged. "I used to run an Amish woodcraft shop. But you know what? I was good at it. I miss working with my hands these days. Nothing is ever going to change the fact that you grew up Amish. Being English doesn't mean you're starting over. I think of it as building on who you already are. And the fact that Amish goods can bring a high profit, well, it's out of your control. I want you to be able to eat, and if quilting on the side is the best way to support yourself, who could argue with that?"

"I haven't told Will about it," I admitted.

"Why not?"

"He'd...he'd want to fix things. He'd figure out how to give me a raise at the bookstore. He'd worry. He'd...I don't know."

"It's up to you, but I think he'd want to know. He cares about you. A lot. I've seen it."

"Yeah?"

"I had a hunch when I came in for that book for Jayne. The day of the accident, well..."

"Pretty obvious?" I shook my head but couldn't hide the smile. "I'm happy about it, even if it did take a while. Will is…he's special." I shrugged, feeling shy. "How's Jayne? I haven't heard from her in a couple days."

"She's good. Busy. Has empty-nester syndrome."

"What?"

"She misses you. Makes huge meals and expects me to eat your share. Keeping the place pretty tidy, but I can tell it's taken a toll. I'm researching the possibility of a housekeeper once a week after we get married. But she's good."

"I'm glad. So—where is the money?"

"At my place. I didn't feel comfortable carrying it around."

I fluffed the back of my hair. "I'd be pretty silly not to accept it, wouldn't I."

"It's entirely your decision, so I'm not going to answer that."

I glared at him, and he mock-glared back.

I giggled. It felt good being with my brother. With family.

"If mom wants to make sure I'm eating, I don't want to worry her. I'll take the money—you can tell her so."

"I will." Levi studied me for a moment. "Have I told you how impressed I am with how you're doing?"

"Not lately."

"I'm impressed. And Will? He's a lucky guy. I'd tell him, but I have a hunch he already knows."

Chapter 32

"You seem distracted," Will said halfway through dinner Saturday night. "Huh?" I looked up from twirling my pasta. "Sorry, what?"

"I said you seem distracted," Will said, spearing a bite of potato. "Is your food okay?"

"No, it's...I...um, I don't know."

"You don't know if your food's okay?"

"No, my food's great. Yummy. I love it. Why?"

"Sara..." Will took the fork from my hand. "What's going on?"

I was about to protest the removal of the fork from my hand, but having Will's hand on mine mollified that impulse. "Nothing's going on."

"Horse manure. We may have started dating only a week ago, but I didn't just meet you yesterday. I know when you're preoccupied." He lifted an eyebrow. "Spill."

There was no help for it. "Sorry. I've been busy lately..." My words dropped off as I realized he wasn't believing any of it.

At least I tried.

"I'm poor," I stated bluntly. "I barely had enough money to get into the apartment, I owe my roommate for the deposit, I have a huge bill from the ambulance after the accident, and I need a car. I've been making quilts to try to make ends meet. But I found out yesterday that my mother sent a significant amount of money to Levi to give to me. The first quilt is up for online auction and up to $1,900, which is encouraging. After it sells, I can pay Livy back. Wow—Livy and Levi, hadn't thought of that. Anyway, I can also pay off the medical bill. The second quilt is cut but not pieced. As soon as it's done, I might be able to look for a car."

I stopped talking. Will didn't say anything. I looked down at my plate. "Sorry. I probably should have said something earlier."

Will took another bite of potato. "It's your prerogative." He put his fork down. "You could have told me."

"I know."

"You'll let me know if you want my help?"

I nodded.

"And you'll ask for help before you fall over from working so hard? Don't think I haven't noticed you've been tired all the time." He leaned forward. "Please?"

"I will."

"In all fairness, I can talk to Richard about giving you a raise."

I winced. "Do you think that's a good idea? I don't want a raise in pay because we started dating and you heard about my financial woes. It's nice of you, but…"

"But what? Our sales have been up since you've come on. The place is cleaner and runs smoother than it ever has. You've passed your three-month mark, so it's a reasonable thing to ask for. Zach wouldn't resent it in the least, not that it's any of his business. But," he said, holding up a hand, "I won't do it if you don't want me to."

"I didn't—I don't think I realized I had made that much of a difference at the store."

"You have. And I'm not saying that to be nice or anything."

I smiled. "I don't worry about that much. I guess if you want to say something to Richard, you can. Just don't badger him about it. Don't fork his lawn if he says no."

"Fork his lawn? As in—sticking plastic forks in someone's yard?"

"Yes."

"Is that something Amish kids do?"

"No, but Jayne did when she was young. Apparently, one of the Safeway employees forked her parents' lawn because he figured out from all of the plastic forks that she'd been buying that she was the one hitting people around town. Oh, and she not only hit the locals but even went down to one of the places for RVs and forked a four-foot-deep rectangle in front of an RV door."

"Your brother's fiancée has quite the checkered past. Don't worry. I'm not a lawn forker. I've never had the patience for that sort of thing." Will smiled. "Did I tell you how pretty you look?"

I smiled back. "Yes, earlier."

"Oh. I won't bore you by telling you again."

I laughed, wondering at how a conversation with Will could make the world seem better.

———※———

"I can't believe you guys are making me do this," Jayne sighed from the front seat of Gemma's car.

"Look," Gemma said, yanking on the parking brake with surprising force. "You want to be a bride, right?"

"Right! I'm already a bride. I don't need to be here to be more bridey."

I patted Gemma on the shoulder. "She's been like this for a week."

"Oh, I'm sure." Gemma fixed Jayne with her stare. "Okay. We can do this the easy way or the hard way. In a few months, you're going to walk down an aisle of some sort so that you can become Mrs. Levi Burkholder, right?"

Jayne crossed her arms. "Right."

"Okay. And since you're not going all Genesis on us and doing it stark naked, and since it will be a wedding, that means you need a wedding dress. We're at David's Bridal because if it's one-stop bridal shopping you're look-ing for, David's your guy. One store, lots of options, and then you can move onto something you'll really enjoy, like invitations."

Jayne wrinkled her nose. "I thought we'd just send out an Evite or some-thing."

"Think of your mother. Think of Miss Lynnie, your Sunday school teacher. Do you think an Evite will work for them?" Gemma asked.

"We're getting out of the car now," I said, taking the initiative and climb-ing out. I opened Jayne's door for her. "Come on. You too."

Jayne unhooked her seatbelt. "You're so bossy."

"I'm bossy?" I lifted an eyebrow. "I could call your sister. I'm sure Beth would love to come down and help you pick a dress."

"You wouldn't."

"I've got her number programmed into my phone."

Jayne leapt from the car. "She'd make me try on something poofy."

I couldn't deny the fact, so I just walked behind Jayne as she made her way toward the front doors of the store.

Gemma presented the girl at the front desk with a piece of paper. "I called ahead," she said. "These are the dresses she's interested in. If you don't have one of them in stock, it's fine to move onto the next on the list. The bride is a 34C, and she'll be trying on mostly size eights, I'm guessing."

Jayne crossed her arms over her chest. "I feel violated."

Gemma rolled her eyes. "Stop whining. Do it for Levi."

"Mmm. Levi." Jayne smiled. "That's not playing fair."

"No, it's playing smart."

We followed the sales associate who had been assigned to us, Petra, to the mirrored dressing rooms.

"Did you want to go through the racks and look at any of the dresses?" Petra asked Jayne.

"Huh-uh." Gemma held up a hand. "She's got to start with the list."

Jayne put a hand on her hip. "What if I *wanted* to go through the racks?"

"You'd tell me they were too white and too shiny and too poofy. Yes?"

"Wow." Jayne turned to me, pointing at Gemma. "She knows me really well. It's like we're friends or something."

Moments later Petra returned with two of the gowns Gemma had requested.

Gemma clapped her hands together. "So. Ground rules. If you hate it, you have to say why. If it doesn't fit, you'll try a different size. If you choose it, you have to love it. No picking something just so we leave, okay?"

"I don't know why you're behaving like this," Jayne said sternly. "It's not like I'm behaving childishly or anything."

"You're funny." Gemma said sarcastically, but I could see her smile.

I stood outside the door while Gemma helped Jayne put the first dress on—the dressing room was too small for three women.

Jayne stepped out a few moments later, tugging at the neckline. She took a look at herself in the mirror. "That's odd."

Gemma fluffed the short train. "What?"

"I don't hate it."

"Of course you don't hate it." Gemma stood and studied Jayne's reflection. "I picked dresses with you in mind, silly. Tell me what you like about it."

I watched as Jayne tried to find her words. "What do you think about the empire waistline?" I asked, prompting her.

"I like it. Very simple. I kind of wish it had straps or something though."

"There are sleeve options," Petra was quick to point out.

"I'm not sure about this beady stuff," Jayne pointed to the beads along the waist. She turned to the side and examined herself. "But I don't hate it."

"We'll put it in the maybe pile." Gemma said. "Next dress!"

Over the next hour, Jayne tried on long dresses and short dresses, dresses with spaghetti straps and dresses with halter necklines, dresses that laced up the back and dresses that zipped up to a portrait back and then buttoned at the top.

I walked with Gemma as she checked the racks to see if she'd missed anything. She pulled out a ball gown to examine it closer, fingering the pickup-style satin skirt.

"I'm not sure that it's very Jayne," I suggested, pulling out one a few gowns down. "Maybe this one?"

Gemma was still looking at the dress she was holding. "Oh, I don't think this is Jayne's taste at all. I like it, though." She replaced the dress. "Maybe someday."

"Why aren't you married?" I blurted before clamping my hand over my mouth. "I'm sorry. That was rude, wasn't it? Forget I said that."

Gemma smiled graciously. "Oh, it's a question I ask myself. I'm busy. I don't meet new people very often—at least not in a way that leads to any kind of consistency. My father thinks I intimidate men." She pointed at the dress I'd found. "That one has potential. Anyway, it's not my time. At least, not yet. One of these days, God may introduce me to the right man, maybe a chef or a restaurateur, who knows? Until then, I've decided to live a full life without regrets. And being single means I have more time to spend with friends who need wedding dresses."

With Petra's help, we added three new dresses to the "to be tried" rack outside of Jayne's room.

"I hate to ask," Gemma said as she examined the new entries, "but have you thought about bridesmaid dresses? And colors?"

"Um, no." Jayne eyeballed the new dresses. "I want to try this one," she said, tugging on a protective plastic bag.

"Okay. That one's next."

Jayne emerged from the room moments later. None of us said anything as she studied herself in the mirror.

The dress was the loveliest on her that she'd tried on. She wore it differently too, as if her muscles were more relaxed, her body language more sure. The style was simple—a cross-over V-neckline with thin straps that crossed in the back. The waist was defined by a three-inch band. The A-line skirt fell in two gentle pleats in the front and several more in the back to give the sweep train fullness. It was simple but not plain. And it was perfect for her.

Jayne broke the silence. "I want it."

Gemma's eyebrows shot up. "Wow—really?"

"I don't want to take it off. I don't know that I've ever really felt that way about a garment not made from flannel."

Petra sprang into action. "The dress is meant to have a crinoline underneath…"

Jayne shook her head. "No. I like it just the way it is. And—" she stuck her hands into the folds of the skirt. "It has pockets."

"It's perfect," I said, coming up behind her. "If you did a veil, you'd want a short one. The style is classic but very modern."

Jayne shook her head. "I don't think I can handle a veil. Or that a veil can handle me."

I reached up. "Your hair up, like this? Maybe a sparkly clip or a simple white flower?"

"I like that."

I smiled, knowing my eyes were growing watery. She was so happy, her beauty radiated from her heart outward.

"This is what I'm thinking," Jayne said, sounding calmer than I'd heard her in weeks. "I don't want to buy this on impulse, and I know my mom and Beth will want to feel like a part of the wedding process, even if I'm not a wedding-y person. Can I put the dress on hold?" she asked Petra. "Maybe they can come down this week and see it before I buy it."

Once Jayne reemerged from the dressing room in her street clothes, she turned to me. "The way I see it, I think you should pick your own bridesmaid dress. We can agree on a color, maybe, and you and Beth can each pick a style you like. I love my sister, but I don't want to put you through the ordeal of what would happen if you picked one for the two of you and Beth didn't like it. Also," Jayne said, choosing her words carefully, "the idea of a color-coordinated wedding makes me want to break out in hives."

I thought about it for a moment. "So, no color. What if you did black or a pewter gray?"

Jayne's face brightened. "Is that allowed?"

"You're the bride. Gray would be nice and neutral for a late afternoon wedding, not drab at all if it's a fabric with some shine. I could take a very basic dress and make some embellishments out of silk chiffon and beads."

"Beth would like that sort of thing. I like the idea of something you made being a part of the wedding. Makes it more special that way. Could you make something that could go on the wedding dress? Nothing too frilly, you know."

"I'd like that," I said, running ideas through my head.

Only a couple of dresses came in gray, but the ones that did, I liked. I envisioned a trail of flowers in ivory chiffon, maybe going down the side, maybe trailing over the shoulder.

Jayne, Gemma, and I went out for gelato once the dress Jayne picked was safely tucked away on hold.

"I've been told," Jayne said, "that someone has to light the candles during the ceremony. Levi and I would be honored, Gemma, if you'd be willing to do that."

Gemma's face lit up. "Really? I'd love to."

"You know that in different circumstances, I'd love to have you as a bridesmaid."

Gemma waved a hand. "I understand—I love lighting candles. The day's about you anyway."

"Oh, only partially. Even I know that. It's about Levi, and my mom, and Beth, and Sara—it's about everyone. We couldn't do it right without any of you."

I tilted my head. "Why can't Gemma be a bridesmaid?"

"I like fairness. If I asked Gemma, I should ask Kim. And Joely. Kim would wear a bridesmaid dress if she needed to—"

"She's got the legs for it," Gemma interjected.

"True. But Joely would rather, I don't know what. Die? Eat tofu? Anyway, she'd rather watch tapes of the O.J. Simpson trial than wear a dress. She'd do it, but it would not be a happy day for her. Add the fact that Levi only has so many men to be groomsmen…"

"Don't worry about it." Gemma put a hand on Jayne's shoulder as she took a bite of her rum-flavored gelato. "I hate having my picture taken anyway."

"Oh—photographer, that's another thing. Do you think Barry does weddings?" Jayne asked.

"He's done some lovely crime scenes," Gemma said dryly. "I don't know how he does it, but I've never seen police tape look so bridal. Hire someone who doesn't work at the paper, please?"

"You're so picky."

"You'll thank me later."

"What about my parents?" I asked, no longer able to hold my words back. "Will you tell them? Will you send them an invitation?" My heart ached, knowing my brother would stand at the front of the chapel without any of his brothers. But then, Jayne would walk down the aisle without her father.

"We'll send an invitation to your parents," Jayne assured me. "And your grandmother too. We'd love for them to come, but Levi and I, we're not…"

"Not getting your hopes up," I finished for her.

My appetite disappeared.

I tried to think about Jayne in her dress, my brother waiting for her, and the silk flowers I would sew for the dresses. I tried to think about the happy parts, but as hard as I tried, the ache wouldn't go away.

Chapter 33

On Monday, sitting in the lobby of the school and waiting for my name to be called, I relived the moments before my admissions interview.

A tall, chic woman stepped out of the administration offices and called my name. I stood, walked to meet her, and offered my hand, feeling very sophisticated and English.

"I'm Caryn," she said. "My desk is this way."

I followed her into the offices, noting the bright colors and updated posters. We turned a corner and stopped at what I assumed to be Caryn's cubicle. "Have a seat," she said as she gestured toward the chair on the opposite side of her desk. "How are your classes going?"

"Good," I said, smoothing my trousers. Granted, I'd been so busy I hadn't been paying nearly enough attention to them. But my first quilt had sold, and the second was nearly done, and by the time they were both off, I'd be ready to face my finals with complete attention. "I've enjoyed the material and learned a lot."

"Very good." Caryn glanced over some papers. "You're planning on staying in the fashion design track?"

"Yes."

"What kind of design in particular, if I may ask?"

"Haute couture, red-carpet gowns." I folded my hands to keep them from fidgeting. "That sort of thing."

Caryn nodded and leaned forward. "So, keeping that in mind, let's talk about how to set you up for success. I checked in with your instructors. They say you've done excellent work in the past, but you're not putting in your full energy these days. I've also heard you've had trouble staying awake in class. Is there something that's keeping you from getting your assignments done?"

"There have been some…challenges lately. I've had to work particularly late hours," I answered carefully.

237

"Is that going to be an ongoing thing, or is it just temporary?"

"Temporary," I was quick to point out. "Things should calm down soon."

"Good. We try to give you the tools to succeed, but fashion design is very competitive, and couture even more so. Your clients will expect perfection, and you'll demand it from yourself as well. Do you have anywhere in particular that you'd like to be working?"

"I—I hadn't thought about it."

"You might want to start. It could inform you of what kind of internships you'll be looking at. L.A. and New York are obvious choices. Italy, France if you're willing to relocate to Europe. You'll be more competitive for domestic internships, but planning ahead is wise."

My head was spinning. Los Angeles? New York? I had never traveled outside of Oregon or seen a city larger than Portland.

"And the Pacific Northwest?" I hated to even ask.

"You know," Caryn said with a shrug, "There just isn't the market for it around here. A shortage of red carpets." She laughed. "Obviously, we do have other design options here. Nike, for instance. Columbia."

Athletic apparel? I restrained a shudder. "Good things to consider."

"Excellent. If you can, try to really succeed during your finals. Finish the term strong."

"I will," I said. "And I'll think about what you said. About the locations."

I left and did exactly what I said I would. It was all I could think about.

<hr/>

I was still thinking about Caryn's words as I walked through the hallways to class. "Sara! Hey!"

I heard Arin before I saw him, turning around to see him jogging toward me. "Hey," he said, "slow down. I never talk to you these days. Are you doing okay?"

In truth, *okay* was not a word I'd use to define myself.

"I'm fine." Actually, I wasn't. The possibility of complete and total failure took up all of the space in my head. I just didn't want to talk about it.

"Wanna get coffee? Talk or something?"

I ran a distracted hand through my hair. "I've got five minutes here, but I really don't have time."

"I…I just wanted to tell you that I didn't like how things were with us last, you know, the last time we went out."

"It's okay," I started to say, but changed my mind mid-sentence. "Well, it wasn't, not really. But I'm over it."

"I really, well, I really like you." I watched as Arin's normally cool facade started to slip. "I just—I mean—are you sure you won't go to coffee with me? Or water, if you're not drinking coffee these days?"

"I know you mean well, but, see—I'm seeing someone from work."

"Work?" Arin's face rearranged itself in confusion. "You and that Will guy?"

Just hearing his name made me like sunshine inside. "Yeah."

"Does he know? I mean, does he know about you—"

"He knows all about my family," I finished for him. I wanted my friends to know, but I wasn't sure I wanted it announced in the hallway.

"He makes you happy?"

I couldn't stop my smile. "He does."

Arin shrugged. "Then he's the better man. Or something like that. Classes going well?"

"Well enough." I said, feeling the knot of dread forming in my stomach all over again.

─────※─────

Tuesday night, Livy was out at a missions meeting of some sort, and Will was helping me look for a car online.

A mysterious place, the internet. I didn't think I would ever get used to it.

We sat on the couch together, me leaning on Will's chest, his arms around me, the laptop on my lap.

"Here's a '95 Honda Civic. Good car, even if it's a cliché." He kissed the top of my head. "What do you think?"

"It's a maybe. I don't know how I feel about being in a creative, competitive field and driving a cliché car." I traced a circle on his knee with my finger.

"Interesting point. What else…a Ford Taurus…I wouldn't. There's a Saturn, they're pretty reliable. Oh—this is interesting. A '92 Subaru Legacy Sedan, and I think it has all-wheel drive. Nice. That's a good deal. Tell me if you hate it fast, otherwise it's going in your definite pile."

"I never thought you liked cars much."

"I like cars as a method of doing things—traveling, moving. It's when they become status symbols by shallow people who can't drive and don't know how to handle their cars…well, that frustrates me."

I looked up at him and smiled. "It doesn't show at all."

"Want to check this car out during lunch tomorrow?" Will pointed at the Subaru onscreen. "It's not too far from the shop."

"We should probably bring Zach a present when we get back. Maybe a cookie or something. Just so he doesn't feel left out."

"That's a good idea." He stroked my hair. "You're smart."

I chuckled. "I'm the fourth of eight children. I know how to keep the masses happy."

"I see how it is." He squeezed me in a hug. "We're just pawns in your game."

"Yes," I said dryly. "Because it's *so* easy to get you to do something you don't want to do. That must be it."

"I was just teasing. Wow, eight kids? I'm embarrassed to say this, but I don't think I actually know how old you are. I stopped asking people after my aunt got her first face-lift."

"Ouch," I said, lifting my hand to my own face. "That sounds painful. I'm eighteen."

I felt Will's breathing pause, then return to normal. "Oh."

It was only fair to ask back. "How old are you?"

"Twenty-five."

I patted his arm. "You're old."

He snorted. "You're young."

I wrinkled my nose. "I don't feel young." I moved the laptop onto the floor. "I feel very, very old these days."

"You've been working hard."

"I'll have a birthday in a few months though, in case that makes you feel better."

Will didn't say anything. I tilted my neck to look up at him. "Does it bother you?"

He sighed. "It should, probably. I've known guys who've dated much younger girls and rationalized it by saying they were mature for their age. But you…you actually are."

"I kind of grew up differently from everyone else. Well, everyone not Amish. Joely calls me Ethel though."

"I heard her do that the other night. Why is that?"

I stretched my arm out. "She says I'm an old soul."

"So she calls you Ethel?"

"Yes."

William mulled that over. "Fascinating. But I'm sure you're right. You were raised with a lot more responsibility and very different expectations."

"True. Most of my friends back home are probably either already married or will be by the fall."

"So my age doesn't bother you?"

I looked up at him. "Should it?"

He shrugged. "Maybe. But it's not a deal breaker for me. You've met my family. I've met the family of yours that I can. We've known each other for a while. It's not like I picked you up in a bar."

"I can't legally enter bars," I pointed out. "So that's very unlikely."

"True. And...we're good for each other. At least I like to think so."

I hugged his arm. "I think so. I have two socks in my drawer that say so."

"I'm glad you feel that way." He was silent for several moments. "If you change your mind, change it about us, any part of us—you'll tell me, right?"

"How do you mean?" I asked, confused.

"If one of us wants out, we'll say so. No finger pointing. No name calling. Just, you know, say something."

I pulled away so I could face him. "What if I don't want out?"

"I don't want out either—don't get me wrong. I just want you to know that communication is important to me." He winced. "Not that I was very good with it for most of the time I've known you. I'll be the first to say I'm probably stunted in some way. But we're in a relationship now, and I want to take care of us."

I shifted so I could pull my knees close to myself. "Have you ever thought about moving?"

"Moving?" The question took him aback. "As in, out of my place above the store?"

"Sure. Or maybe even farther." I was thinking of the conversation I'd had with Caryn earlier that day. "Have you ever thought about leaving Portland? Going back to New York or something?"

Will shook his head. "No, not really. The thought of dealing with New York traffic again makes me want to jump out a window. I have no desire to live in a broom closet again. And if I were honest with myself, I'd admit that I like being close to my family even if they do frustrate me."

"I understand. I do." I felt my stomach tighten.

"You look tense." He stood and stretched, offered me a hand, and pulled me toward him.

"What are you doing?"

"Relax," he said, lifting the hand that held mine over my head, sending me into a gentle twirl. "I'll bet you didn't dance much back home."

"Um, how about never?"

"That's what I thought."

"So you figure skate and dance?" I teased him. "You're a mysterious man, William Blythe."

He twirled me again. "My mom enrolled my brother and me in dance lessons. Twirling is the only part that's stuck."

I laughed. "Clearly."

"So tomorrow we'll go look at that car?"

"Sounds like a good idea."

"Can I tell you something?" Another twirl.

"You said you wanted to be communicative," I reminded him. "So you probably should."

Will pulled me close. "I love you," he said simply. "I just thought you should know."

My eyes widened. "Are you sure?"

"I am."

From the look in his eyes, I didn't doubt him. I hugged him close, hoping that if I hugged him tight enough, the constant ache would go away. "I love you too," I whispered.

※

I couldn't sleep that night. The previous two days' conversations played over and over in my mind. Caryn talking about L.A. and New York and saying how my work had suffered. Will saying he wanted to stay near his family and hated the city.

Will holding me close and telling me he loved me. That part I thought about most.

What would I do? What *could* I do? I loved Will. I loved the way he thought, the way he read books and carried them everywhere in his mind.

I loved the way he persisted in trying to love a family so different from himself.

He made me laugh. He made me feel safe. When I was with him, I didn't worry about making sure I sounded English enough. I could relax and be the person I was when no one else was looking.

And yet…he wouldn't leave Portland. And I wouldn't be able to stay.

Chapter 34

I thought I'd be able to focus better once the second quilt sold, but instead I found myself going through the motions while my head was somewhere else entirely.

Will and I took a look at the Subaru the next day. I liked it well enough and followed through with his suggestion that I have a mechanic check it out.

I made the fabric floral pieces for the bridesmaid's dresses as well as Jayne's dress. It didn't take long, and the pieces could easily be reconfigured into other shapes, depending on the taste of the wearer.

I knew my class assignments were suffering. My sketches were dull and uninspired. Sonnet, Britta, and Meg tried to offer their help and assistance, but I felt dried up inside.

Will sensed something was wrong, I think. He didn't say anything though. Maybe he'd just assumed I was stressed with classes. He would have been partly right. It was part class, part life. The act of living, making decisions—I didn't know how to handle it, not anymore. I didn't know how to be English.

I loved fashion. Enough, obviously, to send me to the English city of Portland. Enough to get my GED and attend the Art Institute. But in the process, I had severed family connections. I grieved over those losses every day. And now there was Will.

Will, who was unlike anyone I'd ever met. Will, who managed to be funny and serious in the same breath. Will, who was content in his small existence the same way my parents were content with theirs.

I knew that not every relationship lasted forever. Back home, I'd seen courting couples drift apart and marry other people. Before the drift, those couples probably couldn't imagine an existence without the other person. Was I naive to think Will and I were different? Silly to think that our short time together carried weight?

Somewhere in my heart, I hoped Will could ease the sense of loss I carried with me from day to day. I had no idea what the future held, but it had the possibility of us as our own family. Of starting over. Of wholeness instead of loss.

I knew Will loved me. I believed him when he said so. But he didn't want to leave Portland. I would not ask that of him. Even if I could, and he agreed, I hated the thought that he might regret it and resent me for the move later on.

Could I leave Portland without my family and without Will? Could I stay but resign myself to designing things I didn't have a heart for? The thoughts occupied my head as I rang up books, cut fabric, took notes in class, ate ice cream with Will, and bought a car.

I searched my head for solutions and found only heartbreak.

——

Friday morning I awoke with one thought clear in my head.
I could go home.

——

I tried to shake the thought, but it followed me through my first class.
"Sara?"

I froze and turned, seeing my instructor walking toward me, intercepting me before I could leave the room. "Yes?"

"Do you have a moment?"

"I do." I followed her to the front of the classroom.

"I have to tell you," she said after the last person had filed out, "I'm worried about you. Your creative work has been very promising, but after the last few weeks—Sara, you're at risk to not pass the class."

"Oh." I took a step back. My extra work, the extra effort…none of it mattered. "I hadn't realized."

"There are still finals to come. But I wanted you to realize the gravity of the situation. Please," she said, seeing the look on my face, "don't be discouraged. Your potential is enormous, and I don't think I'm speaking out of turn when I say that you have more raw talent than most of your contemporaries. But there is still work to be done."

I thanked her, nodded, and left the classroom.

—✶—

I went to work in a haze. Will noticed the moment I stepped into the shop. He put an arm around me and walked me to the back room, holding me close. "I love you, but you don't look good. What's going on?"

A stray tear spilled onto my cheek. I swiped it away. "Sorry. Bad morning. I'm not doing so well in class right now. There's just a lot going on."

I could go home.

"Is it me?" Will asked, his voice strained but strong. "Is it too much right now?"

"No, not at all." I met his eyes and cupped his face with my hands. "You're wonderful."

He bent down to kiss me. The sensation of him—his lips, his scent, his Will-ness, sent another tear streaking down my face.

Will caught it with his thumb. "Don't cry. Everything's going to be okay. What can I do?"

A third tear escaped despite my desperate attempts to blink it back. Will checked the storage shelves for Kleenex and, finding nothing, offered me his sleeve. I shook my head. "I don't want to get makeup on it."

He smiled. "I think I can deal with it."

I wiped.

"Is everything okay with your brother and Jayne?" Will probed.

I nodded.

"And the car's working out for you?"

"The car's fine." At least it was as far as I could tell. I'd only driven it twice.

"Zach and I can handle the store just fine today if you want to go home and work on your class projects," Will suggested. He stroked my face again. "Everything's going to be okay."

But it wasn't. It couldn't. And I couldn't tell him.

"Maybe that's a good idea," I said.

He squeezed my shoulders and then held my face in his hands. "It's going to be okay."

I wanted to weep but maintained control. "Okay."

"You going to Jayne's for movie night tonight? Can I come?"

"Sure. That would be…good."

"I know you've got a car now, but can I pick you up anyway?"

I nodded. "That would be nice. I—I love you."

"And I love you. Go home, get some work done. You'll feel better."

—☆—

I didn't feel better. But then I had come home only to sit on the couch and stare at the texture pattern in the wall. Why did English people spray texture onto their walls? It made no sense to me.

I could go home.

The apartment was quiet. Livy was at work.

I could go home.

The thought wouldn't leave me alone. Maybe it was because it was the only solution that made any sense.

If I stayed in Portland, I could have Will but potentially lose my career, my dream, and my family.

If I followed my career, I would lose Will and still be away from my family.

The whole point to leaving home, coming to Portland, and becoming English was to follow the hope that one day I might be able to work in fashion and sew without worrying about my creations being too "fancy."

If I really, truly followed through on that hope, I faced a future of loss. I couldn't choose between Will and my dreams, and I couldn't ask him to choose between me and his family, his career.

Oh, too many choices.

I would miss Sonnet and Meg, Britta and Zach. Jayne's friends and Jayne herself. But it wouldn't make up for my family, and they wouldn't likely be moving with me if I left for a larger city.

Nothing could be gained from staying. Whatever I chose meant that I lost a chunk of my heart, and I didn't want to have to choose which chunk. Staying meant failure and loss, no matter which way I looked at it. If I went home, at least I'd have my family.

I had to think this through. I couldn't be rash. If I went back to my parents' house, I couldn't predict how my father would react. My mother would be glad to see me. My siblings would be glad to see me. My father, though—I wasn't sure if I could face him. For a man who believed in peace, he could also be fearsome. I didn't know if I could stand up to his disapproval.

I knew I wouldn't just be going home. I would become Amish again. I would have to leave my sketchbooks and fabric behind, my jeans and tubes of lipstick.

I'd have to leave Will's books behind, the ones he'd given me after the wreck.

But even if I didn't have to leave them behind, I knew that keeping them wouldn't truly be an option. Any reminder might have the power to make me change my mind. If I went back, that would have to be it. There was no going halfway.

I dreaded the idea of my father's censure, but Rebecca...I could go to my sister Rebecca's home in Washington. I knew she cared about me—the letters had proved that. And I hadn't seen her or her family since my birthday gathering. The one I'd had before I left in the trunk of Jayne's car. I hoped Rebecca's husband wouldn't remember that much.

But I could stay with Rebecca and get my feet back under me. I could adjust to plain living again, to the simple rhythms of life that did not require difficult choices.

Should I pray? I wanted to pray. But it had been so long, I didn't know if God had forgotten me. Or if He remembered but wouldn't be inclined to answer because we hadn't talked for so long. I had to pray sometime though—I wasn't going to spend the rest of my life without prayer. I would pray this time, but I wouldn't expect an answer.

Guilt washed over me as I remembered my Christmas resolution to understand Jesus better. What reasons did I have? I was busy. Busy doing English things. Busy being fancy.

Lord, I'm sorry. I'm sorry I let myself be distracted with worldly things. I want to change. I need to change. Help me know what to do. Help me to have the strength, I prayed, before succumbing to bitter tears. I knew what I had to do, and I knew it would break my heart.

~~~※~~~

The packing didn't take long. I hadn't been at the apartment long enough to settle in deeply, and some of my things were still in open boxes.

I had moved so quickly that I was done by the time Livy came home from work.

"I have the next month's rent," I said, glad the second quilt had sold. "And I'll send my brother money to have the rest of my things removed shortly. I'm sorry—I'm sorry this couldn't work out."

"Life happens," Livy said. "I understand. If you want to store your things here for a few weeks, just in case…"

"No." I was firm. "Once I leave, I can't change my mind."

"Do you want me to send anything to another address?"

I considered this. "I can leave my sister's address with you. Levi has it as well. They do have a phone, but it's really only used for outgoing calls unless someone is close enough to the feed shed to hear it ring."

"I find all of this fascinating," Livy said, "so you can tell me to stop asking questions. I just figure I'm not likely to have another formerly Amish, soon-to-return roommate. Does Will know? About you leaving?"

My face froze. "I'll be telling him shortly," I said, though that wasn't exactly the truth. I planned on writing him a letter once I got to Rebecca's. Once I was far enough away that he couldn't change my mind for me.

I spent the evening as close to Will as possible, hoping to enjoy my last moments with him as much as I could. He didn't notice anything amiss when he picked me up, only that my eyes still looked worried.

We sat with his arm over my shoulders, my hand in his throughout the films. I tried to file away the memories—Gemma's giving nature, bringing yet another round of hors d'oeuvres and dessert bites to the hungry, uncultured masses. Kim's wise insights and smart-alecky comments. Joely's offbeat humor and the way she looked out for her friends.

And then there was Jayne, who had given me a chance and let me stay in her apartment, taking up space while I figured out who I was. I wished I could explain to her in person, but I would send her a letter.

I would send a letter to Levi as well. He, at least, would understand. At least I thought he would. He had made a life for himself, but we weren't as alike as I used to think. I wasn't as strong. I would miss him terribly though.

And Will? I couldn't think about it.

I made sure to give everyone a hug before we left, made sure to thank everyone for something. Even if it was just something small, like an extra thank-you to Joely for the flashlight, it was my way of thanking each one in person.

Will and I were quiet on the drive back. I rested my head on his shoulder, which in truth was quite uncomfortable, but I wanted to be near him while I could.

"Things will smooth out soon," he said, rubbing his thumb over my hand. "And spring break is coming. You'll have a break, some time to recharge. Maybe we'll hit the museum or something, if you're not tired of it."

"That sounds nice."

He walked me up the steps to the apartment. "I take it your roommate's home."

I nodded.

"I'll kiss you here, if you don't mind," he said with that half-smile of his that I loved.

The feel of his lips, the scent of his skin—I was almost undone. I wouldn't let myself cry. One tear, and it would all be over. He pushed my hair from my face. "See you tomorrow?"

I held him close and looked into his eyes. "I love you," I said. "I really do."

Will's smile broadened. "I know." He winked. "Sleep good. I love you too."

I stepped inside the door. From the peephole in the door, I could watch his descent down the stairs. I heard the car's engine start up and the sound of the tires on asphalt as he pulled out of the parking lot.

Tears pricked my eyes, but I dashed them away. I had things to do. I had a plan.

I needed to change clothes.

Chapter 35

I studied myself in the mirror.

My face was scrubbed clean of makeup. I wore my old dress, my heavy black shoes, and black stockings.

I pinned my short hair up as best I could under my kapp. The face that looked back at me was almost familiar, like an old friend who had been gone a long time but had changed during the journey.

There wasn't much time. I tucked away some extra paper and envelopes, though the most important letters were the ones I'd posted earlier in the day. I couldn't think too much about the hours ahead. I could only move forward.

~~~~

At 12:30 that night—or morning, I suppose—I climbed into my car to begin my drive to Rebecca's home.

It would be a long drive. Springdale was about 390 miles away. If I drove all night, I would arrive a couple hours into their morning. I didn't worry about staying awake. At the rate I was going, I probably wouldn't sleep for a week. Every time I closed my eyes, I saw Will. Or Levi. Or Jayne.

There was no room for second thoughts. With a heart full of resolve, I turned the key in the ignition and began the journey back. I wasn't going home. Not really. But maybe it would be close.

~~~~

The sky began to lighten around six that morning, turning a lovely shade of gray that made me rethink Jayne's bridesmaid dresses. Maybe pewter was too dark. The dove gray shade was so pretty, and would look nice contrast-ing with the flower embellishments I'd made...

I shook my head. Jayne and Levi would have a perfectly lovely wedding without my design assistance. If I wanted to be creative with fabric, it would have to be in quilts.

I hadn't visited Rebecca's home since my nephew, Henry, was born. I felt out of place behind the wheel of a car, but there was no help for it. Early blooming daffodils lined large sections of the gravel road in front of the house. I could see a head in the window.

I waved, hoping it was Rebecca, hoping she would be a little glad to see me. I parked the car by the family buggy before climbing out and approach-ing the door.

There wasn't time to knock—the door swung open while I was still feet away.

"Sara? Oh, goodness—how did you—come in!" Rebecca's hands flut-tered, one landing over her heart, the other over her abdomen.

If I wasn't mistaken, she looked to be five or so months pregnant.

I stepped through the portal only to be squeezed into a hug. "You've been missed!" She said, out of breath from surprise. "Where have you been? Have you been back home? Do our parents know you're here?"

"No, they don't know. I've only just left."

"I'm so relieved you've left! You don't know how I've worried about you in the city. You're so skinny! Come see Henry and Verna—they're so grown, I don't recognize them myself some days. And we've another coming in the late summer." She patted her belly again. "Did you bring anything with you? Are you staying a while?"

"If that's possible," I said carefully. "I would love to stay with you for a while. If that's okay with you."

Rebecca laughed. "I can do with another hand around the house these days, and I'm just glad to see your face. Of course you can stay. Karl's so busy with the farm these days. Henry is into everything, and since Verna's been walking, I feel I never know where she is. Babies are a blessing from God, but my goodness they can wear me out!"

"They're absolutely beautiful, though," I said.

"All children are lovely in God's eye."

"What can I do to help?" I asked, taking off my coat.

"Are you still handy with a needle? I'm very behind on the children's mending. Henry wears a new hole in his pants every day, it seems."

"I can do that." I gave her a hug. "It's good to see you, Bex."

She wrapped her arms around me. "I'm so glad you're back and safe! Have you eaten?"

"I'm not hungry, but thanks. Why don't I get started on the mending?"

I set myself up in the rocking chair, a pile of mending at my feet and a simple needle and thread between my fingers.

───※───

Karl seemed glad to see me, if only so that I might help his wife around the house. I was contented with that. Rebecca set me up in the guest bedroom, telling me I could stay as long as I wanted.

I closed my eyes that night to the sound of buggy wheels rolling by, creaking through the quiet—the sound of a young man in search of a young woman. I thought of Will. But then I tried not to think of Will or of everything I had left behind. Contentedness was a choice. This was my home now. There was no going back.

───※───

My first week at Rebecca's was a blur. If I tried to recall portions of it, all I found in my mind was a series of long, hardworking days followed by sleepless nights.

By the following Sunday, I tried to come back to life. I rose early with the family and helped the children dress for church. I regretted I didn't have a good dress to change into but reminded myself yet again that I was plain, and honoring God with my presence would have to be enough.

The worshippers gathered at the home of Rebecca's friend Lizzie Stutzman. I sat with Rebecca and little Verna on the women's side of the room, listening with an open heart to the sermon and eager to correct the worldliness that had taken root in my heart.

I listened, but upon leaving, felt...not the way I expected to feel. Perhaps I hadn't listened right.

───※───

The days felt long, and the nights stretched even longer. I continued to sleep poorly, my dreams full of memories. Christmas tree shopping with Jayne and Levi. Cupcakes with Sonnet, Britta, and Meg. Looking at yarns with Britta. Maybe I should have brought the yarn—the knitting might have helped to relax me. I thought about Zach and his *Godfather* jokes and Joely teaching me to drive. I thought about the *Godey's Lady's Book* volume at the bookstore and the unfinished sewing projects I'd left behind.

Sometimes the dreams mixed up my recollections. I knew that Jayne hadn't been at Meredith's birthday party. I knew Gemma didn't attend the Art Institute.

Other dreams were less memories than they were loose creative energy trying to find an outlet. After one dream about a pale pink gown with cream organza pleating, I woke up looking for a sketchbook to record the idea.

But my sketchbooks were in Portland and by now may very well have been discarded.

Would Levi throw my sketches away? I hated the thought of those drawings languishing in a compost heap. Would Gemma take care of them?

And then I remembered I wasn't supposed to be worrying about my sketches. I wasn't going to design English clothes anymore. I would sew good, simple clothes for my sister's family and one day my own.

Would I marry soon? I tried to picture my Amish husband. He would grow a beard after we married and wear shirts I had sewed for him. He would share my bed. We would raise a family together. Would I love him? Could I love someone the way I had loved Will? English, proud, stubborn, ill-tempered Will?

⚒︎

"I'm worried about you," Rebecca said on Thursday morning. At least I thought it was Thursday. The days seemed similar, only punctuated by different sets of chores and patterns of housework. "You've grown even paler, you're even skinnier than when you arrived, and your eyes look bruised. There is an excellent chiropractor in town. Do you think a visit would help?"

I frowned. "My back feels fine. I'm just adjusting to a new schedule. I kept different working hours when I lived in the city."

"Changing your hours is affecting your eating? You eat less than a bird these days."

"Oh," I searched for an excuse. "Changing my food has upset my stomach a little. I'll be better in a few days."

Rebecca did not look convinced. Instead of push the matter further, she suggested a stop in town for some fabric. Maybe a quilting project and fabric for new dresses of my own would lift my spirits or at least keep me busy while I adjusted.

I agreed—I could hardly disagree. Rebecca's prematernity dresses fit me well enough, but the sleeves required constant rolling to keep them from flopping over my hands and getting messy while I helped in the kitchen.

We drove the buggy into Spokane for the day. Rebecca was overly animated in an attempt to rouse my spirits, but I felt the sense of dread collecting from the soles of my shoes up as we approached town.

Fabric.

Fabric meant clothes. And clothes—clothes I found myself drawn to, clothes made out of a sense of creativity rather than necessity—were worldly and English. And my Amish sister was taking me into the center of temptation.

I tried. I picked a dull polyester fabric in a smoky blue, a fabric that wouldn't move well, but would hang like a dead fish.

Rebecca insisted on looking at quilting fabrics despite the fact that Henry complained of needing to use the bathroom and Verna began to cry as if she suddenly had started to cut a new tooth.

Rebecca browsed through the sunny florals, but I found myself in front of a bolt of cotton cloth the color the sky had been during my drive to Washington. Nearby, I found a shadowy gray cotton and a creamy ivory. A dark pewter rounded out the neutral palate of shades.

"Are you sure those are the ones you want?" Rebecca asked, trying to be delicate as she frowned at the piled bolts of fabric at the cutting table. "They're so...somber."

I shrugged. "I liked them together." And they matched my insides.

~~⁂~~

"She doesn't look so good," I overheard Karl say to Rebecca Friday evening. I sat on the living room floor, cutting pieces for my new dress while Rebecca served her husband a second slice of chocolate cake. "Are you sure she's not ill?"

"She's not sick, she's just adjusting. The English world was difficult for her," came Rebecca's hushed reply.

"Then why is she getting worse the longer she stays? Maybe you should write your mother. Or my mother," Karl suggested. "Something is wrong with her."

"She's my sister. Nothing is wrong with her," Rebecca said primly. "How is the cake?"

"*Gut*," Karl answered after a pause. "If she is not better by next week, you might think of taking her to the chiropractor. Or even a doctor. She looks like she might fall over."

"She will be fine," Rebecca insisted.

I continued cutting, unaware for the next fifteen minutes that I had cut out four sleeves.

※

On Saturday, I woke with a resolve to be better. Brighter. I would try to eat. I would spend time reading Scripture. I would enjoy the fact that here, I always knew what everyone was talking about. Even if I'd had access to Google, I wouldn't need it.

"I can make breakfast," I told Rebecca. "Do you want me to make pancakes? I can make eggs and cook up some sausage too."

"Oh, thank you," Rebecca said, her hand on her midsection. "I feel so ill this morning, I think cooking would make it worse. Do you mind if I go lay down?"

"Go ahead. I'll take care of things."

"Thank you so much. Let me know if you need something though, won't you?"

I promised I would and then set to work. Forty minutes later, there were steaming stacks of golden pancakes, bright yellow scrambled eggs with melted cheese on top, and browned, peppery sausage.

Karl led us in the traditional silent prayer before loading his plate with food. Rebecca and I each helped the children with their food. I broke the pancakes into manageable pieces for Verna to pick up.

I felt a rare smile spread across my face. Finally, I'd been able to do something right—make breakfast, feed children, and move on with the new version of my old life. It felt good to be plain. I could do this. I could be Amish again.

And then Karl coughed. Henry began to cry. And Verna let out a wail, using her little hands to brush pancake crumbs from her rosy little lips.

Rebecca leapt up. "What's wrong?"

"Tastes bad," Henry sobbed, spitting half-chewed food onto his plate. "*Bad*."

I sat up straighter. "What?"

Karl stood up calmly. "The pancakes," he said, lifting the pancake plate and removing it from the table. "They're bitter."

"They look fine." Rebecca cut a small bite for herself, chewed, and made a face. "They are bad. They taste like…baking soda."

My heart fell. "But…" I took my own bite, although I couldn't deny the four victims before me. Rebecca was right. They tasted strongly of baking soda. "I must have used the soda rather than the baking powder," I said. "I'm so sorry. Eat the bacon and eggs—those are hard to ruin. I'll make another batch of pancakes."

I headed into the kitchen before the tears fell onto my cheeks. I brushed them away as I began measuring the dry ingredients again. Stupid. There was no reason to cry over pancakes. Kitchen mistakes were a fact of life. It didn't mean anything.

I cracked new eggs into a bowl and tried to regain control. There was no reason to have such an emotional response from ruined pancakes. But as I mixed the milk and vanilla, I knew the truth. I wasn't crying over the pancakes.

Chapter 36

K arl took the ruined pancakes to the pigs.
     After cleaning the kitchen—and any evidence of the pancake mistake—I decided to get out of the house. I told Rebecca I was going to town,
saying that I could see if there was mail at the post office while I was at it. A
part of me wanted some time away to think. Another, more rebellious side
of me wanted to see if there was any mail for me.

The buggy felt so slow, and by the time I tied the horse up at the post
office, I wished I'd brought a cushion with me. At least when I'd ridden to
town, I'd had Bex and the kids to distract me. Now, alone, all I could think
about was how long it was taking and how much my rear hurt.

I knew the locals had to be a little accustomed to seeing the Amish in
town, but I still received some stares as I walked inside with the key to the
post office box.

Inside the box I found several envelopes and a soft, squishy package. I
flipped through the envelopes, finding that most were for Rebecca, except
for one—a letter from Levi addressed to me. I pulled that envelope out.

The package also had my name on it. I flipped it over and looked on the
back. No return address.

I wanted to rip both the package and the letter open and discover their
contents on the spot, but I made myself calm down, lock the box back up,
and exit the post office.

I didn't want to read my letter in the parking lot either. I untied the horse
and began the trip back, taking a bit of a detour off of Gill Way and onto
Hawk Haven just long enough to ensure complete privacy.

I read Levi's letter first.

Dear Sara,

I hope this letter finds you well. I just wanted you to know

*that I understand your desire to go back. No matter what you
decide, I hope we'll be able to continue to contact each other.*

*You are strong and smart, and if you decide that you want to
be Amish, I'm confident that you've made the right decision
for yourself. Jayne and I will miss you very much, but it's
important to both of us that you're where you're supposed to be.*

*Know that you're always welcome back. If there's one thing
I've learned, it's that it's never too late to make a change.*

*Give Bex and the kids hugs from me, and maybe pat Karl on
the back or something when he's not looking. Miss you tons,
but wish you the very best.*

Levi

When I finished reading, I folded the sheet of paper back up and tucked
it into the envelope.

The horse, Cocoa, shifted his hooves and snorted. I think he was getting
bored. I climbed out of the buggy to stand beside him and pat his neck.

"I miss them," I said, knowing the horse wouldn't divulge any secrets.
"I thought coming here meant I could be myself again, but I feel more lost
than ever."

Cocoa snorted. I gave him another pat on the neck and hoisted myself back
into the buggy, this time to discover what was in the padded package.

What I really needed was a pair of scissors, but after picking the tape off
with my fingernails—which were due for a trim—I managed to open the
envelope enough to dump the contents into my lap.

Recognition hit a split second later. I couldn't move, couldn't breathe.

In my lap were the socks. Will's socks. The cozy, comfy socks he'd lent
me after the car crash, the socks I'd pulled on my first night at the apartment, the socks he'd let me keep. The ones I'd left behind.

I hugged them close.

Nothing else was in the envelope. No letter, no note of explanation. I
didn't need one. The socks spoke loud and clear.

※

I led Cocoa back to the main road, my mind whirling.

I missed him. I missed Will, missed him so much I ached. All the time, I ached. And I kept hoping it would go away, that I would forget him and the stupid socks.

It wasn't even just Will. I missed my life. I missed my classes and learning and finding out new things. I missed sketching and sewing difficult things and using my imagination. I missed my friends from school, the first people I ever found who thought like me, who saw the world the same way I did.

Was it sin to be this way? Was it sin if God gave me these eyes? I didn't know what to do, but I was so tired of trying to figure it out. No matter what I did, I seemed to hurt myself and everyone around me.

I came back to the Amish to get away from the busy English life, only to find I was just as busy as ever. Maybe it wasn't about being too busy for God and more about making time for Him.

So many questions. So many gigantic questions. Who did God create me to be? Was I being disobedient by being English? By being Amish? Did being obedient to God mean living in Portland? Or New York? Would He call me to such a place?

Had I behaved like Jonah, running all the way to Joppa when I needed to be in Nineveh? Maybe my Nineveh was New York. Maybe it was designing street wear. Either way, I knew now in my heart that I had run.

I hugged my arms to myself. *Lord, tell me where to go. Tell me who to be.*

No words answered mine. I waited, holding still, ignoring the brisk breeze that pulled on my sleeves and brought a chill to my arms.

No words. Only a sliver of understanding. It was time to stop running. I needed to go back. I just didn't know what to go back to.

"What—what happened?" Rebecca asked the moment she saw me.

I handed her the stack of envelopes with her name on it. "These are yours."

"Sara, please talk to me. Come to the kitchen. You've hardly eaten anything in a week."

"I'm not hungry."

"Sara," Rebecca's voice grew stern. "You *must* eat. There is still chocolate cake—would you eat that?"

She cut me a slice before I could respond.

The house was quiet. I looked around. "Where are Henry and Verna?"

"Asleep. Karl is in the barn." She pushed the slice of cake toward me. A fork followed. "Please, Sara, please eat."

I reached for the fork. Could I eat? I wasn't sure. Rebecca was right. I probably needed to eat sometime. But did I have to eat now? My stomach was so unsettled, I wasn't sure what would happen if I put food into it. But I had a hunch it would get ugly with my sister if I didn't at least try. I pushed the fork through the cake and lifted it to my mouth.

Rebecca watched as I chewed and swallowed.

"Everything is okay," I said, trying to reassure her with another bite of cake.

"No, it's not okay." She sat at the table across from me. "It's not okay that my little sister is hardly eating and hardly sleeping. Are you sick? And what happened in town?"

There was no use in being anything but honest. "I had two pieces of mail in your box. One was a letter from Levi—" I held up a hand as I watched her tense. "Telling me that he hoped I was well and he respected my decision to come here."

"Oh," she said, relaxing. "That was kind of him."

"It was. He's a good man, our oldest brother. He leads a good, honorable life with the English."

She gave a soft smile. "He was always a good boy. You said you received two pieces of mail? What was the other?"

I took a deep breath. "A pair of socks."

Rebecca frowned. "Socks?"

Without quite intending to, I told her the story of the socks. But to tell it right, I had to start at the beginning, at the bookshop with Will. I was sobbing by the end.

Rebecca came around to my side of the table and hugged my shaking shoulders. "Shh. You were always different. I'll bet no one ever told you that. When you were little, you were so upset if your doll's clothes became dirty. You always chose the brightest, most colorful fabrics for your clothes, and when clothes were made for you, you wore the most colorful ones." She patted my head. "Don't tell the bishop I said this, but maybe you aren't supposed to be Amish. I don't understand the ways of God—they are mysterious to me. But I've watched you grow thinner and thinner in just a few days, and if being Amish means you wasting away, I don't want you to stay."

I shrugged. "I don't know what to do. If I went back—" I shook my head. "I know I've hurt a lot of people."

"You can make things right. You're strong."

"I miss my family when I'm gone."

"And we miss you. But we want you to be healthy and happy." She tapped my plate. "Another bite, please."

Under Rebecca's eye I managed more dinner than usual that night, as well as a heaping bowl of ice cream.

Sleep came quickly that night. I awoke in the morning knowing I'd had dreams but not able to remember them.

I dressed for church in my new dress, the blue dead-fish dress.

The adults were quiet throughout the drive to the morning church service, but Henry filled the silence with a running commentary on the cows as we drove along.

Rebecca and I sat next to each other during the service as we had the previous week. Only this week, there was a difference. This week, I knew I didn't belong.

I looked like I belonged. My clothes fit in. I wore my kapp, and not a single bit of makeup had touched my face. But my heart was different. God had called me to something else. A different life. A different way of worship.

A different love.

I squeezed Rebecca's hand. She squeezed back and then patted my hand. I looked up to see her blinking away a tear. She knew. We both did. I needed to go home.

I gave the children hugs before I left, taking a moment to tickle Henry's tummy and smell little Verna's sweet head.

Rebecca clasped me in a warm embrace. "Drive safe. Write to me when you are back so I know you've arrived well. Tell Levi hello for us. And Jayne as well. Think of that—an English sister-in-law."

Karl cleared his throat. "Come visit us after the babe's been born. I'm sure Rebecca would enjoy that."

"I'd love to," I said, deciding not to embarrass my brother-in-law with a hug.

I continued to wave goodbye as I drove down the long gravel driveway, continued until I could see the house no longer.

※

I drove to Levi's house first but continued driving when I didn't see his truck in the driveway.

A few miles later, I found it in the parking lot of Jayne's apartment.

I pulled my car in next to it and turned off the ignition. Here I was. What would I say?

I didn't have time to sit and figure it out. With a deep breath, I climbed the familiar stairs to Jayne's door and knocked.

I heard footsteps on the other side and the bolt sliding back. There was my brother and Jayne just behind him.

I think the neighbors heard the joyful shouts.

hung on to your things," Levi said as Jayne rooted through her refrigerator, pulling out and reheating everything not past its expiration date in an effort to feed me. "It's all in my garage. And I could be wrong, but last I heard from Gemma, I don't think Livy's found another roommate yet."

I shook my head. "I'll figure that out later. There are other things I need to do first. I'm really glad you kept my sketchbooks though."

"You're welcome."

I started to run my hand through my hair but stopped at the kapp. Without wasting another moment, I yanked it and the pins from my hair, giving my head a shake. "Oh, that feels better."

"You're welcome to stay here until you figure out where you want to be," Jayne said. "Obviously your bed's not here, but I've got a couch."

"My place is open too," Levi said.

Jayne put a hand on her hip. "My closet is more fun to raid."

I shrugged. "She's got a point."

———※———

In the end, Levi left to bring over some of my things. I took a hot shower, dried myself with one of Jayne's miraculously fluffy towels—I'd forgotten about the joys of English towels—and pulled on some of Jayne's clothes.

"Glad to have you back," Jayne said when I emerged. "Levi was pretty worried, although he was trying not to. Are you okay? You look—"

"I look awful," I said flatly. It was true. Now that I was back in a home with a mirror, I understood Rebecca's concerns. My eyes were dark hollows, my skin gray and dull. In the two weeks I'd been gone, I'd lost a noticeable amount of weight.

"To be honest, I'm amazed you drove here safely. Let me put another pot of tea on—my guess is you're dehydrated as well."

I opened my mouth to argue but thought better of it. "You're probably right."

"I'll make some chamomile. I found a new blend I really like." A few moments later, the kettle had begun to whistle, and Jayne had poured us both tall mugs of tea, sweetened lightly with honey.

I held my mug with both hands. "I need to see Will."

"Have you heard anything from him?"

I told her about the socks.

"Powerful socks," Jayne commented. "You love him, don't you."

I nodded, miserable.

"If you want to go see him, I'm not stopping you. I'll be here later, and so will Levi."

"Levi—"

"He'll understand." She gave a short laugh. "Believe me, he'll understand."

"But Will—what if he…"

Jayne rested her tea on the countertop. "You won't know until you ask."

⸻

I left Jayne's apartment with damp hair, borrowed clothes, and no trace of makeup, but I didn't care. I climbed into my car and started off in the direction of the shop.

The trouble was, I wasn't entirely sure how to get to Will, assuming he was home. I'd left my key to the shop behind when I left my apartment. I couldn't get to Will's door without getting into the back of the shop first.

I tried to call him on the way, but every call went to his voicemail. What if he was ignoring my calls? My stomach twisted, but I drove to the shop just the same. I had to apologize. I owed him that.

After calling, I realized I had voicemail on my phone. I dialed in and listened to the messages.

There was a message from Britta calling to check on me since I'd missed class and a message from Sonnet saying she'd gotten my letter and wished me the best. Several blank messages followed.

The last message was from Zach. "Hey Sara. Hope you're good in Amish

land. You might want to come back, though. Will's all depressed and playing Guitar Hero, like, three hours at a time. It's kind of freaking me out.
Thought you'd want to know. About Will, not me freaking out. See ya."

I really didn't know what to make of that.

I parked in my usual spot in the alley lot behind the shop. From my seat
inside the car, I could see a light on in Will's apartment.

So he was home.

I tried the phone again. No answer.

I looked around. A pile of concrete rubble rested against the opposite
building. I sifted through briefly until I found a piece small enough not to
do any damage. Serious damage, at least.

With an unpracticed arm, I aimed for Will's window. The bit of concrete
clinked against the window and fell to the ground.

Nothing.

Listening, I realized there was a definite bass line coming from above.
Was Will listening to music? Was he having a party?

Determined to be heard, I found a slightly larger piece of concrete and
lobbed it toward the window. A split second before the rock hit, the music
paused. The rock met with the window with a louder clink than before.

I waited.

Nothing. My muscles tensed in frustration.

I chose a bigger piece, not noticing that the music had ceased. I threw
the piece at his window…maybe a little harder than I should have.

Rather than bouncing off as the other pieces had, this one seemed to
have gone through. As in, broken through. Oops.

The next thing I knew, the apartment lights brightened, and Will's head
appeared in the window. I felt myself freeze in place.

Will lifted the unbroken section of the window. "Hey! What's—"

The second he saw me, the words died on his lips.

"I didn't mean to," I called up. "I'm sorry about your window."

And then he left. I crossed my arms and waited.

The back door to the store opened with a whoosh to reveal Will. My heart
stopped, just looking at him. He stood stiffly in the doorway, arm braced
against the frame. "What are you doing back here, trying to get mugged?"

"I don't have my key."

"That was stupid."

"I know." I tried to read his expression. "Can I come up?"

"If you want."

I reached into my car, retrieved the jacket with my wallet, and turned off the headlights. "I want."

I met him in the entryway. He closed the door after us, barely pausing before turning and going up the stairs. I followed him up to the apartment.

The open door revealed a plastic guitar-looking thing on the floor in front of the TV. Stacks of dishes and glasses littered the sink, as well as several old takeout boxes.

Inside the apartment, I got a better look at Will. He was even scruffier than usual. My guess was that he hadn't shaved for at least a week. His eyes were about as dark and hollow as mine. He wore one of his oldest rugby shirts. His jeans had seen better days.

He was a mess. Just like me.

"So?" he asked. "What's up?"

"I, um," I fiddled with my fingers. "I'm back."

"Huh." He walked to the kitchen and poured himself a glass of water from the fridge. "For how long?"

"I don't know what will happen after I graduate from the design program, but until then, I'm here to stay." I cleared my throat. "Thank you for the socks."

He seemed to soften around the edges a little. "I thought you should have them. Levi found them in your things."

"I liked getting them. It—it was sweet. I wanted to come and tell you that I'm sorry I left like that. I'm—I'm sorry."

"Why are you back?"

"Because I couldn't stay," said, steadying myself with one of the kitchen chairs. "I finally realized that everything I really wanted in my life were things I couldn't have and be Amish at the same time. I wanted to be creative with fabric, to learn new things. I wanted to worship a God who encourages creativity in His children. And I—I realized I couldn't be without you."

"So why'd you leave?" His voice sounded hurt. "You said in your letter that it was about your family. It was something else, wasn't it."

"Can we sit down?" I shot a longing glance at the couch.

"Knock yourself out."

I cleared away several days' worth of newspaper to make a spot for myself. After a moment, Will perched himself on the opposite end.

"It's true that I missed my family," I said slowly. "But I also thought that not being here was for the best."

"Why?" Will's voice was husky.

"If I continue with the fashion program and do the work I want to do, I can't stay here. If I want to work, I have to be in a larger city, in New York or L.A. And I love you with my whole, whole heart, but your family is here. Your life is here. I can't ask you to leave your family the way I did mine."

"But—"

I held out a hand. "I need to finish. I was so distracted with everything going on, I wasn't doing well in my classes. I felt like I was failing at everything and missing my family through it all. If I couldn't have you, and I couldn't have my family, there was no reason to stay in this place where I hardly know what's going on half the time." I shook my head as I felt my eyes grow watery. "So I ran away. It wasn't right, and I shouldn't have, and I'm sorry. I'm so, so sorry."

An instant later Will closed the distance between us and gathered me in his arms. "It's okay."

"No, it's not okay!" I pulled myself away. "It's not okay at all! I should have talked, should have communicated."

"Shh." He pulled me close again, stroking my hair as I rested my head on his chest. "Sure, I like living in Portland. I like my job. I like not being far from my family, even though they're all loony. But I love you. And if being with you means moving away from Portland, fine."

"You'd resent me," I said, my voice ragged.

"Sara, listen to me—" He tipped my chin so I could see his eyes. "I love you. Do you hear me when I say that? If there's anything I've learned this week, I've learned that I really don't like living without you."

"Me too," I said with a hiccup. "Can we—can we be together again? Can we love each other again? Because you're my home, Will. I hated being away from you."

"I hated it too. You know what I think?" he asked, sitting up and pulling me away so I could face him.

"What?"

"I think we should get married."

I couldn't have been more shocked if he suggested that we join the circus. "What!"

"Think about it. I love you. You love me. Right?"

"Right."

"We tried being apart, and that didn't work very well."

"No, it didn't."

"And you're gorgeous, but you look like a cholera patient right now."

"You're so sweet," I said dryly.

"And I'm a train wreck myself. We tried being apart, it didn't work. Another week, and I probably would have needed to be institutionalized."

"Zach left a message on my phone saying you'd been playing something called Guitar Hero for hours every day. What is that?"

Will looked sheepish. "It's a video game." He nodded toward the plastic guitar object on the floor. "It…I…it wasn't a good time for me."

"I started a gray quilt when I was at my sister's."

"Interesting. He stroked my cheek with his thumb. "Look. I'm good at what I do. I've had offers from university libraries in the past. I can work wherever, live wherever, just as long as you're with me."

"I'd design sports shoes," I said, nose wrinkled, "if it meant I could be with you."

"You should see the way your face is scrunched up." Will tapped the end of my nose. "I would never ask you to design sneakers. Like I said, we're kind of a mess without each other. I want to be your husband. I want you to be my wife. I don't want us to be apart any longer than necessary."

"But—we've only known each other, what, three months?"

"Do you think waiting would change how we felt about each other?"

I thought about it. "No."

"Do you think that, even if we weren't in love with each other, we'd still want to spend time with each other, just talking?"

"Probably. Yes."

"I know I would. I love you, Sara. The way I see it, marriage is two people committed to loving each other and working together through conflict. I want to work together with you. Only you." He shrugged. "We could live here together while you finish school. You'd be close to classes—"

"Close to work," I pointed out.

"True. And we'd be together."

I looked at him. "You really want to marry me?"

"I do."

I tilted my head. "I always thought I'd marry an Amish farmer."

"I'm sorry I'm not an Amish farmer," he said, although he didn't look sorry at all.

"No, you're a former figure skater. You do smell better though."

"Thanks."

"I thought English guys asked on their knees or something," I asked, an eyebrow raised.

"You want me to get down on my knee?" He knelt beside me on the couch, took my hand, and lifted it to his lips. "I love you, Sara Burkholder. I think I started falling for you the morning you showed up for work with your short hair, ready to conquer the world. I can't imagine life without you. Will you marry me?"

"Yes." I couldn't contain my smile.

We looked at each other, stupid grins plastered across our faces.

Will stood, reaching his hand out to pull me up. I took it and faced him, our noses inches apart. He cupped my face and drew me into a long, gentle, winsome kiss. "Thank you for coming back," he said, breathless.

"You're welcome," I answered, before giving an impish smile. "So—if I'm going to live here—we probably should do something about the broken window sometime."

Laughing, we looked for a broom together.

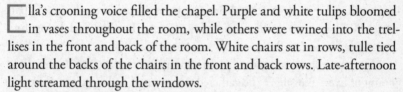

Ella's crooning voice filled the chapel. Purple and white tulips bloomed in vases throughout the room, while others were twined into the trellises in the front and back of the room. White chairs sat in rows, tulle tied around the backs of the chairs in the front and back rows. Late-afternoon light streamed through the windows.

"How does it look?" Jayne tugged at her white gown.

"It's perfect. Stop fussing with your dress. It fits perfectly," I said. "I did the fittings, I should know."

"You're so bossy."

"Do you have your bouquet?"

"Beth's got it. She won't let me hold it until we line up. You'd really think someone with a five-year-old would be easier to distract, but she's like a wolf or something."

"I think it's a firstborn thing." I moved a stray piece of hair from my face. "Does my makeup look okay?"

"You look like an angel. Well, if angels wear pewter gray, strapless dresses. Which I don't think they do. You look lovely, though."

There was no time to bask in the loveliness. Gary, Beth's husband, seated Jayne's mother. When he returned, Beth took it upon herself to organize the wedding party—all five of us, not counting Jayne and Levi—handed us our bouquets, and lined us up behind the double doors to the side of the chapel. Will took my arm, and Gary took Beth's. Jayne's young niece, Emilee, wearing a frilly white dress and carrying a basket of flowers, started down the aisle first, following her mother's directions to walk toward Levi.

Three minutes later, Gary led Beth down the white-carpeted aisle. The crowd chuckled when Emilee, seeing her parents, gave an exuberant wave.

Will kissed my cheek. "You look pretty," he said, smiling into my eyes.

"Thank you." I turned to stand in his arms. "I like your suit."

He straightened, broadening his shoulders. "Glad you like it."

"You're handsome. Though I have to say I'm not used to seeing you clean-shaven."

Jayne poked me in the back. "Hey—I want to get married today. Start moving!"

With a laugh, Will and I passed through the doors, under the first trellis, and down the aisle. I looked ahead to see my brother standing at the front next to the minister looking proud, handsome, and a touch nervous.

As Will and I walked forward, I could see Gary walking to the back of the chapel, having deposited Beth up front. When it came time to part ways, Will squeezed my hand and winked at me. I smiled back before finding my place next to Beth.

The music changed again, this time to a piano rendition of "Come Thou Fount of Every Blessing." The gathered guests stood and faced the door, waiting. A moment later Jayne emerged on Gary's arm, glowing.

I could tell the instant Levi saw his bride—his demeanor changed. His shoulders relaxed, his smile broadened. They would be so happy.

The ceremony passed in a whirl of lit candles, spoken vows, and heartfelt words. I looked at the familiar faces in the crowd—Gemma, Joely, and Kim sat near the front. Jayne's boss, Sol, was in attendance with his wife, as well as Levi's friends and former coworkers, Grady and Spencer.

Zach sat near the back, no doubt looking forward to the reception at DiGrassi & Elle. Britta, Meg, and Sonnet were seated nearby. Next to them sat an elderly lady Jayne had introduced to me as her former Sunday school teacher, Miss Lynnie.

Will's parents sat in the very back, as well as Will's brother Carter and his girlfriend, Allison. I knew Meredith was particularly excited not only to have the opportunity to see her son in a tailored suit but also to meet Gemma's parents, the restaurateurs, during the reception.

Livy had come as well. She hadn't minded in the slightest that I had moved back in with Jayne because her then-boyfriend Clay had proposed, and they began to make concrete plans for going overseas together. She had decided to downsize into an even tinier but much cheaper apartment. If she was happy, I was happy.

In the month and a half since my trip to Rebecca's, I found myself with a sense of renewal in everything I did. My instructors had all agreed to give me incompletes in my classes. I caught up in all of them during spring break and received high marks for my work.

Never in my life had I felt so strongly that I was where I was supposed to be. I loved my classes, loved my friends, loved my job. Though truly, I loved Will most. And I finally understood God's journey for me in this season. It wasn't the journey I'd ever thought I'd be on, but it was beautiful.

The sight of a familiar head distracted me from my thoughts.

My heart stopped. It wasn't just one person, but two. My mother and grandmother sat in the very back, wearing their Sunday best, tears shimmering in their eyes as they watched Levi and Jayne take their first communion as a couple.

Will noticed my sudden attention shift and caught my eye. I gave a slight shake of my head—there was no good way to infer that my mother, whom I hadn't seen in nearly a year, sat in the back.

Here I was, standing in a strapless, knee-length dress that was arguably the least clothing my mother had seen me in since I was baby. She had to have seen me. What did she think? Would she still love me, even if I was English now?

I knew that no matter what, I was loved by God, and I was loved by Will. But a piece of me still wanted my mom's approval. Could I live with it if she refused to give me that approval? Yes. It just wouldn't be my first choice.

I tore my attention away from the back of the room during the final prayer. Jayne and Levi held hands and stood close together, foreheads touching. It was beautiful.

My heart fluttered in nervous anticipation as the minister declared them man and wife and invited Levi to kiss his bride. Levi took Jayne into his arms and kissed her like the gift she was.

Shutters snapped. Flashes flashed. With triumphant grins, they marched back down the aisle together, hand in hand. Will and I followed.

He leaned over to kiss me as we passed under the back trellis. "See you in a couple minutes?"

I nodded, breathless. He winked.

I squeezed his hand goodbye and followed in Jayne's footsteps back to the bridal dressing room.

"Are you ready, Sara?" Jayne asked, her eyes shining, a crazy smile plastered on her face.

"I am," I said.

Meg, Sonnet, and Britta filed in seconds later, with Beth on their heels.

Beth gasped when Jayne started to unzip her wedding gown. "What do you think you're doing? We're taking more pictures—you need your wedding dress on for wedding pictures. And the reception. Didn't you get the memo?"

"Don't worry, we'll take pictures," Jayne said, stepping out of her dress. "Hurry up, Sara, I'm half-naked over here."

"Just a second," Meg said as she finished unlacing the back of my pewter bridesmaid's dress. I shimmied out the second the ties were loose enough and then handed the dress to Jayne. "There you go."

Sonnet unzipped the garment bag that hung by itself in the closet. "We really should get class credit for this, you know."

"Totally," Britta agreed.

Beth stuck her hands on her hips. "What is going on here?"

"I'm getting married," I said, stepping into the white silk shantung dress with Sonnet's help. "Surprise!"

"For the next few moments," Jayne explained, taking advantage of her sister's rare moment of silence, "Sara and Will's friend Zach is going to play a lovely piece on the piano."

"Who knew he played the piano?" Britta said, placing my white heels on the floor in front of me.

"When he's finished," Jayne continued, "the minister will sweetly ask everyone to pick up their chair and rotate it by 180 degrees."

Understanding dawned in Beth's eyes. "That's why you insisted on the second trellis."

"And the rented chairs. Pews are a little tricky to flip like that. Can you lace me up, Sis, be a pal? You know, I really wanted to choose bridesmaid dresses that could be worn again. I just didn't think I'd be the one wearing it."

"The lace-up back was genius," Sonnet said. "A nice panel-inset for modesty, lacing for fit. The white accents are perfect too. You're going to go far, Sara."

"You should speak." I said, looking at myself in the mirror. "I just tweaked an existing piece. This dress is amazing."

Meg and Sonnet had designed and made my dress together—a knee-length strapless sheath with ruche along the bodice that was asymmetrical from the hip down. An origami-like detail fanned out from my waist, adding a three-dimensional aspect that I loved.

Britta helped me into the shrug that she'd made, an airy mohair and silk confection with tiny capped sleeves. The look was complete with a freshwater pearl choker, matching drop earrings, and a small net blusher veil that made me feel like Grace Kelly.

A knocked sounded at the door. "It's me," Levi called through the door. "Everybody ready?"

"Come in!" I called.

"The chairs have flipped. Only one vase got knocked over." Levi stopped when he saw me. "I'm so proud of you, Sara. You make a beautiful bride."

"Hi, honey." Jayne closed the distance between herself and her new husband, planted a kiss on his lips, and then wiped the trace of shimmery lip gloss from his mouth. "You make a handsome groom. And groomsman."

I hugged them both. "Thank you both. Thank you for sharing your day with us."

"Are you kidding?" Jayne wrapped her arm around me. "I'm loving this. Beth was speechless. Talk about a perfect wedding gift."

"Hey!" Beth stuck a hand on her hip, but I could tell from her smile she wasn't offended.

I looked at Levi. "I saw Mom and Grandma in the audience earlier."

"I hope you don't mind the surprise. We weren't sure until they arrived if they'd be able to make it or not," he said. "But I knew they desperately wanted to be here for our day."

"They know?"

He nodded.

"Speaking of," Beth asked, breaking the moment, "who all knew about this?"

"Aside from my Mom and Grandma," Levi's eyes twinkled, "just the four of us, as well as Sara's couturiers. And the minister."

"Not even Zach?" Meg asked.

I shook my head. "No. He only knew that he was being asked to play some nice music. Surprises are good for him. Keeps him young."

"There might be something with your name on it," Levi said, pointing across the room.

I followed the direction of his finger. Sure enough, there was a wrapped package on the dresser against the wall that hadn't been there before. I walked and read the tag.

To: Sara

From: Your favorite bookstore coworker.

Open before the ceremony.

I smiled as I carefully removed the wrapping paper. Underneath, I found a wood box with a hinged lid. With anticipation, I lifted the lid. And gasped.

Nestled in the silken lining lay the *Godey's Lady's Book.* I set the box down back onto the dresser and lifted the front cover to look at the illustration near the front. "It's wonderful," I said. "Breathtaking, even."

"We should probably start," Levi suggested. "Crowd's getting restless."

"Your bouquet!" Sonnet pressed the gathering of white camellias into my hands.

Beth and my friends filed out of the dressing room to retake their seats.

I took Levi's arm and waited behind the doors as Jayne reentered the chapel by herself, this time dressed as a bridesmaid. I heard the stifled gasp from the audience and giggled.

Levi squeezed my elbow. "Are you ready, Sara?"

"Absolutely," I answered, feeling more calm than I had for a week.

Will's eyes lit up the second he saw me. His brother stood next to him, looking confused and bewildered.

Those confused and bewildered expressions were echoed in Kip and Meredith's eyes, but I saw smiles on their faces as well. As for my mother's face—I was afraid to look. What if she looked unhappy—would it ruin the day?

Another look at Will told me no, it wouldn't. The way his eyes looked at me, nothing could shake the joy that wrapped around my heart. From this day forward, he would be my family.

After an eternity, Levi and I made the twelve-foot voyage from the door to my place beneath the trellis, next to Will. Levi gave me away with a hug and took a seat next to our mother, clasping her hand in his.

I caught the expression on her face—it almost rivaled mine for happiness.

The minister led us in a word—several, actually—of prayer. We had planned the ceremony to be short and sweet because neither Will nor I were the sort of people who enjoyed being the center of attention. Will recited the vows he had written for me while I held his hands in mine. "I love you

Sara," he said at the end, his voice unwavering. "I am so humbled that you love me and that God has enabled us to experience this life together."

I recited my vows to him, my heart full. Here we were. Getting married. From traveling in the back of Jayne's car to Portland, to standing with Jayne beside me as I married an English man—what a journey. What a crazy journey.

And I wouldn't have it any other way.

Before I knew it, we had lit candles and taken communion together, and the minister pronounced us man and wife.

Will lifted my veil with one hand and cupped my face with the other. Cheers erupted when he kissed me.

I blushed but couldn't contain my grin.

The moments after the ceremony were a blur. Instead of walking back out of the chapel together, Will and I stayed to greet our parents.

Kip and Meredith met us first. "What a surprise, what a wonderful surprise!" Meredith wrapped her arms around me. "Welcome to the family, Sara. We couldn't be happier."

"Though if we'd known, we might have brought a gift," Kip said dryly.

"And I would have worn a different tie." Carter extended his hand to Will. "Congratulations, bro."

After another round of hugs from Will's family, I pulled my new husband away so he could meet my mother and grandmother.

"I'm honored to meet you, Mrs. Burkholder," Will said formally.

My mother patted his hand. "I'm so, so very blessed to meet you," she said, her eyes bright yet damp with tears. Her gaze fell on me. "You are the most beautiful bride." Before I knew it, she had pulled me into her warm embrace. "I'm so proud of you," she whispered.

I couldn't cry. Not now. Not today. "I miss you."

"I miss you too." She pulled back and looked into my eyes. "I pray it will not always be this way, though."

"Dad?"

"His heart has experienced many changes. Give him time. Know that we love you"—she grasped Will's hand—"both of you, very much."

Grandma pulled me into a hug next. "Oh, my sweet girl." She winked and lowered her voice. "Fancy suits you. Come visit me soon. Bring your young man with you."

"Can you come to the reception?" I asked them both, hopeful.

They exchanged glances. "We need to get back on the road soon," my mother said. "But have a wonderful time."

I nodded. "I understand."

From the corner of my eye I saw Jayne return to the chapel, dressed in her wedding gown again. "I'm sure you want to see Levi and Jayne." I hugged my grandma and then my mom again. "I love you," I said. "Give everyone hugs for me."

"I will." She patted my cheek. "Now go. Have a wonderful time."

Will put his arm around me as we made our way through the crowd. "Your mom was here. She saw you get married."

I nodded, unable to speak.

"I love you, Mrs. Blythe."

I looked up at him. "I love you, Mr. Blythe." I smiled up at him. "Thank you for the book."

"You're welcome." He squeezed my hand. "Thank you for the wristwatch. Are you ready to go to the reception? I hear there's a tower of cupcakes waiting for us."

"I'd love to." I rested my head on his shoulder.

It was good to be home.

Discussion Questions

1. Sara makes clear in the opening chapters that she isn't ready to visit any of her family from back home, even her grandmother. Do you think she did the right thing?

2. We know that Jayne loves Levi. Why do you think she is reluctant to set a date for their wedding?

3. Sara and Will do not get along when they first meet. Have you initially disliked someone who eventually became a good friend?

4. What character in *Simply Sara* do you identify with most? Why?

5. In many ways, seeing the *Godey's Lady's Book* was a launching point for Sara. What books or objects have inspired you?

6. Will and Sara's relationship changes during the Christmas season. Did your opinion of him change? How so?

7. Sara's desire to move out is rooted in a need for independence, but she finds an apartment with the help of others. When have you had to rely on other people's assistance?

8. Jayne observes that the Amish help people stay in one place, while the English help people move away. What do you think about that statement?

9. At Rebecca's, Sara concludes, "Maybe it wasn't about being too busy for God, and more about making time for Him." How might that be true in your life?

10. The end of *Simply Sara* took me by surprise. How did you feel about it?

Fastnacht Kuecheles

(pronounced like "fas not keek gells")

Sara's decision to make *fastnacht kuecheles* was the result of a recipe contest Harvest House Publishers offered on www.amishreader.com. Rhonda Bergsten sent in the winning recipe and added this note:

> *This German recipe has been in our family for years. It was always made during the Lenten season. When I was a little girl, I watched my German grandma make this recipe every year on Shrove Tuesday (or what some might call Mardi Gras Tuesday), the day before the beginning of Lent. I was always amazed when I watched these little "cakes" fry in the hot oil. The sugar coating and the nutmeg in the batter made these a special family treat each spring. They became a fast favorite in my very own family years later.*

Ingredients:
1 package active dry yeast (2¼ teaspoons)
¼ cup lukewarm water
1 tablespoon sugar
4 tablespoons butter (¼ cup)
⅜ cup sugar (6 tablespoons)
1 teaspoon salt
1 cup milk, scalded and cooled
1 teaspoon nutmeg
1 egg, beaten
4–5 cups flour
Oil for frying (such as vegetable oil)

In a small mixing bowl, mix together the yeast, water, and 1 tablespoon of sugar. Set mixture aside to begin to rise.

In a large mixing bowl, cream together the butter and ⅜ cup sugar. Then add the salt, milk, nutmeg, and egg.

Now, add the yeast and water mixture to the butter/sugar mixture. Continue to add 4–5 cups flour—enough to make a soft dough.

Cover the bowl and let dough rise until doubled in size (approximately 1 hour). When doubled, take the dough out and place on a floured board. Roll out the dough until it is ½ inch thick. Cut into round shapes. Gently pull the dough so the center of each circle is much thinner than the outer edges.

Place each round on a floured surface and cover with a cloth. Let rise for 30 more minutes while you get the oil ready to fry.

Heat oil to 375 degrees in a deep frying pan. Fry a few of the rounds at a time in the hot oil, turning each when golden brown. Then remove and allow to drain on brown paper bags (that is what grandma always used to do). Dip each one in granulated sugar when ready to eat.

About the Author

Hillary Manton Lodge is a graduate of the University of Oregon School of Journalism and the author of the bestselling book *Plain Jayne*. When not working on her next novel, Hillary enjoys photography, art films, and discovering new restaurants. She and her husband, Danny, live in the Pacific Northwest.

Check out Hillary's website at
hillarymantonlodge.com

"Smart, fast-paced and chock-full of endearing characters...a keeper, plain and simple."
—*Publishers Weekly*

Plain *Jayne*

HILLARY MANTON LODGE

Jayne Tate loves her life as it is—living in a big city, working as a reporter for a fast-paced newspaper, and dating a guy who knows nothing about her past. But when she looks for a story in an Amish community and meets the mysterious Levi Burkholder, she begins to wonder...

Where does God fit in all of this? And what's a green tea-drinking, laptop-using, motorcycle-riding reporter to do when a little Plain living starts to change her?

More Great Amish Books from
Harvest House Publishers...

The Homestyle Amish Kitchen Cookbook
Georgia Varozza

Straight from the heart of Amish life, this indispensable guide to hearty, home-cooked meals is filled with hundreds of recipes for favorites such as Scrapple, Amish Friendship Bread, Potato Rivvel Soup, Snitz Pie, and Graham "Nuts" Cereal. "Amish Kitchen Wisdom" sections highlight fascinating tidbits about the Plain lifestyle.

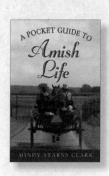

A Pocket Guide to Amish Life
Mindy Starns Clark

Full of fun and fresh facts about the Amish people, who abide by an often-misunderstood faith and unique culture, this handy-sized guide covers a wide variety of topics, such as beliefs and values, clothing and transportation, courtship and marriage, shunning and discipline, teens and *rumspringa*, and education and work.